Twelve Stories

TWELVE STORIES

BY

STEEN STEENSEN BLICHER

TRANSLATED FROM THE DANISH BY

HANNA ASTRUP LARSEN

WITH AN INTRODUCTION BY

SIGRID UNDSET

1945

PRINCETON UNIVERSITY PRESS

PRINCETON

FOR THE AMERICAN-SCANDINAVIAN FOUNDATION

NEW YORK

LONDON: GEOFFREY CUMBERLEGE, OXFORD UNIVERSITY PRESS

CONTENTS

STEEN STEENSEN BLICHER

BY SIGRID UNDSET

In an autobiographical sketch, written in his fifty-seventh year, Steen Blicher ends his record of a life spent in tireless activity and almost constant misfortune, with the following words:

"Finally, he has made numerous contributions to the public journals—at first sometimes anonymously—through which he has mainly tried to call attention to imperfections and abuses, to arouse the spirit of his people to a more vigorous life, and to further patriotism at the expense of selfishness. He has had—and still has—to fight misfortunes and heavy sorrows. Several times he has been in peril of his life from accidents when driving, from runaway horses, from illness. . . . But during all his tribulations he has held firmly to his chosen motto: 'Lord, when Thy hand is heavy upon me, Thou makest me strong.' "

No doubt Blicher was in perfectly good faith when he wrote these words, convinced that he had stated two vitally important facts about himself. His conscience assured him that, in spite of the scant and tardy recognition he had met as an author and a poet—and he cannot have been unaware of the fact that in his vast literary output were some short stories and poems of rare originality and exquisite beauty—he had never flagged in his unselfish devotion to his people and in his efforts to serve the material and spiritual needs of his native land. And even if it seemed to him as though an unkind fate had persecuted him ever since he became a man, the poverty-stricken village pastor remained steadfast in his trust in God. He had grown up among a people whose lives were bare, harsh, and difficult, and he had accepted the fact that God does not coddle His children. He treats them as grown-up sons and daughters, who must be able to face misery and carry the responsibility for what they bring upon themselves and their fellow men. After all, this life is short, uncertain—like a mirage; for hope of adjustment and consolation a man must look beyond the sunken graves where withering grass and dead flowers rustle in the wind from the moors. In spite of his shortcomings as a pastor, dire as they were, Blicher was in his own way a deeply pious man. And in his own strange way he was also a man of rare fortitude.

I

Steen Steensen Blicher was born on October 11, 1782, in the parsonage of Vium in Jutland, where his father, Niels Blicher, was a minister. For five generations the forefathers of Steen Blicher had been clergymen. Most of his relatives on his father's side were parsons.

Since the Lutheran Reformation such families, wholly devoted to the ministry, had become quite common in the Scandinavian countries. A peasant's son who had managed to work his way through the Latin school and the University, ending up as the minister of a country parish, would make every effort to prevent his children from sinking back into the ranks of the common people. He would strive hard to make it possible for his sons to study divinity, and try to marry his daughters to curates and vicars. Usually a minister's income was very modest. And if his predecessor had left a widow, she had a right to be pensioned from his tithes, the basic income of the living. It might even happen that there was more than one minister's widow in the parish. When Steen Blicher was given the living of Thorning and Lysgaard, no fewer than three widows claimed their share of his income. Small wonder that the country parsons were often inordinately eager to make some extra money at the expense of their parishioners—"Parson's purse is never filled," says an old proverb—or that they often were denounced for neglecting their duties as shepherds of souls, while they devoted their energies to the tilling of the parsonage acres, to literary work, or whatever extraneous activities they had a natural inclination for.

Yet the Church offered by far the easiest way for a lad who wanted to escape from the unfree and uncertain conditions to which the peasants, at least in Denmark and Sweden, were subject. The lack of personal liberty and security was far worse than the economic stringency, for, in spite of the latter, farmers sometimes managed to become quite well-to-do. But under a rural system where all but a handful of the peasants were tenants under great or small landlords, and bound to work on the fields of the manor, even if they had to neglect their own holdings; where the squire had the right to inflict bodily punishment on his tenants; where the *Stavnsbaand* institution held the men tied to their native village as long as they were of an age to serve in the militia in case of war; and where the lord of the manor could send a young man away to be made a soldier if he had a grudge against him, the opportunity to change this life of virtual serfdom for the life of a clergyman must have seemed immensely tempting. Yet the commoner, even as a clergyman, did not escape the domination of the nobleman, who to a great extent possessed the right to give away the living attached to the church or churches on his domain. Many of these country squires might be kind and pious men, yet they could not help regarding the clergy as just an order of upper servants; in fact, it was not unusual that the minister had for a time served as valet or tutor to sons of the squire, while he was trying to finance his studies in the Capital. The situation of the parson between his patron and his parishioners, and subject to the former, was as between the bark and the wood. And the parishioners were prone to regard their parson with suspicion and accuse him, justly or unjustly, of toadying to his lordship and trying to squeeze as much as possible in emoluments out of his flock.

Nevertheless, the minister had come a long way from the status of his humbler ancestors. He was addressed as Herr— Herr Sören, Herr Jens (not until the eighteenth century did it become usual to address him by his surname). And a young man who had a genuine yearning after knowledge and was inclined to the pursuit of literature and scholarship would usually have to approach such goals by way of the Church. The marvel is not that the spiritual life of the Scandinavian countries lagged in the first centuries after the Reformation, nor that the moral and intellectual standard of the clergy on the whole was none too brilliant. The marvel is that, in spite of so many obstacles, a number of clergymen were still able to achieve as much as they did, as scholars, poets, educators of the people, and as men of erudition.

Niels Blicher lived up to the best traditions of his class, when he tried to introduce improved methods of agriculture among his parishioners, and made propaganda for inoculation against smallpox. He joined the company of those eighteenth-century clergymen who wrote "topographical descriptions" of the district where they lived and worked, storing up for generations to come an immense amount of information about the soil and climate, the health conditions, the farming methods, the morals and customs and superstitions of the country people of the times. Niels Blicher's book about his parish of Vium is delightful. His numerous exercises in Latin verse-making at least amused himself.

He had married Christine Marie Curz, a minister's daughter, descended from the famous Bishop Bang of Odense, who in his turn claimed descent from the illustrious house of Hvide—that great and noble clan which in the Middle Ages had given to their country a number of heroes of ballads and history. They had been great warriors, great statesmen, founders of cities, builders of churches and abbeys, loyal servants of the great kings of Denmark, until one of them turned regicide and several of them rebelled against less great kings, and made war on their native land. Blicher mentions this relationship of his with the Hvide lords, but it does not seem to have occupied his fantasy unduly. (To poor Herman Bang a century later the thought of his descent from the house of Hvide became an obsession.) But Steen Blicher had ever since his childhood had an intimate knowledge of the rural aristocracy of Denmark, and for him it did not possess much glamour. Like his contemporaries, Blicher took for granted that a nobleman ought to be a noble man, and sometimes was. But he also took for granted that people very often are not what they ought to be. He was keenly aware of the way a man's outlook on life and his behavior is conditioned by the virtues and vices of the class he has been born into, and he quietly enjoyed the rich variety of manners and tastes and ambitions brought about by different environment. But good or bad, funny or vicious in an entertaining way, to Blicher the squire and his lady, the poor and the wealthy peasants, the gypsy and his woman flitting across the lonely Jutland moors outside the border line of ordered society, were just human beings, of whom no two are alike but all deserving of interest and sympathy.

Blicher scarcely ever mentions his mother. No memory of Marie Curz seems to have entered into the world of his imagination. He was her eldest son. Two children died in infancy. A fourth, a boy five years younger than Steen, survived. According to the scanty information that has been gleaned about Niels Blicher's wife, she was queer and melancholy almost from the beginning of their married life. Soon after the birth of her youngest son she became hopelessly insane.

Her uncle was *Etatsraad* Steen de Steensen, owner of the manor of Aunsbjerg. The *Etatsraad* (Counsellor of State, an honorary title not involving practical duties) was a kindly man; and probably because his small namesake could not be properly cared for at home with the invalid mother, Steen was frequently carried off to Aunsbjerg to spend some time with this distinguished relative and his strong-minded lady. Another relative of his mother's was Fr. von Schinckel, owner of Hald—of all Danish country seats the richest in legends and traditions. Beautifully situated on an inland lake near Viborg, the old capital of Jutland, the von Schinckel home was surrounded by the ruins of a prehistoric stronghold, a medieval castle, and an earlier manor. The Schinckels took their turn in caring for the little boy, who for all practical purposes was motherless. Indeed, it seems as if the only taste of womanly tenderness and a woman's caresses Steen Blicher had as a child were the kisses the wanton young Charlotte Schinckel showered upon him, when she was in the mood. At Aunsbjerg the boy felt as if he were in a cage, and Hald was not much better. Yet what he had heard and observed from his footstool of the doings of the grown-up people about him, stayed in his memory, and a belated understanding of the things he had seen happen at Aunsbjerg and at Hald became an important part of his inspiration later on. A number of his finest tales have for a setting these two old Jutland country houses.

In those days, however, he always longed to get away from these strict ladies, to go home to Vium and the parsonage. His mother's condition may have been something dark and frightening that children often evolve an elaborate technique to ignore or circumvent. And his father tried to make up to his two young sons for the shortcomings of their home. He was their tutor and their friend; he let them accompany him on his visits to the poor and the sick of the parish, and on his excursions to collect material for his "Topography of the Shire of Vium."

At that time the parish straddled the border line between the fertile eastern plains and gentle valleys of the east coast and the vast and desolate high moor, *Ahlheden*, which occupied the interior of the Jutland peninsula all the way from the northern sandy spit of Skagen down to the marshy lowlands of Slesvig, continuing with some interruptions into the moors of northwestern Germany.

Since the dawn of Danish history the Jutlanders had enjoyed the reputation of being the toughest, shrewdest, most stubborn of Danes. Nowhere else had the peasantry fought so hard and so long for their ancient Northern freedom against the system of oppression from the South, which slowly and gradually engulfed the rural populations of Denmark and Sweden during the later Middle Ages and the time of the Reformation. Fierce uprisings of the peasants had to be crushed in blood before the State and the aristocracy could subdue them—and in Jutland the peasants were never wholly subdued. Nevertheless, the reason why Jutland even during the centuries of rural unfreedom had the largest percentage of owner-farmers in Denmark may not have been the much-vaunted stubbornness of the Jutland mind. On the contrary, cause and effect probably worked the other way around, as in Norway. There the resistance of the peasants against attempts to deprive them of their old freedoms was helped by the natural conditions of the country, which did not favor the building up of large estates, since most of the arable land was in scattered patches separated by rocky and infertile ground; and the independence thus preserved strengthened the peasants' individualism and sense of personal dignity. So in the parts of Jutland where small and isolated farms nestled among wide marshes and on the outskirts of the barren moorland, the greedy noblemen were not tempted to build up their estates. Here the farmer-owner survived, while the fertile eastern counties, where the peasants had always lived in villages and tilled their land under a system of strip-farming, came under the domination of the gentry. But even here the Jutlanders never tamely submitted to their master. If he was too unjust or arbitrary, he was met with grumbling obstruction or sullen resistance. The rebellious peasant who retaliated against a beating or an insult to his girl by killing the squire or his overseer could still escape to the great forests and the moor—haunts of the numerous robber gangs who made the highways unsafe. As everywhere, when the common people suffer oppression, the rebel outlaws became popular heroes, their deeds of daring and their generosity towards the poor, the stuff ballads and tales are made of. As a child Steen Blicher must have imbibed a great deal of this robber lore.

Behind the village with its green pastures and fields was the somber world of the moor. Wave upon wave of hills, dark with brown heather, rolled all the way towards the distant horizon, where the rows of great burial mounds from the Bronze Age topped the ridges—memorials of the time when the ancient *Hærvej*, the trail of the Danish warriors of old, traversed the peninsula from north to south. In between the hills, sluggish creeks and stagnant swamps daubed the murky landscape with patches of pale green. In the hollows, copses of stunted oak bowed to the winter storms and managed to keep alive, yielding shelter to the game birds that abounded on the moor. The roads of the moorland had made themselves: they were the ruts dug out by the creaking wooden wheels of oxcarts, or yellow and sandy tracks worn by the hoofs of innumerable cattle, which the drovers bought from the farmers along the Limfjord and herded south to fatten in the marshes of Sönderjylland, before they were marketed in Hamburg or northern Germany. To a sensitive boy with a vivid imagination they were also the roads leading back through the history of his country, into the dim past of the race.

Sometimes the wanderer on the moor would suddenly come upon a tiny homestead with low walls of turf and clay almost disappearing under the overhanging thatched roof. A slender column of yellow peat smoke curling upwards under the wide sky, some shy, barefooted children fleeing at the sight of a stranger, a few sheep seeking their meager food in the heather, told of a life lived many miles away from the nearest neighbor. Yet the inside of the cottage might look snug, or even prosperous, with solid furniture, curtained beds swelling with bolsters and linen sheets, an array of copper pots and pewter tankards by the fireplace. The challenge of the infertile moorland had been accepted by an industrious and thrifty population, which turned to sundry home industries. The only domestic animals that could be kept in any number were sheep, and so the spinning of wool and the knitting of woollen garments kept whole families busy, men as well as women. Scattered among the hills were pits of a kind of clay that made excellent pottery, and the "Black Jutlanders," handmade pots and pans and dishes, were carted all over Denmark and shipped from Jutland ports to neighboring countries, even as far as to the Netherlands. Usually middlemen skimmed the cream off the business, but even so the makers might achieve a modest competence and by the thrift of several generations amass a small fortune.

The love of the moor was planted in the heart of Steen Blicher when as a child his father took him along on his trips—

and it was also his father who initiated him in the noble art of the hunter. It seems that Niels Blicher let his boys have a gun as soon as they were big enough to tote one; and his friends in the manors of the neighborhood, who appreciated the parson as a member of their hunting parties, let the lads run along with the men. The spell of the wild and desolate dark land, which would turn into a riot of purple and rose colors for a few weeks in blossom time; the everlasting trill of the skylarks under the immense vault; the hot summer days when the distant grave-mounds seemed to float above ground and dance in the hot, trembling air; the teeming life of wild things, birds and hares and foxes, in winter time even now and again a stray wolf; the tales about outlaws and gypsies; the friendliness of the moor-land people, hospitable as the Arabs of the desert—these were the treasures Steen Blicher laid up in his boyhood. Later the moor was destined to become his inspiration, his happy hunting ground, his refuge from misery and heartbreak.

II

According to Blicher, he was a frail child and dull at school. Finally, though, he must have made some progress with his studies, for when he was admitted to the Latin School in Randers at the age of fourteen, he was placed in the third form, among boys most of whom were his seniors. He may have had private tutors at home, but evidently Niels Blicher had himself been the chief instructor of his sons.

Just before he left his home for school, something happened to the adolescent that probably influenced his whole life for the worse. His father had recently been promoted to the living of Randlev, and here young Steen made the acquaintance of a girl of sixteen, newly married to a doctor, but staying for a few summer weeks as a guest with relatives. The girl took it into her head to flirt outrageously with the thirteen-year-old lad— hugging, petting, kissing him lavishly in public as well as when they were alone. Avowedly, the young grass widow merely indulged in an innocent pastime; technically, the parson's boy was still a child. Moreover, according to the tastes of the time, "page-love" was so sweet, the admired pattern being the love of Cherubino for the Countess in Mozart's opera. To the boy the caresses of the plump and pretty little brunette were a dangerous intoxication—a stormy awakening of his emotions and his senses (though Blicher goes out of his way to deny that his passion for the doctor's wife had much to do with sensuality). When the lady left Randlev to return to her husband, Steen waved a last adieu to his beloved from the stone fence of the vicarage garden. Afterwards he grovelled in the grass, wishing that his heart would really break, and that he might die.

Friends of Ernestine Blicher, the sixteen-year-old widow Steen Blicher married fifteen years later, describe her almost in the same words as he has used about his first love—small and plump and pretty, with an abundance of nut-brown curls. So it is very likely that the romping of a flighty married girl with the schoolboy Blicher had a good deal to do with his marriage to a woman who helped to make his life a tragedy.

The Latin School at Randers was a good one, according to the standards of the day. The headmaster and some of the other masters were gifted teachers who knew how to make the strong meat of classical learning palatable to young boys and foster in them a genuine zest for intellectual activity. Steen Blicher was not quite seventeen years old when he left school for Copenhagen, where, according to the pattern of studies of the time, the final examination and the graduation from school to University took place. Steen acquitted himself very honorably and settled down to the study of theology—certainly not because he felt any special vocation for the ministry, but because he had always been destined for it.

He witnessed the attack of the British Fleet under Nelson and Parker on the navy of the "Twin Kingdoms," Norway and Denmark, April 2, 1801. Blicher enlisted in the Students' Volunteer Defense Corps, but this time he was not called upon to prove his valor. The naval engagement had ended in a stalemate, with heavy losses on both sides. The Danish and Norwegian seadogs fought back with fierce courage and considerable skill. But Nelson called for a parley and pretended that, unless an armistice was entered upon, he would have to burn the captured Danish ships with the men in them. The Crown-Prince-Regent Frederik was a very brave man, but he was also very tender-hearted. The undecided battle of Copenhagen was turned into a diplomatic defeat. Denmark and Norway had to quit the League of the Armed Neutrals and submit to letting England search their merchant ships for contraband. Moreover, Denmark's ally Russia at the same time signed a peace treaty with England. For six years Denmark stayed outside the Napoleonic wars, enjoying a period of unusual prosperity.

Ever since he had taken over the rule for his insane father, Crown Prince Frederik and his Cabinet had worked untiringly to liberate the Danish peasantry and improve their condition. The right of the squire to inflict bodily punishment on his tenants was abolished; tenants could not be evicted from their farms without having the case tried in a court of justice, and the eviction must be made by rural policemen, not by the squire's people. Most important of these amendments was the abolition of the *Stavnsbaand*, which took the recruiting out of the hands of the landowners. In place of it, conscription based on a census of all adult males was introduced; and in the mind of the Danes a national conscripted army and personal freedom for all men became twin ideas. Credit institutions were established expressly to help the farmers to buy their homesteads on easy terms. The transition of the peasants from tenants to freeholders made new strides in these years of prosperity. Several estates were bought by so-called "manor butchers," to be parcelled out and sold on speculation. But the driving force in this work of emancipation had been the Crown Prince and his helpers, most of them noblemen from the highest Danish aristocracy. It was only natural that the common men of Denmark should look upon their autocratic monarch with a love and a loyalty which none of his later disastrous mistakes could weaken, and also that the Danes on the whole should regard their noblemen as the cream of the nation, in spite of the black sheep and the dullards and the crackpots in their ranks. They really had seen a number of their great lords stand out as men of true moral greatness. Revolutions might be all right in other countries, but in this enlightened corner of the world similar reforms were brought about peacefully, and now, with enlightenment about to penetrate the whole nation, there was no telling how far small Denmark might go as an example to the world of a model country.

This smugness and conservatism of the Danes in the beginning of the nineteenth century and their excessive royalism were to have fatal consequences in the long run, but in the days of Blicher's youth these were scarcely apparent. In his tale "A Fortnight in Jutland" his, or rather his father's, memories of the Jacobin Club of Viborg have become a source of rich fun, and the fact that the Baron of the tale is an out-and-out rascal does nothing to mitigate Blicher's scorn of the provincial revolutionaries.

Blicher was not called upon to fight for his country in the summer of 1801, but the nervous tension of the time may have had something to do with the breakdown in health he now suffered. A sunstroke together with a chest trouble prostrated the sensitive youth, and the doctors held out no hope of recovery from what they called his "incurable hectic condition." It seems to have been a case of advanced consumption. But Blicher's Jutland stubbornness was roused by this death sentence. He did not care to linger on as an invalid; he would try to cure himself by drastic treatment, or else succumb quickly.

Though he was so weak that he could scarcely cross the room without becoming exhausted, he went for a walk every day, and little by little he was able to extend his promenades. To strengthen his ailing lungs he started playing the flute. And when his health had improved somewhat he took a situation as tutor to young Lauridz Foss, whose wealthy bourgeois father had bought a manor on the island of Falster. In an age when ideas about infection and contagious diseases were of the haziest kind, nobody objected to the consumptive Mr. Blicher's acting as tutor to a lad only a few years his junior. The situation offered ample opportunities of outdoor life for mentor as well as pupil. The two young men went duck-hunting in ditches and marshes, sometimes soaking wet for days on end; tramped across the country with guns and dogs; shot seabirds and seals from a rowboat; or during the winter, when the fjord was icebound and bitter winds cut through their clothing, went hunting on skates among the outer islets. As by a miracle, this indifference to the state of his health turned the wan and emaciated candidate for death into a lean, tanned, sturdy young man—at least that is what Steen Blicher tells us. Moreover, he insists that, except for a few attacks of acute illness, he ever after enjoyed a gloriously robust health, which none of his adversities could shake.

In the time left over from their outdoor activities, Blicher and his pupil managed to get along with their studies well enough for Lauridz Foss to pass the examinations at the University of Copenhagen in due time and graduate with distinction. And the friendship between Steen Blicher and Lauridz Foss lasted all their lives. Meetings, sometimes made happier still by hunting trips, and the exchange of letters and greetings kept green the attachment between the two men, and after the death of Steen Blicher his former pupil wrote some very touching reminiscences of the good man and great genius he had loved so faithfully.

During his stay in Falster Blicher made one more acquaintance that became a lifelong love with him. He discovered the poems of Ossian. Macpherson's book was still widely held to be a genuine translation of ancient Gaelic lays. To young Blicher from Jutland, the highland moors of Scotland, where heroes and bards of old moved to their tragic fates in an everlasting mist, and lovely maidens mourned their dead lovers to the strains of the harp, merged with the moors at home. Family traditions and old wives' tales he had heard as a boy were glorified in the sorrows of the blind Ossian and the faithful Malvina.

Probably Blicher already toyed with the idea of translating Ossian into Danish during his stay in Falster, though he did not start work on it until later. His translations of Ossian appeared, one volume in 1807, a second in 1809. Opinion about Macpherson's rank as a poet has changed since the time when Ossian was the craze of the literary world all over Europe. I still think he was no mean poet, and my lingering love for Macpherson's misty world of gloom and doom dates back to a summer in my maternal grandfather's old-fashioned Danish garden, where as a schoolgirl I read Blicher's rendering in the green shadow of the elder arbor.—To Blicher "the Bard of Morven" remained a kind of tutelary spirit as long as he lived. In the dark years that lay ahead he was to find consolation in communing with the heroes and heroines of Ossian's world, flitting about him on his own moors. His second daughter, his favorite child, he had named Malvina after the widowed bride of the dead Oscar.

But the young man who returned from his stay in Falster in 1803 to resume his studies for the ministry in Copenhagen had no misgivings about the future. He was, according to his own words, quite a "mahogany fellow," which in the slang of the time meant a dandy. He was musical and played several instruments with more or less skill, he had a nice singing voice, he danced, was sociable and keenly interested in poetry and public matters. And there would always be an opportunity to get out of town and go hunting when he felt like it.

Yet he does not seem to have been a member of any of the literary clubs or coteries that flourished among the Copenhagen students and young writers. The stir caused by the introduction of the Romantic movement from Germany evidently left him cold. In spite of the British outrage against Denmark, Blicher loved English poetry and literature, though not uncritically. Byron he disliked. But he liked the English. Their politicians might be ruthless and unhampered by moral niceties, but he loved their language, and he liked the humaneness of the English people. Germany was another story. As a Jutlander he knew his and his ancestors' neighbor, whose political intrigues and policy of infiltration in the southern part of Jutland were backed by a mean and greedy people.

He was terribly poor, but he was used to straitened circumstances from his home. And when after a while he was given a scholarship that included lodgings in one of the colleges for indigent students, of which Copenhagen had several, he immediately offered to share his quarters with a friend who was as poor as himself. In justice to Blicher it should not be forgotten that, if later he degenerated into an inveterate borrower, hopelessly unreliable in money matters, he was always willing to share what he had, if he had anything at all, with whoever happened to come along.

Meanwhile it became evident that Denmark could not possibly be kept out of the European wars much longer. The sympathy of the people was with England, but the plight of Germany under the heel of Napoleon made the Danes forget their old grudge against the nation which innumerable times had played the aggressor against Denmark. "We want to keep what is ours, but we want all other people to do the same." A Danish army of defense was stationed at the southern frontier to fight off a possible French invasion. But among the measures proposed at the meeting in Tilsit between Napoleon and the Emperor of Russia was an "invitation" to Denmark to lend her navy for an attack on Great Britain. Reckless, and not too well informed on European matters, the British Government of Canning decided to forestall this eventuality, and in the late summer of 1807 a large British fleet appeared in Danish waters. Denmark was offered "protection" and colonies after the war as payment for the "loan" of her navy to the English. The Crown Prince refused: "With what would you pay for the honor of Denmark?" Then the British landed their invasion army and shelled Copenhagen until approximately one third of the city was razed and burnt to the ground—among buildings that suffered were the cathedral and the University. After a defense of four days, the city capitulated. The British carried away the large and modern navy together with much war material, and six hundred vessels of the merchant marine. Denmark was in the war on the side of Napoleon until his defeat, and had to pay the price.

Steen Blicher had fought with the defenders of the city. When he returned to seek his lodgings after the capitulation, they were gone, and so were all his earthly possessions, including his first manuscripts. For a while he had to go home to his father in Jutland. Napoleon had sent an army, mainly of Spanish auxiliaries, into Jutland, as he had planned a joint French and Danish attack on Sweden. The attack never came off, but Blicher made the acquaintance of a number of French and Spanish soldiers and officers, and liked them. He acquired a fondness for their languages—according to himself strong enough to make him learn both French and Spanish quite well.

He returned to Copenhagen, and in 1809 he was able to finish his studies and graduate "with distinction." Then he applied, not for a living in the Church, but to be appointed teacher at his old school in Randers.

The teachers of the "learned schools" were appointed by royal decree. And as the King, Frederik VI, who had succeeded his insane father in 1808, was the very type of paternalistic monarch who manages to keep an eye on an incredible number of his State employees, it is likely that the way Blicher acquitted himself of his duties as a teacher was remembered and held against him for years in the offices of the government in Copenhagen.

Soon after his arrival in Randers the new "Adjunct," as was Blicher's title, married the widow of his uncle, Pastor Peder Daniel Blicher of Spentrup. The bride, Ernestine, was not quite seventeen years old and the mother of a baby boy. Her father was a petty government official who had been imprisoned for embezzlement, and after the breaking-up of her Copenhagen home the girl Ernestine came to Pastor Blicher as a nursemaid for his children by his second wife. She was considered very good-looking, small and plump, with an abundance of dark curls. She was also said to be very flighty. She had been a widow only for a couple of months when she became engaged to a young agriculturist, but when he was killed in an accident she was reported to have exclaimed, "How lucky—for I have just become engaged to the overseer of Hald!" Then she married Steen Blicher.

He was evidently in love with his "sweet Neste"—his pet name for his wife. She may have reminded him of his first love. But it certainly would not make her less attractive that her late husband had left her a tidy sum of money. Blicher immediately invested part of it in a house.

It was a bad thing that the house was situated so far from the school that Adjunct Blicher habitually came late for his classes. But it was worse that he very soon began to neglect his duties as a teacher shamelessly—cancelling classes, or simply not turning up at the school for a day or a couple of days, without giving any excuse. All we know is that Blicher was a welcome guest at the hunting parties of the neighboring landed gentry and farmers, and that he enjoyed the duck-shooting in the estuary of the river Gudenaa.

In a little more than a year he had made himself impossible as a member of the staff of his country's "learned schools." He had also made away with Ernestine's fortune. His own explanation is that the money was lost because of the deterioration of the Danish currency during the war years. That is probably true as far as it goes. But he was always a bad manager of his finances, and it seems that he had already in Randers forged the first links in that chain of debts which he dragged along until his death. The house in Randers was sold, and it is uncertain whether Blicher succeeded in saving anything at all out of his first financial shipwreck.

III

His damaging record as a teacher was probably the reason Blicher did not try to get another position under the government. Instead he returned to his father in Randlev, to take over as the pastor's tenant the farming of the land that belonged to the vicarage. Occasionally he aided his father in his ministerial duties, but it was understood that farming was to be his real job.

Now Blicher was keenly interested in the problems of agriculture. The rotation of crops was still a new departure among the Jutland peasants. Blicher practised the method himself and preached it to his neighbors. The breeding of sheep was the mainstay of the agriculture of Jutland, but according to time-honored custom the farmers let their sheep run loose, herded by small boys or girls who were unable to hinder them from doing a great deal of harm to the crops. Blicher invented a movable sheep-pen, a large frame on wheels which prevented the animals from doing damage and kept the field evenly manured. He also advised the peasants to cultivate a greater variety of crops and to produce more for home consumption, as a means to improving the health of the coming generations. He proposed that the villagers should enlarge their arable land by co-operative draining of the low-lying marshes, of which the parish had vast areas. He recommended cultivation of flax on the fertile lands of the east coast in order that a linen industry could supplement the woollen industry of the moors.

Blicher's theories were usually sound enough, but he preferred to write and make propaganda for his ideas instead of toiling steadily in his own fields and barnyard. As a practising farmer he was never a success. He was simply incapable of sticking to the tasks it was his business to mind, when he felt like doing something else.

Having begun to write for the newspapers, he discovered more and more topics he wanted to write about. He wrote about the Jews, fighting with might and main whatever was to be found in Denmark of anti-Semitic prejudice. He proposed the founding of "Magdalen homes," where fallen girls could be reclaimed and reintegrated into respectable society. The cause of the Greeks, struggling to throw off the yoke of the Turks, fired his enthusiasm, and he even composed a proclamation in English verse, calling upon Britain to make war on Turkey. He wanted his country to abolish capital punishment, "that the government who first of all struck off the fetters from our black brethren may also give the world the first example of a more humane treatment of criminals." (Denmark had been the first country to abolish Negro slavery in her colonies.)

His journalistic efforts got him involved in a number of newspaper controversies, some of which went on for months. Now and then he had written verse, enough to make a slim volume which was published by an obscure Jutland firm. The collection contains one of his loveliest and most famous poems, "My native land is the brown land of the heather—." No anthology of Danish poetry would be complete without it.

Meanwhile Blicher's economy had become a sorry mess. And he had a family of young children. He had to try and get into the ministry in order to earn a living. But for some time it seemed as if all his applications for vacant parishes were in vain. In 1819 he composed an advertisement: "A graduate in theology wants a situation as gamekeeper or forest ranger in a gentleman's establishment. Besides his main work he offers in his spare time to give instruction in the Latin, Greek, German, French, Italian, and English languages. Can produce first-class recommendations as to his skill as a hunter."

It may be questioned if Blicher really had intended to advertise in the newspapers for a job as gamekeeper. He showed the draft to a hunting companion of his, a gentleman of some influence, and through his good offices he was at last appointed vicar of the parishes of Thorning and Lysgaard. The church of Lysgaard had formerly been served by the parson of Vium, so here Blicher was to mount his father's old pulpit. He returned to that part of Jutland which he loved with his whole soul, the somber moor and the poor, sandy soil he had tramped as a small boy. In 1819 he moved into the vicarage of Thorning with his wife and six small children, the eldest being his stepson.

He dragged with him a burden of debt. Among other things he owed taxes for several years. The income of the parishes of Thorning and Lysgaard was modest, and the buildings of the vicarage were badly in need of repairs, which the parson had to make mainly at his own expense. Struggling with his private difficulties, he nevertheless took time to work for the betterment of the village schools in his twin parishes, for the improvement of the peasants' methods of farming, and for a number of causes which he considered beneficial to the common people. And when he had worked till he was tired, writing and talking about matters of public welfare, Blicher felt that he had really deserved a long, lonely stroll, with his dog and his gun, in among the hills, to look for grouse and woodcock in the heather. His parishioners were not quite satisfied with the way he fulfilled his duties as minister. Particularly the people in the village of Lysgaard complained that Mr. Blicher had not held the number of divine services in their church to which they were entitled. But when he proposed that they should send horses and carriage after him, as his own carriage was the worse for wear, the Lysgaard farmers refused.

IV

In the city of Aarhus lived a printer, a certain Mr. Elmquist, who at this time decided that, as a sideline to his printing business, he would cater to the reading public of Jutland with a magazine offering short stories, popular articles, poems, and so on. This kind of publication, the precursor of the pulp magazines of today, enjoyed an immense popularity in Germany. Mr. Elmquist borrowed for his venture the title of one of the most popular, *Lesefrüchte*, which means "windfallen fruit." But Elmquist translated it *Læsefrugter*, "fruits of reading," and intimated his intention of filling its pages with translations which he could print without paying for them. However, Mr. Elmquist also approached Pastor Blicher to ask for his collaboration. In order to add to his meager income, Blicher for six years provided the Aarhus magazine with "translations" from sundry European languages, that is, he retold stories he had read, abridging or altering them according to his fancy. But he also let Elmquist print some of his poems and a number of original tales, for which he drew mainly upon his memories of the Jutland of his childhood, on old traditions, and on his intimate knowledge of his countrymen, from the gentry to the gypsies. Thus were printed for the first time a number of short stories, some of them peerless masterpieces of Danish prose-writing. In 1823 Elmquist first published "The Journal of a Parish Clerk."

To give an American public some idea of how *Steen Steensen Blichers Noveller* are beloved by his Danish admirers, one might possibly compare his position with that of Jane Austen among the British. But the Danish Blicher-worshippers are a much larger proportion of the nation, for in Denmark the "highbrows" are to be found among fishermen and farmers as well as among the elite of Danish artists and scholars. Moreover, Blicher's tales have a more profound human appeal than those of the brilliant Englishwoman, while his artistic skill, when he is at his best, is as consummate as Jane Austen's. You will meet lovers of Blicher—men and women, who have read and re-read his tales any number of times to enjoy again the old remembered beauties and discover new perfections—on trains or in boarding houses, at a family party or by a café table, when a casual mention of Blicher's name will unite you in a kind of delightful freemasonry. (I was initiated in the cult when my Danish mother read to me the first part of "Marie," ending with the words of the old fisherman's wife when her husband permits the adoption of the babe saved from the ocean, "In Jesus' name! She is a loan of God's from the sea." Some years later I was entrusted with the precious volume and read for myself the sequel, which nearly broke my heart. And when my first book had been published, my mother gave me "for remembrance" an edition of Blicher's poems about the bird life of Jutland, *Trækfuglene*, with a dedication, "that as a writer you will always look up to Steen Blicher as your model, for profound integrity, fearless acceptance of life as it is, and truthfulness in telling what you know.")

The time of Steen Blicher is known as the Golden Age of Danish literature. The impact of the Romantic movement in Germany had touched off an explosion like fireworks of young geniuses in the North. The liberation of emotion, the faith in intuition, the yearning for unity of nature and spirit, the rediscovery of the secret places of the mind, created a new kind of poetry. The battle cry of freedom for the nations, the pondering on the past of the races and on that mystic entity called the soul of a nation, fired the enthusiasm of the young writers of Denmark and Sweden. (Norway had regained her national independence in 1814 under difficult circumstances, and her energies and emotions were occupied with practical problems, almost to the exclusion of the arts and literature, until the coming of Henrik Wergeland—and he did not belong to any movement; he was a movement and a literature in himself.) But the Romantic movement in Denmark rapidly developed a character of its own. After all, freedom for the whole people was no new idea in the Northern nations; it was rather a resurrection of the spirit of the fathers of old who, in the words of the Swede Thorild, were "no man's masters, no man's slaves." But this liberation had been well under way in Denmark a long time before the Romantic movement started. Interest in the past of the Northern nations had never been dead, and now it became an inspiration not only to the scholars but also to the poets and artists, who invested the Northern past with glamourous beauty. To the Northern people interest in real men and women with the weaknesses and strength of our common human nature had always been greater than their enthusiasm for ideal constructions of heroes and heroines. It is this taste for real life, its glories and its miseries, which makes the Icelandic sagas so vital that they appeal to us still by their timeless human quality as something contemporary, while most of the great literature of the Middle Ages of which they were a part seems to belong to another world than our own. Instead of dreamy nostalgia for the faraway, the world beyond the horizon, Oehlenschlæger and Grundtvig, and later Hans Christian Andersen and Christian Winther, gave their love wholeheartedly to the men and women of their own native land, to the past and the present and the future of their country, the sights and sounds of Denmark's nature. No hankering for the "Blue Flower" of Romanticism— the roses and the wild flowers, the oaks and beeches rooted in the soil of their homeland were all they desired.

A strong undercurrent of realism was present also in the Romantic literature of Denmark—even when the writers looked for the usual romantic stuff in a Southern or Oriental background and wrote of picturesque countries which they did not know much about, but dreamed all the more vividly. Yet however much the world of their imagination was rooted in the realities they knew and loved, their aim was to invest this world with the grandeur of fates larger than everyday life, and transfigure it with beautiful and noble emotions. Like the painters of their age, they made their studies in the field, but used their sketches for carefully composed canvases of balancing lines and rich colors. And when they wrote of their own land they wrote as lovers and glorified the things they loved. With a warm and healthy sensualism, as innocent of the convulsions of passion as of the repressions due to fear or bad conscience, the Danish poets exulted voluptuously in the loveliness of Denmark—the silence and the cool dusk of the beechwoods, the blue Sounds flung like embracing arms of the ocean around the sea-born country, the waving field of yellow grain bordered with cornflowers and poppies. And voluptuously sweet were to them the women of Denmark, fair-haired and white-bosomed, virtuous yet friendly and warm—adorable sweethearts, loyal wives, strong and tender mothers. The common men of Denmark were "the merry sons of nature," sturdy, brave, clever, and honest. Many of the writers of the Golden Age were the sons of country parsons and had spent their childhood among the peasants, or they came from the homes of the poor. But they did not feel called upon to tell about their origin, except to praise the attractive sides, and forecast the ideals they aimed at and fondly hoped their countrymen would live up to in the future.

Blicher loved his native Jutland without any desire to idealize either his home or his own people. The world he knew was full of good and evil things, of bitterness and bliss and humdrum trivialities, but he accepted everything—it was his world. He accepted it as a loyal son accepts his mother, or a faithful husband the wife who has been his partner through a long life. Jutland belonged to him, and he belonged to Jutland. Underneath his conscious love of this corner of the earth was a deep, almost unconscious conviction that he could no more uproot himself from this soil and this people than he could cease to breathe.

In a nation as highly cultured as the Danish of his time, where the art of good writing was so widely appreciated and the love of poetry so intense, a genius like Steen Blicher's was bound to be discovered and recognized before long, even if he did publish his work in an obscure provincial magazine. Literary circles in Copenhagen became aware of this lone bird who liked to call himself "the heath lark," this country parson who wrote in a way all his own, different from the others, but sometimes, oh, how splendidly well! "Realism" was a word that had not yet become fashionable, but the critics of Copenhagen praised Mr. Blicher's originality: his tales were profoundly true to nature, his scenery new and interesting, and his style had the directness of oral narrative.

En Landsbydegns Dagbog ("The Journal of a Parish Clerk")[1] is probably the most widely beloved of his tales. Certainly it combines all the qualities of his finest work.

The matter of the story Blicher has partly taken from the history of the celebrated Mistress Marie Grubbe who, like Blicher's Miss Sophie, was born at Tjele. Her first husband was

---

[1] *A Degn*—parish clerk—in the Lutheran churches of Scandinavia is the minister's assistant during divine service, leading the singing of hymns and reciting some of the prayers. He was also traditionally the schoolmaster of the village elementary school. As a man of some education his position was an intermediate one between the clergy and the villagers. Sometimes the *Degn* was a student of theology who had failed to pass his examinations—as happened to two of Blicher's sons, who became village *Degns*.

Count Ulrik Frederik Gyldenlöve, natural son of the King, and governor of Norway. Marie ran away from him with her sister's husband, a dissolute Danish nobleman, and for years the couple travelled all over Europe, dissipating a tidy fortune. Then Marie had to return to her father at Tjele. The double divorce of Gyldenlöve from Marie and of Ane Grubbe from her adulterous husband left the lady with a damaged reputation, and in the opinion of all sensible people she ought to have been grateful for her good luck when a neighboring squire nevertheless asked for her hand in marriage. But she came to detest her second husband, too, and took for her lover the overseer at Tjele, Sören Möller. After a thundering scandal and a second divorce, Marie Grubbe married her peasant lover. When the young Professor Holberg in 1711 fled plague-stricken Copenhagen, he went to stay at a very modest inn on the island of Falster and discovered that the innkeeper was Sören Möller and his landlady the former Countess Gyldenlöve. Marie evidently took pleasure in meeting once again a young man of culture and wide reading. To the quietly friendly Norwegian she spoke freely of her unusual life and told him how she had loathed her first husband, who was considered the handsomest and most accomplished gentleman in the Twin Kingdoms. And none of her other highborn lovers had been able to hold her affection. But she was perfectly satisfied with her present husband, even if he beat her occasionally when he was drunk. A short time afterwards Sören Möller killed a man and was sentenced to hard labor for life. Marie carried on, keeping the inn for sailors and fishermen, and died a year or so after her husband had been taken away from her.

J. P. Jacobsen used the story of Marie Grubbe for an elaborate psychological novel. Blicher has simplified the tale. His Miss Sophie is a giddy young girl who has an affair with her father's gamekeeper and elopes with him. When Morten Vinge, who loved the fair and gay young creature, meets her again, she is a coarse and embittered and ugly old harridan. Her sordid story is entirely without glamour, and it fills the heart of Morten

Vinge with revulsion and terrible sadness. Blicher also has moved the story forward in time. Marie Grubbe was born in the middle of the seventeenth century—Blicher's story is set in an eighteenth-century milieu, the age he knew intimately from living tradition. Blicher was quite well read in history, but like Sir Walter Scott he is rarely able to make his stories come to life unless he tells about the times of his father and grandfather. To him, as to Scott, the atmosphere and the language of this age are the atmosphere and language of his own childhood: here he had no need to imitate old letters and writings—he culled the quaint and old-fashioned expressions from the living lips of the old people around him, those he was fond of and those he was afraid of or amused by, and he knew every shading in the old folks' way of expressing human emotions. In that other masterpiece of Blicher's, "The Parson at Vejlbye," the entries in the diary of the young judge pulsate with the troubles and hopes of an upright, high-spirited, and warmhearted man. The sedate language adequately expresses his indignation at the attempt to corrupt his integrity, his love for the parson's sweet daughter, his concern for his hot-tempered father-in-law, his horror and his despair as the tragedy unfolds.

For "The Parson at Vejlbye" Blicher also utilized an old story, but again treated it in his own way. According to the documents in the case, some twenty years had passed since the disappearance of the servant of Sören Quist, parson at Vejlbye, when plotters framed the evidence and bought false witnesses who sent the luckless clergyman to his death under the headman's axe. With his strong feeling for close-knit composition, Blicher makes the discovery of the remains of Niels Bruus occur immediately after the man's quarrel with the irascible Herr Sören and his disappearance from the vicarage. The sleepwalker motif is Blicher's own invention. It adds to the grimness of the tragedy that the framed minister ultimately lets himself be persuaded to believe he must be guilty, though unwittingly, of the murder of his hired man. But to the fundamentally straight and honorable Herr Sören it is a consolation to believe that he dies a victim of

justice and not of injustice. To him it would have spelled despair if he had been able to see through the full hideousness of
the plot that was his undoing.

The best tales of Blicher are those in which he tells the story
of such simple, strong, and loyal souls. This does not mean that
these people are simple-minded. Morten Vinge has a keen,
curious, and adaptable mind. The boy who spends his few pennies on a stack of Latin books just to keep up his knowledge of
the beloved language, even after he has had to give up his hope
of going to a Latin School, takes up quite as eagerly the study
of the French language which he hears the gentry speak. He
thoroughly enjoys his initiation in the gallant sport of hunting;
for all his kindheartedness he feels a healthy satisfaction when
he has proved he can fight and make a good soldier. His journal
mirrors his adaptable mind, but his heart never changes: from
boyhood to old age Morten Vinge remains the same true and
good man, grateful towards whoever befriends him, humble before God, and upright among men. The parson at Vejlbye and
his son-in-law, the judge, are canny Jutlanders with plenty of
sound common sense, but their emotional life is beautifully simple and pure. The emigré French nobleman who ends his days
as gamekeeper with a rustic Jutland gentleman is a kind of
psychological detective, shrewdly unmasking the murderer of a
young peasant girl. Then he marries the other girl, for whose
sake the murderer killed his sweetheart, and gives his name to
the unborn child of the criminal. About his life with the young
wife he married out of chivalrous pity, enough is said when
Blicher tells how the widow died of a broken heart a short time
after her elderly husband had been found dead out in the
heather. The gypsy woman Linka Smælem, who carries her
crippled husband on her back, as they wander homeless all over
Austria, Germany, and the Jutland peninsula; Marie, the waif
saved as a baby from the Western Ocean; and Cecil, the
daughter of the prosperous hosier, can no more take back their
hearts, once they have given their love to a man, than they can

stop their hearts from beating. Faithfulness with them is scarcely a virtue, since it is the very essence of their being.

But so is their roguery to his knaves and thieves. Horrible, or merry and winning, they follow the bent of their natures with perfect simplicity and no conscience to trouble them. And his loose women cannot possibly be called fallen women; they are amoral far more than immoral, creatures to whom the rules and restrictions society tries to impose upon their appetites have no real meaning. They overstep them as lightly as they would a stile in a hedgerow. Miss Sophie, and Charlotte Schinckel in "An Only Child"—whom Blicher had known when he was a small boy—follow the bent of their natures without shame or remorse. If they have to learn by experience that the primrose path leads to a sad ending, they may turn bitter or subdued, but not repentant. In "Tardy Awakening," written after Blicher had made the shattering discovery of his own wife's unfaithfulness, he has drawn with a few light and sure touches the picture of a promiscuous woman. Lazy and demure, she has lulled her husband into an illusion that he is a happily married man: "*Die holde Sittsamkeit bey Tage*," is his whispered, rather indiscreet confidence to his friend. The quotation is from Wieland and the whole passage runs: "*Die Wohllust ist sie in der Nacht, die holde Sittsamkeit bey Tage.*" He never suspected he was sharing her "love" with almost any man who happened to be with her in a convenient situation.

The narrative style of Blicher is based partly upon the art of the peasants who had been handing down their traditions and legends by word of mouth and partly upon the way the old ladies and gentlemen of his childhood used to talk. He must have possessed an unfalteringly sensitive ear for variations in the inflections of voices and in the ways people express themselves. His tales "Marie" and "The Hosier and His Daughter" both tell the stories of young girls who lose their minds when their deep and faithful love for a young man has been frustrated. In both of them he uses the same device of letting an old woman tell the tragedy of the girl. But what a subtle difference in the way they

tell it! The fisherman's widow from the stern west coast who
says, "Look, out there where ships are sailing now, there my
cradle stood," whose men are laid to rest somewhere out there
beyond the sand bars, with all her pity for Marie and Jörgen, is
inured to hard fates and misery; and she tells the story of the
ill-fated lovers quietly and tersely. The hosier's widow is much
more voluble, and interrupts her narrative of the ghastly end to
the love between her daughter and the poor suitor—when he returned prosperous and acceptable to Cecil's father—with sighs
and sorrowful exclamations. She has so long felt safe in her life
of comparative ease, and the terrible thing that destroyed her
comfortable household has left her broken, longing for sympathy even from the stranger who happens to come to her door.

Of course the style developed by a more or less illiterate people for entertainment in the form of storytelling, and for the
oral preservation of their traditions, is always highly elaborate,
and at its best usually of consummate beauty and vigor. Blicher
loved and appreciated the values of this rural art of storytelling.
In his tales *Bette-Fanden* (Little Scratch) and *Tre Helligaf-
tener* ("Three Holiday Eves")[2] he uses it with perfect mastery.
The rules and theories of the rising school of Copenhagen
esthetes, led by the young and energetic Johan Ludvig Heiberg,
he despised, and he had not much patience with that brilliant
would-be dictator of taste in Denmark. Blicher, the realist before Realism, knew masters he liked better. It was a custom in
his part of Jutland for the peasants to gather sometimes in a cottage or in a farm kitchen, to entertain each other with singing
and storytelling, while young and old, men and women, busily
knitted the stockings and mittens which were to earn for them
the ready money upon which their modest prosperity was built.
The dialect of Jutland—so different from the language of the
educated part of the nation and also from the dialects of the

[2] Lutheran Protestantism could never make the Scandinavian people give up
the old custom of keeping the eve of the great feasts of the liturgical year as
half-holy days, with celebrations in the evening—the Vigils of Catholic times.
The evening before Christmas is still in Denmark and Norway the holiest and
best beloved feast of the year.

islands, that to Danes outside the peninsula it is difficult to understand and sounds funny—had scarcely ever been committed to
writing, or at least only as a comical element in plays and poems
written in the common language. Blicher loved this homely dialect, and in tales and poems where he used it, brought out all its
latent beauty and power to express the shy and sweet emotions
of a reticent and stronghearted people, the courage of men and
women faced with grief and hardship which they accept uncom-
plainingly, the sly humor of a tribe who in an eminent degree
have been gifted with the Danish virtue of self-irony. When his
collection of dialect stories and ballads was published in 1842,
under the title of *E Bindstouw* (The Knitting-Bee), fifteen
years of loving labor lay behind the slim volume, which has become a treasured classic of Danish literature.

Later, when his genius seemed on the wane, the danger of
this narrative style became apparent, and much of Blicher's work
during his decline is merely wordy and a little tiresome (though
"Three Holiday Eves" was written only a few years before he
died). He himself was aware of his tendency to become chatty
and created an alter ego, his "Cousin Peer the Fiddler" as the
narrator of his loosely knit, usually only mildly amusing, humorous tales. The wistfulness and resigned sadness of "Alas, How
Changed" is unique among the stories attributed to Peer Fiddler
—many of his own emotions during a life filled with frustrations
went into it.

V

In 1825 Blicher was promoted to the living of Spentrup and
Gassum, where his uncle, Ernestine's first husband, had been
pastor. In fact, when he wrote his application for this appoint-
ment, he mentioned that it would mean the fulfillment of his
wife's dearest hope, if she might return to the scenes of her
happy youth. The income of the living of Spentrup and Gassum
was good enough, and together with the money he could make
by his writings it might have saved him financially, if he had not

already been so deep in debt, the father of a family of seven children besides a stepchild, and a hopelessly bad manager.

However, to Steen Blicher the outlook for a while seemed quite bright. He was reinstated in the good graces of the King, who even a couple of times granted him modest sums of money from his private funds, as an aid to pay his debts. According to the custom of the times, Blicher addressed his supplications to the paternalistic monarch and asked for assistance when his need became too pressing. In 1823 he had edited a volume of poems called *Bautastene* (Memorial Stones) about great and good Danish men. It contained contributions from several well-known authors. The best known today is Blicher's own ballad on Sören Kanne, the peasant who saved a group of shipwrecked sailors. To the Danes, an unmilitary but fiercely courageous people, the heroism of a lifesaver has always seemed the finest kind of courage. Blicher now enjoyed some recognition as an author, and in 1825 he severed his connection with Mr. Elmquist and his *Læsefrugter* and started as an editor with a magazine of his own, *Nordlyset* (The Northern Light). A printer in near-by Randers was willing to act as publisher. However, when a tragedy of his, *Johanna Grey*, at long last, after several delays caused by a management which did not have much faith in Blicher as a dramatist, was produced at the Royal Theater in Copenhagen, it proved a failure and was taken off the boards after three performances.

Of literary friends Blicher had only one who remained really close to him through the years. Bernhard Severin Ingemann and Steen Steensen Blicher seemed in many ways to be absolute contrasts—they were of different natures, had different fates, and lived very different lives. The young Ingemann had begun as a writer of highly exalted poetry, romantic horror stories (some of them deserving to be included in the volumes of spine-chillers that have again become the fashion, as they are really good in a gruesome way), and had been very successful with his romantic tragedies in smoothly flowing verse. He married his first love, a young lady of delicate beauty and angelic virtue, and

was given a professorship at the academy of Sorö, a medieval
abbey converted into a public school on the lines of the English
institutions. In a beautiful villa on the shores of a charming inland lake, Ingemann lived a happy married life, the happiness
somewhat damped by childlessness and by the frail health of Mrs.
Ingemann. His historical novels of the Danish Middle Ages have
been favorite reading for generations of Danish children. But
his lasting fame among the poets of Denmark he won by his
Morning and Evening Hymns, in which profound piety is
blended with the keenest sense of the moods and sights and
sounds of the Danish countryside. In verse of exquisite purity and
naturalness he hails the risen Christ in the sunrise of a Sunday
morning in summer time. Awakening birds and little children
singing their hymns in the village orphanage unite in a chorus
of praise to the God of love. Nightfall, when the woods are
swallowed up in darkness and silence under the stars, brings to
his lips the words of the disciples on the road to Emmaus, "Remain with us, dear Master——."

Yet Ingemann was the one faithful friend who always understood Blicher's genius, so unlike his own, and who never joined
with those admirers who murmured that, granted the poor parson of Spentrup was really an extraordinarily gifted writer, more
was the pity that he made such a sorry mess of his life, and by
and by became a disgrace to the cloth.

Blicher embarked upon his duties in his new parish with a
great display of energy—especially to promote the material well-
being of his flock with a number of projects of the kind he loved
to make propaganda for. Passionately as he loved his moors, he
nevertheless dreamed of making at least parts of the wide waste-
land add something to the natural resources of his country.
When the *Ahl*, the hard crust of stonelike sand or porous sand-
stone, was broken, it must be possible to plant hardy evergreens
some places on the moor and by and by get a crop of fuel other
than the peat the Jutlanders were wont to burn. And perhaps
some time, when the land had been prepared by the planting of
pine forests, it might become arable. Blicher's idea of utilizing

the moors was taken up by Colonel Enrico Dalgas, after Denmark in 1864 had lost Holstein and Slesvig to Germany, under the slogan: "What we have lost without can be won within." Under Dalgas' untiring leadership the reclamation of this barren though beautiful part of Jutland became a reality—today the parts of Blicher's Jutland that are still left untouched by cultivation are protected as national parks. But Blicher had the vision—and at great expense he planted in pine some outlying land belonging to the vicarage. Never chary when he could lay hands on a bit of cash, he gave the money for a bathing pool and gymnastic equipment for the village school, so that the children would get some athletic training. He resumed his advocacy for the cultivation of flax, for the draining of marshy meadows, and a number of other causes which he considered of national importance.

Since the Blichers had moved to Spentrup, old Pastor Niels Blicher, no longer able to fulfill the duties of a minister, had made his home with them. Steen Blicher and his father were deeply attached to each other. Theirs were kindred natures with the same love of the land and the folkways of Jutland, and the close companionship between father and son was a source of much happiness to both men. But Blicher's wife could scarcely have been pleased to have a father-in-law, who was gradually growing blind and dependent on other people's help, added to the household.

It seems that Blicher did not suspect, until Fate dealt him the blow from which he never recovered, that there was anything wrong with his marriage. He was satisfied with his "sweet Neste," and if she scolded him for his untidy habits, indifference to his personal appearance, and disregard of his clerical dignity, if she complained of their straitened circumstances and the crowd of young children teeming all over their poor home, her husband listened calmly, with some vague consoling words. He took for granted that such scenes occurred among all married couples. He made no bones about the fact that he was partial to his hunting flask, and when among boon companions he freely

imbibed the national beverage of Jutland, *Thevandsknægt*—hot
strong tea liberally laced with the cheap rum that flowed plenti-
fully into Denmark as long as she possessed her colonies in the
Virgin Islands. He felt sure that if his family was not better
provided for, certainly it was not his fault. He was a hard-
working man, always busy with his numerous activities. Moreover, he was a tender father and an affectionate husband—
surely Ernestine had no serious reason to be dissatisfied, now
they were settled in her dear old home in Spentrup.

Some among Blicher's biographers have made out a case
for the defense of Mrs. Blicher. Certainly she had plenty of
reasons to complain of her lot as the wife of Steen Blicher. The
modest fortune left to her by her first husband had disappeared
in no time at all under his hands. Ernestine liked to have a nice,
comfortable home, and she was a competent housekeeper, but
it was impossible to keep her house well ordered, clean, and neat
with all those children about and her husband trampling all over
her scrubbed floors in muddy boots, dirty from the fields, dirty
from duck-hunting, letting his dogs run all over the place, dropping his guns and papers and samples of his agricultural and
other experiments at random. A woman born to be a poet's wife,
with an understanding of her husband's genius, might have had
the patience and forbearance necessary to put up with Blicher's
lack of domestic virtues and make their marriage a success of a
sort in spite of all. Ernestine was not in the least interested in
the literary efforts of her husband and boasted that she had
never read a line of the "trash" he wrote. She liked lively company and going to great and noisy parties, she loved dancing
and flirting, and when the well-to-do farmers of the neighborhood with their servants and guests gathered for an evening's
merrymaking, as the local custom was, Mrs. Blicher would appear and take part in the fun with more abandon than her husband's confreres and especially their wives thought seemly for
the wife of a minister.

In the Scandinavian countries December 11 is Term Day,
popularly called the Devil's birthday. Blicher in his memoirs

darkly hints at a Term Day which forever terminated his illusions about happiness on earth. On December 11, 1827, the birthday of Ernestine Blicher had been celebrated in the vicarage of Spentrup. In the night after the party Blicher chanced to surprise Ernestine and one of their guests in a situation that no wishful thinking could explain away. Early in the new year Blicher wrote to his bishop that circumstances had forced him to separate from his wife.

It never came to a legal separation. Mrs. Blicher took rooms in the neighboring town of Randers, and her husband himself drove her to her new abode. Outside her front door he solemnly kissed his wife, saying, "Good-bye, sweet Ernestine, now we two are never to meet again." Before long it was the talk of the town that Pastor Blicher called on his wife almost every day. When her baby was born it seems that Blicher refused at first to acknowledge it, but after a while he accepted the paternity and even came to be quite fond of the boy. Less than a year after the fatal Term Day, Ernestine Blicher was back again in the vicarage. But the patched-up marriage rapidly deteriorated. A tenth child was born to the Blichers—a feeble-minded little girl. Steen Blicher and Ernestine drifted apart more and more. Soon they rarely saw each other or exchanged words—they stayed under the same roof, and that was all. Ernestine developed a taste for young and brawny farm hands. At one time her husband's coachman was her favorite. And he had successors. A neighboring parson sadly commented on the conditions in the parish of Spentrup, "The Pastor is a drunkard, his wife Magna Adultera."

Yet Steen Blicher carried on his efforts to promote a number of causes aimed at the improvement of the material and spiritual conditions of the people. His work on a description of the Shire of Viborg and another on the Shire of Skanderborg furnished him with excuses for rambling widely all over Jutland. And the old complaint that he neglected his duties as clergyman were raised in Spentrup and Gassum, as they had been heard from Thorning and Lysgaard. His insatiable curiosity about human nature and his kindly understanding of all sorts and conditions of men made him seek the hospitality of laymen and colleagues everywhere, but he could not help feeling that he was not everywhere a welcome guest. It was a long, long time since the young Steen Blicher had been a "mahogany fellow." The Pastor of Spentrup was disgracefully indifferent to cleanliness and looked a fright in his dirty old clothes; and as everybody knew, he drank too much, whenever he had an opportunity to do so.

It may have been a feeling of kinship, a mixed emotion of pity and envy, which made Steen Blicher devote so much of his interest and sympathy to the study of the alien, dark-skinned people that flitted mysteriously all over the Jutland peninsula, with no fixed abodes, even if they had their favorite haunts in out-of-the-way places on the moor. They called themselves Wanderers or Travellers, but the peasants' name for them was *Natmænd*, nightmen, or *Kjeltringer*, rogues. Undoubtedly there was a strong gypsy strain in the Jutland rogues—drawings by contemporary artists as well as old photographs in the files of the police show that much. But they had forgotten their native Romany language and adopted *Rotvælsk*, the secret language of crooks and thieves in Germany and Austria—in fact, many of them extended their wanderings from Jutland far down into Central Europe and back again. Besides his famous tale of the faithful gypsy woman and her crippled man, Blicher wrote a great deal about the Wandering People in his topographical as well as in his fictional work. In a short story, "The Unbaptized," he tells about the faithful love of two gypsy brothers from the day they stood as small boys by the corpse of their mother, killed in a roadside brawl, until their death as old men. In "A Fortnight in Jutland" he has sketched the famous female robber chieftain Big-Margrethe, not without sympathy. And to the end of his life he took a keen interest in their language and their habits.

VI

In 1835 the leading Copenhagen publishing house of Reitzel decided to bring out an edition of Blicher's collected short stories. And in 1836 he managed to get financial aid, so that he could make a journey into Sweden, apparently in connection with his plan to write a dictionary of peasant dialects. This was the only time Steen Blicher ever left his native land. Almost all the other Danish writers who were his contemporaries travelled widely abroad—in Germany, France, and above all in Italy, which to the Danish painters and poets of the Golden Age became another spiritual mother country. Hans Christian Andersen, who in spite of his innumerable handicaps was a man of terrifying vitality and indomitable will power, even managed to see Turkey, to make a voyage on the Danube, to visit princes in Germany and Dickens in England. Steen Blicher after his short trip to Sweden never had another opportunity to go abroad. He yearned to see England and Norway, but even the short voyage to the latter country he was never able to make.

His transfer to the relatively good living of Spentrup and Gassum, and his income from his literary work—at times quite considerable—nevertheless failed to help him out of the financial quagmire which more and more engulfed poor Pastor Blicher. He was the father of ten children and had for years cared for his old blind father; also for some time he had sheltered the three orphaned children of his younger brother in his home. Now his older children were growing up, and it soon became evident that they could not possibly be called promising young people, at least not as to their prospects of worldly success. Of his sons only the eldest, Peder Daniel, ever graduated from the University of Copenhagen. Following in the footsteps of his forefathers, he became a minister in one of the smallest and poorest parishes in Denmark. He was never promoted to a better one and resigned, while he was still a fairly young man, eking out an existence on his small pension and whatever money he could make by teaching. Blicher's second son, Jens Fredrik, lingered on for years as a student of divinity in Copenhagen, but never passed the final examinations. Finally he married and became a *Landsbydegn*. And a *Landsbydegn* also became the third son, Francisco—named by his father after a Spanish officer, a friend of his youth. For the younger Blicher boys a University education was out of the question. According to their father, one was "in the transportation business," that is, he became an omnibus driver in Copenhagen. Another was an assistant in a bookshop, another employed "in agriculture." His stepson, Niels Blicher, had been considered a wild, bad boy ever since he was an adolescent—which probably was not entirely the fault of young Niels. In the opinion of their neighbors, his mother hated the boy and did her best to drive him out of the home. So Niels enlisted for service with the troops on the Virgin Islands, got into trouble, was somehow redeemed by his stepfather, but afterwards went from bad to worse. Among the tribulations of Steen Blicher's last years was the periodic appearance of Niels, a tramp and a drunkard, not unacquainted with the police in several places of northern Jutland.

Blicher evidently was a tender father, even if he was utterly unable to influence his offspring for their own good. In his various supplications for assistance he speaks of all his children as "dependent," years after the older ones were of an age when they ought to have been self-supporting. The children evidently preferred to stay in the poor and disorderly home, dependent on their easygoing father whom they loved and admired, and whose shortcomings and faults they copied, with sad consequences to themselves. The judgment of people who had known the sons of Steen Blicher is rather unanimous: they were all nice, friendly men, but, more is the pity, they were quite unable to resist the temptation of the bottle.

Of Blicher's daughters the eldest, Christiane, was supposed to keep house for this family of lazy and inefficient males. His second daughter, Malvina, was his favorite child. When Blicher in 1837 was taken seriously ill with rheumatic fever, Malvina nursed him in a way that earned for her her father's touching gratitude, expressed in simple and moving stanzas. Next summer she married a landless farmer, Rasmus Berg, and the couple took over the farming of the parsonage acres of Spentrup. They did not succeed as farmers either in Spentrup or any of the other places where they tried their luck, and according to the talk of the neighborhood the fault was mainly Malvina's. She was no good as a farmer's wife, spending her time reading, playing, and singing and doing a little fine needlework, but never putting her hands to honest hard work. Her husband gallantly insisted that he was to blame for this, he loved her so much, he would not permit her to become a drudge. Malvina Blicher is said to have been very pretty, taking after her mother as to looks, but, thank God, not as to morals.

Complaints of the way Pastor Blicher fulfilled, or failed to fulfill, his duties as a minister piled up. So did his debts. He was in arrears with his taxes for years, and unpaid bills flooded the vicarage. Sorrow and troubles, together with the memory of his late serious illness, filled him with a new, resigned sadness. In the opening stanzas of his poem *Trækfuglene, En Naturconcert* (Migrating Birds, a Concert of Nature) he speaks in simple and beautiful lines about his own death, which may be approaching—he too is a migrating bird, and he has heard the voice of Winter; maybe the cage will soon be opened and the prisoner of life set free. But his intimate knowledge of bird life and his eternal love of Danish nature allowed him to forget his melancholy, as he lovingly observed and vividly sketched the annual procession of migrating birds over Jutland, in one of his loveliest works.

Undaunted in spite of all his misfortunes, Steen Blicher busied himself with all the questions and causes he felt in duty bound to support as a Danish patriot. As he advanced in years, his outlook had become more and more liberal, not to say radical. In so far he followed a trend common to an increasing number of Danes. Though their love for the person of their old King Frederik VI was as warm and sincere as ever, the nation had seen how his policy had time and again led Denmark to the very brink of disaster. Now it was evident to most Danes that the old trust in an autocratic monarch who singlehanded, or almost singlehanded, managed the vital interests of the country, was outdated. The times of the eighteen-thirties were serious, the immediate future seemed fraught with grave dangers. Now the nation must demand its right to participate when the fate of Denmark was to be decided.

One of the burning questions of the day was the growing tension between the kingdom and the united duchies of Slesvig and Holstein. Holstein was German land and had always been peopled by Germans, Slesvig was fundamentally and purely Danish. But according to an old treaty of 1460 it had been declared that under one Duke the two principalities were to be *"up ewig ungedeelt"*—never to be separated. The German minority within the realm of Denmark had unearthed this old document and worked it for all it was worth as an excuse to hasten the German infiltration of Slesvig, the introduction of the German language in the church and in the schools, of German usages and bylaws, of German officialdom in Slesvig. The plan of the Holsteiners was to join the league of German principalities and drag Slesvig along with them. The fact that the King was growing very old, that he had no son, and that the right of his cousin, the Crown Prince, to inherit the Dukedom could be disputed according to the Holstein rules of succession, aggravated the situation.

To meet the emergency of the troubled times, in 1831, King Frederik by a decree had created advisory councils, to be elected by representatives of the Estates of the realm. There were to be four of these Advisory Assemblies, one for the Danish Islands, one for Jutland, one for Slesvig, and one for Holstein. Though they were given only advisory powers, the statutes granted them a great deal of real influence. They were empowered to propose new laws and amendments, and all new laws of the realm were to be presented for them to scrutinize and express judgment upon, especially laws pertaining to taxation and matters which might impose new burdens on the people. However, when the Assemblies, according to the opinion of the King, were too outspoken in their criticism of the financial situation, which certainly was bad, and when a crop of newspapers, most of them devoted to criticism of the government, sprouted in the wake of the Assemblies, King Frederik became indignant and in a proclamation to his subjects told them that We, the royal We, are alone capable of judging the true interests of Our kingdom. This of course gave new impetus to the budding political radicalism in Denmark. Yet, when the old King died in 1839, all Denmark mourned him wholeheartedly as a good man of profound integrity, a true father of his people, and a man tried through great and bitter misfortunes.

His successor, Christian VIII, was received with great expectations. As a young prince he had been governor of Norway in 1814, when the Union with Denmark came to an end and the Norwegians took their fate into their own hands, proclaiming, in defiance of all the European powers, that their country was free, sovereign, and would be independent. Elected to be king of Norway under the name of Christian Frederik, he promulgated the Norwegian Constitution of May 17, 1814, at that time the most radically democratic any European state had dared to write for itself. But when it became evident that to preserve her independence Norway would have to make her peace with Sweden and accept Bernadotte as her future king on condition that he leave the Constitution intact and the sovereignty of Norway respected, Christian Frederik loyally abdicated and left the land he had loved with youthful ardor. "To save the Constitution is the all-important thing." Now the Danes hoped he would listen to the public demand for a democratic constitution and give to Denmark something like the Constitution of Norway. However, with Christian VIII youth and youthful ardor were things of the past. He was perfectly aware that the time for absolute monarchy was over, but he believed in gradual progress, and the introduction of democracy by stages—not least because of the perils rampant in a realm with a strong minority of German nationality intriguing and looking for opportunities to make trouble and tear a bit of Denmark away from the mother country. For, above all, Christian VIII had become a Danish patriot, passionately eager to secure the welfare of his country.

Meanwhile, Steen Blicher all on his own had started agitation for an idea which—like so many of Blicher's ideas—was to succeed only partially during his lifetime, but nevertheless was destined to become an influence in the spiritual life of the Danish people in times to come. He would summon Danish men and women to a meeting on the Himmelbjerg, the highest point in Jutland—and, for that matter, in all Denmark. Here, during a popular festival assembly, representatives of all classes and walks of life in the nation were to meet in a patriotic endeavor to strengthen the national consciousness of all Danes and make them pledge themselves to work for the good of their native land.

Himmelbjerg means "Heaven Hill," and the Danes, when teased because of this ambitious name for a hill of very modest elevation, will eagerly explain that the name was not given because any Danes imagined their highest hill as soaring towards the skies, but because the view from the summit is of heavenly beauty. At the foot of the wooded slopes lovely lakes, surrounded by great forests, feed the calm rivers and rivulets that meander towards the distant horizon and the expanse of dark moors, through beautiful valleys where fine farms nestle in the folds of the landscape. Blicher had discovered this glorious view on one of his long hikes, away from domestic troubles and the tedious duties of a parish priest. He had used it as a backdrop for one of his tales, and the rather indifferent story is relieved by beautiful word pictures of the landscape. Evidently he had never forgotten his first impression of the spot, where the glories of his beloved land had unfolded so movingly before his eyes.

The first Himmelbjerg festival took place in 1839, with Blicher as the leader and main speaker. It was a great success, even if the participation was not too large—for it was a new departure. But the young people who had gathered under his pulpit were enthusiastic about the whole idea, and the singing of Danish songs and the merrymaking were all Blicher could have hoped for. Among his topics was the new national army based on extended conscription, which he hailed with jubilation; since among the Danes service in the army of their country was considered a privilege and an honor. He called upon all Danes to pledge themselves to a sacred cause, the strengthening of true Danishness. His fanciful idea, that the Danes ought to introduce a "national costume" and free themselves from dependence on the fashions of foreign lands, as well as his proposal that all Danes should address each other with the hearty *Du* (Thou) of the peasant dialects, were more in the line of fads, fondly cherished by this unconventional clergyman.

Meanwhile his private affairs had arrived at a crisis. In the fall of 1839 an auction was called at the vicarage of Spentrup. Furniture, livestock, etc., belonging to Pastor Blicher was to be publicly auctioned away to cover his unpaid taxes and sundry other debts. Among articles to be sold the advertisement mentioned the iron stoves of the house. This at last roused the admirers of Blicher the poet, and the leading newspaper of Jutland, the *Randers Avis,* in moving words called upon the readers to contribute to the collection it had started, to "pay a first installment on a sacred national debt" and relieve the Bard of Jutland of his financial embarrassment. The collection turned out a success: well-to-do people responded with donations, some of them very generous. But what touched Steen Blicher to the quick was the innumerable contributions of small sums from the common people, many of them veritable widow's mites. The auction was staved off, and for a time Steen Blicher's economic misery was substantially relieved.

In 1840 the Himmelbjerg festival very nearly failed to come off. The owner of the grounds protested that his crops and pasture lands had been so badly damaged by the crowds making their way to the summit, he did not want to see them there another year. Blicher let loose his scorn and fury in the papers. But King Christian VIII came to the rescue; he bought the

grounds where the festivals were to be held as well as the right
of way up to the top of the hill. Now the future of the Himmelbjerg meetings seemed secure. And Blicher joyfully accepted the
nickname, given him first by scoffers at the proceedings, the
Himmelbjerg Parson.

The Himmelbjerg festivals were attacked with considerable
bitterness by German and German-minded newspapers. After
all, the peninsula of Jutland from Holstein to the spit of Skagen
is a small area, and the leaders of the attempts at Germaniza-
tion of South Jutland were perfectly aware that the counterblast
launched by the Danish poet-pastor might easily become a grave
menace to their activities. Blicher replied with a call to all Danes
to liberate themselves from German bureaucracy—he hated
with all his heart this hardy perennial weed.

But from 1843 on Blicher was quietly pushed aside from his
post as leader of the Himmelbjerg festivals and deprived of his
cherished part as the soul and spirit of the meetings. There were
various reasons. And in spite of the fact that this loss of leadership was to Steen Blicher a heartbreaking tragedy, it is not too
difficult to understand why many of his original co-workers
tried to put the old man in a less conspicuous place at the
festivals.

The Danes have a word for a drunkard; they say he is *forfalden*. *Forfalden til stærke Drikke* is the whole phrase, and it
means a man is enslaved by his love of hard liquor. But taken
singly the word *forfalden* also means disintegrating, ruined. And
it seems that even the most fervent admirers of Steen Blicher's
genius could hardly refute the charges made against him by
decent everyday people—such as his fellow ministers of the
diocese, and well-to-do citizens of the district, not to mention
his poor parishioners: genius or no genius, Mr. Blicher was
sadly *forfalden*, disintegrating as a character, and a disgrace to
the cloth.

Once, when as a young girl I visited my mother's home in
Denmark and discussed with a young lad, a friend and fellow-
Blicherite, the merits of the master's work, my old great-aunt,

herself a parson's daughter from Jutland, interrupted us brutally, "Oh, yes, he was a very gifted poet. But, children, if you had seen him! He visited us once at Læstrup—he was forever wandering all over the country; he never stayed in his parish. He was filthier than any of the beggars that used to come to our back door. And lousy—oh, yes, he was that, too. The maid who had to clean his room when he left us the next day was quite sick with disgust.—No, I never met Mr. Blicher—Mother would not permit us girls to come into the living room when he called at our home." I shall never forget the pang of grief and pity I felt at the words of the old lady, nor the fury of my friend at her narrow-mindedness. The worst of it was that this aunt of mine was really an exceedingly broad-minded old woman. Imbued with the ideas of the eighteenth century, she was so broad-minded as to scare and scandalize the bourgeois mind of another generation by her opinions on life and human nature.

But worse than by his filthy habits and his lack of restraint when the bottles appeared on a convivial table in cottage or hall, Steen Blicher disgusted even admirers of his literary work by his brazen attempts to borrow money from friends or stray acquaintances. The relief afforded him by the national collection proved to have been temporary—very much so.

His mismanagement of his ministerial duties had become a scandal that had to be stopped. So in 1841 he was granted from public funds a subsidy that would enable him to engage a curate and devote himself to his writing and other activities. It was intimated that if his son, Jens Frederik, would finish his studies, so that he could be ordained and return to Spentrup as his father's curate, that would be a very satisfactory solution. But Jens Frederik did not pass his examinations. And so a certain Mr. Lakiær moved in as curate to Mr. Blicher.

To celebrate his liberation from the onerous duties of his parishes, and to look after his interests with the publishers, Steen Blicher travelled to Copenhagen and remained for several weeks in the capital. But he did not get in very close touch with literary circles. He took a fancy to the low taverns that line the old canals, the haunts of sailors, but also of all the riffraff that prey on sailors ashore. Blicher, who always felt perfectly at ease among the so-called common people, may have enjoyed the company as much as the bad liquor. But when he emerged, drunk and quarrelsome, he several times collided with the Copenhagen police—and rumor probably did nothing to minimize the disgraceful nature of his escapades in the underworld of Copenhagen.

Meanwhile it looked as if Mr. Lakiær got along very well with the family in Spentrup, and soon he became engaged to marry the eldest daughter, Christiane—according to the time-honored custom of Scandinavian clerical homes, where the curate usually marries the minister's daughter, if such a female is available. But one Sunday morning, when Christiane entered the bedroom of her fiancé to bring him the usual Danish morning snack, a cup of tea and some slices of bread and butter, before he had to get up and go about his duty in the village church, Mr. Lakiær lay dead in his bed. He had committed suicide, putting a bullet through his brain.

To Blicher and his family this was a shattering grief. And the vacancy after Mr. Lakiær was never filled; Blicher was not to get another curate. Jens Frederik had accepted a situation as a *Landsbydegn* and given up the idea of becoming a minister. Blicher and his parishioners had to get along as well, or as badly, as they could.

But in this time of his deepest misery Steen Blicher was still able to write some of his artistically most finished short stories. And even if most of *E Bindstouw*, his garland of dialect stories and poems, had been written years ago, he must have put the finishing touches to this masterpiece of his before it was published in 1842. And there is other evidence that Steen Blicher possibly was not so ruined by drink as his kind neighbors would make out to be the case. His Jutland stubbornness as well as his ingrained dislike of order, cleanliness, and rules of conventional behavior may have induced him willfully to appear more broken down by an irregular life than he really was. One of his biographers—Jeppe Aakiær, I believe—has unearthed a number of small notebooks in which Blicher after his hunting trips used to enter the bag of the day. These entries prove that almost up to the end of his life he was the same splendid marksman he had been since he was a mere youth. And it seems improbable that he could have retained such sureness of eye and hand, if he had been as badly *forfalden* as he was supposed to be.

When Reitzel in 1846 published his collected short stories and poems in six volumes, Blicher had won nation-wide recognition: together with a great deal of dross and many things stamped with the carelessness of too hasty production, there were gems that will be treasured by his people as long as the Danes speak and write Danish. But next year, in 1847, the inevitable happened: Pastor Blicher was requested to apply for a release from his office as minister to the twin parishes of Spentrup and Gassum.

Pastor Blicher had to apply, so that he could be "graciously relieved" with a pension. And while his fate, and the fate of his former parish, was still pending, Death mercifully relieved Steen Blicher from the sorrows and cares of life.

Christian VIII died on January 20, 1848, and with grave misgivings the Danish people saw his son and heir, unreliable, unpredictable Prince Frederik, ascend to the throne in a time of dire peril to the country. And on March 23 open insurrection broke out in Holstein. But when it happened Steen Blicher was on his deathbed in his bare, poor study in the vicarage of Spentrup. A lingering typhoid fever slowly drained the life out of him. His son Francisco and his daughter-in-law, who had been sent for, were the only ones to be with him when he passed away, quietly as a candle burns out.

The "Prisoner of Life" was set free; the strange bird who had always known that his life on earth was a migration towards another world had left the land that had become too wintry for him. Of the ideas he had broadcast so liberally, with such disregard for what ordinary common-sense people mean by happiness and the respect of one's fellow men, very many became firmly rooted in the soil of Denmark, to flourish in times of adversity and in times of prosperity for the nation, spreading like the forests he had dreamed of, which were to make his barren moors fertile and life-giving to his people, even if the price must be the passing of that wild and melancholy beauty that had been the true home of his heart. His fame as one of the great masters of the Danish tongue, and as a mind that knew the mind of his own race more intimately than most others, has grown through the years—overshadowing the memory of his frailties and his misfortunes, until the tragedy of Steen Blicher's life only made his genius dearer to his nation.

THE JOURNAL OF A
PARISH CLERK

[En Landsbydegns Dagbog, 1824]

FÖULUM, January 1, 1708.

GOD give us all a happy New Year! and preserve our good Pastor Sören. He blew out the candle last night, and mother says he will not live to see next New Year; but I dare say it means nothing.—We had a merry evening. When Pastor Sören took off his cap after supper, and said *"Agamus gratias,"* he pointed to me instead of to Jens. It is the first time I have said grace in Latin. A year ago today Jens said it, and then I opened my eyes wide, for then I didn't understand a word, but now I know half of Cornelius. Just think if I could become pastor at Föulum! Oh, how happy my dear parents would be if they might live to see that day. And then if the Pastor's Jens could become bishop of Ribe—as his father says—well, who can tell? It is all in God's hands. His will be done! *Amen in nomine Jesu.*

✧

FÖULUM, September 3, 1708.

Yesterday by the grace of God I completed my fifteenth year. Now Jens is not much ahead of me in Latin. I work harder at home than he does; I study hard while he is running about with Peer Gamekeeper. That's hardly the way to become a bishop. I am sorry for Pastor Sören; he can't help seeing it. The tears come into his eyes sometimes when he says, *"Mi fili! mi fili! otium est pulvinar diaboli."*—At New Year we shall begin the study of Greek. Pastor Sören has given me a Greek Testament. "They're queer crow's feet, are they not? They must seem like a whetstone in your eyes," he said kindly, and pinched my ear, as he always does when he is pleased. But heyday, won't he be surprised when he finds that I can read it quite fast already!

FÖULUM, *die St. Martini.*

Things are going badly with Jens. Pastor Sören was so angry with him that he talked Danish to him all day. To me he spoke in Latin. I once overheard him saying to himself, *"Vellem hunc esse filium meum."* He meant me. And how Jens did stammer at his Cicero! I know very well why, for day before yesterday, while his father was attending a wedding in Vinge, he was with Peer Gamekeeper in Lindum woods, and—God help us!—a wild boar had torn his breeches. He lied to his mother and said the Thiele bull had done it, but she gave him a good box on the ear—*habeat!*

❖

FÖULUM, *Calendis Januar, 1709.*

Proh, dolor! Pastor Sören is dead. *Væ me miserum!* When we had sat down to the table Christmas Eve he put away his spoon and looked long and sadly at Jens. *"Fregisti cor meum,"* he said with a sigh, and went into his bedchamber. Alas, he never rose again. I have visited him every day since then, and he has given me much good advice and admonition; but now I shall never see him again. Thursday I saw him for the last time. Never shall I forget what he said, after a very moving address to me, "God, give my son an upright heart!" He folded his thin hands, and sank back on the pillow. *"Pater! in manus tuas committo spiritum meum."* Those were his last words. When I saw the mistress put her apron to her eyes, I ran out of the room, feeling very unhappy. Jens was standing outside the door, crying. *"Seras dat poenas turpi poenitentia,"* I thought, but he fell on my neck and sobbed. God forgive him his wildness! That is what has grieved me most.

❖

FÖULUM, *Pridie iduum Januarii MDCCIX.*

Yesterday my dear father went to Viborg to arrange for my dinners when I am to go to school. How I long for that time to come! I study all day, but the days are so short now, and mother says we cannot afford to use candles to read by. I can't make head or tail of that letter to Tuticanus. No—things were different when the good Pastor Sören was living. *Eheu mortuus est!*

It is a terrible winter. Heaven and earth are one whirl; there is a snowdrift that reaches to the rooftree of our barn. Last night Jens shot two hares in our vegetable garden—he seems to have forgotten his poor father. But if Peer Gamekeeper finds out about it, there will be trouble.

FÖULUM, *Idibus Januarii MDCCIX.*

Father has not come home yet, and the weather is as bad as ever. If only he does not lose his way! There is Jens on top of our barn carrying his gun and a brace of birds in his hand—he is coming in here.

They were partridges he had shot on Mads Madsen's dung-hill, and he wanted mother to roast them for him, but she was afraid of the squire, and refused.

FÖULUM, *XVIII Calend. Februar.*

Alas the day! My dear father is frozen to death. The man at Kokholm found him in a snowdrift and brought him home in his cart. I have cried till I can't see out of my eyes—and mother, too. God help us both!

FÖULUM, February 18, 1709.

I hardly know Jens; he had gotten a green coat and a green feather in his hat. "There, you can see," he said. "Now I'm a hunter. What are you? A schoolboy, a Latin grind!"—"Yes, God help us," I replied. "There will be no more Latin. I can become a pastor where you're a bishop. My mother is not going to starve to death while I sing at people's doors in Viborg. I

have to stay home and earn a living for her. Oh, Jens, if your
father had lived!"—"Don't let us talk about it," he said. "Anyway, I'd never in all my days have learned Latin—devil take
the stupid stuff! Why don't you try to get service at the squire's?
There you'll have a fine time and live well."—"How should I
get in there?" I replied.—"We'll try anyway," said Jens, and
ran away. After all, Jens has a kind heart, but he is wild and
flighty. Six weeks ago he buried his sainted father, and three
weeks ago his mother followed her husband. But now it is as if
it didn't concern him. He can cry one moment, and laugh the
next.

THIELE, May 1, 1709.
So now I am a servant in the squire's family. Good-bye pastorate! Good-bye Latin! Oh, my precious books! *Valete, pluri-
mum! Vendidi libertatem* for twelve dollars. The eight must
go to my poor mother, and the squire has promised her besides
a part in all the trees that are felled in the forest, so she will
neither freeze nor starve. It is really Jens who has gotten me
this place. He has a lot to say here in the big house. He is a devil
of a fellow, or rather cock of the walk. The housekeeper put
a big piece of cake in his hand; the dairywoman smirked at him,
the chambermaid likewise, and even one of the young ladies
nodded kindly as she passed him. It looks as if he may become
gamekeeper in place of Peer. The worst of it is that he has
gotten into the habit of swearing worse than any sailor.

THIELE, March 12, 1709.
I am getting along very well, God be thanked. We are six
servants to wait on the master and mistress, the young master,
and the two young ladies. I have time to read, and I don't
neglect my beloved books. Of course it is not of any use, but I
can't leave them alone. Yesterday the books of our dear Pastor
Sören were sold. I bought for two dollars and got as many as I

could carry away. Among them were a number of Ovidius; one is entitled *Ars amoris* and another *Remedium amoris*. I am going to read them first; I do want to know what they are all about. Once I happened to get hold of them in Pastor Sören's study, but he snatched them away from me, saying, "*Abstine manus!* Hands off! That's nothing for you."

❖

THIELE, June 3, 1709.

If I could only learn French! The family never speak anything but French at table, and I don't understand a word of it. Today they were speaking about me, for they looked at me several times. Once I came near dropping a plate. I was standing right behind Miss Sophie's chair, when she turned and looked me full in the face. She is a beautiful young lady, Miss Sophie—it is a joy to look at her.

❖

THIELE, September 13, 1709.

Yesterday was a day full of commotion. The family from Viskum were here, and there was a big hunt. I was along and had one of the squire's guns. At first all went well, but then a wolf passed close to me. I was so frightened, I almost dropped the gun, and quite forgot to shoot. Jens was standing by my side and shot the wolf. "You're a blockhead," he said, "but I won't tell on you." Soon after the squire passed me. "You're a bungler, Martin," he said. "You must have been bribed."—"I humbly beg your pardon, sir," I replied. "I am quite innocent, but someone must have slandered me. God helping, I will serve you honestly and truly, sir." At that he was pleased to laugh, and said, "You're a great bungler." But that was not the end of it, for when the family were at table they began to talk about the wolf again, asked me, "How much did he give you?" and so forth. I don't know just what they meant, but at least I could understand that they were making fun of me in French and in Danish, too. Even Miss Sophie was laughing at me to my face—that hurt me most of all. I wonder if I couldn't learn that snuffling gibberish. Surely it can't be more difficult than Latin.

✧

THIELE, October 2, 1709.

It's not impossible—I see that now. French is nothing but garbled Latin. In a box of old books that I bought there was a French translation of *Metamorphoses*—it came in quite pat. The Latin I had learned before. But one thing seems odd to me. When I listen to them talking up there, I can't make out a French word in what they are saying—it's certainly not Ovidius they're discussing.

I must learn to shoot. The squire wants me to go along when he hunts, but there I can never please him; he either scolds me or laughs at me—and sometimes he does both at once: I don't carry the gun right, I don't take aim right, and I don't shoot right. "Look at Jens!" says the squire. "He's a hunter. You carry the gun as if it were a scythe slung over your shoulder, and when you take aim you look as if you were falling backward." Miss Sophie, too, laughs at me—but laughing is very becoming to her; she has such beautiful teeth.

✧

THIELE, November 7, 1709.

Yesterday I shot a fox; the squire called me a good *garçon* and made me a present of an inlaid powder horn. Jens's instruction has borne fruit. This shooting is quite good fun.—I am getting along better with the French; I am catching on to the pronunciation. One day I listened at the door when the French governess was giving the young ladies their lesson. When they were through and had gone upstairs, I contrived to look at the book to find out which one they were using. Good gracious! How surprised I was! It was one that I too have, one called *L'École du Monde*. So now I stand outside the door every day with my book in my hand, listening to them. It works very well. After all, the French language is much prettier than I realized; it sounds lovely when Miss Sophie speaks it.

❖

THIELE, December 13, 1709.

Yesterday God saved my gracious master's life by my poor hand. We had a battue in Lindum woods. Just as we were opposite Graakjær, a wild boar rushed out and made straight for the squire. He fired, and hit it all right, but did not kill it, and the boar went for him. The squire was not frightened; he drew his hanger and was about to plunge it in the breast of the boar when it broke in two. Now, what was to be done? It all happened so quickly that no one could reach him. I ran toward him, but in the same moment I saw the squire on the back of the boar, and off it dashed with him. "Fire!" he cried to the bailiff, who had been standing next to him on the left—but the bailiff didn't dare to. "Fire, in the devil's name," he called to Jens as he passed him. Jens's gun missed fire. Then the boar turned and passed close to me. "Fire, Martin, or the boar will ride to hell with me," he screamed. In the name of God, I thought, and aimed for the animal's hindquarters, and was lucky enough to crush both its thighs. Glad was I, and happy were we all, the squire especially. "That was a master shot," he said. "And now you keep the gun, since you can use it so well. And listen," he said to the bailiff, "you mollycoddle! Mark me the biggest beech in the forest for his mother. Jens can go home and fix his gun." Then, when we came home in the evening, there was a questioning and narrating. The squire patted me on the shoulder, and Miss Sophie smiled on me so kindly that my heart was in my throat.

❖

THIELE, January 11, 1710.

A *plaisant* weather! The sun rises red as a burning coal. It looks so *curieux* as it shines through the white trees, and all the trees look as if they had been powdered, and the branches hang around them down to the ground. The old Grand Richard is badly battered; a couple of its limbs are broken already. It was just such a day a week ago when we drove to Fussingöe, and I was standing on the runners of Miss Sophie's sleigh. She wanted to handle the reins herself, but after about fifteen minutes her small fingers began to feel cold. *"J'ai froid,"* she said to herself. "Do you want me to drive, Miss?" I asked.—*"Comment!"* she said. "Do you understand French?"—*"Un peu, made-moiselle,"* I replied. She turned round and looked me full in the face. I took one of the reins in either hand, and thus had both my arms round her. I tried to hold them far apart in order not to come too near her, but whenever the sleigh gave a jolt and threw her against me, it seemed as if I had touched a hot stove. I felt as if I were flying through space with her, and we were at Fussingöe before I knew it. If she had not called out, *"Tenez, Martin! arretez-vous!"* I should have driven on to Randers or to the world's end. I wonder if she isn't going out driving to-day! But there is Jens with the squire's gun, which he has cleaned—so I suppose we are going out hunting again.

❖

THIELE, February 13, 1710.

I don't feel well. It is as if a heavy stone were weighing on my chest. I can't keep my food down, and at night I can't sleep. Last night I had a strange dream. It seemed to me that I was standing on the runners of Miss Sophie's sleigh, and then suddenly I was sitting in the sleigh and had her on my lap. My right arm was around her waist, and her left around my neck. She bent down and kissed me, but in the same moment I awakened. Oh, I wanted so much to go on dreaming!—It is a fine book she lent me. I amuse myself reading it every night. Oh, if one could be as happy as the Tartarean prince! The more French I read the better I like it; I am almost forgetting my Latin on account of it.

THIELE, March 13, 1710.

Yesterday, as we were coming home from hunting snipes, the squire said to me, "And I hear that you understand French?"—"A little, sir," I replied.—"But then you can't wait on table; we couldn't open our mouths with you there." —"Oh, sir," I cried, "you don't mean to send me away?"— "*Point de tout*," he replied. "From now on you shall be my *valet de chambre*. And when Master Kresten goes to Paris, you shall go with him. What do you say to that?" I was so moved that I couldn't say a word, but kissed his hand. But although I look forward to going, I dread the thought of leaving, and I really think my health has worsened since then.

✧

THIELE, May 1, 1710.

Wretched creature that I am! Now I know what is the matter with me. Ovidius has described my distemper exactly. If I am not mistaken, it is called *Amor*, which means "love" or "infatuation," and the person I am enamored of must without a doubt be Miss Sophie. Miserable fool that I am! What will this lead to? I must try his *Remedia amoris*. A few minutes ago I saw her standing in the hall and talking to Jens. It cut me to the heart as with a knife. I could have shot him through the head, but then she skipped past me with a smile—I felt as when I am out hunting and the quarry comes within range of my gun; my heart pounds against my ribs, and I can hardly get my breath, and my eyes are as if they were glued to the animal—*ah, malheureux que je suis!*

✧

THIELE, June 17, 1710.

How empty and tiresome the house seems. The family are away and won't be back for a week. How shall I get through it? I don't want to do anything. My gun hangs there dirty and rusty, and I don't care to bother about cleaning it. How can Jens and the rest of them be so gay and happy! They're

jabbering and roaring with laughter till the yard gives echo—
while I sigh like a bittern. Oh, Miss Sophie, if only you were
a peasant girl or I a prince!

❖

THIELE, June 28, 1710.

Now the house looks to me as if it had been newly whitewashed and embellished. The trees in the garden have taken
on a lovely light green color, and everybody looks kind. Miss
Sophie has come home. She came in through the gate like the
sun piercing a cloud; but nevertheless I trembled like a leaf.
It's both good and bad to be in love.

❖

THIELE, October 4, 1710.

We had a magnificent hunt today. Three hundred beaters
were posted in Hvidding copse, for they had come from Viskum
and Fussingöe with all their hounds. We of Thiele were on
the spot at dawn. There was no wind, and a thick layer of fog
covered the land; only the beacon hills could be seen above it.
Within the fog we could hear the heavy footsteps of the beaters
and occasionally the baying of a hound. "There they are coming from Viskum," said the squire; "I know Chasseur's bark."
—"And now they are coming from Fussingöe, too," said
Jens. "That's Perdrix baying." Still we couldn't see anything
on account of the fog, but as they came nearer we heard the
rumbling of the carts, the breathing of the horses, the talk and
laughter of the gamekeepers. The huntsmen were already putting the beaters in their positions; we could hear them whispering and hushing those who were inclined to talk too loud,
and sometimes using their sticks. From the west and the south
the gamekeepers came driving in, and behind them came the
carts with the hounds, their tails wagging over the side of
the carts and sometimes a head protruding—only to get a box
on the ear from the huntsmen's boys. Now the squire himself

posted us all down the long valley that runs through the copse. When he was ready, he blew his whistle, and the hornblowers started to play a merry piece. The hounds were loosed, and it was not long before they began baying, first one, then two, then the whole pack. Hares, foxes, and deer darted back and forth in the brushwood on the hills. Now and then a shot rang out, echoing down through the valley. We could not see the beaters, but we heard them shouting and calling when a hare or a deer tried to break through. I held my place and shot two foxes and a buck before lunch. While we were eating, the hounds were called in and tied up, but the hornblowers played. When it was over, off we went again. Just then two carriages stopped at the entrance to the valley with the ladies, among them Miss Sophie. That saved a fox, for while I was looking up at them, he slipped past me. Before nightfall the copse was cleared of game. We must have shot about thirty animals, and Master Kresten, who had killed the most foxes, was honored by a piece played on the bugle.

❖

THIELE, December 17, 1710.

Yesterday I followed my dear mother to her last resting-place. The new pastor—God reward him for it!—honored her passing with a funeral sermon that lasted an hour and three quarters. She was a good and loving mother to me. God give her a blessed awakening!

❖

THIELE, January 23, 1711.

What a miserable winter! No sleighing yet! I have been longing for it ever since Martinmas, but in vain. Rain and wind, southerly gales, and dreary weather. Last year at this time we drove to Fussingöe. When I think of that night! The moon shone as bright as a silver platter on the blue sky, throwing our shadows to the side of the road on the white snow. Sometimes I leaned over till my shadow mingled with that of Miss Sophie; then it seemed to me that we two were one. A

cold wind blew in our faces and carried her sweet breath back
to me; I drank it in like wine. Oh, fool that I am!—lovesick
fool that I am! What good do such thoughts do me? Sunday
I am going to Copenhagen with Master Kresten, and there
we are going to stay all summer. I dare say I shall be dead
before Mayday.—*Ah, mademoiselle Sophie, adieu! un éternel
adieu!*

✧

AT SEA BETWEEN SAMSÖE AND ZEALAND,
February 3, 1711.

The sun is setting behind my dear Jutland; the reflection lies
over the calm sea like an endless path of fire. It seems to
bring a greeting from my home. Alas! it is far away, and I
am getting farther and farther away from it. I wonder what
they are doing now at Thiele! My right ear is burning—perhaps it is Miss Sophie who is talking about me? Alas, no! I
am only a poor servant; why should she think of me?—any
more than the skipper who is walking up and down on the
deck with arms crossed. Every little while he looks toward the
north; I wonder what he sees there? "A Swede," he says. God
help us in His mercy and goodness!

✧

KALLUNDBORG, February 4, 1711.

Now I know what war is. I have been in battle, and—the
Lord of Sabaoth be praised!—victory was ours. It was, as the
skipper said, a Swedish privateer. Early this morning, as soon
as it was light, we saw him only two miles away from us; they
said he was chasing us. "Are there any of you passengers,"
said the skipper, "who have courage and stout hearts and would
like to try a bout with that Swedish fellow?"—"I have a good
rifle," replied Master Kresten, "and my servant has one. What
of it, Morten, shall we try this kind of hunt for once?"—"As
you please, Master Kresten," I said, ran down into the cabin,
loaded our rifles, and brought them up on deck together with

powder and shot. There were two soldiers from Jutland who came up from the hold, and they had each a blunderbuss, and the skipper had a Spanish gun as long as himself. The mate and the sailors armed themselves with axes and marlinspikes. "Can't we sail away from him, my good skipper?" I asked.—"The devil we can," he replied. "Don't you see he's gaining on us for all he's worth? We shall soon be hearing his cannon. But if you're scared, you can go home and crawl into your mother's bureau drawer." In the same moment the smoke poured from the Swedish ship, and then we heard a terrific noise and a whizzing over our heads. Before long there was another explosion, and then another, and the last cannon ball tore a splinter from our mast. Then a strange feeling came over me; my heart pounded, and there was a ringing and a buzzing in my ears. But when the Swede came so near that we could reach him with our rifles, and I had taken my first shot, then I felt as if I were out hunting. The Swede came nearer and nearer. We stood in the shelter of the cabin and fired at him across our stern as fast as we could. Several of his people fell, most of them hit by the young master or me. "If we can shoot a snipe, Morten, surely we can hit a Swede, when he stands still," he said.—"Brave fellows!" said the skipper. "Do you see the Swedish captain, the man with the big sabre, who's walking up and down? If you can pick him off, we've won the game!" I aimed at him, pressed the trigger, and as I took my rifle from my cheek, I saw him fall and strike the deck with his nose. "Hurrah!" cried the skipper, and we all cheered. But the privateer turned round and sailed away. With the Danish flag flying aloft we sailed into Kallundborg Fjord, proud and happy, for not a man had been wounded, although the cannon balls flew over and through the ship. The tutor, Monsieur Hartman, was the only one who saw his own blood, and that happened in a curious way. He was lying in the skipper's bunk smoking his pipe when the battle commenced. A little later I came down to fetch tow for the bullets. "*Martin*," said he, "*quid hoc sibi vult?*" But before I could answer, a bullet flew through the cabin window and shot away his pipe which he was holding out over the edge of the bunk—and the mouthpiece pierced his palate.

Now we are in port and on dry land, where rest is sweet after such a bout.

✧

COPENHAGEN, June 2, 1711.

My head is full of all the strange things I have seen. I can't dispose them in my mind, for one chases the other like clouds in a wind. But the most curious thing is that I have almost gotten over my lovesickness. The longer I stay here, the less it seems to me I long for Miss Sophie, and I am almost ready to believe there are just as beautiful maidens in Copenhagen. If I were to write a footnote to *Ovidii Remedium amoris*, I would recommend a trip to the Capital as one of the best cures for that dangerous malady.

✧

ANCHORED UNDER KRONBORG, September 12, 1711.

Oh, gracious Heaven! What have I not lived through! What wretchedness and misery have I not seen with these my eyes! God has visited our sins upon us and stricken the people with boils. They died like flies round about me, but I, unworthy that I am, was saved from the jaws of death. Oh, my dear young master! What shall I say when I come back without him? But I did not leave him till he had drawn his last breath; I risked my life for him, and yet God preserved it—praised be His name! When I think of those days of horror, my heart is ready to break. Silent and full of fear, we sat from morning till night in our lonely apartment, gazing at each other and sighing. Once in a while we looked down into the empty streets that used to swarm with people. Now and then a mournful figure would walk across the pavement like a ghost. Inside the windows we could see people sitting like prisoners, most of them as immovable as if they were painted portraits. But when they heard the hollow rumbling of the dead-carts, they would rush away from the windows in order not to see the dreadful sight. I saw it but once, and wanted no more. There those black angels of death drove their long carts, full of corpses piled up like dead cattle. In the back of one cart hung the head and arms of a young woman; her eyes stared horribly in the blackish-yellow face, and her long hair swept the street. Then my young master was shaken for the first time; he tottered into his bedchamber and lay down on his deathbed; but I sighed in my heart: "Like sheep they are laid in the grave; death shall feed on them. But God will redeem my soul from the power of the grave: for He shall receive me. Selah!"

❖

THIELE, September 29, 1711.

So now I am here again. When I went in through the door my heart pounded in me almost as on the day we fought the Swede. And when I came in to the family and saw them all in black, then I wept like a child, and they wept, too. I could hardly speak for tears, and before I had finished the *affreuse* story, the squire turned away and went into his bedchamber. God comfort them in His mercy, amen!

❖

THIELE, October 8, 1711.

Today we went hunting for the first time since my return. Alas, it was not as in former days and gave but little satisfaction! "Martin," said the squire again and again to me, "we miss Master Kresten!" He sighed so that it cut me to the heart. We came home long before nightfall with one poor little hare.

❖

THIELE, November 2, 1711.

The house is getting lively again; we are expecting exalted company: His Excellency Lord Gyldenlöve and retinue. He is going to stay a few weeks and amuse himself with the chase. Yesterday the family discussed the matter at table. "He is of royal blood and a perfect gentleman," said the mistress, looking at Miss Sophie. She blushed, looked down at her plate, and smiled, but I grew cold as ice through my whole body. Alas, alas! I thought I had been cured of my foolish infatuation, but I feel the distemper has come back in even greater force. I struggle like a partridge in a snare, but it is of no avail. Oh, that I were a thousand miles from here!

✧

THIELE, November 14, 1711.

At last His Excellency has arrived, in all his glory and grandeur. Two running footmen with tall, silver-trimmed caps came trotting into the yard half a mile ahead of him. They posted themselves with their long motley staves on either side of the big door. The mistress waddled in at one door and out another; never have I seen her in such *égalité*. Miss Sophie was standing in the drawing room and looking now at the mirror, now out of the window. She didn't even see me when I passed through the room. At last he himself came in a carriage drawn by six yellow horses, a handsome and *magnifique* gentleman. He looked both distinguished and gracious, and yet I felt there was something repulsive about him. His smile seemed to me sickly sweet, and his eyes blinked as if he were looking at the sun. Though he bowed to each member of the family, it seemed as though he only bowed in order to draw himself up all the higher. When he came to Miss Sophie, the blood rose slightly in his face, and he whispered or lisped a long French compliment. At table he never took his eyes from her, not even when he was speaking to someone else. She threw a glance at him occasionally; but I burned my hand on the plates, and today it is full of blisters. Would it were only the hand that pained me!

✧

THIELE, November 20, 1711.

Yes, it's certain enough; there will be a *mariage*. One need only look at the mistress. When she sees Miss Sophie, she lays

her head back like a duck that has got its crop full, turns as if
she were on the point of going to sleep, and then she gabbles:
"*Un cavalier accompli, ma fille! n'est-ce pas vrai? et il vous
aime, c'est trop clair?*" Yes, more's the pity, it is plain enough;
and she loves him in return, that is plain, too. May she be happy.

✧

THIELE, December 4, 1711.

As yet His Excellency has not profited much from the chase.
Twice we have set out, but each time he has wearied of it before we had gone half way. There is a quarry in the house at
home that draws him like a magnet. Alas! Would that I had not
left Copenhagen!

✧

THIELE, December 8, 1711.

Today the *mariage* was declared. The wedding is to be in a
week. Where shall I hide till then? I can't bear it. When he
puts his arm around her waist, it is as though someone stuck a
knife into my heart—

Good heavens! I believe Jens is as badly smitten as I am.
When I told him about the *mariage*, he thrust his gun so hard
against the ground that the butt broke, and then he dashed out
on the heath with the broken piece in his hand. So I am not the
only fool in the world.

✧

THIELE, December 16, 1711.

Miss Sophie has the smallpox. Oh, how I tremble for her
life! Would that I might die in her place; but they say I can't
get this sickness more than once. Her lovely face is full of
blisters.

✧

THIELE, December 19, 1711.

Here is great sorrow and lamentation. Miss Marie is dead,
and the squire is inconsolable, but the mistress speaks only about
the funeral and how that is to be arranged. Miss Sophie will

probably be the next to go, for she is very poorly. His Excellency, her fiancé, is getting ready to leave—good riddance!

❖

THIELE, March 13, 1712.

So now I have risen from my long illness. I thought it would have been my last, and prayed to God in my heart for deliverance. But it seems that I am to wander in this vale of tears yet a while—it is His will—let it be done! It seems as though I had risen from the dead, and I feel as though this illness had lasted three years instead of three months. Yesterday I saw her for the first time since I was stricken, and I kept my countenance. I could almost believe that the illness had taken with it my foolish infatuation.

She was a little pale and did not look particularly happy. Nor has she any reason to be happy, more's the pity. His Excellency is surely a great libertine. The other day I saw through a crack in my door how he caught hold of the mistress' maid and that in a very unseemly manner. Oh, my poor young lady! If I were His Excellency I would worship her as an angel from heaven.

❖

THIELE, May 1, 1712.

His Excellency has gone away and left his fiancée here. He is plainly tired of her already, and—God forgive me!—if I don't think she is tired of him, too. She certainly is not pining for him; for she is just as merry and *vive* or even more so; but once in a while she is a bit overbearing. Sometimes she speaks to me as if I were a beggar, sometimes as if I were her equal. I almost think she wants to make game of me—poor creature that I am! I am afraid I have not yet come to my senses, for she can make me happy or depressed as she pleases.

❖

THIELE, June 3, 1712.

My health is gone forever, and my youthful gaiety is a thing of the past. I am dull and heavy in my whole being and have no pleasure in anything. I don't care to hunt, and I don't care to read; my gun and my *Ovidius* are both equally dusty. French, which used to give me so much enjoyment, I cannot bear either to hear or to read—it is a deceitful language.

❖

THIELE, June 24, 1712.

I have exchanged bedchambers with Jens. He was bent on getting mine, because he was afraid to lie near the cemetery, the silly fool! After all, that is where some time he will lie forever. I am well pleased with the change; from my window I can see the graves of my dear parents—they are at peace—God give their souls great joy in heaven! Over there is Pastor Sören's grave; the thistles are growing on it already—I must pull them up!

❖

THIELE, December 13, 1712.

The mistress' maid has a little son. She has declared a lace-peddler to be the father, but everybody in the house knows who is the guilty one. Miss Sophie has even joked about it. I don't see how she could, but she takes things lightly—such is not my nature.

❖

THIELE, February 27, 1713.

Am I dreaming or am I awake? Have my senses deceived me, or was she really mine? Yes, she was mine—I have embraced her with these my arms; she has lain on my breast, and covered my face with kisses—with hot kisses. Now I wish I could die, for I shall never be so happy again. But, no! What is the matter with me? What have I done? Oh, I don't know what I am writing—I believe I am going out of my mind.

❖

THIELE, March 5, 1713.

Let me recall in my memory those douce moments! Let me reflect on the rapture I felt; it is only now that I seem to awaken as from an intoxication.—The squire came home from the chase, while Jens had stayed behind in the forest to dig out Tax who was stuck in a pit. I knew very well that he would not come home before daylight, and I had an impulse to lie in my old room. I had just gone to sleep when I was awakened by a kiss. Startled, I sat up and was about to cry out, when I felt a soft hand on my mouth and an arm around my neck, and a sweet voice whispering—heavens! it was hers—hers whom I don't dare to name. Then—then—oh, sinner that I am! hardened sinner that I am! I have betrayed my master! and I can't even repent it from my heart. Whenever I want to do penance, I am held back by a secret rapture which mocks my remorse. I feel it: I long to repeat the transgression which I ought to curse. "Ever mine!" were the first words I could utter, but then she tore herself from my embrace with a low cry, and—I was alone. The door creaked and I sat up in bed; I wondered if it had been a wraith. Oh, why did she flee? Why then did she come of herself, uncalled, untempted? Has she loved me as I have loved her, silently, deeply, passionately?

❖

THIELE, March 6, 1713.

Oh, world, world! How art thou false! Honesty has passed away, virtue and honor are trampled under foot! Yet why do I complain? Am I better than he? Is my sin less because I believe my love is greater? Ah, I only got my deserts; one of us is as good as the other—one betrays the other. Ha, you deceitful woman, you Potiphar's wife! That was why you cried out and fled when you heard my voice. So it was old habit, a beaten path, when you sought my bed—no, Jens's bed! Old love, old sin! While I worshipped you, while I looked up to you with veneration as to a holy angel, you were whoring with my fellow servant!

It was midnight. Intoxicated with sweet memories I strolled around in the garden. In a dim walk I saw something stirring— something that told me it was she. With quickened steps I hurried to the spot—it was she! Yes, it was she, but how did I find her? On Jens's lap, with her arms around his neck. Quickly they started away from each other, and I stood as if I were sinking into an abyss. The sun found me in the same place; I shivered with cold, trembled like an aspen leaf. Oh, thou wretched, thou false, thou corrupt world!

❖

THIELE, March 9, 1713.

I have seen her for the first time since that night of sin. A quick blush passed over her face; she let her eyes flit around the room in order not to look at me. I felt myself getting hot and cold. As soon as we were alone, she passed me rapidly saying with half-closed eyes, *"Silence!"* She was out of the door before I was quite conscious of something pressed into my hand.

❖

THIELE, April 13, 1713.

Everything is discovered. The master, the mistress, the entire household know it, and it is Mademoiselle Lapouce who has found them out and exposed them. Miss Sophie sometimes amused herself by raillery at her expense, and this she had taken note of. No one has suspected that the sly woman understood a word of Danish, and so they must have said something carelessly in her presence from which she got wind of what was happening. She has followed the scent until she ran them down. Heavens! what a commotion! The squire ran around with his gun threatening to shoot Jens; but Jens was on his horse and already far away. The young lady was locked in the corner room in order that the squire should not lay violent hands on her. Good heavens! What will be the end of it! I tremble whenever I hear his voice. My conscience condemns me and makes a coward of me. Remorse and fear have so overpowered me that they have driven love and jealousy out of my heart. I wish I were fifteen leagues under the ground.

THIELE, April 14, 1713.

The young lady is gone! Last night she escaped through a window. Jens has surely been here and abducted her; for about midnight someone saw two persons on one horse, but on account of the dark, he could not see whether both were men. They were on the road to Viborg, and we have been out, every man of us, all day long hunting for them. We came back without finding them. I heard a rumor that they had crossed Skiern bridge, but I shall certainly take care not to come near them. Alas! alas! what a world we live in! My poor master! I am afraid he will take his death over it. He lies on his bed, and doesn't allow any human being to come near him.

❖

THIELE, April 20, 1713.

Today I was called in to the squire. Oh, Thou gracious Saviour! How pale and shrunken he was! He will not live, that I could plainly see. "Martin," said he, when I came in, "is that you? Come over here to me." As soon as I heard his voice I burst into tears. Formerly it sounded as if he were speaking out of a barrel, and when he called out of the big door, "Martin, bring the dogs!" the house shook, and chickens and ducks flew up startled. But now he spoke so low and his voice was so feeble that my heart was ready to break. "Martin," he said, "have you seen any snipes?"—"No, dear master," I replied sobbing. "I haven't been out at all."—"Oh, haven't you?" he said. "I shall never shoot any more."—"Oh, you may," I said. "God can yet help you."—"No, Martin," he said, "I am nearing the end. If I had only had Kresten!" At that he pressed two tears back into his hollow eyes. "Where is Vaillant?" he asked.—"He is lying in front of the fire," I replied.—"Call him," said he. The dog came and laid his head on the edge of the bed. The master patted him a long time and looked sadly at him. "You have been a faithful servant," he said. "You have not left me. When I am dead, you must shoot him and bury him under the big ash outside the cemetery, but shoot him carefully and don't

let him suspect what you are about to do—promise me that!"—
"Yes, dear master," I said.—"I don't want him to belong to
strangers," he said, as he sank back on the pillow. "My hunter
and Donner (his favorite gun) and my sword-belt I want you
to have. You must never part with my Blis. When he gets so
old that he can't eat any more, you must shoot him."—"Yes,
dear master," I said; I could hardly speak for weeping.—"And
there on the table is a wad, that's for you, for your faithful
service. Go now, Martin, and pray to God for my sinful soul."
I kissed the hand he held out to me, and stumbled down to my
own bedchamber. Oh, may God give him a blessed end! He
was a good and gracious master to me.

❖

THIELE, May 3, 1713.

So now he too is departed! Now I have not a friend on
earth. Here I cannot stay; I must out in the world and get rid
of my melancholy thoughts. Poor Vaillant! When I took my
gun he leaped joyfully around me; he did not know I was leading him to his death. No, such a shot I will never fire again as
long as I live. When I pulled the trigger, and he heard the
click, he began to wag his tail and look around as if he expected
a quarry, and least of all suspected that he himself was the object. When the shot was fired, and he writhed in the throes of
death, I felt as if the heart would burst out of my breast. Oh,
my dear blessed master! That was the last, the hardest service
I have done you.

❖

SAILING PAST THUNÖE, May 17, 1713.

For the second time—perhaps the last time—I am saying
farewell to thee, my beloved native land. Farewell, thou green
forest, thou brown heath! Farewell all the joys of my youth! It
was with a lighter heart that I ploughed these wild waves two
years ago. Then I had my kind master; now he is in his grave,
and my young master, too; she—whom I would like to forget

—is roving around in the wide world, God knows where and how. I too shall try my luck and eat my bread among strangers. Yes, I am going to try war, it will give bread or death. Blis and I shall go together, he is my last friend on earth.

❖

SWEDEN, June 13, 1716.

Here I sit, a captive in a foreign land. That is what my sword has brought me to. My colonel and I cleared a space among the enemy, but we were only two against ten. Alas, my old Blis! You found death, would that I had found it, too!

❖

STOCKHOLM, August 14, 1717.

This cannot go on much longer. They have dragged me from one fortress to another, tempted and threatened me to make me enter their service, but I would rather starve to death in a dungeon than fight against my rightful king and lord. But rather than that I would win my freedom. I will try it and find either that or death.

❖

NORRKÖPING, February 3, 1718.

So I became a Swedish soldier after all! However long I fled and hid like a hunted beast in forests and mountain clefts, they found me at last. What could I do? Better be under God's open sky among swords and guns than within the four walls of a prison! They have promised me that I should never have to fight against my countrymen, but only against the Muscovite— perhaps he has the bullet with the name of Morten Vinge.

❖

SIBERIA, May 15, 1721.

Lord my God! How strange are Thy ways! Many thousand miles from Denmark, I go about in a rough and dreary land; I walk over frozen rivers and wade in snow to my knees, while at home forest and field are putting on their green summer dress. Outside my old chamber window the apple tree is blossoming, the linnet is chirping in the gooseberry hedge, the starling sits on the well-curb and whistles a jolly piece, and the lark is singing overhead. Here wolves are howling, bears are grunting, hawks and ravens are crying in the black forests. Where, I wonder, is the end of this wilderness? And where is the end of my miserable life?

✧

RIGA, September 2, 1743.

Shall I really live the day when I see my native land once more? Four and twenty long, sorrowful years, four and twenty winters I have hunted sable and marten in the forests of Siberia. How weary of life have I not been this long, long time! But I will wait patiently till my Lord and Saviour calls me. Perhaps He will lay my weary limbs to rest in my native soil. Ah, there I see the Danish flag with the precious sign of the Cross and of our salvation. My soul, praise the Lord, and all that in me is His holy name!

✧

FALSTER, October 23, 1743.

Once more near death, and once more saved from it! In storm and bad weather I approached my beloved native land. The waves crushed our ship and threatened to devour us; but the Lord succored me, His hand upheld me—nor will He withdraw it from me now, though I wander, poor and half naked, among strangers.

✧

CORSELIDSE, November 2, 1743.

I have found a place of refuge, a shelter from the storms of the world, a godly and generous lord who has taken me into service and promised to provide for me to the day of my death. So I shall not move again before I am carried to my last home.

CORSELIDSE, May 1, 1744.

What a lovely land this is! Everything in full bloom! The woods are green and the meadow is green. Flowers everywhere! In Siberia it is still winter. God be thanked for such an exchange! My master is very fond of me. I often have to sit for hours telling him about the war and about all the countries I have wandered through. And if he likes to hear, I like to talk; I take pleasure in recalling to memory the innumerable misfortunes I have endured.

✧

CORSELIDSE, July 2, 1744.

Oh, Thou Father of Mercy! Was this bitter cup still left for me! Were the old wounds to be opened again! Ay, for such was Thy will.—I have seen her—her? Ah, no, not her! a fallen angel I have seen, an apparition of darkness. Often have I wished for death, but now—now I loathe my life—I cannot write any more.

✧

CORSELIDSE, August 8, 1744.

It is not for my pleasure that I once more take up my pen; but if anyone after my death should come upon this journal, I want him to see how sin rewards its children.

On that distressful day I was enjoying a walk in our beautiful garden. As I passed the open gate, I saw standing there a man whose face seemed familiar to me in spite of a thick black beard streaked with grey and a lowering look in his eyes that almost frightened me. "So you are here, too?" he said with a strange grin. The cane fell from my hand, and I trembled in every limb—it was Jens! "Good Lord my God!" said I. "Do I find you here! Where is Miss Sophie?"—He burst out with a loud oath, "No longer Miss or Madame either, but if you want to see my dearly beloved wife, she's lying down there, weeding. Sophy!" he cried, "here's an old acquaintance." Then she turned half around, looked at me for a moment, and went on weeding. I could not see the least sign of emotion in her

face—this face!—this once lovely face! How changed it was!
—pale and wan, wrinkled, sullen as if it had never smiled. A
ragged hood with long tatters of black lace made it look still
darker. Dirty remnants of clothes that had once been handsome and fine hung about her heavy, ill-shaped body. I felt as
if I were almost getting sick, and not a tear came into my eyes.
A fear, a loathing, as when one suddenly sees a viper, seized me.
I could neither speak nor stir from the spot. Jens roused me
from my stupor. "Now she isn't as handsome," he cried, "as
when she crept into bed with you." I shuddered. "The gilding
has worn off," he went on, "but she still has her fine spirit, high
and mighty she is still, and spiteful, and she can cackle. Hey,
gracious lady, talk to us!" She was silent, and pretended not to
hear, though he spoke loudly enough. "Now it doesn't please
her to speak," he said, "but when we get home, she'll set her
mouth going. Haven't you got something for a drink, Morten,
for old acquaintance's sake?" I gave him something, and went
up to the house like a sleepwalker. My master was standing by
the garden door. "Do you know those people?" he asked.—
"Ah, good God," I said. "Yes, I have known them many years
ago."—"They're a bad lot," he said. "She is shrewish and full
of cussedness, and he drinks like a sponge. They have lived for
a couple of years in a house down on the beach. He fishes, and
she works by the day in the garden. They say she is come of
decent people?" Then at last my tears began to flow, and relieved the pressure on my heart. I told him who she was, and
his horror was as great as my sorrow.

✧

Corselidse, September 14, 1744.
I doubt that I shall stay here. I no longer feel happy, since I
know that she is near me and I can't avoid seeing her often. As
yet I have not spoken with her, for I shun her as an evil spirit.
Jens seeks me with an importunity that pleases neither me nor
my master. When I smell his breath reeking with brandy, I

feel as if someone were offering me poison to drink. He has told me their story—oh, how terrible it is, how loathsome. They have strolled around from one place to another in Denmark and Germany; he played the bugle, and she sang and played the lute. In this way they made enough to subsist, and when it was not enough, she practised another trade which it wrings my heart to think of. At last that had to be given up, and they would have died of want if my kind master had not taken pity on them.—God forgive me, but I could almost wish I was back in Siberia.

❖

CORSELIDSE, May 1, 1745.

God bless my kind, generous master! He has understood my wish: to end my days in the place where I was born; and so he has arranged—without my knowledge—for a good place for me with the new family at Thiele. On Tuesday I shall take ship at Stubbekjöbing. God reward him for it in all eternity.

❖

AT SEA BETWEEN ZEALAND AND SAMSÖE,
June 4, 1745.

"Fear not them which kill the body, but are not able to kill the soul: but rather fear him which is able to destroy both soul and body." I feel the force of these words of the Saviour. When in my youth, on these waters, I stood before the bullets of the Swedes, I felt better than in the garden at Corselidse when I saw the fallen angel of my youth. Swords and bullets, stabbing and cutting, wounds and death are as nothing against the wasting of a soul, against the destruction of an innocent soul. If I had seen her beautiful body torn by wild beasts, it could not have wrung my heart as now when I found her ruined, corrupted, contemptible, lost beyond redemption. As she lay there digging in the dirt, it seemed to me that she buried my last hope, my last vestige of faith in honor and virtue. But I will say, as the old Turk who shared my captivity in Siberia used to say even amidst the greatest sufferings: "God is great." Yes, and merciful. He can do far more than we poor human beings understand.

❖

THIELE, July 4, 1745.

At last I have entered my winter haven. For more than thirty years I have been tossed about on the wild ocean waves of the world, in order to end where I began. What have I achieved? What have I gained? A grave—a resting-place with my parents. That is something, indeed not so little; I have friends and acquaintances here both above and under the ground. The apple tree still stands outside my window; it too has grown older, there's a canker in its trunk, the storms have bowed its head, and its limbs are covered with moss like the grey hair on the head of an old man. On the way to the church I see the big ash under the roots of which I buried poor Vaillant. So I remember many a tree, many a heather-grown hill, and even the dead stones that have stood here unchanged and seen one generation after another grow up and pass away. The generation that I knew is gone. New masters, new servants—I am a stranger, and an alien among them all.

❖

THIELE, September 2, 1749.

Today it is fifty-six years since I first saw the light of this world. Lord my God, what has become of these years? of these many thousands of days? Where are the pleasures of my youth? They are gone with the friends of my youth. It was at this time of the year that we used to enjoy the delights of the chase. How merrily it went when we set out in the morning; the huntsmen calling, the hounds baying, and the horses stamping, as impatient as we ourselves. Sometimes we went after the black cocks on the heath, sometimes after the wild game in the forest. Singing and with horns blowing we rode out and came back. Now it's quiet as a monastery; the new master doesn't care about the chase. Silent and solitary, the gamekeeper goes out, and quietly he comes home. This generation is joyless like myself.

❖

THIELE, January 12, 1751.

A calm, glorious winter night! Everything that I see is blue or white. The moon has driven away the stars and shines alone. So beautifully it shone many, many years ago when I was coachman for Miss Sophie. My young soul shone as brightly and merrily as the moon, and hers too was pure, unspotted as this newfallen snow. Now my soul is dark as the heath when the snows of winter have melted, and hers—if she is still living— must be like a Siberian valley after a flood: darkly furrowed by streams of water, thickly strewn with tussocks, stones, and fallen trees. Yea, Lord, Lord! "When Thou with rebukes dost correct man for iniquity, Thou makest his beauty to consume away like a moth: surely every man is vanity."

❖

FOULUM, May 12, 1753.

Last Sunday I officiated for the first time as parish clerk of Thiele and Vinge. The squire called me on his deathbed. I am now living in my father's house; but I am living here alone. All the friends of my youth have long since gone to rest; I alone am left as a stripped tree on the heath, but in due time I shall be gathered to them, as the last of my line. These pages will be the only memorial of me. If anyone—when I am dead and gone— should read them, he will sigh and say: "As for man, his days are as grass: as a flower of the field, so he flourisheth. For the wind passeth over it, and it is gone; and the place thereof shall know it no more. But the mercy of the Lord is from everlasting to everlasting."

THE ROBBERS' DEN

[*Røverstuen*, 1827]

THE STAG RIDER

THE islands of Denmark wear such a charming, friendly, peaceful aspect that when we try to imagine their origin, our thoughts are never carried back to any violent convulsion of nature; they do not seem to have been cast up by earthquakes or furrowed by mighty floods, but rather to have risen gently from the falling waters of the sea. The plains are level and wide; the hills are few, small, and gently rounded. No steep bluffs, no deep hollows remind us of the labor pangs of the earth. The forests do not cling wildly to sky-high mountains, but range themselves as hedgerows around the fruitful fields. The brooks do not dash down as frothing waterfalls through deep, dark clefts, but glide along, clear and tranquil, between reeds and bushes.

When we leave the lovely island of Fyn and sail to Jutland, we feel at first as if we had only crossed a river and can hardly convince ourselves that we are now on the mainland, so nearly related to the islands is the countenance of the peninsula. But the farther inland we get the more the landscape changes: the valleys become deeper, the hills more precipitous; the forests look older and more decrepit; many a rush-grown bog, many a bit of ground covered with low heather, great rocks on the high backs of the fields—all testify to a lower state of culture and a smaller population. Narrow roads with deep ruts separated by high ridges indicate less travel and less intercourse between the inhabitants. The houses of the people become poorer and poorer, lower and lower, the farther we go, as if they were ducking before the violent onslaught of the west wind. As the moors become larger and more frequent, the churches and villages are fewer and farther apart. On the farms the light frames for drying hay give way to stacks of black peat and the orchards to cabbage plots. Great bogs covered with heather, carelessly and wastefully used, proclaim: here are plenty of them. No hedges, no rows of willows make division between man and man; one might think that all was held in common.

When at last we reach the backbone of Jutland, immense flat plains are spread out before our eyes; at first they are strewn with grave-mounds, but gradually the number is lessened, which would indicate that this region was never cultivated in olden times. Not without reason we imagine that this high back of land was the first part of the peninsula to appear—lifting itself up from the ocean, tumbling the waters down on either side— and that waves rolling down have washed up hills and hollowed out valleys. In the eastern part of this heather-grown plain we occasionally encounter groups of low, shrubby oaks, which serve the wayfarer as a compass, for the crowns of the trees are all bent toward the east. Otherwise we see but few touches of green on the great heather-clad slopes; an occasional patch of green grass or a young aspen with its quivering leaves surprises us into asking: how did you come here? If a brook or a river runs through the heath, no strip of meadow or bushy growth proclaims its presence; deep down between hollowed banks it winds secretly and with speed, as if it were hurrying to get out of the desert.

Across such a brook a young, well-dressed man was riding one fine autumn day. He was headed for a small rye field which had been cultivated by turning the crust and burning it to ashes. The owner and his family were just engaged in reaping it, when the rider approached and asked the way to the manor of Aunsbjerg. After the peasant had answered the question with another, as to where the traveller came from, and had told him what he already knew, namely that he had lost his way, he called a boy who was stacking the sheaves and told him to show the traveller the road. But before the boy could obey the order, an apparition appeared that for the moment held both rider and harvesters spellbound. From the top of the nearest heather-clad hill there dashed down toward them, with the velocity of a

storm, a stag with a man on its back. The man—who was tall
and burly and dressed in brown from top to toe—was caught
between the antlers of the royal stag, which were thrown far
back after the manner of these animals when they are running
at full speed. The strange rider had probably lost his hat during
the ride, for his long black hair flew out from the back of his
head like the mane of a galloping horse. His hand was in constant motion trying to stick a knife into the neck of the stag,
but the mad pace prevented him from taking aim. When the
stag rider came near enough to the amazed beholders—which
did not take long—he was recognized by the peasant, who
called out,

"Hey, Mads, where are you going?"

"The deer and the devil know!" replied Mads, but before
the answer was out of his mouth he was so far away that the
last word hardly reached the ears of the questioner. In a few
minutes both stag and man were gone.

"Who was that?" asked the stranger without turning his
eyes from the spot where the centaur had disappeared.

"Oh," said the peasant, "he's a poor fellow who's called
Mads Hansen, or Black Mads; he has a little house on the other
side of the river. I guess food is pretty scarce there—he has a
lot of kids—so he gets along as best he can. He comes over on
this side once in a while and takes a deer—but today it looks
as if the deer had taken him—if it was a real deer," he added
thoughtfully. "God deliver us from evil! Mads is a reckless
chap—but still I don't know anything but what's honest and
decent about him. He shoots a bit of a deer once in a while, but
what of it? There are plenty of them—too many, if one might
say so. You can see for yourself how they've nibbled the ears off
my rye. But, halloo! There's Niels Gamekeeper. See if you can
catch Black Mads! Today he's better mounted than you."

As he spoke, a hunter came riding at a long, rapid trot from
the same direction where they had first caught sight of the stag
rider.

"Have you seen Black Mads?" he cried out to them from a distance.

"We saw someone riding a deer, but we couldn't make out whether he was black or white, for he went so fast it was all we could do to keep our eyes on him," replied the peasant.

"Devil take him!" said the hunter, as he reined in his horse to allow it to breathe a moment. "I saw him up in Haverdale, where he was sneaking 'round after a stag. I kept behind a hill so's not to disturb him. He fired, the stag fell down, and Mads jumped on the back of him to kill him. But when the stag felt the knife, he got up, caught Mads between his antlers, and halloo! I got his gun, but I'd rather have had himself."

With these words he started his horse at a trot and hurried after the poacher, one gun on his pommel and the other slung over his back in a strap.

The traveller was going in about the same direction and started off with his guide as fast as the boy could run after divesting himself of his wooden shoes. When they had gone a good mile, and had gained the top of a hill that sloped down to the stream, they caught sight of both riders. The first had come to the end of his mad ride. The stag had fallen dead in the river at a place where the water was very low. Its slayer was still standing astride it, trying to free himself from the branches of the animal's horns which had pierced his clothes. Just as he had gotten loose and sprung ashore, the gamekeeper —who had lost sight of him—came dashing past our traveller, holding the reins with one hand and the gun with the other. A few yards from the unlucky stag rider he stopped his horse and with the comforting words, "I'll be the death of you, you son of a bitch!" lifted his gun to his cheek.

"Wait, wait!" cried the culprit. "Hold on a bit, Niels! What's your hurry? Let's talk it over."

"No more talking," said the enraged hunter. "Now I've caught you red-handed."

"Oh, just wait a little bit!" repeated the other. "Just let me say an Our Father!"

"So you're going to pray, are you?" said Niels, as he lowered his gun slightly from his cheek. "You won't get to heaven anyway."

"Then it'll be your fault, Niels," said the other, "when you want to kill me right in the midst of my sins."

"Serves you right, you stag thief," cried Niels, once more laying his cheek against the butt end of the gun.

"Hey, hey!" cried Mads again, "wait just a wee bit! If you shoot me now, then——oh, do take that gun from your eye! I can't stand to have anybody pointin' at me with a loaded gun." Niels lifted his head once more. "If you shoot me, you'll be broken on the wheel yourself."

"The devil I will!" replied the gamekeeper with a forced laugh.

"Niels, Niels!" cried the other. "Here are witnesses. But, listen, I'm goin' to give you another piece of advice. Now you've got me sure enough; I can't get away from you. Why don't you take me up to the house? Then the squire can do what he pleases with me. That way we'll both keep our lives and you'll get a good big reward besides."

At that moment the traveller rode up, and called to the gamekeeper, "For God's sake, my friend, don't do anything rash, but hearken to what the man says."

"The man's a scoundrel," said the gamekeeper, but nevertheless uncocked his gun and laid it down on the pommel. "But since the strange gentleman begs for him, I'll spare his life. But you're crazy, Mads," he said turning to the poacher, "for now you'll be pushing the wheelbarrow all your life. If you'd let me shoot you, there would have been an end of it. Well, come along then, you scoundrel, and keep next to me. Shake your legs now!" With that they started out, and the traveller, who was also going to Aunsbjerg, joined them.

They went on for a while without speaking a word, except that the gamekeeper now and then broke the silence with a grunt or an oath or a word of abuse. At last the poacher began talking along a new and less passionate tack.

"Don't you think it's rather hard on me to have to wade in this tall heather?" he said.

"You're used to it, you dog," replied Niels.

"You might let me sit up behind you," said the poacher with a sly glance, but in a tone which showed that he did not expect his appeal to be favorably received.

"Ho, ho!" replied the gamekeeper with a guffaw. "You've ridden enough for today. Now you can stir your long stumps."

"Now then, Niels Gamekeeper," murmured the other. "Don't take on so. You're so darn contrary today."

Niels Gamekeeper made no reply to this, but whistled a tune while he took his tobacco pouch and pipe from his game-bag. When he had filled his pipe, he was going to light it, but the tinder wouldn't catch fire.

"I'll have to help you," said Mads, and without waiting for an answer, he struck fire with his own tinder, blew on it, and handed it to the gamekeeper, but while Niels received it, Mads caught the butt end of the gun which was lying across the pommel, tore it out of the strap with a mighty pull, and leaped three paces backward in the heather. It was all done with a swiftness which one would hardly have believed the heavy and rather elderly poacher to be capable of.

"Now it's my turn," he said. "Don't you think I might smash you like a toadstool, my dear Niels? But you were reasonable before, and that's your good luck now."

The poor gamekeeper, pale and trembling with rage, looked at his enemy without being able to say a single word.

"A little while ago," said Mads, "you were raging so that anybody else couldn't get in a word, but if I hadn't heard then how you used your mouth, I might be thinking you'd left it home at Aunsbjerg. Light your pipe, or the tinder will go out— you're looking at my tinder box—I guess you don't think it was a good exchange you made. Sure, this is better"—he patted the butt end of the gun—"but I'll give it back to you if you'll let me have mine." Niels reached over his head, took the poacher's gun and gave it to him with one hand, at the same time as he held out the other to receive his own.

"Wait a bit," said Mads. "First you must promise me—but never mind, you won't keep any promise anyway; but if some day you should hear something pop out on the heath, then don't get mad, but think of today and Renard Foxtail."

He turned to the traveller. "Is your horse used to shootin'?"

"Shoot away!" said the stranger.

Mads held the gamekeeper's gun like a pistol with one hand and fired up in the air.

"It sounds just like hitting a door with a clay pot," he said.

Then he took out the flint and gave the gun to his opponent, saying, "Here's your shooter. It won't hurt anybody now. Good-bye, and thanks for today!" So saying, he slung his own gun over his back and walked off in the direction where he had left the stag.

The gamekeeper, whose tongue seemed to have been bound by some magic power, now let loose his pent up rage in a stream of oaths and curses, beginning, "Now may the devil," etc., etc.

It is unfortunate for you as for me, dear reader, that my Muse is not genuinely humorous, for if she had been, I should have had the best opportunity here to embellish my story with the most forceful oaths, compared to which those that enliven our comedy stage would sound like the yapping of a lap dog against the roaring of a lion. But my Muse has never been able to understand the inner meaning of conversation at Gammel Strand; therefore you will have to fill out *ad libitum* the numerous lapses in the conversation of Niels Gamekeeper and other geniuses of his kind. I will simply relate—though with all proper reservations regarding the said Niels Gamekeeper's legal right to the devil and his kingdom—the further conversation between him and the stranger on their way to Aunsbjerg.

The latter, whose sympathy had turned from the escaped poacher to the almost despairing gamekeeper, tried to console him as best he could.

"But you have really lost nothing," he said at last, "except the miserable pleasure of ruining a man and his whole family—"

"Lost nothing!" exclaimed the gamekeeper. "That's all you know about it. Lost nothing! As sure as I'm a sinner, that dog has spoiled my good gun."

"How so?" said the traveller. "Spoiled your gun? Load it and put in another flint."

"Shucks!" said Niels with an angry laugh. "It'll shoot neither hare nor deer after this. It's bewitched, I tell you, and only one thing can help—ah, there's one sunning itself in the wheel rut—he won't eat any more young larks today."

With these words he stopped his horse, put a flint in the gun, cocked it, and jumped down. The stranger, who was quite uninitiated in the science of hunting and knew neither its terminology nor its magic, also stopped in order to see what the green-coat would do. Dragging his horse along, he advanced a few steps, and with the barrel of his gun poked at something lying in the road. The stranger now saw that it was a viper.

"In with you!" said the gamekeeper, prodding it with his gun. At last he got its head into the barrel, held the gun up and shook it until the snake was entirely inside the barrel. Thereupon he fired off the gun with its strange wadding, not a single particle of which remained. "If that doesn't help," he said, "then no one can cure it except Mads or Renard Foxtail."

The stranger smiled a bit skeptically both at the witchcraft and the curious way in which the spell was broken, but having already made the acquaintance of one practitioner of the black art, he wished to learn something about the other, who bore such an unusual and meaningful name. In reply to his questions, the gamekeeper, as he loaded his gun, told the following:

"Renard Foxtail—as they call him, because he can lure all the foxes in the country to come to him—he's ten times worse than Black Mads. He can make himself proof against both lead and silver buttons—the son of a bitch. Once I and the squire came upon him down in the valley there standing over a deer he'd just shot and was skinning. We rode right up to him, and he didn't see us till we were within twenty paces of him. But do you s'pose Renard was scared? He just looked 'round at us and went right on with the deer. 'Now we've got you,' said the squire. 'Niels, let him have it! I'll answer for everything.' I gave him a load of slug right in his broad back, but he didn't mind it any more than if it had been a popgun. The fellow just turned his face to us for a minute and went right on with his skinning. Then the squire himself fired—and it was just the same. He was just cutting the skin from the head of the deer, and not till he had rolled it up did he pick up his little rifle, which was lying on the ground, looked at us, and said, 'Now I guess it's my turn, and if you don't get away from here, I'll try if I can't shoot a hole in one of you.' That's the kind of fellow Renard Foxtail is."

After this tale, which is just as strange but more true than many which we import from abroad, the travellers continued on their way to Aunsbjerg.

AUNSBJERG

IF YOU, dear reader, begin the perusal of a Danish book which, mind you, is not a translation, and if this book should find favor in your sight, then you will certainly propound the reasonable question, "Who has been this author's example and model?" For that a Danish writer—*in specie* a poet—should have the temerity or self-confidence to venture out on the slippery ice of authorship without foreign guidance is neither conceivable nor advisable. If furthermore you read the critical reviews—*in specie*—the Danish Pasquino—you will be confirmed in your supposition; for in these reviews you will often read: "Our author has evidently formed himself on A. or B. or C.," and— if he is one of those bearing the stamp of approval—"Our poet has succeeded in capturing the spirit of D. or E. or F.," or—if he is one of the unprivileged—"This product is a poor imitation of G. or H. or I." Now then, if my little stories or—if you prefer—novelettes have pleased you, have you not asked your-self, "Who is this author's example and model? L . . . . ? No, for that his heroes and heroines are not angelic enough. V . . d . . V . . . . ? No, not that either! For that they are not devilish enough. Furthermore, he doesn't begin his chapters *ad modum*: 'In his large-flowered green damask dressing gown, with the snow-white red-topped cotton nightcap on his vener-able head, the eighty-five-year-old gentleman sat in his grand-father's chair, softly-cushioned with orange-yellow silken fleece,' etc., etc., or: 'On a spirited, chestnut-colored Arab, chewing its foam-flecked silver bridle, the wondrously beautiful maiden rode through the vaulted portal of the castle,' " etc., etc. "Is it possible," you ask further, "that our author may have formed himself on H . . . . or R . . . . . . or A . . . ? No, for that his adventures are too reasonable, too credible and commonplace; he has too little commerce with ghosts, goblins, trolls, werewolves, vampires, and devils." "Who in the world can it be?" you persist. "It must be someone. W . . . . . S . . . . ? On my word, that's the man!" Alas, dear kind reader, you have not found the right one even yet. You do me too much honor; his perfections are his own and neither I nor anyone else can take them away from him, and his faults—if he has any— I will leave to C . . . . . . and others who can fill a sheet with the description of a shawl and how it is worn, writers who cannot introduce us into a peasant's hut without making us acquainted with every chair in the room, every hen on its perch, every rag the innocent children have on, who wherever they convey us refuse to pass a stick or a stone in the road without making us read an elaborate description of it. After all, this Scotch manner pays better in other countries than here, where people would rather borrow books than pay for them, where lending libraries and reading societies see to it that authors should not leave their marriageable daughters manuscripts for a dowry. No, my esteemed reader, if I had followed this practice, we should still have been standing at Karup river, lost in con-templation of its heather-grown banks, or we should have fol-

lowed its winding course with the accuracy of a surveyor right
to the place where the Limfjord would have stopped our
progress. If I had been S .... we should at this moment have
been pleasantly employed in counting the brown spots on Niels
Gamekeeper's white pointer (of whom we haven't yet said a
single word) or the grouse in his game-bag. But—it cannot be
otherwise—I gang my own gait, though crooked and unsteady.
If you will follow me, I shall regard it as an honor and a
pleasure. Sometimes I stand still, then I walk, then I run, and
once in a while I take a start and make a mighty leap, as now
for example from Karup river to Aunsbjerg. And if you want
to give me a pattern, let it be the author Siegfried von Linden-
berg—in view of this long, chatty, parenthetic introduction.

To sum up, A. and B. and C. have their peculiar beauties—
which let them keep! And perhaps they are not entirely free
from faults—what should I do with them? I have enough with
my own. No, I would prefer that you should not say, "The
voice is Jacob's voice, but the hands are the hands of Esau"; I
would rather you should say, "It is Esau wholly and altogether." And if I should not always please you, if my Pegasus
should sometimes run too fast, sometimes be balky, then kindly
remember that it has not been trained by an equestrian artist,
but has its own crochets, which neither you nor I can cure it of.
Mount it, my honored friend, and ride with me in through
Aunsbjerg gate and let us see what kind of an adventure—short
or long, credible or incredible—we shall meet there.

I seldom hear the word "manor house" without thinking of
ghosts. These venerable remains of antiquity—once inhabited by
doughty knights and decorous ladies, whom we think of as
stern and serious, stiff as to dress and manner, rigid as to mind,
hard and stark even in love—these fathom-thick walls, these
long, dark, narrow passages, these vaulted cellars seem to us
to invite the spirits of midnight; the wide, open fireplaces seem
made for those airy creatures that would rather pass through the
chimney than the door. Nor do I think there is any old manor
house that does not harbor such nightly visitors, and that has not

at least one gloomy chamber, a corner room or a tower closet, where everything is not as it should be and where no one likes to sleep alone.

I am happy to state that Aunsbjerg is in this respect as well equipped as any manor house in the country; and I hope soon to see the night when I can treat my reader to a genuine phantasmagoria; but all in good time! Therefore I will now proceed with my story in chronological order.

When the two riders had entered the gate to the farmyard, they turned toward the stable, the gamekeeper showing the way, and each unsaddled his own horse. From there they walked through the shady lane of lime trees up to the court in front of the manor. The house consisted of three wings. The main building to the left was two stories high and had an attic which enjoyed the designation "tower," perhaps because it was felt that no manor should be without a tower, and a name —as we know—is often enough to satisfy people. I have heard a room containing a bookcase and a score of books thickly covered with dust, a cupboard with bottles and glasses, a table with writing materials, and a cushioned easy chair called a "study." I have seen a cluster of a couple of hundred stunted trees called "the forest" and a carp pool called "the lake." In the same way a clothes cupboard is called a "wardrobe," a couple of peasant farms and half a score of houses an "estate," and the rent collector of this domain a "manager" or an "inspector."

The central wing, which was also faced with brick but was only one story high, housed the numerous servants, from the bailiff to the boy that took care of the dogs. The right wing was the home of the tenant farmer. In the corner between the two stood the wooden horse, at that time just as indispensable in a manor house as the escutcheon of the noble house over the main portal.

In the same moment when the gamekeeper opened the gate leading to the inner court, a window was opened on the ground floor of the main building, revealing a head and bust picture

which I think I ought to describe in order to assist the reader—
who has seen similar pictures painted—in guessing the period
when the present events took place. The lord of the manor,
whose heavy figure filled the broad window, was clad in a dark
green velvet jacket with a row of buttons coming all the way
up to the throat, large revers, and pockets with big buttons. A
black periwig—not of the solidly built-up kind, but with a roll
extending all around the head—concealed his hair entirely. The
part of his dress that was visible consisted therefore of only two
simple pieces, but inasmuch as his whole person will appear later,
I had better, in order to avoid repetition, mention the other
three parts of his costume; on top of the periwig he wore a
tight-fitting green cap with a brim standing out to both sides,
something like the black shovel-hat which parsons and afterwards parish clerks wore within the memory of men now living; his feet were covered with a pair of high, wide, spurred
boots, and long black trousers of the kind that a few old peasants
even in our time have worn under the name "rolled breeches,"
completed the visible part of his costume.

"Niels!" the squire called. The gamekeeper showed his companion the door where he was to go in, and then, with his small
three-cornered hat in his hand, stepped over to the window,
where the honorable and well-born squire regularly, rain or
shine, gave audience to the servants in the house and the tenant
farmers on the estate. The gamekeeper here had to observe the
same ceremony as everybody else, although when out hunting
the relation between master and servant was less constrained;
as long as that lasted, the strict rules of etiquette were suspended.

"Who's that?" began the squire with a nod sideways in the
direction of the stranger.

"The new clerk, my lord," was the answer.

"Is that all? I thought it was somebody. What have you got
there?" asked the squire nodding toward the game-bag.

"The old cock and two chickens, my lord." (This "my lord"
we will omit for the future, but it must be understood as following every remark.)

"That isn't much after two days' hunting," said the squire. "Didn't you get any deer?"

"Not this time," said Niels sighing. "When poachers use stags to ride on, there can't be any for us." This cryptic utterance of course required an explanation, but as the reader already has heard the story, we will direct our attention to what was going on behind the squire's broad back.

There stood the young engaged couple, Junker Kaj and Mistress Mettë. The young man was five-and-twenty, handsome, elegant, and perfectly dressed according to the latest mode. In order to show by what means a maiden's heart was attacked and conquered in those days, I must not neglect the account of the young man's outward appearance, and I will begin with the feet, in order to rise in my description. The said feet were encased in broad-nosed, low boots, the tops of which flopped in wide folds around the small of his legs. From them white silk stockings extended to a handbreadth above his knees, where they ended with a strip of the finest lace. Then came a pair of tight-fitting black velvet breeches, of which only a little was seen, because an enormously long vest, also of black velvet, came down over them. A coat of crimson cloth held together with a clasp over the frilled shirt front, with a row of large covered buttons, and short sleeves reaching only to the wrist but having cuffs turned up to the elbow, completed his costume. All his hair was brushed smoothly into a long, stiff queue which was tied in the back of the neck.

I should deserve but little thanks from my feminine readers if I did not with the same accuracy portray the gracious young lady, but in her case I can be more brief, summing her up in three main articles: 1) The pointed, high-heeled, silver-buckled shoes; 2) the little red, gold-laced cap coming down in a tongue on her forehead and completely hiding her hair, which was brushed up under it; 3) the dress of damask with large flowers on a sky-blue ground, the sleeves coming only a little below the elbows, the waist long, but not tight-laced, and leaving the shoulders and bosom uncovered. To those who know

and properly admire the beauty of the present styles it will seem
inconceivable that a lady so attired could strike fire from a
masculine heart, since the only attractive part of the picture
was the bare shoulders and bosom; but I must add that Mistress Mettë's face was really so exceedingly beautiful it might
easily make one forget her clothes.

These two handsome young people then stood behind the old
gentleman, hand in hand, and—as it seemed—engaged in
playful love-making. The young gentleman tried every little
while to snatch a kiss, but the young lady just as often turned
away her face, not exactly with aversion, but with an arch
smile. The strangest part of it was that every time she bent
her head back she glanced past her father into the court, although there was nothing to be seen (for the gamekeeper stood
too near the wall under the window) except the wooden horse
and the new clerk who, as soon as he had entered the office,
seated himself by the window. The fact that, although he had
the title of clerk, he was a handsome young man signified little,
for in the first place he had a huge scar cutting across one
cheek, and secondly, thirdly, fourthly, and fifthly, he was
dressed simply as a clerk and nothing else. What this costume
looked like I do not feel it is proper to relate, now that I have
just described the costumes of persons of quality. Nor do I
think it necessary to dwell long on Mistress Mettë's mother,
the good Mistress Kirsten, who sat by another window, contemplating with a pleased smile the amorous play of the two
young people.

The good old lady had every reason to be gratified at this
match, since it was her own doing from first to last. In a
whole herd of junkers—as the squire expressed it jokingly in
the language of the chase—she had got the scent of the fattest,
and was the first to give tongue after him. Inasmuch as the
young man was an only child, heir to Palstrup and several other
estates, and, as for his birth, had sixteen known ancestors, the
marriage was soon decided upon by the parents and their decision announced to the children. The bridegroom, who had just

returned from Paris when Mistress Kirsten sighted him, was well satisfied, and why should he not be? Mistress Mettë was young and beautiful, an only child, heir to Aunsbjerg, where the deer, the wild boars, and the crofters were just as good as at Palstrup, while the grouse and ducks were much better. As for the bride, she was so perfectly submissive under the iron will of her parents that for the present we will leave unanswered the question of whether her own fancy turned to the young man. We know that the heart of a maiden prefers to make its own choice, and sometimes a suitor is rejected for no reason but that he is the choice of the parents. Nevertheless, if Junker Kaj is but the first, we need have no fears for him.

After this—not wholly unnecessary—digression, we will go on with our story. When the gamekeeper had rendered an account of his mishap—which he did not dare to conceal, inasmuch as the clerk, the peasant boy who had acted as his guide, and even the stag rider himself might tell the tale—the squire, almost beside himself with rage, burst out into a torrent of the most heartfelt curses on the poacher; and during this rain of invective some drops fell on poor Niels, who in his fear of the angry master had to swallow his own equally hearty curses.

As soon as the first gust of stormy wrath had subsided and given room to reflection, a plan was made for prompt and sufficient revenge: the audacious miscreant was to be seized and, as one easily convicted of poaching, was to be turned over to the arm of the law and, after proper procedure, sent to the prison of Bremerholm. But to catch him—there was the rub; for if he got the least wind of danger, he would flee and leave his wife and children behind him. The squire, who had been wounded in his tenderest spot, was for setting out immediately. There was enough left of the day to enable them to reach the hut of Black Mads at nightfall. But the mistress, whose revenge always showed more careful planning and more mature consideration, argued with her impetuous lord and master, saying that darkness would also aid the flight of the criminal or—if that were prevented—a desperate defense on his part. It would be better, therefore, to start a little after midnight; then the entire armed forces could encircle the hut at daybreak and conquer it. This proposal was unanimously adopted, and the visiting junker was invited to share the dangers and honors of the expedition. The bailiff of the estate, who came to report the arrival of the new clerk and to present his letter of recommendation from the bailiff of Vestervig, was ordered to hold himself in readiness together with the gardener, the overseer of the farm, and the stablemen, and was told to engage a peasant cart to follow the expedition.

THE NISSE

Who does not know—at least by name—this creature whose pranks almost always are just good-natured frolics? Who has not heard of his chubby little figure and his red Jacobin cap— symbol of uninhibited liberty? Who does not know that the house he chooses for his abode is perfectly safe from fires and other disasters? (In order not to forget it I will mention at once *in parenthesi* that there is also a ship Nisse whose function it is to plan during the night—in a sort of shadow drawing—all the work that has to be done the next day: weigh anchor or cast it, hoist the sails or take them in, furl them, or reef them, which means a storm. He doesn't even think he is too good to swab the deck, but will do this humble work very nicely. Those who know him say that this *spiritus navalis* shows his kinship with the house or land Nisse by his pranks. He turns the weather vane, blows out the light in the binnacle, teases the ship's dog, and if there is a passenger on board who is prone to seasickness, one can see the rogue with a heart-rending expression vomiting into the bucket. If the ship is about to be lost, he will jump over-board the night before it sails, and either climb on board another ship or swim ashore. Finally, I must remark that, inasmuch as very few people are privileged to see this airy sprite, his warnings are not often heeded.)

The house Nisse, which is the one that concerns us especially, is a real blessing to the home which he honors by his presence; it is safe against fire, storm, and thieves. Who then would be offended by the little fellow's capers? When sometimes he takes a ride on the horse in the stall, it is no doubt only in order to give the animal healthy exercise. When he milks a cow before the maid gets there, it is only to make her rise earlier in the morning. And even if he steals an egg in the hen-house once in a while, chases the cat in the attic, or upsets a chamber pot, who would be angry with him for that or begrudge him the dish of Christmas porridge which no thoughtful housewife fails to set out for him in a corner of the attic? It is only in case this is neglected that he shows a slight trace of vindictiveness. Then the housewife may be pretty sure that her porridge will be burned, or her soup will get bitter, or the ale will turn sour, or the milk won't curdle, or she can churn all day and not get butter.

Well, then: such a little domestic hobgoblin had haunted Aunsbjerg from time immemorial and is probably haunting it yet, although it would seem that this manor was not his only place of abode, for sometimes years would pass in which no one would notice him at all. But just at the time of our story he seemed to have resumed his doings—or undoings, if you prefer.

The gardener would occasionally miss some of his loveliest flowers or several of the largest and ripest peaches; the strangest part of it was that both would sometimes in the morning be found in Mistress Mettë's chamber, from which one would naturally conclude that the lady stood very high in the favor of said Nisse. Furthermore, the stablemen declared that many a night there was something wrong with the horses and in the morning one of them would be as dirty as if it had been used for a long, wild ride. They vowed—and who would doubt them?—that they had often run out into the stable, but then everything had all of a sudden been perfectly quiet. Once only they had thought they caught a glimpse of the unlucky red cap, and after that they did not mix in the affairs of the Nisse, which was certainly wise on their part.

Weight was added to these tales when Niels Gamekeeper, one night he came home from Viborg and was neither drunk nor crazy, nevertheless had not been able to find the road from Demstrup to the manor, although it was straight as a string, and there was moonlight. Whether he wanted to or not, he was forced out into the elder bog, where the red cap several times peeped out between the stems of the trees. As he was a brave man, he called out to the sprite, but every time he opened his mouth he would fall, and then he would hear a ghastly laughter that sounded like the cackling of a black cock or the neighing of a horse-snipe. When at last, with clothes muddy and torn, he had managed to get out of the boggy wood, he heard behind him the troating of the roe deer, and the whistling of the gambet, although it was not the mating season for either roe deer or snipe. Such exceptionable testimony did not fail to make an impression on the personnel of the manor, especially the feminine part of it. And even the squire himself received such tidings in thoughtful silence.

Such was the state of things when the expedition against Black Mads was undertaken, an event which made an epoch in the history of Aunsbjerg and for years to come was used as a point to measure history from, as thus: "It was the same year that we went hunting for Black Mads," or "It was two, or it was three years after," etc. Those who remained at home waited all day with tense expectation for news of the attacking army. Noon came—evening—midnight—and yet nothing was seen or heard of it. They consoled themselves by thinking that perhaps the culprit had been taken directly from his home to Viborg; in that case the day might have gone, and after such an exhausting march it was only fair that the troops should be given an evening's refreshment and a night's rest in town. With this plausible hypothesis both the family and the servants went to bed, and only one servant kept watch. Finally, an hour after midnight, Junker Kaj and his groom returned. But before I go on, it would be most proper to explain the reason for their late return and the failure of the others to come at all.

The poacher's hut, which he himself had built in the most primitive fashion with walls of green turf, and roof of heather resting on rafters made of oak branches bent and tied together, had an excellent strategic position considered as a fortress. Right in the middle of a great bog measuring fully eight miles in circumference, there rose a little hillock which was never under water even in the most violent sudden thaws, and to which at least no horseman could come except by way of a narrow strip of firm land that went winding among turf-pits and quagmires. On this hillock Black Mads had built his idyllic house, and there he with wife and four children lived by the chase. The larger game animals were eaten fresh, salted, or smoked. The smaller were sold secretly together with the skins of deer and foxes, and for the money they bought bread and salt. Milk the wife and children begged of the farmers in the neighborhood.

The day was beginning to break when the Aunsbjerg squire and his army reached the bog. Niels Gamekeeper, who knew the locality, rode ahead and successfully led the united forces to the place where the hut was supposed to be. No hut was to be seen, and yet there was light enough to see it if it had been there. The first thing Niels had recourse to—as usual with him in all trouble and bewilderment—was a long and vigorous oath. The squire, who rode up to learn what had occasioned this heartfelt outpouring, gave his gamekeeper an equally heartfelt good-morning, and accused him of having lost his way and taken them to the wrong place. But Niels, who was sure of his point, declared and even called a dozen of the black angels to witness that the hut was there, but that Mads had made it invisible, no doubt with the aid of his good friend of the horse's hoof, for he certainly knew how to bedevil your eyesight.

The squire was almost ready to accept this explanation as the most plausible, when Junker Kaj, who had ridden ahead, exclaimed, "There's been a fire here!" At that all crowded in, and soon they discovered that the hut was reduced to an ash heap in which a few embers still smouldered. This discovery led Niels to the conclusion that "the said long-tailed person had taken him and his whole brood." Junker Kaj, however, was of the opinion that Mads had himself first burned down the hut and then fled. During this debate it had become full daylight; the site of the fire was searched, but nothing was found except ashes, embers, bits of coal, and charred bones which the hunters identified as those of deer. Acting on the hypothesis of the junker, they decided to search the surrounding heaths, for after all the fugitive with family and baggage could not have gone very far. With this in view, the pursuers were divided into four parties to scour the country in all four quarters. Junker Kaj with his groom and one other man chose the eastern way, possibly to be nearer Aunsbjerg and his ladylove; but all his efforts were fruitless, he rode hither and thither, exhausting himself, his men, and his horses, but all in vain. Sometimes he thought he saw something moving in the distance, but closer investigation proved it to be sheep or stacks of heath turf. Once he was sure that he saw human beings just about in the spot where the German church now stands, but the nearer he approached, the more indistinct grew the figures, and at last they disappeared entirely. The groom explained this optical illusion by telling an old legend: in olden times a battle had been fought here, and the spirits of the fallen would sometimes re-enact the bloody game. As a herdsboy he had often at sunrise seen whole regiments marching, mounted officers dashing up and down before the ranks, enemy armies mixing and fighting, now one forced back, now the other. In his grandfather's time they had even been able to hear the commands of the officers, the blaring of trumpets, the clashing of arms, the cries of the wounded. But the junker, who had heard something about fata morgana and who at sea had witnessed similar phenomena, laughed at his visionary servant, and in his heart cursed the black poacher and all his descendants to the fourth generation.

Unfortunately the organizers of this ill-fated excursion had forgotten—which sometimes happens in more important wars— to provide that necessary foundation for heroism, food. One third of Junker Kaj's division was therefore sent out to forage, but when evening came and the man had not returned, the starving young gentleman decided to turn his face homeward. But this was more easily said than done, for the horses were just as exhausted and just as hungry and thirsty as the riders. They made very slow progress and did not get out of the heath before darkness fell. The result was that they lost their way and did not get to Aunsbjerg till after midnight.

In order to avoid doubling on my tracks again, I will now briefly relate what happened to the other three divisions. They had just as poor luck and found nothing of what they were looking for. In vain they searched every peat bog; in vain they encircled every valley and hollow, every mound and hill; in vain they questioned people in all the near-by villages and farms: no one had seen or heard anything of Black Mads. The day passed, and it became necessary to look for a place to spend the night. The squire himself landed at Rydhauge, where he spent two pleasant days shooting grouse before he returned to his home.

My honored readers, particularly my feminine readers, as many of you as start to read this true story! for your own sake I advise you: do not read what follows alone or by candlelight; but if you are several in company, it would do no harm if you would draw as close together as possible—we are going to have a ghost story!

When the tired junker had satisfied his hunger, he began to think of sleep. He ordered the servant to light him to his bed-chamber, but as the man was about to open the door, the key broke and the nib remained stuck in the lock. What could now be done? To curse the door, the lock, the key, the locksmith, the servant, and—for good measure—Black Mads was tried, but did not help the situation. To remove the lock would require hammer and screwdriver and would besides make a noise that would rouse the household. Of what use then that he had been so quiet and—in order not to disturb the sleep of the ladies— had been satisfied with a piece of cold roast meat which the servant had managed to procure for him in some secret way!

In such cases the first impulse is often the best, and the servant was ready with his advice. "The tower room," he said in a low voice and with an uncertain look at his young master. At the mention of this well-known but ill-famed room, Junker Kaj shuddered slightly, but he tried to conceal his fear both from the servant and from himself by a forced smile, and by the question, thrown out in an indifferent tone, as to whether the bed was made up? The answer was Yes, for the mistress always kept a bed made up in the room for emergency, though in the memory of man it had never been used. She herself kept the keys of the other guest rooms, but thought such a precaution unnecessary in this case, since there was nothing in the room but a bed, a couple of chairs, and a table, and besides the ghostly safeguard was sufficient protection against thieves. Evidently no excuses or objections could be brought forward. So Junker Kaj allowed himself to be shown to the room. The servant undressed him, left the candle on the table, and went away, shutting the door after him.

It was a dark autumn night. The waning moon was approaching the last quarter; its curved half-circle stood low in the heavens, and shone in through the tall, narrow, arched window which was the only one in the room. The wind was blowing; small clouds were scudding quickly, one might almost say in measured time, across the moon; their shadows slipped like pictures in a *camera clara* over the white wall and disappeared in the stove. The leaded window clattered under the gusts; the wind whistled and howled in the panes; the chimney rumbled; the door of the stove rattled. Junker Kaj was no coward; indeed his heart was pretty much in the right place. But the quality we call courage is quite relative, and just as varied in its manifestations as the circumstances that call it forth. Many a warrior who faces shot and bayonets without trembling will feel his heart pounding if he tries to enter a church alone and in the dark. He who bravely seizes a banner from the enemy ranks could perhaps not be persuaded to fetch at midnight the missal from the altar or a skull from the charnel house. The soldier who stands firm on land may perhaps tremble on the unaccustomed, terrible ocean. And the sailor who laughs at storm and waves may become very serious among guns and sabres. He who commands a regiment may not have courage to command a wife, and another who keeps his wife under the lash may shrink timidly before the eye of an angry man. There are those who fear nothing but their own conscience; others know how to subdue this rebel, though in all other respects they are timid as hares.

Nor was the courage of our young gentleman whole and perfect. He was not afraid to meet his adversary or to ride his horse—even if it were a Bucephalus—in short, he feared no living, or rather, no physical creature, but for spirits he had a great deal of respect. The hour, the circumstances, and particularly the ill-repute of the room sent his blood coursing more quickly, and all the ghost stories he had heard forced themselves uninvited on his heated imagination—Phantasus and Morpheus struggled for possession of him, and the first was in the ascendant. He did not dare to close his eyes, but stared constantly at the opposite wall, where the formless shadows seemed to take on shape and meaning.

Under such circumstances it is a comfort to have one's back free and to face all one's enemies. He therefore sat up, drew the curtain away from the head of the bed, and looked around. The bed stood in a corner; at its feet, though a little farther on, was the window. Right in front of the bed was the one wide wall, the stove, and behind it the door. His eyes passed on to the rear wall. There hung an ancient portrait of a doughty knight clad in mail, with a face as large as a pumpkin framed in thick, waving black hair. This picture held his searching gaze. It appeared and then vanished again, as the clouds left the moon clear or hid it. In the light the face seemed to broaden in a smile; in the shadow, it shrank in sinister gloom. Perhaps a former owner of the manor, which had passed to strangers after the extinction of his own family, had been relegated to this obscure corner, and perhaps his nightly visits were in revenge for the indifferent and contemptuous treatment accorded him by late comers. Like the shadows on the wall, courage and fear chased each other through the soul of the junker. At last by main force he made his courage prevail, lay down, and gave himself completely into the hands of Morpheus.

When greatly exhausted one does not always sleep well. He had slept perhaps only half an hour when he was wakened by a noise as of a rusty doorlock. Startled, he opened his eyes; they fell on the door opposite, where a white figure appeared and vanished almost in the same moment—the door closed with a slight creaking noise. A numbing chill passed over his head, such as we express by saying that one's hair stands on end. Nevertheless he mastered his fear; his imagination had not yet got the better of his cool common sense. "It may have been the servant," he thought, "who—though undressed—wanted to see if the candle had been put out." His mind somewhat set at rest by this idea, he withdrew his gaze, but then it fell on the window where he saw the dark upper half of a human figure. The outline of the head and shoulders was quite clear and the edges were touched by the light of the moon. It seemed to be turning its back to the room. Fear got the upper hand and almost stopped his breathing. The figure sighed, lifted one hand, and wrote something on the window pane. Then the courage of the junker vanished. Like Belshazzar, his "countenance was changed, and his thoughts troubled him, so that the joints of his loins were loosed, and his knees smote one against another."

What was to be done? Flight could not be thought of; for if he went out of the door he might run into an ambush; the window defended itself, and other exits he had not seen. True, there was one other refuge which many people might resort to in such circumstances—to crawl under the coverlet; but it is well known that some ghosts are cruelly playful enough to pull the coverlet down on the ground, and I cannot therefore absolutely recommend this expedient. Our young gentleman either did not know about it, or he was ashamed to use it. In fact his natural courage once more rose to such a height that he challenged the figure with a "Who's there?" At this call, it made a sudden turn, but did not answer; after a few seconds it sank slowly beneath the window, and then nothing more was seen or heard.

No lost wayfarer can long more ardently for the light of day than did the poor junker. He dared not shut his eyes for fear that when he opened them again he would see something that he did not wish to see. He went on staring anxiously at the door, the stove, and the window; he listened with more and more tense expectation, but he heard nothing except the soughing of the wind, the rattling of the windowpanes, and his own breathing. At last day broke, and as soon as it was light enough to distinguish all the objects in the room, he got up and searched it with the greatest care. In vain: he found no traces of the nocturnal visitors. The doors of the stove were closed, the door to the room likewise; the windows were fastened with all their hasps, and any other exits he had not seen. So he had conviction brought home to him, and hurried to leave this disturbed lodging, sincerely determined that he would never more set his foot there.

As soon as the family had gathered at the breakfast table and Junker Kaj had given a report of the luckless expedition, the mistress of the house asked him the natural question as to how he had slept after all this toil and moil.

"Very well," was the answer.

Mistress Mettë smiled. "Didn't you sleep in the tower room? I thought my maid said something about it."

Junker Kaj said Yes, but not wishing his fiancée to know how frightened he had been, he felt the need of denying his nocturnal acquaintances. The young lady seemed equally bent on forcing a confession from him. She declared she "could see by his eyes that he had not slept, and he looked very pale."

In order to make an end of this painful examination, he declared the maligned room to be quite purified, and added that she could very well sleep there herself if she dared.

"Then," she said laughing, "I believe I will try it some time."

With that the subject was exhausted and the conversation turned to other matters.

After the return of the old gentleman, several days passed before the subject of the tower room was brought up again. First everybody was fully occupied with devising, presenting, and discussing all the different ways in which Black Mads could have been caught, and in surmising where he was most likely to be hiding. Then a long time was spent in narrating circumstantially and in detail the story of the two days' grouse-hunting at Rydhauge. When this subject too was exhausted—that is, when the full history of every bird shot or missed had been told, satisfactory explanations made of every miss, expert comparisons of dogs and guns threshed out, etc., etc.—then Mistress Mettë led the conversation to the ill-reputed room, telling her father that her fiancé had slept there and calling attention to his unusually serious expression. In this second examination he had two inquisitors, and the young lady especially pressed him so hard with her roguish teasing that at last he thought it best to take back his former denial and confess that he would not care to sleep there again.

"Is that befitting a cavalier," said the young lady, "to be afraid of a shadow? I am only a woman, and yet I'll try to stand such an adventure."

"I'll wager my sorrel," answered Junker Kaj, "that you don't dare to!"

"I'll put up my Bella against it!" she cried.

They thought she was joking, but when she insisted on carrying out the wager, both her father and her fiancé tried to dissuade her from such a dangerous undertaking. She was not to be moved. Now Junker Kaj felt that he had to make a clean breast of it all. The old gentleman shook his head. Mistress Mettë laughed and said he had dreamt it, and in order to convince him, she felt more than ever bound to fulfill her promise. The old gentleman, whose fatherly pride was flattered by his daughter's courage, now gave his consent. All that Junker Kaj gained was the promise that a bell-rope should be placed near her bed, and that her maid should sleep on a cot in the same room. On the other hand, the young lady exacted the promise that all the people in the house should stay in their beds, in order that no one should say the ghost had been scared away, and that no one should have a candle lit after eleven o'clock. Her father and her fiancé were to take up their quarters in the so-called gold guest-chamber, which had access to the tower room by a long passage. The bell with which the young lady could ring the alarm if need be was to be in their room. The mother—no less heroic than her daughter—willingly gave her consent to the adventure.

THE ELOPEMENT

IF I should have roused in anyone expectations of a new ghost story, I am truly sorry, and all the more so as perhaps the first may now be susceptible of a natural explanation and may end with a "Pshaw! was that all!" But on the other hand, I am happy in that, instead of a real ghost story, I can serve up an elopement as regular as any that ever was found in a novel: an elopement, not in the daytime, but in the night; not through the door, but through the window; not in a carriage, but on a horse.

The eventful night that was to decide the future of the sorrel and the isabella brought little sleep either to the family or the servants. All lay there in tense expectation of things to come. The mewing of cats, the hooting of owls, the howling of dogs drove away the sandman whenever he came stealing in. The stablemen heard the horses breathing, snorting, and kicking; the farm overseer was sure that sacks were being dragged along the floor in the attic; the dairymaid thought it sounded exactly as if the rocking churn were going; the housekeeper plainly heard someone rummaging in the pantry. Nor was there any more sleep in the gold guest-chamber; the squire and the junker lay silently glancing every little while at the silver bell that hung between them, but it gave no sound. When the

clock in the tower struck one, Junker Kaj began to think he
had lost his wager, but consoled himself with the thought that
losing anything to your wife is only giving from one hand to
the other. In short, the night passed—at least as far as the
tower room was concerned—as quietly as if there were no ghosts
in the world.

With the first glimmer of daylight the two gentlemen, who
had only partly undressed, got up and hastened to say good-
morning to the brave young ghost-tamer. They rapped on the
door; no *"Entrez"*—perhaps both were sound asleep. Papa
opened the door; they went in. *Peste!* the young lady's bed was
empty and the coverlet thrown aside.

"Bravo!" cried Junker Kaj, "she has fled, and the isabella is
mine."

The old gentleman said not a word, but turned to the maid's
bed. She was not to be seen either, but when he lifted the coverlet, she was lying there flushed and perspiring as if in a violent
fever. Upon being eagerly questioned by the squire, she first
answered nothing, but stared at them with a wild look in her
face. Then at last she found her tongue and told her story in
disjointed sentences: shortly after midnight she had seen a terrible ghost coming right through the wall. She had been so
frightened that she had crept under the coverlet and hadn't
dared to remove it; what more had happened she didn't know.
But it was evident enough; the window was open, and down
below stood a ladder—Mistress Mettë had been abducted, but
by whom?

What an uproar in the whole house! What a wailing and
screaming and lamenting! Curses without an object, questions
without an answer! "After them!" was the next impulse of the
father and the bridegroom; but whither? The mistress, who
was the most cool-headed of them all, advised a general muster,
and the squire personally called the roll of every living creature. He finally declared that he didn't miss anyone, and the
entire drawn-up garrison was of the same opinion, until Mistress
Kirsten asked, "Where is the clerk?"

"The clerk! The clerk!" went from mouth to mouth. They looked around, they looked at each other—no! The clerk was really not there. The bailiff and two other men ran to the office, and the squire called to the grooms, "Saddle the horses and bring them to the door, like thunder and lightning!"

The bailiff came back, breathless and frightened, saying that the missing man was really gone; his bed hadn't been slept in, his spurs and riding whip were not to be found. In the same moment one of the stablemen came running and said that Jezebel was gone. All stood as if turned to stone, looking at each other and saying nothing, until Mistress Kirsten broke the silence.

"Our lady daughter," she said, "could not elope with a clerk. He has sneaked in here as a spy. I suspect the robber comes from the west—see if you can't trace them on the road to Vium, and now be off! It may be possible to catch up with them, for the isabella can't run very far with two."

Her guess proved to be true. Tracks of a horse in full trot were seen on the road mentioned, and as a further proof a ribbon bow and a little farther on a glove, both the property of Mistress Mettë, were found not far from the house.

Armed with guns, pistols, and swords, the squire, the junker, the bailiff, the gamekeeper, and four other well accoutred men rode out briskly; and the mistress called after them, "Bring them back dead or alive!" We will accompany the Aunsbjerg squire on his second expedition for a part of the way. The track was plain as far as to Vium, but there the pursuers would have lost it, if a peasant of whom they made inquiry had not told them that a couple of hours before daybreak he had heard the trotting of a horse going out of the town toward the west. They followed this hint and found the track again pointing in the same direction past Hvam Tavern. There they learned that a couple of hours ago the dogs had made a great noise. Evidently the speed of the fugitives was slowing, and this could be seen also from the tracks. The pursuers came to Sjörup. Here a man who was standing outside the house for a certain purpose had heard a horse passing and thought he could make out two people on it. But now the trail was lost. Several roads ran out from here, all with deep and narrow wheel ruts—which was the right one? The fugitives had not followed any of them—probably from fear that the horse should stumble in the ruts—but had ridden into the heather. Of the three main roads one ran to the northwest, one to the southwest, and one right between. While these were taken under advisement one after another, the talk turned also on the great event of the night and on the suspicious clerk. One of the men said he thought he had seen him before, when he served in the cavalry, but he couldn't remember where. Another had seen a stranger speaking with him secretly a couple of days ago in the woods, and it seemed that the stranger had addressed him as "Cornet." At that a light flashed upon the old gentleman.

"Ha!" he said. "Then we follow the middle road! It goes to Vestervig. I'll swear the clerk is none other than the major's third son who was a cornet with the Cuirassiers. I remember Mistress Kirsten once warned me against him, saying he was hot on the trail of Mistress Mettë. And what of you?" he cried to the bailiff.

"My lord," replied he, "you yourself saw the letter from the bailiff at Vestervig. It's he that has fooled us all, or else the letter was a forgery. Besides the fellow was so quiet and decent and hard-working, so polite and humble, that I would never have dreamed of taking him for a nobleman."

"His estate lies in the moon," said the old gentleman, and put his horse to a trot. "A dollar to him who first catches sight of the runaway!"

The troop had still to ride six miles before it could reach the ford across Karup river. Meanwhile, by your leave, my reader, I will run on to the ford and follow the fugitives, who are just now touching the farther shore.

The poor isabella, weary from her double burden and the forced pace for many miles, walked slowly and with tottering steps up the heathery hill. The cornet—for it was really he—

often turned back with a worried look, and each time he snatched a kiss from his sweet Mettë who, dressed in her riding habit, sat behind him, clasping him with her arm.

"Do you see anyone yet?" she asked anxiously, for she didn't dare to look for herself.

"Not yet," he answered, "but I am afraid—the sun is quite high already; they must be on their way after us—if only the mare can hold out."

"But your brother's cart?" she asked after a pause.

"It should have met me by the river at daybreak," he answered. "I can't understand what has happened to it. We still have eight miles before we get out of the heath, and if meanwhile they have found the right trail—"

As he was speaking, they reached the top of the bank, and the great western heath spread out before them like an ocean; but no cart, no living creature was to be seen. The cornet reined in the horse to let it breathe and half turned round in order to get a better view of the eastern part of the great heath which they had passed over. That, too, was bare and desolate: nothing to be seen but a few peat stacks; nothing to be heard but the cackling of the black cocks, the rushing of the river, the breathing of the isabella, and their own sighs. For a few moments they stood there; then the young lady broke the silence with the question.

"Isn't there something stirring way over there?" She spoke in a low voice as if she feared that it might be heard on the other side of the desert.

"We have no time to lose," he said. "I am afraid it's your father coming out there." With that, he turned to the west again and spurred his horse.

"Oh, my father," she sighed and clasped her abductor more closely.

"In Hungary," he said, "—it's now just five years ago— we had taken up our quarters for the night in a village. In the morning we were surprised by the Turks. When I got on my horse, there were already several houses on fire; we had to retreat, and I was one of the last. About half a mile out of the village, a little Hungarian, a boy of ten or twelve years, came running after me, pursued by a troop of Janizaries. He was half naked. I saw he couldn't hold out long. So I turned back and took him up on my horse. Just then the first Janizary reached me. Before he fell, he gave me this memento of him across my face. But I saved my little Hungarian. He is at my brother's, and was to have met us today. My dearest, then I felt better than now."

He looked around again. "They seem to be gaining on us—if I drive the mare harder, she'll drop."

They rode on a way—he with a depressed, she with an anxiously beating heart.

"I shall have to walk," he said, dismounting, "that will help her. Don't look back, dearest lady."

"Oh, God!" she cried. "Is it they?"

"There are seven or eight of them," he said. "So far as I can see, they're mounted."

"How far away are they?" she asked again.

"A little over two miles, perhaps three," he replied. In spite of his admonition, she looked back.

"I don't see anybody," she cried.

"Neither do I now," he said, "but they're most likely down in a valley—there's one coming up, and another—Come, come, poor Bella!" he cried and tried to pull the horse after him. "Usually you arch your neck and lift your feet high enough, now you're dragging them along the ground and stretching your head like a fish that has to be pulled out of the water by main force."

After a little while the young lady asked, "Do you think they can see us?"

"They're riding right after us," replied the cornet, "they're gaining on us more and more—"

"Heavens!" she cried, "if they reach us! Oh, I'm afraid my father will kill you; but I will protect you with my weak body, dearest Holger. I can't live if they kill you!"

During this nervous, constantly interrupted talk they had covered about two miles from the river into the western heath. The pursuers were now close to the eastern river bank; they could be plainly seen and counted. The fear of the fugitives had now almost become desperation—there was no gleam of hope. The cornet breathed almost as hard as the horse; the young lady wept.

Suddenly there rose from the tall heather a large man clad all in brown and carrying a gun in one hand and a low-crowned hat in the other. The fugitives stopped.

"Who's there? Where do you come from?" cried the cornet in his military fashion.

"From where the houses stand outdoors and the geese go barefooted," answered the man. "Where are you from, and where are you going? But wait a bit, haven't the two of us met lately? Aren't you the person who begged for me when Niels Gamekeeper was going to do for me?"

"Black Mads!" cried the cornet.

"That's what they call me," replied the poacher; "but how does it happen that I meet you here so early in the morning and with such a young lady? Maybe you've been poaching, too? If I can help you with anything, say so."

"In need the nearest friend is the best," replied the cornet. "I am the major's son at Vestervig, and have fetched me a sweetheart at Aunsbjerg. Her father is after us with a whole troop of mounted men. If you can save us, or hide us, I'll thank you as long as I live and reward you as well as I'm able. But it must be soon," he added quickly, as he turned around, "for there they are right on the other side of the river."

Mads held up his hat to shade his eyes from the sun. "I'll say so! There he is with all his men. Nobody worse than your own kin, said the fox when the red dogs were after him. If you'll promise never to tell about the place I'm taking you to, I'll see what I can do."

The young lady promised, and the cornet swore it.

"Now listen, children," he went on, "they're just riding

up the last hill on the other side of the river. Before they can get up on this side, it'll take a little while, and they can't see what we're doing. So now we'll put up a fence that they can't jump over."

As he said so, he laid down his gun, took out his tinder box, and struck fire. Then he pulled up a few handfuls of dry moss, covered the tinder box with it, blew on it till a flame rose, and then threw the moss in among the heather. Instantly there was a crackling and roaring fire which spread rapidly. During this work, which the fugitives did not at first understand the purpose of, Black Mads gave vent to his thoughts in short, disjointed sentences.

"The wind's on our side—the heather's dry—now Niels Gamekeeper can light his pipe—it's the second time my tinder box has helped him—the squire will scold and curse about his grouse because I'm roasting them without gravy—but needs must—God helps him who helps himself—there now, she's burning!"

Then he got up and said to the cornet, "Now do as you see I do. Pull up a tuft of heather, light it, run ten paces to the north, set the heath on fire, then pull up a tuft again, set fire all along to the north as far as that knoll you see over there, about two gunshots away. I'll do the same to the south, and then we'll run back here just as fast. The young lady'll have to stay with the horse. It'll only take a minute. Now we begin: Light before and dark behind!"

With this formula the poacher began operations. The cornet followed his instructions, and in a few minutes a stretch of the heath two miles wide was in flames. Both the firemen rejoined the trembling lady.

"Now you've earned your breakfast," cried Mads, "if you'll come with me and put up with what we have. But, heyday! what'll we do with the mare?" He gave the isabella a slap with his flat hand. "Can you find the way home alone?"

"Oh," said the young lady, "she follows me wherever I go."

"No, by the Lord, that she mustn't! She'd lead them to where we were. The door of my house is too narrow, and we don't dare to leave her outside.—You're too good to waste— but we've got to think of ourselves."

The cornet, who realized his purpose, took his lady by the hand and drew her aside as if to guard her against the flames, which were in fact coming nearer—though slowly—against the wind. The poacher took his gun, cocked it, put it behind the ear of the horse, and fired. The young lady turned with a scream and saw the poor isabella sink down in the heather without a sound. A few tears of pity ran down the girl's pale cheeks.

"The nag's dead as a herring," said Mads to comfort her. "She didn't as much as hear the report." And with that he took off the bridle, put the saddle and bundle on one shoulder, slung his gun over the other, and set out. He urged the fugitives to follow him as quickly as they could, and cheered them with the assurance that his palace was not far away.

"And don't look back," he said, lengthening his stride; "remember Lot's wife."

The young girl, though dressed in her riding habit, could not long keep up the pace in the tall heather. She often stumbled and got caught in the branches. So the cornet, without asking permission, picked her up in his arms, and in spite of her protest, carried her.

Although the specific weight of a pretty girl must be equal to that of a homely one, nevertheless I have been told that the former is much easier to carry, especially for a young cavalier who is in love. I hope, therefore, that no one will doubt my veracity when I say that the cornet carried his lady without resting for about half a mile. Black Mads offered once or twice to exchange burdens with him, but the cornet shook his head, and we can readily see that such an exchange would not have suited anyone. As the young lady had one arm around his neck and with the other hand constantly lifted his hat, fanned him, wiped the perspiration from his face, while she kissed his flushed forehead, that naturally made her lighter and him stronger.

"Here we are!" cried the leader at last, throwing down the saddle and bundle at the foot of a small heather-clad hill.

"Where?" said the cornet, as he too set down his burden. He looked around without being able to discover anything that looked like a human habitation. A suspicion quickly arose in his mind, but vanished almost in the same moment: if the man had meant to rob and murder them, he could easily have carried out his purpose and with no risk of resistance while his intended victim in a literal sense had both hands occupied.

"Here," said the poacher, as he lifted a very large and broad piece of heather turf and put it to one side. "A few days ago I was living above ground. They wouldn't let me stay there, but it's a poor mouse that hasn't got more than one hole." As he said this, he moved aside four or five stones that were large but not too large for a strong man to handle, revealing an opening roomy enough to crawl through.

"Why, this looks as if you had dug out foxes," said the cornet.

"That's what it's s'posed to look like," replied Mads. "But before we go in we'd better look around—not for the Aunsbjerg people, they can't have got past the fire yet—but there might be others around."

They scanned the heath in all four quarters: toward the south, the west, and the north there was not a living creature, and the entire eastern horizon was hidden by clouds of smoke, so thick that the rays of the morning sun couldn't penetrate them.

"Please go in, but you'll have to stoop," said Mads, as he crawled in on all fours. "Just you follow me! The door is low, but the house is big enough for us all. I'll get your things right away."

With some difficulty they followed their guide and soon found themselves in the underground dwelling. It was a good-sized room with walls of large stones and a ceiling of logs lying close together. A lamp was suspended from it and with its dim light barely revealed the furniture, consisting of on one side two beds, one large and one small, on the other side a bench, a table, a couple of chairs, a chest, and a pair of hanging cupboards. In the small bed lay three naked children who, at the arrival of the strangers, hid under the coverlet like wild ducklings. On the edge of the large bed sat Lisbeth Madame Mads knitting a stocking, which in her amazement she dropped with both hands in her lap. At one end of the table stood a small, red-haired man dressed in skins from his chin to his knees, whom Mads introduced as his good friend Renard Foxtail.

"We were digging out his half-brother here," he added smiling, "and then we found this hiding-place. Renard thinks it may have been a robbers' den once upon a time, but it may have been a burial mound, for we found some black pots with ashes and bones in them."

At the mention of a robbers' den the young lady shuddered slightly. Her lover noticed it and said in French,

"Don't be alarmed, my dearest! We are safe here. But I am sorry that the first house I bring you to should strike you with fear and repugnance."

"I'll show you my whole palace," continued the poacher, as he opened a door in the background. "Here's my kitchen, but we don't dare to make a fire here except at night. It's my pantry, too," he added, pointing to a salt-trough and some legs of deer that were hung to smoke over the fireplace. "I have bread and meat and a drop of mead, too, that I bought in Viborg for the last deerskin." With these words he set a jar and a wooden dish with food on the table. "Eat and drink of what we have! And when you want to start out, we'll get a safe guide for you."

The cornet pressed the hand of the honest troglodyte, saying, "At this moment I can offer you nothing but my heartiest thanks—"

"I don't want anything," Black Mads cut him short, "only promise me that you'll never let on about me or my den."

This easy promise was given with assurances by everything sacred; and the lovers sat down to a breakfast which hunger and joy over their escape combined to make all the more palatable.

Acting on the advice of their host, they decided to wait till evening before resuming their interrupted journey. Meanwhile Renard offered to go out reconnoitering, both to see where the pursuers had gone and to find out what had become of the cart from Vestervig. The first time he got no farther than the entrance to the den, where he observed that the pursuers had now ridden around the fire and started out in two divisions toward the west. A few hours later he ventured a little way out into the heath, and came back with the report that they had now ridden toward the northwest and that the heath would most likely be safe from them, as they could hardly imagine that the fugitives were still there; it seemed they must have been given information that had thrown them off the scent. A little after noon he and the host went out again, the former to order a cart from one of the villages in the west. The latter came back after half an hour and reported that out there he had come upon a young fellow who looked rather queer. From the way he talked, he might be a German. He inquired about the way to Hvam Tavern and asked if there hadn't passed some travellers that day. The cornet asked more particularly about the man's appearance and dress, and from the description he was sure it must be his Hungarian. Then they both went out and were lucky enough to catch up with him about a mile from the den.

We shall not dwell on the Hungarian's account of why the wagon had not shown up; the reason was simply that he and the driver had mistaken for Karup river a more westerly stream, where the cart was now waiting. Furthermore, we shall only mention briefly that a little before noon he had been stopped and questioned by the pursuing riders and had not only managed to answer in such a way as to allay suspicion, but had sent them off in a direction where he supposed the fugitives would not be—though all the time in the most painful uncertainty about their fate.

Finally, I think it unnecessary to go into details about the development of the catastrophe, but will hurry toward the conclusion after the manner of novel writers. The cornet and his sweetheart arrived safely the next morning at Vestervig, where they were made man and wife, and to begin with received from the owner, the oldest brother, a small manor at Thy where they could live. Junker Kaj got first a long nose and secondly —about a year later—a still richer heiress in Fyn. The Aunsbjerg squire and his lady cast off their daughter entirely and —in spite of all humble and repentant letters from her and her husband—refused to forgive them.

THE HORSE PASTURE

TOWARD the west end of Aunsbjerg woods there is an open place, quite a good-sized green surrounded by venerable beech trees. Every year, on the afternoon of Whitsunday, most of the people who live in the surrounding parishes gather there. Many houses are standing empty that day, or they are guarded only by the blind and the bedridden; for the lame and the cripples— provided they have their eyesight—must at least once a year enjoy the forest newly in leaf and bring home a light green beech bough—like Noah's dove—to the dark dwelling which is often a Noah's ark in miniature.

What fun! What crowds! The horse pasture—for that is the name by which this gathering-place is known—is like an enormous beehive: constant stir, everlasting thronging back and forth, in and out, all busy only with sucking up the honey of joy, drinking in the exhilarating summer air. How they hurry, how they flutter from flower to flower, greet each other, touch hands, part again, intimately, lightly, hurriedly! How many a young swain has not here found the queen of his heart! How faithfully the lovesick boy follows his queen bee! Far from the great hive one hears an incessant humming and buzzing—the bees are swarming. As we get nearer, the noise grows louder and the monotonous mass of sound dissolves itself into cries, singing, laughter, snapping of beech leaves, music of fiddles and flutes. The crowd surges in and out of the green edges of the forest, the peasants in their Sunday best, the gentle-folk in smart summer clothes, the gentlemen in black, the ladies in white. Is there dancing? Yes, a ball in the forest, dancing on the elastic greensward. Don't you see over there by the beech the village fiddler high above the surrounding crowd? Don't you see between the flower-trimmed hats how quickly his bow flies up and down? And there is a real quadrille, a genuine schottische.

"Am I in the Deer Garden? or in Charlottenlund?" you ask. "Look at the vehicles, the handsome carriages! Coachmen in livery, horses with silver-mounted harness, tents with restaurants, serving cold cuts and pastry! Coffeepots over the fire! Families gathering in the grass around their lunch baskets!"

You are in the horse pasture. This is the vespers on Whit-sunday in Lysgaard district, the day of homage to beautiful and ever-young Nature, the levee of the forest, the triumph of summer. Thus it is celebrated till the sun goes down, and the forest is once more left to the birds and animals that have been for a time frightened away. Formerly only the peasants in the two or three nearest parishes assembled here. But the innocent, joyous feast itself is surely an old custom, perhaps as old as the forest itself.

Ten years after the event concluded in our last chapter, the summer festival was held as usual in the horse pasture. A man from whose grandson I heard the story in my young days has described it as follows:

"It was the first year I served at Kjærsholm as bailiff of the estate. My sweetheart lived at Vium; she was distantly related to the pastor's family. Whitsunday she had asked me to meet her in the horse pasture, and we both came so early that we were the first couple there. We walked around for an hour or two until the noise and the sound of a violin told us the people were gathering. We went over there and sat down to look at the dancers. Presently I saw a party approaching on the path from Aunsbjerg, consisting of two fine gentlemen, a lady, and two little boys. As I was a stranger in the neighborhood, I asked my sweetheart who they were.

"Hush," she said. "It's the family. The large, stout man is the old squire, who became a widower five years ago. The young man with the scar on his cheek is his son-in-law, the woman his daughter, and the two little boys their children. Ten years ago the young gentleman carried her off in the night. As long as the old mistress lived, any reconciliation was out of the question, but after she was dead the old squire relented, and asked them to come and live with him. When he dies they will inherit the house and the estate."

They remained standing there a while, amusing themselves by looking at the peasants and giving them some money for drinks. On a windfallen trunk two elderly men were sitting with a mug of ale between them and smoking their pipes. The gentlefolks went over to them, and at that they rose and took their pipes out of their mouths.

"Don't get up," I heard the young gentleman saying. "Now you're better friends than when you struck fire for Niels's pipe at Karup river."

"Yes, my lord," said the older of the men addressed with a smile. "There's no animal so small it doesn't fight for its life. It looked bad, but turned out well."

The gentlefolks laughed.

"Take care," said the old squire as they went away, "that you don't get caught in the antlers of the stag you're riding there."

Again they laughed heartily, and I could hear the guffaws of the Aunsbjerg squire, which sounded hollow as the call of the bittern deep in the woods. I asked my sweetheart what all this meant and who the two old men were.

"The one," she said, "in the green coat with the gray hat is the gamekeeper. The other, in the brown suit, is Mads, the under-ranger, who lives near by and whom the young gentleman brought with him when he came. That talk about the stag I'll explain to you."

As she was doing so, and at the same time telling me the whole story of the young people's secret engagement, my eyes fell on a couple who were dancing all by themselves while all the others stood gaping at them.

"Who are they?" I said, "they look rather out of the ordinary, the young fellow especially, with his yellow leather breeches and the blue jacket with such a lot of buttons and with the queer cap on his head."

"He's no young fellow," she said, "but a married man, and it's his wife he's dancing with."

"It's a curious dance," I cried; "he stamps so hard in the ground and struts around her like a bristling turkey cock. That's no country dance."

"They say it's Hungarian," she answered, "for he's from Turkey and came here with the young master back from the war. He's clerk and gardener and jack of all trades at the manor. His wife has been maid to the mistress for many years, and they do say it was she who helped her the time she ran away from her parents."

And so the story is at an end. Several generations lie between it and us. Bells have rung and hymns been sung over many of their descendants since the persons I have written about went to rest. Both the old squire and the young master have long since been forgotten, and no one knows anything about Black Mads. The manor has often changed hands, the land has been sold and divided. Only the robbers' den lives on in a dark and confused tradition. In the great heath, miles west of Karup river, there are some heather-grown hills which are still called, and always will be called by that sinister name. But no one remembers that it was once a refuge for tender and faithful love, a heaven under the earth.

TARDY AWAKENING

[*Sildig Opvaagnen*, 1828]

I CANNOT remember any death that has caused a greater sensation than that of my friend of many years' standing, Dr.
L—— in the town of R. People stopped each other in the
street, they ran from house to house, asking, "Have you heard
it? Do you know about it? What could have been the reason?
Could he have done it in a fit of madness?" and so on. He was
a very genial man, universally liked and respected, an excellent
physician with a large practice; happily married, so far as we
knew; the father of six fine children, the two eldest sons
already launched in the world, the daughter married to a
worthy civil servant, the next one just grown up, and the
two youngest ten and twelve years old. Furthermore, he had
a fortune, kept open house, and enjoyed social diversions. He
was forty-eight years old and had never been ill.

Suddenly there came a rumor that he was not well. His
patients waited for him a whole day in vain. People sent to
inquire about him; they came to call, but he did not receive
them; visitors were told either that the doctor was sleeping or
that he was not well enough to see anyone. The other physician in town, though not called in, was at least admitted.
When people asked him about Doctor L——, he shrugged
his shoulders and said that he did not understand what was
the matter with him. He refused all medicines. I was his pastor
and the only person whom he allowed to pay him long daily
visits. He didn't want to see the children; when any of them
came in, he turned his face to the wall. He lay like that for
eight days, and on the ninth he shot himself.

The other doctor said that he had committed suicide in a
fit of delirium, and he received an honorable burial. I had
meant to speak a few words at his grave, but my voice broke
with grief, and I could hardly read the burial service for weeping.

Before his death he had told me the hidden reason for his terrible deed. But that which was a secret then could not long be concealed, since five people knew it; one of them, stung by jealousy and just indignation, was unable to be silent about a crime which had better have been interred with the victim and brought only before the bar of eternal justice. The story, which at that time was only a sinister rumor stealthily circulating by word of mouth, can now well be set down on paper, provided the names of the persons concerned are omitted. Of these none are living except three of Doctor L——'s children —who are residing abroad—and his wife, who is the chief figure in this tragedy.—But I will begin my story a little further back.

It was just five and twenty years before the catastrophe I have described that I came to R. I was a candidate for orders and had been offered a position as a private tutor, for the school in the town was in ill repute. Shortly after my arrival L—— and I made each other's acquaintance, and not in the pleasantest way. He had recently settled in the town as a practising physician. We met at a ball. I was only a year older than he, gay and thoughtless, a skillful and impassioned dancer. I soon discovered who was the best dancer among the ladies, and she was also decidedly the prettiest. I must confess, however, that it was in the former capacity she impressed me most. I asked her to dance one of the dances fashionable at the time, and she accepted with a bow. It was my turn to lead, and I had just clapped my hands as a sign that we were to begin, when Dr. L——, whom I had never seen before, stepped up to my partner, bowed and reminded her that she had promised him that dance.

Miss W—— blushed and excused herself by saying that she thought it was the next dance for which she had engaged herself. "But if my partner will allow me," she added, "we can still change."

"By no means," replied L—— rather sharply. "I resign, and consent to being Number Two, more especially as I am no doubt a poor dancer compared with this gentleman."

"Who is the best dancer has nothing to do with the matter," I said, "but if you are not satisfied with my partner's proposition, I beg you to let us begin—the entire quadrille is waiting."

He was standing right between us. "Both begin and end," he replied with a sneer, and stepped aside.

When I came to the end of the quadrille, I saw him standing at the end of the line with one of the clumsiest figures to be found at the ball, and I noticed that in the chain he would not give my partner his hand. She smiled almost imperceptibly at me, and I thought I felt a slight pressure on my fingers. The fellow was jealous, that was plain. I could not help thinking that he must have other rights than those given by the laws of the ball. After the dance I therefore went over to him and apologized for my short answer. This approach met a courteous response, and we were soon touching our punch glasses and drinking to our better acquaintance.

I danced once more with Miss W——. When I left her, and perhaps kissed her hand rather warmly, I received and answered the second pressure of her hand. I am sure that neither my heart nor my senses felt the slightest excitement; it was only my vanity that was pleasantly tickled. It was not the first time that I had received such a sign from a maiden's fair hand in the heat of the dance and the whirl of pleasure; I well know that such an impulsive expression of a tender and happy heart's emotion is as fleeting as the salutation that two travellers exchange in passing and the next moment forget. But when a few months later I learned that Miss W—— at that time had been secretly engaged to L——, I mentally made a note of this pressure of the hand. A girl who is free and unpledged may venture such an advance—though she ventures more than she perhaps knows or suspects—but when an engaged girl permits herself to do such a thing she thereby reveals herself as a flirt, and if she is a married woman, any man who is not entirely inexperienced will put her down for what she is or will become —a harlot. It was, however, the first and last time I noticed anything suspicious in Miss W——, and after I had observed her modest and virtuous manner and behaviour both as maid and wife, I began to think that I had been mistaken about the pressure of her hand and about her, that perhaps she had not even been conscious of the act.

I have had a strange and often saddening experience confirmed by too many instances: that the first impression a person's face—or rather countenance—makes upon me is to be relied on, that it gives a sure glimpse into the soul, an infallible view of that person's true character. I have often been angry with myself for what I thought was a mere fancy: I have even punished myself for my gratuitous harsh judgments, and secretly made amends for my secret offense when later I saw a behaviour and a conduct quite the opposite of what my first impression had led me to expect, when I saw not only a different character but quite a different countenance. And yet— alas! though it pained me I must confess that, sooner or later, rational arguments have been put to shame by a mere fleeting fancy. It was not so much the pressure of Miss W——'s hand as the first look at her face that whispered to me, "This beautiful girl is not for one man." There was nothing in her eyes of the sweetly languishing or the ardently inviting, of the tenderly conceding or the deeply exploring; her smile was neither sweetish nor roguish, still less bold; there was nothing voluptuous in the movements of her erect, perfectly beautiful figure, nothing that suggested sensual pleasure; and yet there was in the bland, passionless face something furtive, something stealthy; it seemed to hide some deep, terrible mystery, or perhaps rather it boded a crime not yet conceived in thought which the future would reveal. Twenty-five years later I was reminded in an awful way of this long unremembered foreboding.

If vampires were anything but the abortive fancies of an unbridled imagination, then I must have seen one of these creatures—outwardly living, inwardly lifeless, bodies without soul, lumps of flesh without heart. I knew her as a girl of eighteen, and as a wife and mother; I saw her in the ranks of the dancers and of the worshippers; with playing cards in her hand and with a nursing baby at her breast; at the wedding of her daughter and by the dead body of her husband; but she was always the same: gentle, quiet, attentive, and controlling herself perfectly. I have recently seen her—she is now not far from fifty —but she is almost unchanged, enjoys blooming health and an even, calm cheerfulness. The two darkest days of the year (after the tragic event, while I was still living in R.) were those on which I had to give her the sacrament. In my communion sermons I have occasionally tried to shake her conscience and awaken it, but there was nothing to awaken. If these pages should meet her eye, I am sure she will be able to read them without dropping a stitch in her knitting or making a mistake in her embroidery.

But I am running too far ahead of my story; let me go back again.

The acquaintance between L—— and me, which had begun so inauspiciously, was continued and soon grew into a friendship that nothing but death could dissolve. Three months after that ball he confided to me that he was and even then had been engaged to Miss W——. It struck me; I remembered the pressure of her hand, and asked him—though without betraying my suspicions—whether he had taken counsel not only of his heart but also of his intelligence? if he knew her? and if he felt assured that she would and could make him happy? His answer was the warm outpouring of a heart in love. He assured me that she loved as tenderly and sincerely as he, but that she was able to control herself perfectly and let no one even suspect her preference; this was all the more necessary inasmuch as her stern and hard-hearted father would assuredly have broken her engagement to a young man without any fixed means of livelihood. As soon as he got a position, he would propose and had no doubt that her parents would consent.

Six months later the district physician in the town died; L—— became his successor, and soon after Elise W——'s happy husband. I have never seen a more rapturous human being—he was almost wild with pure joy. He would neither sit nor stand for long in one place; a sweet restlessness drove him hither and thither, and finally—as soon as it was at all possible —back in the charmed circle of the fairy. During these honeymoon days—which lengthened into weeks and months—his patients got short visits and short prescriptions, but all the more comforting and joyous hopes, for in this period no illnesses were mortal; he was master of them and of death, too. And it was true, I remember it very well: his cures were all successful. I almost think he cured his patients with his happy face and merry talk. His wife seemed to be happy, too, but her joy bore the stamp of moderation. The wife was exactly like the engaged girl, and the bridal bed had made no visible change in her.

Once when he described his rapture to me in unrestrained dithyrambs, I could not help expressing a wish that she might "share it in an equal degree."

"Wilhelm," he whispered, *"die holde Sittsamkeit bey Tage"* —here he paused, put one hand on his heart and the finger-tips of the other on his lips, as he looked heavenward with an enraptured expression.

"Well, well," I said smiling, and never asked for any further comment. Nevertheless I could not help doubting whether there could be any emotion underneath that calm, mirror-smooth surface. If there was any warmth in that beautiful body, I felt it must be—if that were not a contradiction in terms—what I would call a cold fire, or at least a smouldering glow which never could burst out in flame—and perhaps could as little be extinguished.

Eight months after the wedding Elise presented her husband with the first son. He was drunk with joy. At the christening party there was great merrymaking. It was at that period of our social life when Phoebus and Bacchus were inseparable guests at every assembly, when there was constant interplay between them, and both acted irresistibly on all their worshippers. The cup had to be ushered in with song and the song ended with toasts. Mine was the last; at the end of the party I was handed the letter of presentation of the curacy at R. Two years later the rector retired, and I entered into the living. Now I could marry my Henriette, to whom I had been engaged since my early university days. We carried on a constant and very friendly intercourse with the L——s.

His wife had borne her second son and mine the first, when a third family joined our circle. Lieutenant H—— was transferred to the regiment garrisoned in R. He was one of the most genial and cultured officers I have ever known, and married to a wife who was handsome, witty, and sprightliness personified.

The doctor and the lieutenant (or rather the captain, for he soon got his promotion) lived side by side and I across the street from the doctor's. In view of this, we called our little closed circle, among ourselves, the triangle; L—— was the right angle, H—— one acute angle, and I the other. As a rule we would meet in one of the angles every Wednesday night, but outside of this routine, L—— and H—— often gave larger parties, which were then called assemblies, for both had means; the doctor had inherited money from his father-in-law, the captain from his own parents.

We lived in a state which seemed to me too happy to last. The only thing the captain lacked was children, but he made up for it by more excessive gaiety.

We three men without a doubt had the three handsomest and best wives in R.; their characters and ways were very different, but this divergence was—I think—one reason for the perfect harmony among us. My wife was quiet, gentle, and shy; she seemed to be subordinate to the other two, although in reality she possessed the deepest feeling and the clearest intelligence. Mrs. H—— was always in high spirits, full of merry jests and sallies, and she was the most talkative. Mrs. L—— was quiet, but there was something commanding about her, something that suggested a superiority of mind which, however, she did not attempt to assert, and she was treated by the other two as an elder sister, though actually she was both the youngest and the least cultured of the three.

If similarity of character were the foundation of matrimonial bliss, we six people should have been quite differently matched; there should have been a complete change-about. My even temper and natural gravity, which was strengthened by the dignity of my office, should have been united with Mrs. L——. Her frank, merry, brisk, and bold husband would have found his congenial match in Mrs. H——. And my gentle, meek, and mild wife should have been chosen for the captain's companion on the way of life.

The captain had nothing warlike about him except the uniform. In civilian dress he looked like a modest, bashful candidate for matriculation. Not that he wasn't a capable officer, and recognized as such by the whole regiment, high and low. At the muster his company always acquitted itself best, although his men were better acquainted with his purse than with his stick, which only dangled from his wrist as a matter of show. His courage, integrity, and nobility of mind were known and appreciated by all. In the case of quarrels he was often chosen as arbiter, and in that capacity he prevented many a duel. In short, he had a very winning personality and was far more dangerous for feminine hearts than he himself seemed to be aware of.

How we all longed for Wednesday! We would meet at teatime, devote a couple of hours to music, in which all except Mrs. L—— took an active and rather creditable part. After supper we three men had a quiet omber, and the ladies had their private talks, enlivened by Mrs. H——'s sallies and merry laughter. She often caused a player to be looed and prevented a codille, when we broke up our game to join our merry wives.

About a year passed without any rupture in our pleasant relations and cheerful intercourse. But suddenly there was a noticeable change in the captain; he was often absent-minded and made mistakes both in the music and in the omber; sometimes he was gloomy and silent—sometimes excessively gay and talkative, although his talk was often disconnected. My wife called my attention to this strange metamorphosis and hinted that she thought there was something not right between him and Mrs. L——. I hushed her and tried to set her mind at rest on the subject—but I knew more than she. Against my will I had witnessed a scene which will never be eradicated from my memory, and which for a while gave me stuff to rack my brains with.

We had for a long time talked of getting up a masquerade; and I think it was Mrs. L—— who first suggested the idea. At last arrangements had been completed, masks and costumes provided, and the evening fixed upon. It was to be held in the club. Inasmuch as I could not myself take part in such an entertainment, I had agreed with three other omber devotees in town that we would have a game of cards. But in the evening I had an attack of headache which I am sometimes subject to. I got someone else to take my hand and went away to try to sleep it off. I asked the host to show me a quiet room where I hoped half an hour's rest would dispel my rheumatic attack. I was shown into such a retreat, so far from the ballroom that the distant sound of music and noises only tended to lull me to sleep. I sat down in an easy chair in a corner by the window and soon dozed off.

I had not slept long before I was awakened by the creaking of the door. I could hear that two people entered the room, but I saw nothing, for it was quite dark. It must be a man and a woman, but masked, as I could hear from the indistinctness of their voices.

"Now then, what do you want, dearie?" said he.

"Dearest, you are so wonderful tonight," lisped a feminine voice.

"But, wifie," he said again, "what are you thinking of? Do we need to steal away together as if we were straying on forbidden paths?"

No answer—the sound of a "hush" allowed me to guess that they had unmasked. I was on pins and needles; what should I do? My headache, which the sudden awakening had intensified, rendered me unable to take any resolution. The door creaked again, but whether they went away or stayed I was unable to make out. All was quiet and I heard nothing but a brawl out in the yard. So I sat for a little while and listened, vainly trying to go to sleep again. But the fracas out in the yard grew more noisy. Someone came out with a lantern or a candle which cast its rays through the window and on the sofa opposite. Myself unseen, I saw Captain H—— in Mrs. L——'s arms. A terrible mistake had been made, but whether it was intentional on either side I could not then decide.

The captain jumped up with a cry of horror; Mrs. L—— sank back and hid her face—as in despair or shame—in her hands. It was dark again.

"God forgive us both," he said. "Everlasting silence and—if it were possible—everlasting oblivion!"

It seemed to me that she was sobbing. He heaved a deep sigh of distress, and went out; a few minutes later she followed, and I was alone.

I sat there a long time, quite confused and stunned by what I had unwittingly learned. When I entered the ballroom again, the guests had just unmasked. The doctor and the captain wore exactly similar costumes, as Don Juan. Mrs. H—— wore the dress of a Turkish woman; I was sure that Mrs. L—— had worn the same costume when I saw her on the sofa; now she was a shepherdess—which seemed to me both strange and suspicious. The doctor was in high spirits; he teased Mrs. H—— and declared that she had met him alone in the passage and embraced him, thinking he was the captain. The latter was standing near them and tried to laugh, but the attempt was unsuccessful and ended in a forced cough. Mrs. L——'s face did not show the slightest change; she smiled as calmly as she always did to the playful remarks of her friends. I began to doubt my own eyes; if she had been guilty, how could she have maintained this—I came very near saying—hellish calm? The Turkish woman in there might have been someone else who looked like her. In short, I had almost recovered my faith in her innocence, when my wife—who is a nice observer—some time afterwards said to me confidentially that she was "afraid the suspicion she had expressed on a former occasion was not unfounded." That a great change had come over the captain since that masquerade was strikingly evident. He was often absent-minded and lost in thought. His old even temper was gone and had given place to a curious gaiety that would break out by fits and starts, sometimes without any occasion. The reason for this change—remorse for his unwitting crime—I well knew, but I didn't tell my wife. I tried to defend Mrs. L——, but did not enter into any explanations of the captain's behaviour.

"Dear wife," I said, "be on your guard against suspecting anyone!—And it's so unlike you. Do you know anything? Have you seen anything?"

"Only a single look," she replied, "but it was a look that made him blush and me turn pale; so we must both have understood it. It was quick as a distant gleam of lightning on a cloud at night, but clear enough to give light. The two of them were alone in the room, and my face was turned away, but I saw it in a mirror."

I shook my head, as if I didn't believe her and enjoined silence. "Let us not discuss the matter even with each other," I said. "You can so easily be mistaken; a look may mean more than one thing—why believe the worst?"

She too shook her head; and after that the subject was not mentioned between us for fully twenty years.

Meanwhile my wife and I continued our secret and separate observations, but nothing—not the least thing in the world— was discovered. The captain gradually regained—not his former frank cheerfulness—but at least a certain poise in his manner, which, however, had a more serious, perhaps a duller, tinge. After all, he was getting older day by day, and the sweet hope of fatherhood retreated more and more into the distance. Time, which carries us along on our course, wears off the sharp edges of our youthful emotions; imperceptibly we gain either firmness or flexibility, strength or bluntness, until at last all our passions leave us, to begin their play in younger and softer hearts.

The triangle remained undisturbed, the assemblies likewise. We had our musical evenings; we played our omber. Our children grew up, added their voices to our singing, and sometimes took our places at the card-table, if world news absorbed our interest.

The doctor's two eldest sons had taken their degrees in medicine and surgery, my son his in divinity. His eldest daughter was married and mine engaged, when the volcano which so long had been smouldering in the dark suddenly burst its crust of secrecy and by its unexpected eruption destroyed the earthly happiness of two families.

I had just returned from a journey which had taken several days, when my wife met me with the sad news that the major was very ill. I divested myself of my travelling clothes and hastened to his house. He was asleep. His wife, looking worried, stood with folded hands at the head of the bed; a pained smile was her greeting to me. I approached softly and in a whisper asked about our dear patient. She only shook her head, while she continued to look at him through the tears that welled up in her eyes. His sleep was restless; lips and fingers moved incessantly, and the eyeballs seemed to be rolling under the lids.

I sat down in order to wait for his awakening. Meanwhile his wife's aunt was telling me the story of his illness. He had caught a cold at the drilling of the regiment, had been overheated, and then had drunk cold water. As soon as he had come home he had felt ill, had gone to bed, had rapidly got worse, and every afternoon had a fit of fever. Our friend the doctor called several times a day, comforted him—as he always did, but he had nevertheless looked rather serious. Mrs. H——made a sign asking her aunt to do something or other, and she left the room.

Shortly afterwards, the major awakened. His eyes were wild; one could see that he was not in his right mind. He looked at his wife and threw himself back in the bed.

"Elise!" he began (his wife's name was Charlotte), "Elise! What do you want of me? It's enough now—it's too much. If the doctor or my wife found you here in bed with me, what would they say? Go, go! and leave me alone!" He stretched out both hands as if to push someone away.

The wife's eyes met mine—she changed color. The sick man went on in his delirium, "It was an unlucky idea about that Turkish costume. I certainly didn't know but that you were my wife." Mrs. H—— listened with anxious attention. I could see that she didn't know what he was talking about, but I understood him only too well; the scene at the masquerade was still vivid in my memory.

I went over to the poor woman and caught her hand. "Try to be calm, dear madame," I said. "Your husband's illness seems to be at its height—he is raving——"

Her only answer was a deep sigh.

"Hush! hush!" he whispered, "they might hear us down below—you know, Elise, that the storeroom is right above the mangling-room, and if anyone should discover the secret door in the summerhouse——"

Mrs. H—— clutched the bedpost; she had turned pale—a terrible change came over her face.

"Dear madame," said I, pretending that I noticed only one reason for her excitement, "would it not be best to send for the doctor? His presence would perhaps reassure us—this crisis may not be so dangerous as it appears." She answered with a nod and quickly left the room.

The eyes of the sick man closed—he slept, but it was a restless sleep. I looked out into the yard. Mrs. H—— was walking rapidly in the direction of the mangling-room. It was true that the storehouse for soldiers' uniforms was right over it, and the summerhouse in the doctor's garden, which was two stories high and built of planks, adjoined it. A terrible suspicion seized me and was not far from becoming a conviction. I had often had tea and played omber in that summerhouse and remembered that from it one could hear if there was anyone in the storehouse. No doubt there was a foundation of miserable truth in the ravings of the sick man.

While Mrs. H—— was outside—no doubt in order to search the premises in the light of the hints she had received—the doctor came of his own accord. With a troubled expression he went over to the bed, examined the patient, felt his pulse, looked anxiously at me, and shook his head.

The major awakened—he stared fixedly and with a look of terror at the doctor. "What?" he exclaimed. "What does this mean? You made me believe that your husband had gone to see a patient in the country and would be gone for the night, and here he is, large as life. Why did you want to fool me? Why did you give the sign? Didn't you pin the red ribbon on the curtain in the summerhouse? Go, go! and sleep with your own husband! You're altogether too rash—the pitcher may go to the well once too often."

I stood there in an agony. I drew the doctor over to the window; I wanted to prevent him from hearing or remarking anything more.

"What do you think?" I asked.

"He is very delirious," he replied; "his illness is taking a bad turn."

"His ideas are perfectly crazy," I said.

"Oh, no," cried the major who had heard what I said, "I know perfectly well what I am saying; and I tell you once for all, Mrs. L——, that now everything must be at an end between us! It's a sin against both your husband and my wife, and neither of them has deserved such treatment from us."

Now the doctor began to be attentive. He cast a hasty glance out at the summerhouse, the upper window of which was visible from the sickroom. I followed the direction of his glance and—inside the window the major's wife was standing with clenched hands lifted, but the next moment she disappeared.

Good heavens! then she must have found the secret door which the sick man was raving about. He was dozing off again.

The doctor turned pale. I caught his hand and whispered, "For God's sake, dear friend, surely you're not attaching importance to what a man says in his raving? In a paroxysm of fever like that a patient may imagine the most unreasonable things in the world." He looked at me thoughtfully, but said nothing. In his glance there was something which could be interpreted, "You don't mean what you are saying." In the same moment the major's wife came in. Her face was flushed— her expression almost as wild as that of the sick man. The doctor met her with quiet self-control, comforted her, and asked some questions about the patient. She answered them rather carelessly and indifferently; her glance flickered from one to the other. But presently a flood of tears relieved the pressure at her heart. She rushed over to the bed, threw herself down on her knees, and pressed the hand of the sick man to her breast.

"Oh, God," she prayed in a low, hurried voice, "spare his life only this once so he can receive my forgiveness if he is guilty or my repentance if I am wronging him." (I heard only a word here and there, but could fill in the rest. The doctor heard nothing; he did not have a sensitive ear.) "Unhappy you!" she went on, pressing her forehead against his hand, "you are the one who has been seduced, but she—" here she sprang up and turned to the doctor.

I caught her hand and pressed it hard. "At this moment," I said, "it is for the physician and no one else to speak. Subdue your fear and your pain—if you value your husband's life," I added in a low voice that only she could hear.

She controlled herself, and suppressed the dangerous words that were already trembling on her lips. She was one of the fortunate natures who combine with strong feelings a quick judgment and a clear intelligence which her feelings could never quite obscure. Her heart was tender, but not weak. Alas, it was after all not strong enough to stand up under the much more dangerous test to which it was soon subjected.

I was sent for, I had to attend to duties of my office. She went with me into the passage, and I tried with all my might to set her at rest in regard to the dark hints in her husband's speech.

"Inasmuch as I have been present and heard it—" so I ended my warning—"you will not think it presumptuous meddling in your marital affairs if I speak of it. I can judge more quietly of matters that confuse and bewilder a loving eye. What may seem probable isn't always true; and there may be many conceivable explanations besides the worst. For heaven's sake, use your clear intelligence! Spare yourself and your sick husband! And whatever you do, don't let the doctor get the least inkling of it all, or we may have a double tragedy which might after all be due to a mistake." Sighing, she pressed my hand, and went back to the sickroom.

I had a great deal to occupy me; in my absence the work had piled up. This was in the morning, and it was toward evening before I was free. I was about to go to the major's again, but decided that I would first speak with the doctor in his own house in order to hear what he really thought about our friend's illness.

His wife was in the country with the second grown-up daughter. The two youngest were invited out to friends in town. The maid said the doctor was in his office. I went up there.

He was standing with his face toward the door and his back leaning against his escritoire. In his left hand he crushed some papers, while the right was clenched against his breast; in his face was that cold, mute despair which shuts out both hope and fear. My heart turned to ice; I saw at once that all was discovered, that suspicion had ripened into certainty. He gave me a hasty glance as if he did not know me.

How can consolation enter a heart which the winter storm

of calamity has encased in an icy sheath? I lifted up my hands to the Lord whose mercy begins where hope ends.

I know of no task more difficult or hopeless than to console those who need consolation most, that is, those who cannot console themselves. To say to anyone whose entire earthly happiness has suddenly been destroyed, "Be a man! Resist! *tu contra audentius ito!*" is just like telling someone who has fallen and broken his leg, "Come here to me, I'll help you rise," or to one who, without knowing how to swim, is plunged in a rushing stream, "Use your strength! You can save yourself if you only try." Some people attempt to comfort with that hope which the unhappy one has lost; others speak of the healing of time, the very thought of which torments him beyond endurance; and others again act like Job's comforters—who had much better have stopped with their silent pity and sympathetic tears—as they throw out hints of God's punishment, of open and hidden sins committed; instead of pouring balsam in the wound, they drip venom into it. Truly, the sufferer may well say in the bitterness of his lacerated heart: "I have heard many such things: miserable comforters are ye all. Shall vain words have an end? or what emboldeneth thee that thou answerest? I also could speak as ye do: if your soul were in my soul's stead, I could heap up words against you, and shake mine head at you."

When anguish constricts the breast, when it cannot even find a vent through the lips, what can melt the frozen heart unless it be the silent tears of a compassionate friend? Mine flowed freely and wet his hand, which I drew from his own breast to mine. In the unhappy man those floodgates were opened by which both sorrow and joy are poured out; he leaned his forehead against my breast and wept like a child.

But not for long. He lifted his head and threw it back, while the tears returned to their secret springs. "There, there!" he cried, as he vehemently pressed the papers into my hand. "There are prescriptions, legibly written—easy to understand —specific medicines against romantic notions, love, faith in woman's virtue, in friendship—" he threw himself on a chair, gnashed his teeth, and emitted some sounds that had a resemblance to laughter.

While I read the papers—letters, the contents of which I will tell presently—he stared fixedly at me with, I might almost say, envious eyes, and with a repulsive, bittersweet smile such as one may see long after life has departed on the faces of people who have frozen to death.

The letter which was lying on top and which, like the other two, was addressed to the major, but had neither date nor signature beyond "Your E.," (Elise) was undoubtedly the latest, and read as follows:

"Yes, my beloved, I cannot, I will not hide from you that under my too weak heart I carry a secret pledge of our hidden love. My conscience reproaches me with the sin against my husband, but love knows only one sin—unfaithfulness toward the beloved; it has only one duty—to do everything for the dear object of affection, to give it both body and soul and if necessary sacrifice both. Frantz, you were childless, it vexed my heart. If I have forfeited bliss beyond the grave, I did it to give you happiness here. Now, my beloved, I have nothing more to give you."

The other was evidently written shortly after that unlucky masquerade.

"What is done is done," she wrote; "but it is fate, mysterious fate itself that brought us together. Fate itself has united us—who shall now part us? I feel it, I know it; since that night I am yours forever; I have a new heart, a new soul. I am quite changed; my thoughts, my wishes, my longings have but one goal—you, you beloved, adored man! Oh, don't hate me! don't despise me! It is not sensuality that draws me to you; no, my love for you is pure; but I must speak to you, must pour out my agonized heart, and beg forgiveness for a sin that fate alone must answer for. I don't know what I am writing—at eleven tonight I shall expect you—my husband is in the country—have pity on   Your unhappy E."

"Secrecy," said the third, which was most likely in point of time the middle one, "is the life principle of love; without it the myrtle lacks both root and top. If anyone knew that I loved you, if I were your wedded wife, then perhaps the impossible might happen. But what a temple for our secret joys! a storeroom full of uniforms and hempen cloth!—This evening my husband goes to P. By eleven o'clock everybody will be in bed except the one who awaits you with burning heart. The sun doesn't rise till seven. Ah, it will be a long time before I say: 'Frantz, Frantz! *Steh auf! der Morgen graut.*'"

When I had finished reading, and the last letter fell out of my hand, L—— rose, caught me by the shoulders, and asked with a piercing look, "Well, my good parson?"

"How did these letters fall into your hands?" I said. "Are you sure they are genuine?"

"As genuine," he cried, "as *cortex peruviana selecta*, but not quite so good for one's health, and I have them directly from the paramour himself."

(The unfortunate Mrs. H—— told me afterwards how it had happened. When the doctor had returned in the afternoon to see his patient, the sick man had begun to rave again, and had spoken still more plainly than before. At last he had ordered her—still mistaking her for the doctor's wife—to bring him a certain drawer in the escritoire. The drawer had a double bottom, and by pressing a peg the upper one flew open, revealing the letters. Then he had handed them to her with the words, "There, Elise, are your letters. Tear them up, or burn them!" She tore up some other papers, went behind his bed, and read the letters. No longer able to control herself, she had handed them to the doctor, and with that the blow had fallen on the cruelly deceived man.)

"My poor unhappy friend!" I sighed. "What decision are you taking? What do you mean to do?"

He let go my shoulders, and walked quickly with clenched hands round and round the room. "What will I do?" he repeated many times.

"In the first place," I spoke again, "I suppose these unfortunate letters ought to be destroyed—"

"Destroyed!" he cried. "These letters?" He quickly took possession of them again. "What? These sweet, blessed pledges of love!" He pressed them to his breast with the vehemence of a lover. "No, pastor, I will not part with them; they shall follow me into the grave and from the grave up where all such pledges shall finally be redeemed."

"Oh, my friend, my friend!" I said. "Are they not long since registered there? Why do you want to be her accuser? Neither vengeance nor judgment belongs to you, but to God, whose justice is exalted far above our fleeting passions."

He paused, looked heavenward a long while, and then gave them back to me. "There," he said quietly, "keep them! destroy them! but promise me one thing first: that when I am dead and gone you will show them to her."

I promised, but added, "Why, dear doctor, do you speak of death? You have had a hard, a terrible blow—you are losing a wife whom you love—an unworthy, contemptible creature; but you still have your children."

He looked hard at me and burst out into a wild fit of laughter. "Whose children? My children?—No, the major's children—"

"The two eldest," I interrupted, "were born before he came to town, and no one, after even a hasty glance at them, can mistake their father."

"And the others?" he asked, smiling bitterly, "which of them, how many of them are mine? Haven't you read the letter, and don't you think they look the very image of him?—Oh!" and he beat his forehead with his clenched fist, as he began again his impetuous walk around the room.

I was silent—I could not at once think of anything to say; for when I turned the matter over in my mind, I felt that his suspicion was not entirely unfounded, especially in the case of the married daughter. Her likeness to the major was unmistakable. "Fancies," I said at last rather slowly and half dubiously, "may also affect—"

"Ha!" he broke in, "here we don't need to draw on our fancies; the harlot has herself confessed it."

Just then the two youngest daughters came in and ran over to him to embrace him. But he stepped back as far as the room would allow, put out his hands as if to push them back, and stared at them with horror and loathing in every mien. The poor little girls were frightened, trembled, burst into tears, and fell on each other's necks—they thought they had done something wrong. I put my arms around them and my tears fell on their fair, curly heads. Then his hardness too melted in pity; the old tenderness returned and—for a little while—drove out the demon of doubt. He sat down, took them on his knees, and caressed first one, then the other. The little ones now wept with joy.

In this more favorable mood I thought I might venture to leave him in order to attend to my unfinished official duties. I left him to the gentler feelings of his own kind heart and to the mercy of Him whose grace is all-powerful.

When I visited him the next morning he was lying in bed, undressed but wide awake. The next to the youngest daughter, a girl of twelve, was sitting at the bedside and trying to make him drink a cup of tea. He refused it and looked at us both with a dark, cold, distant expression. I made a pleading gesture, pointing to the child, and he then took the tea, lifted it to his mouth, but as if it had been bitter medicine, he set the cup down on the coverlet again. In order to get the little girl out of the room, I asked her to bring him breakfast, and then I turned to the unhappy man, trying once more to open his closed heart.

He put away the cup and folded his hands. Either he did not hear me, or he did not understand me. "My life," he said at last, slowly and in a low voice, "will return to Him who gave it—the poison is acting: I have emptied the cup to the last drop, and for me there is no antidote but death. I have awakened from a long, sweet dream. I have been granted a lucid moment—as is often the case with people who are out of their minds—and I know it for a warning of dissolution to come. Oh, my God, my God! take me away from here before that snake comes back!" He closed his eyes as if he feared the sight of her. "I loved so tenderly, so faithfully," he went on after a pause, "with my whole heart, soul, and mind; for twenty years I imagined myself living in an earthly paradise, while I was walking on a volcano secretly burning under my feet—the thin crust that separated heaven and hell is broken, and I have fallen into the flaming abyss—merciful God! let my body be consumed and receive my poor soul!"

I prayed with him, prayed for strength and patience; I comforted him with God's almighty goodness; I tried to make him think of his two hopeful young sons and of a more bearable future separated from the unworthy one. He shook his head quietly. "I can't live," he said, "in the world where she breathes; we can no longer have one sun in common. Separation from bed and board and house and native country—that means nothing; light and darkness, life and death, time and eternity must be between us; otherwise we are not parted."

The oldest daughter (alas, I can't say *his* daughter) came in with her two-year-old child on her arm. The infant stretched out its arms to the supposed grandfather and tried to stammer that name which up to now had been so sweet to him. With an expression of lacerating inner pain he turned his face away. The distressed mother set the child down, and tears streamed from her eyes. I had to lead them both out of the room and use all my art and inventiveness in an attempt to soothe the poor young woman. I was only partly successful—she felt a foreboding of calamity.

As far as my time allowed, I remained with my unhappy friend as his attendant, nurse, and comforter for the next seven days. I had a hard task: to take care of him, keep visitors away from him, and calm the children.

The other doctor came a few times without having been called in, but as there was nothing for him to do, his visits ceased.

I wrote to the sons in Copenhagen; I hoped their presence might have a good effect on the poor sufferer—they came in time only to follow his inanimate body to the resting-place he had ardently longed for and forcibly wrested from fate.

With every day my friend grew more quiet, gloomy, and taciturn: it seemed to me that he was brooding over some terrible plan or other.

On the eighth day after the tragic discovery the major passed away: he had been lying in a stupor and died without recovering consciousness. I brought the news to L——; he received it indifferently, and only said, "We shall soon meet."

Mrs. L—— was expected home the next day. I asked her husband what measures were to be taken in view of her arrival, if it would not be best to have her sent away? He answered that he was quite prepared for her return and that everything would turn out all right. This made me suspicious, and I said so. With a quiet smile he gave me his hand, saying, "And if I have a sure premonition of my death, would you then begrudge me the satisfaction of the only wish that is left to my crushed heart? The chains that bound me to life are loosening link by link—there is only one left; as soon as I see her, that will break."

There was a double meaning in these words; I ought not simply to take the worst. Yet I continued to admonish him, bringing to bear the arguments of reason and religion. Alas! reason can do nothing with a despairing heart, and religion can comfort only those who have previously been guided by it. And Dr. L—— had been too thoughtless or too happy to possess any deep religious feeling. He had had faith, but it was a flimsy faith, which had never been tested and strengthened by grief or serious reverses. He was a son of joy, and parted from that constant companion on the course of life, he became an easy prey to sorrow—to the most terrible of all the passions against which a weak human soul has to struggle here.

I stayed with him till far into the night. When I was about to go, he stretched out his arms to me, and pressed a kiss of farewell on my lips. A few tears still glistened in his dull eyes, and with an almost breaking voice he spoke only the words, "Thanks, and good-bye, for a while!"

I went home and lay down half dressed, fully resolved to go back to him early the next morning, partly to keep a watch over him, partly to prevent—if possible—a meeting between him and his faithless wife, or at least to be a much needed third party at the scene.

But exhausted as I was, I overslept, and none of my household wanted to disturb my rest. I was awakened with the terrible news that Dr. L—— had shot himself. I hastened over to the house; he was still lying in the bloody bed with his breast pierced. None of the family were there, but the other doctor, the mayor, and the maid. The maid had been present when the deed was done. She stated that, with the doctor's consent, she had relieved me in watching with him; that his wife, who had been informed by the oldest daughter of her husband's illness, had hastily returned to town, and at daybreak had unexpectedly entered the room. As soon as he saw her, he had sat up in bed, spoken a few words in a language which the maid did not understand, had then taken a pistol from under the coverlet, and fired it against his breast.

I will not dwell on the misery that followed. In the beginning of this story I have briefly told how a sensual and unscrupulous woman's crime brought ruin to two families, and to many others a sorrow that gave deep pain for a long time and will never wholly be forgotten.

ALAS, HOW CHANGED!

[Ak, hvor forandret, 1828]

As I am a good-for-nothing fellow, tolerated only because I don't do any harm (that is directly, though sensible people declare that indirectly my poetic twaddle may work mischief in more ways than one), and as my flighty nature has prevented me from ever acquiring a permanent office (once I did hope to be made chief of firemen, another time I aspired to be parish clerk, and a third time I meant to become sexton and undertaker; but each time I was disappointed), as I therefore have nothing particular to do, I have a good deal of time on my hands which I use to look around in the world as much as I can.

THE VISIT

No sooner had I returned last spring from my visit to Copenhagen, during which I renewed acquaintance with a friend of my youth, the happy Counsellor of Justice S——, than I decided that I would look up another old friend who lived in a quiet corner far away in Jutland. I had witnessed domestic bliss in the metropolis; now I hastened to seek it in rural seclusion. I had not seen my now reverend friend, Pastor Ruricolus, for more than twenty years, but he and Counsellor S—— and I had once been a fine three-leaf clover. All three were jolly fellows, full of high spirits, enjoying the pleasures of youth in every decent and legitimate way; but Ruricolus was the most elegant of us, both in dress and deportment. I cannot say that he was exactly a dandy, far less a coxcomb, but he was always dressed in the latest fashion and looked, as my poor, dear mother used to say of him, like a peeled egg. He had an ineffable knack of tying his cravat and the knee-bands of his black silk breeches, and yet there was perfect symmetry in all his garments. When on a Sunday in summer we would walk in Frederiksberg Park, he attracted most glances from the ladies, although S—— too was a handsome chap, and I was almost six inches taller than either of them.

But let me be honest and confess: it was not only longing for a friend of my youth that drew me; in the place where he was now living I had nineteen years ago experienced my twentieth love affair. It was there I first saw Maren the Second,[1] the lovely, angelic Maren Lammestrup, the pearl among all Vendsyssel girls. It was there I for the twentieth time gave away my tender heart and for the twentieth time had it returned to me without dent or flaw. Allow me, my fair feminine reader, to relate my innocent adventure.

Ruricolus and I made a summer excursion from the City within the Ramparts, in order to cast a few rays of light over the peninsula of Vendsyssel. (Our voyage to Aalborg deserves a special description, and with the aid of the Muses it shall be written when, by studying our great models in this field, I shall have made myself perfect in the style of travelogues.) We two Copenhageners—I a native, he naturalized—made a sensation by the Wild Bog; our broad-brimmed hats, short vests, and long trousers attracted well-deserved admiration. It was only the proprietor of Tyreholm, Mr. Mads Lammestrup—a rude, uncultured, boorish fellow—who took the liberty of scoffing at our costumes. It was the first time anyone in Vendsyssel had seen long yellow nankeen trousers and gaiters to match with points reaching all the way down on the toes. The brute said we looked like flat-footed cock-pigeons. His daughter, Maren, the sweet dove, found a more flattering simile in our tender and amorous cooing; indeed I attributed—and I believe with good reason—to these same yellow gaiters a good part of the hit we two blades made with her and the other Vendsyssel girls.

My heart is made of tinder—no! that metaphor is misleading, for though it catches fire easily, it is not consumed; tinder burns but once, my heart any number of times.—My heart is of gunpowder—but, no! that isn't right either, for though it

---

[1] Not to be confused with Maren the First, daughter of the town musician, see *Nordlyset*, February, 1827, page 233.

catches fire in a moment, it burns steadily and quietly, without smoke or explosions.—Now then, my heart must be of asbestos —hm! that won't do, for asbestos doesn't burn at all. Well, then, without any metaphor or figure of speech, I will say that from the first moment I saw her I was over head and ears in love with Maren Lammestrup, the fair maid and sweet flower of the rose.

There was to be a haymaking feast at Tyreholm the same day that we arrived at the parsonage in Kringelborg where my Ruricolus's father lived. His reverence received us very affectionately.

"Welcome, Hans Mikkel!" he called to his son. "Who's the swain you're bringing with you?"

Hans Mikkel explained. The good pastor shook my hand, and said, "Welcome indeed, Mr. Copenhagener! What'll you have? A drink! Hey, Barbara! Bread and brandy!—You come just at the right time, children, for there's to be a party at Tyreholm tonight. Well, Mr. Copenhagener, what can we use you for? Can you play Polish bezique?"

"Yes."

"That's fine! Can you shoot a hare?"

"I'm afraid not."

"Why, that's bad luck! Do you smoke?"

"Not that either, pastor."

"Fie, shame on you! That's too bad! You'll have to learn. Can you drink a tart?"

"I can eat a tart."

"Ho-ho! You don't even understand this *terminus technicus*. Can you stand a tea-punch?"

"Hm, I think so—if he doesn't punch too hard. I'll take a look at him." (I didn't in the least know what he meant.)

The good man laughed till the perspiration stood in beads on his round, reddish-brown face.

"Well, well! Just wait," he said still laughing, "when you get to Tyreholm, Miss Maren will introduce you to the Jutland tea-punch; she knows how to brew it."

Just then a large hunting dog came in. The pastor turned quickly from me to the dog, put both hands on his sides, and cried, "By all the periwigs! Where do you come from? Are you alone, Argus? Or is your master with you? Have you been down in the goose-bog—hey?"

While he was still examining Argus, the owner of the dog, a landed proprietor of the neighborhood, appeared and offered to take the pastor along to the party. Both gentlemen were soon deep in a discussion of hunting, and I particularly remember that they both dwelt a long time on the dogma that the mallard duck in slyness was almost equal to the fox, an assertion which they illustrated with a good many striking examples. Meanwhile the carriage came to the door, and the five of us—including Argus—set off for Tyreholm.

A RURAL BEAUTY

It would be a pity to say that life was formal at the old manor house; of the old nobility's pomp and stateliness there was nothing left but the bare walls, and the present owner had not even the graces and dignity of a valet. Not that he lacked haughtiness or vanity—by no means! But it was not the noble pride that is based on parchments, genealogical trees, ribbons and decorations. Mr. Lammestrup was proud of his money and of nothing else. He had a measuring rod of silver by which he classified everybody without respect of persons; a beggarly tradesman ranked exactly as a beggared nobleman. A good man, according to his linguistic usage and that of the neighborhood, was synonymous with a rich man; a poor man was the same as a villain. I have still a vivid picture in my mind of his big, stout person standing at the door to receive us, his hands under his coat tails. His fat, shiny face grinned at us with a self-satisfied and cunning expression, but he didn't stir from the spot till we were all out of the carriage. Then he extended his broad fist slowly, gave first Chamber-Counsellor Svirum (Argus' companion on the hunt) his whole hand and then Mr. Ruricolus two fingers; we two young men got a nod between us.

"Have you seen my bullocks?" were the first words I heard from his lips. "Then, deuce take it, you must see them—they're no wooden-shoes—come, they're standing right outside the yard here." As he spoke, he put his hands in his pockets again and waddled ahead. The counsellor and the pastor followed him full of reverent anticipation, but young Ruricolus and I stood there without quite knowing what to do.

Mr. Lammestrup half turned when he was midway across the courtyard, and called out to us, "You young fellows, I suppose, don't care for such things. You can go in to the women meanwhile."

We did so.

It was unlucky that one of them should absorb my attention so completely that I had no eyes for anyone else, but this one was really a *non plus ultra* of rural beauty. I saw at first glance that she was perfect of her type. Such a wealth of charm, blooming, buxom, and yet formed on lines of perfect beauty, I felt I had never seen before. My reader must not imagine a round, chubby, strutting dairymaid! No Miss Flamborough or Betsy Bounce, who without stinting could each be divided into two young ladies! No, Miss Lammestrup was truly a model of graceful proportions both as to her face and figure. And as for her soul, believe me, dear reader, I am not speaking ironically when I say that this Jutland Maren possessed unusual culture, which I easily discovered after a few brief conversations. She had read and been moved by her La Fontaine, and I had only to mention "Lotte" and "Marianne" to bring tears into her heavenly clear eyes. Besides these perfections, she danced like an elf, sang like an angel, and played with taste and skill on her piano—probably the only instrument of its kind to be found in the whole of Vendsyssel. In what hothouse this fair field flower had been thus improved I cannot say, but one thing is sure—that Mr. and Mrs. Lammestrup had no part in it.

I have already said—and no one can now wonder at it—
that I immediately gave this excellent girl my heart. But I
will add: I am not in the habit of giving away my apple before
I have a pear in sight, and on this occasion I felt that I could
expect a fair exchange, for not only did her beautiful eyes
brighten with pleasure when they first beheld my person, but
gradually I detected several signs of a budding passion, among
which I will mention only the most conspicuous. In the first
place, I noticed that when I struck my favorite attitude (knees
bent, the left one quite far in front of the right, right hand
on my hip, left fist in my side with elbow bent forward, shoulders also thrown forward and slightly raised, head bent, eyes
wide open, upper lip drawn up toward the nose, giving a look
of pride—what the French call *dédaigneux*—something like a
soldier in a bayonet charge) when I stood in this position, she
secretly whispered to one of the other girls, glanced at me,
and smiled.

Secondly, when we came out in the hayfield where we were
to earn our share of the supper by forming a haycock, and took
the occasion to throw hay at each other, I was almost entirely
spared, while my friend Hans Mikkel was made the victim. My
sweet Maren threw the first handful of hay at his head, and
all the other girls followed suit. He resisted, and I came to his
aid like a brother. In vain! The madcap females stormed in
at him alone. He stumbled, and in a moment he was buried
under a mountain of hay, and with that we had lost the battle.
I was really sorry for the vanquished one when I saw him
standing there brushing his nice clothes and picking bits of straw
and moss off them, while the seven Amazons stood around him
and laughed; but none laughed louder than my roguish Maren.

Third and most evident sign of the dear girl's love I noticed
during the dance. I can say that I had acquired great facility
in the figures that were then the mode. They called for great
wagging of the posterior with long leaps and vigorous throwing out of the legs while the head was bent to one side over
the shoulder and in this position used to butt one's way through

a closely packed crowd. In this I had no equal; I could leap as much as four or six feet, and my fellow dancers took good care not to come too near me. But of course this exercise was rather violent and threw me into a perspiration. The blessed girl noticed how exhausted I was at the end of our first dance, and when I asked her for the next—which was a waltz—she excused herself in the kindest, most courteous manner—and why? Simply from delicate consideration for me. She had no such compassion on Hans Mikkel, for she allowed him to lead her away at once. With secret joy I saw how the little minx kept it up with the very last couple, only to tire him out and in one day defeat him twice—in the ballroom as on the hayfield. But I am sure it is unnecessary to cite more proofs; it must be clear to everyone what was the state of Maren Lammestrup's innocent little heart. I rightly considered it as my property, but I purposely postponed the mutual declaration; it's so nice to have something to look forward to.

THE HAYMAKING FEAST

As I have already said, I make great leaps in the dance, and that no one can object to, but leaps in telling a story may not please the thoughtful reader. Therefore—with due apologies for the hop, skip, and jump my heart did with my pen—I will now return to the sober and orderly description of the feast at Tyreholm.

The first object of our attention shall be the tea-punch. (As the composition of this popular drink is no longer a secret, I shall not dwell on the description of it.) So then: there sat the queen of the feast, Maren Lammestrup, by the steaming urn, brewing and handing out cups to the host, the counsellor, the pastor, and five or six other gentlemen, till they were themselves steaming urns emitting volumes of smoke from their pipes. I could not refuse to sit among them, but when I had consumed my "tart," I hurried out in the open air, for I began to feel sick. The punch, the smoke from the vilest Virginia tobacco, and added to that, the conversation—which was quite bestial, for it dealt with nothing but bullocks, horses, dogs, mallards, and other wild animals—had such an overwhelming effect on me that I had to seek solitude and lean my forehead against the old, venerable walls of Tyreholm.

Inasmuch as I knew that it is honorable to imbibe freely but contemptible not to be able to stand it, I tried to put on a brisk air when I returned to the steam-factory, but I was not very successful. My host, who must have found my sudden disappearance suspicious, looked fixedly at me with his large, milk-blue eyes, took his pipe out of his mouth—which it seemed to leave reluctantly—and said with a broad smile, "Seems to me our good friend is looking pale; I'm afraid Maren has made the brew too strong."

This sally was met with general laughter, first on the part of the originator, then on the part of the whole tea-punch assembly. I kept my countenance and joined in the laughing chorus, but after the finale I declared that my indisposition was due rather to the journey than to the strength of the punch. The arrival of other guests cut short this scene which was so amusing to all but me.

After the newcomers had received their share of the Vendsyssel nectar, the company adjourned to the hayfield. And it was here the battle took place which I have already described in anticipation. I shall therefore go right on to the dance.

The music was very ordinary—one fiddle. Our solo performer, I remember, was more notable for vigorous bowing than grace of execution, and he made up for the lack of other instruments by a kind of double note, the like of which I have never heard from any other master. Besides, he had various mannerisms that by their newness drew half my attention from Maren Terpsichore. He beat time with both his head and his foot and accompanied his instrument with a kind of nasal tone like the low snuffling of a mourning trumpet. Nevertheless we danced merrily to this music till the small hours, when someone suggested that we should play parlor games for a change, and these as usual gave occasion for a great deal of bussing. We played forfeits, and paid all the penalties; we "went to confession," "attended Polish church," "stood on the broad stone," "ground mustard," were "hanged" and "fell into the well," until the carriages came to the door and, with a heart as soft as melted wax, I took my leave of Tyreholm and the charming fairy Maren Lammestrup.

If anyone would like to know how her respected father, the counsellor, the pastor, and the other old gentlemen passed the night, I can only say that from the two card tables in the corners of the ballroom I constantly heard such expressions— puzzling to the uninitiated—as "Clubs, diamonds, spades, hearts, pass, looed, trump, knave of clubs, take your trick in," and so on; and every now and then a blow with a fist on the table, or an oath, or a roar of laughter, or sometimes a moment of deep silence would announce an important event. Two or three times Pastor Ruricolus cried loudly, "Shame on all peri-wigs!" from which I concluded that his reverence must have been sadly and undeservedly looed.

When the party broke up, the counsellor invited all the gentlemen present to a duck hunt in Svirumgaard lake.

I cannot be content to close this chapter without sharing with the reader a reflection which on such occasions is often forced upon me. True, it is neither cheerful nor pretty, but it is natural and answers to the mood of the soul after a wakeful though not necessarily a dissipated night.

What a change—I have thought—in the space of a few hours! We never notice the flight of time or its effect on us— which ordinarily seems slow, gradual, measured, almost imper-ceptible—as on the morning after a ball. Where now is that lively gaiety, that childlike joy, that sweet anticipation with which the dancers met, where that formal grace with which they greeted each other when they took their places for the first dance? How neat and smart both ladies and gentlemen were! Not a ribbon, not a flower, not a pin out of place; not a mote of dust either on the white dresses or the black coats;

not a crease, not a wrinkle but those that should be there. Every shirt frill, every bit of lace, had just the right fall; not a cravat but it was snow-white and fitted neatly under the chin; not a pompadour but rose properly; not a ringlet but glistened and waved in its right place—a snare for every unwary masculine heart.

With shining eyes and gently flushing cheeks, the lovely row of girls stood there, impatiently waiting for the first signal. Attentive, almost solemn, the gentlemen followed the movements of the leader. Gloves are drawn on—the leader steps back—looks at the orchestra—bows to his partner—claps his hands—and now the music starts and the dance commences.

But look at the same party at the end of the ball! It is day; the sun shines in through misty windowpanes; the candles burn dully and sleepily, like many eyes that a short time ago were sparkling with joy. Where is the neatness, the smartness, the grace of the night before? The clothes of the gentlemen are dusty, their hair is tousled, the shirt frill wrinkled, the cravat no longer fits under the chin, the bow is askew. And the ladies! the once so festively attired, so elegant ladies! The whiteness of the dress is gone and so is the flush of the cheeks. The glorious ringlets have lost their elasticity and hang disheveled down over the bosom which last night looked like marble and alabaster but today looks like a wall that has not too recently been whitewashed. Here a flounce, there a frill of lace has been torn; here a bow has been lost and there a pin. And what about the sweet faces? Alas, the brightness is gone from the eyes, the smile from the lips, the delicate flush from the cheeks; pale, dull, sluggish (if I may use such an expression), they seem to have enjoyed the fleeting pleasures of youth to the point of satiety, and in a single night to have become experienced, staid, almost sullen matrons.

But my sweet Maren, had she escaped that heart-chilling transformation? Well—yes. As a human being, she was of course subject to the law of change, but not to a heart-chilling degree. Indeed, her just perceptible weariness and the slight disorder of her dress simply gave her a more languishing appearance. I need only say that it was on this occasion, in fact the very same forenoon, that in a fit of stormy ecstasy I composed one of my most successful poems, "To Maren, the Morning after the Wedding."

THE DUCK HUNT

IT took me a long time to make up my mind as to what kind of style I should use for this important and interesting chapter. The subject was worthy of heroic treatment, but—to be quite frank—I find the heroic style difficult to handle; the purely historical seemed to me too dry. Moreover, I looked in vain for any forerunners on this boggy path. True, one of our poets once ate roast duck—it is uncertain whether they were tame or wild ducks; I imagine the latter—for lunch, and went about with waterproof boots, but all that doesn't make a duck hunt. In short, all my sources consisted of oral traditions and my own brief experience. I shall therefore have to draw on these as best I can.

The noonday sun was shining on Svirumgaard lake when we hunters, booted and armed, gathered for a luncheon which was almost a dinner (*déjeuner dinatoire*) in order to strengthen and harden us against the influence of the water. The meal was enlivened by homemade Danish whisky and spiced with interesting stories of former exploits, in the telling of which the sportsmen vied with each other in bold fiction. Being without experience, I could not take part. Nor did I reap full benefit from the instructive conversation, for many of the words and phrases were quite puzzling and mysterious to me. I afterwards secretly—in order not to betray my ignorance—asked my friend the young Ruricolus to explain them to me.

Now we set off. Our host, Counsellor Svirum, was the leader, and posted us all in our places. Passages had been cut through the reeds and rushes from the land out to the open water to enable the hunter to see and shoot the ducks as they were chased by the dogs. At the end of such a passage, and as it happened the last one, I was placed. Before the chief left me, he gave me various kind and fatherly admonitions.

"My young friend," he whispered, "I am told that you know how to handle a gun, but that you're not much used to hunting. Duck-hunting, my dear, is a dangerous sport. Take care that you don't shoot anywhere except through the open passage; and be careful about us in the boat when we get in your way; and for heaven's sake, don't shoot any of the dogs!"

I answered in my natural voice, making the most solemn promises.

"Hush, hush!" he said softly, but a little pettishly, as he struck out with his hand. "Don't speak loud when at your post." With that he hurried off to enter the canoe that was waiting at the other end of the lake. There was silence for a good quarter of an hour.

The weather was fine; the sun shone warm, the air was clear and calm, the lake as smooth as a mirror. Now and then a fish rose, stirring the shiny surface for a moment, whereby the reflection of the Svirumgaard houses and the trees in the garden was disturbed and I was awakened from my sweet fancies. So, I thought, our most beautiful hopes are disturbed, so our splendid castles in the air disappear, so the first tranquil, pure love is changed into the restlessness of passion. But it is of no use to be sentimental when duck-hunting; I tried to drive away such thoughts, which had no place here, and turn all my attention to the business of the day and the duties I had taken upon myself—not that I thought them very arduous, for I had not yet seen or heard a single duck and came very near regarding the whole hunt as nothing but a maneuver, a mockery. I was strangely mistaken.

I was very much incommoded by mosquitoes and flies, impudent guests which I hardly dared to chase away with my hands, both because I remembered the admonitions given me, and because my neighbor, the elder Mr. Ruricolus, every time I moved an arm, shook his head disapprovingly and hissed out between his teeth a sibilant "Hush!" I stood almost at the mercy of my enemies and hardly dared to defend myself except by breathing and moving the muscles of my face, when—when a plunge in the water and a scream, the most hideous I have heard in all my life, sounded from the other end of the lake and was echoed by the hills and by the houses and trees at Svirumgaard.

I thought it must be an accident and cried in terror, "Mr. Ruricolus! The counsellor must have fallen in the lake." His reverence answered with a laugh which, as it was a crime against the laws of the hunt, he tried, at first in vain, to suppress, but which finally died away in a snicker. With a shake of the head and a gesture of his hand, he ordered me to be silent and at the same time relieved my fear. As the air was so still, the other men must have heard my childish exclamation and been amused by it, even though they controlled themselves. This was my first blunder, but it was not to be my last.

Now then—the scream, or rather the roar I heard really came from the throat of Counsellor Svirum, but it was only a hunting signal, a kind of trumpet call which indicated that the hunt was now to begin. The splash in the water came from the dogs which, eight in number, all plunged in the lake at once. Soon after they began baying. (At the supper table I was unlucky enough to mention that they barked, but Mr. Ruricolus replied seriously and instructively, "Hunting dogs, my good friend, don't bark, they bay." I promised I would never again be guilty of such a mistake.) The dogs, then, bayed, first one, then several. The ducks began to quack; some flew up over the reeds and fell down again; others rose higher and made wide circles around the lake.

The hunt advanced, the dogs came nearer and nearer, their commander in the boat likewise. Soon the first shot sounded. The report was thrown back from the houses and then rolled like thunder down over the lake till it died away in the distant heather-clad hills. It was my neighbor who had fired. Then the next man fired and then the others, and a lively shooting went on for over an hour. Meanwhile the boat and the dogs had passed me, and I wondered very much why I didn't get a chance to fire a shot, as most of the ducks must have crossed my beat. This riddle was soon to be solved.

Nevertheless, though only an idle onlooker, I enjoyed the new and unusual spectacle. Dogs and men, equally eager and spirited, were incessantly in motion; the dogs ran around in the reeds and rushes, splashed, panted, bayed; the men fired and loaded, took aim and dropped the guns. But no one that day surpassed our brave host; he was in restless activity, he dashed from one place to another, wherever his presence was most needed, fired, called to the dogs—he alone was allowed to speak—and from his repeated eager, "Fetch it! Ha-ha! Good dog!" I rightly concluded that there must have been a great deal of game killed.

At last he regarded the first hunting-ground as pretty well cleaned out, and all we hunters gathered around our bold admiral, each with his booty—I alone came empty-handed. When he had mustered us all and distributed due praise, especially to Argus who had covered himself with glory, he turned to me, and said, "But you haven't fired your gun at all!"

"I haven't had anything to fire at," I said. He shook his head. "I assure you," I repeated, "I haven't seen anything but some fishes swimming past me in the surface of the water; not a single duck."

There was an outburst of laughter like that on Olympus when the lame Hephaistos took on himself the form of a servant and waited on table; and when they couldn't laugh any more, they all told me that what I in my ignorance had taken for fishes was nothing but mallard ducks.—We each got a glass of whisky, and so ended the first act. The scene was now changed to another inlet of the bay.

There the passages cut out to the open water were so long that one could not shoot through the whole length of them. Our leader, who foresaw everything, had made a wise—but for me, alas, unlucky—arrangement. Midway between the land and the open water two poles had been driven in and a wide board laid across them; from this outpost the hunter could cover the entire passage. The counsellor himself took us out in the boat and posted us all on our respective platforms.

When I had mounted mine and my leader left me, he said with a mischievous smile, "Look out now, when the fishes come swimming past you, that you don't fall in."

The gibe in the first part of his speech I swallowed, but the warning in the second part I brushed away with a confident, "Don't worry, Mr. Counsellor; I'm not dizzy."

Vain self-conceit! How soon to be punished! When the dogs gave the alarm I saw some of those creatures which I still thought belonged to the fish family, but which the others classed as birds. My opinion was unchanged until one of these amphibia swam so near me—in fact under me—that I had to acknowledge the truth and admit that it really was a mallard duck swimming with only half its head above water and the rest submerged in order to fool the dogs. Now I was about to shoot, but before I was ready, in fact with the first movement of my gun, the duck dived under and got away. It was not long, however, before another slipped out from the reeds; I cocked my gun, took aim, pulled the trigger, and—fell backward into the lake. It was not so deep but that I soon had head and shoulders above the water.

In the same moment I heard a well-known voice calling, "In the name of all periwigs! Who was it that fell in?" Another voice answered, "The long-legged Copenhagener," and a third, "Shove the boat along and fish him up!" It was so done, and wringing wet, crestfallen, and ashamed, I was taken to land, and then I trotted back to the house.

The counsellor expressed regret at my accident, but I thought with a suppressed chuckle, and told me to see his wife who no doubt could find some dry clothes for me. My friend Hans Mikkel accompanied me, and the others continued their interrupted sport, which now had lost all attraction for me.

STILL ANOTHER COOLING OFF

WITH the help of my friend I had soon changed my clothes, but, alas, what a travesty! From the wardrobe of the counsellor I was equipped with a full set of garments: a coat or jacket of rough, heavy green cloth, which was both too wide and too short, and hung around my slender body in great folds but didn't reach down to my wrists; a yellow plush waistcoat, and knee-breeches of the same material which crept up over the knees with every step I took; blue woollen stockings and a pair of boots that slobbered around my legs. I didn't know myself, and alas, my sweet Maren would hardly know me either; *nec mirum;* for this attire was a hideous contrast to a fashionable black coat, embroidered silk waistcoat, yellow nankeen pantaloons and gaiters to match! No, I am sure I am not mistaken when I ascribe to this confounded outfit the misfortune that fell upon me—the total change in the sentiment of the lovely Miss Lammestrup toward me, which until recently had been so favorable.

If I had even known that she, the adored of my soul, was in the house, truly, I would have stayed in my lonely room till my clothes were dry; but Fate, inexorable Fate, which now for half a century has made me the sport of her caprices, had determined otherwise. With a jest on my lips about my own comical appearance, I stepped into the living room, where I expected to see only the hostess, but—the room was full of ladies, and my jest was not needed, for the laughter came of itself. However, this I could have borne, and could even have joined heartily in it myself, if she before whom I would rather have appeared in nobler attire had not been present. She stepped forward, dropped a deep curtsy, addressed me as Mr. Counsellor, and asked how I felt after the hot night and the cold bath. My reader must not think it was her intention to make fun of me—by no means. It was rather a mask she assumed in order to hide her real feelings; for even through her merriest laughter I heard—and perhaps I alone—the unmistakable voice of the heart.

When a quarter of an hour had passed, during which I had been a target for the arrows of the roguish young maidens' wit, I suddenly had an idea which must surely have been inspired by my evil genius. I proposed that the feminine part of the company should enjoy the lovely weather and look at the hunt, which was still going on, as we could hear by the frequent reports of the guns. My unlucky proposal was accepted, and we went—I went—toward my undoing. Near the lake and the hunting-ground was a hill from which I decided there would be a good view. In order to reach it we had to cross a little brook, over which there was a footbridge, but without a railing. I passed over easily. (My friend Hans Mikkel had already returned to his duties at the lake.) But when the ladies were to cross, they were all seized by fright, and no one wanted to be the first. One pretty little foot after another was stretched out on the plank and just as quickly withdrawn; they screamed, they laughed, but didn't get any farther.

Then a demon whispered to me, "Carry them across! Then you'll have a chance to hold your beloved in your arms." My innocent heart leaped with joy. I made the offer—it was accepted. Still, when I went back for them, and longingly stretched out my arms, no one wanted to be the first to entrust herself to them; each one was ready to let another have the honor.

At last the brave Miss Lammestrup came up to me and said, with a gracious smile, "I'll try it; but don't drop me in the water, and remember you've had one bath today."

Full of vain conceit, I assured her that she had nothing to fear, lifted her up, and set her on my arm. I remembered the words of Earl Haakon, "How do you like your seat?" etc., but I said nothing, for I felt too much. Her arm lay like a feather, like a hot flatiron, like an electric machine on my neck —I was in a state of bliss, ready to carry her not only over the water but through it for a lifetime—so I thought, poor fool

that I was! Yes, the beginning was made, but that was all.
Ha! tenfold cursed be the tailor who made Counsellor
Svirum's breeches! for it was they that crept up on my knees
and made my walk unsteady. Reader, do not laugh, your laugh-
ter is cruel, sinful—but you, my tender feminine reader, weep!
Peer Fiddler fell in the brook with his lovely burden!!! Pause!

Would that the brook had been Lethe! Then neither you,
my sympathetic feminine reader, nor I would have wept over
my black misfortune. Yes, black, for the brook was more mud
than water; it was dirty as Styx itself. Ha! once again, why
wasn't it Lethe?

Don't ask me, compassionate reader, how we got out of it,
what I said, what she said, how loud she screamed, how loud
the others screamed, how we came home, and so on—I know
nothing of it all. I heard nothing, saw nothing. I was in a
trance and didn't quite awaken until I heard an exclamation,
"Counsellor Svirum, your yellow plush breeches are certainly
in a state!"

At these words I mechanically stuck my head out of the bed
where I was lying.

"Deuce take the breeches!" cried Mr. Lammestrup, "but
Maren, what do you think she looked like?"

"Is she alive?" I asked anxiously. "Is she out of danger?
And will she forgive me, wretch that I am?"

"Afterwards," he said, "it's easy to laugh. She and the
other girls are sitting down there gossiping and having fun over
certain people who stumble over their own legs."

The last words he said with a malicious grin. But I turned
my face to the wall like a dying man and sighed with the poet:

> "All ties between us now are severed,
> Branded in all eternity I stand,
> And never can this blot be cleansed—
> One thing alone I would advise
> All who set store by mind or life,

> Let no mortal on that deucéd bridge
> Presume to set his foot!
> Let it be instantly destroyed,
> It's poisoned—"

"In the name of all periwigs," whispered his reverence, "he's raving; he's making verses—You stay with him, Hans Mikkel, while the rest of us go down and get a drop of tea-punch."

At that the sportsmen stole out, leaving me to my bottomless misery.

✧

On the third day after this my friend and I were rocking on the waves of the Cattegat.

TWENTY YEARS LATER

AT the end of my story I must refer to the beginning, in which I said that after my trip to Copenhagen I made an excursion to Vendsyssel. I shall now describe the results of it.

On my yellow Norwegian pony I rode from Sundbye toward the scene of the youthful adventures I have related. My legs are no shorter than they were, and as the horse walked in the deep wheel ruts, I could easily brush the dew from the grass with the toes of my boots, and occasionally support the wobbly gait of my horse. Half riding, half walking, I reached old Tyreholm, the lovely Maren Lammestrup's birthplace, about noon. I rode over the hayfield where once that famous battle was fought. The haycocks were there yet, as then, but the lovely Amazons were gone. *"Die hübschen Mädchen die bleiben fern—Traum der Jugend, o goldener Stern!"* I asked a man who was working there whether Mr. Lammestrup still lived in the house.

"No," he said, "he's dead many years ago. Peer Madsen is living here now."

I wanted to have asked about my old Maren, but although one-and-twenty maidens' pictures—if I remember right—had somewhat overlaid her image since that golden time, nevertheless I didn't want to hear that perhaps she too was dead and gone. I rode on, and in passing cast a thoughtful glance at the house to which her presence once lent glamour.

I approached Svirumgaard. The lake with its wreath of rushes spread out before me. My eyes looked for the brook, that pestiferous brook which swallowed up one of my fairest hopes. See! my curse had worked! The footbridge was no longer there; no doubt it had been consumed by fire—an altogether too light punishment! The meadow had been changed into a cultivated field, and the brook had become a dry ditch.

"Does Counsellor Svirum live here?" I asked a man whom I met.

"He's dead many years ago," was the answer.

Then rejoice, ye ducks!—I thought—and swim with lifted heads around on your peaceful lake! No Argus will nose out your hidden nests, and my heavy body will not disturb your clear element!—I rode on rapidly.

By the government office list I knew that the friend of my youth, Hans Mikkel, had succeeded his father; from himself I hadn't heard a word since he left the city. *"Aus den Augen, aus dem Herzen!"*—Whether the old Ruricolus had moved to another parish or had retired, or whether he too perhaps was dead, I knew nothing about.

When for a fifth of a century one hasn't seen a former friend, when so many years—rich in happenings, fruitful of experiences, sad as well as joyous—have passed since that gay companionship of youth, then the heart beats with a strange, happy uneasiness as the hour of reunion draws near. But we very seldom find what we expect, because we have not prepared ourselves for the powerful effect of time. We want our friend to be what he was, and forget that nothing remains as it was. I still thought of my dear Ruricolus, the handsome, fashionable, well-groomed student, the favorite of the ladies, the amiable, pleasant companion, always ready to help a friend, enjoying life but temperate and free from vices, an able divinity student, but a connoisseur also of polite literature—it was our sharing this taste that had made us inseparable. Therefore I was longing to leap from my horse and throw myself in his arms with the exclamation, *"Es waren schöne Zeiten, Carlos,"* etc. But it fell out quite differently.

The first person that met my eye as I rode into the parsonage yard was a fat, red-faced man in a threadbare grey coat, wooden shoes on his feet, and an old low-crowned hat on his head. This person—I should have taken him for the parson's coachman or head servant if an enormous meerschaum pipe-head in his hand had not suggested a tenant farmer—this person was standing on top of the dunghill, surrounded by chickens, ducks, geese, and turkeys, which he seemed to be counting with forefinger stretched out.

"Is the pastor at home?" I asked, lifting my hat slightly.

"Eighty-seven, eighty-eight, eighty-nine, ninety. I'm the pastor," was the answer.

I opened both my eyes wide and—recognized the friend of my youth.

"But, pastor!" I exclaimed, "do you really not know me?"

He descended from the dunghill and came toward me, but slowly and carefully in order not to step on any of the blessed little ducklings.

"Hm!" he grunted with a staid smile, "yes, it seems to me—"

"So you have quite forgotten your old Pietro?" I cried.

"Ah, is it you?" he replied and held out his hand to me. "Well, I must say! Come nearer, my dear old friend!—Morten, take the stranger's horse.—Is it used to standing in the stable, or would you rather have it in the pasture? You'll stay overnight, of course?"

"I mean to stay in the house," I said, "and my horse prefers to be outdoors."

"It's a nice little kitten," he said, walking around the horse as I dismounted, "but a little weak in the forelegs.—Oh, Morten, the dun cow is rutting, don't forget to take her to the bull.

—Well, you certainly are welcome.—Put a tether on this little nag and put him out in the pig-pasture. And don't forget to put a ring in the snout of the big sow, she's rooting the potato patch. —Please go in now"—I did so—"and rest yourself. What'll you have? Some tea-punch? And how have you been since we saw each other? You've aged. Maren, let us have some tea!" The last words he called out through the kitchen door.

This reception drove any kind of poetic outburst back into my somewhat chilled bosom, and the embrace failed to come off. Meanwhile one child after another stuck its head in from the kitchen door to see the strange man, and I also saw some faces at the windows which disappeared as soon as I looked in that direction.

"Are they all your children?" I asked. "How many have you?"

"One for each finger," he replied with a dark and sullen look. "I don't know what I am going to do with them. I hardly know how to keep them in clothes. To send any of them to the University is impossible. What's to become of them?"

Now his wife came with the tea. I greeted her.

"Do you know him?" Ruricolus asked her. "He's the man who dipped you in the brook at Svirumgaard."

Yes, indeed! It was she, but alas, how changed she too was, in face, figure, and manner!

"Ah, yes," she said with a forced smile, as she arranged the tea-table. "I am glad to see you again—it's a long time since we have had the honor. Will you have cream or rum?"

But why weary the reader with descriptions of a scene that had an effect on my warm blood like cream of tartar! So time can blot out, smother, destroy beauty, wit, gaiety; and what time might perhaps leave, will surely succumb to financial worries, the faithful ally of time.

In a bad humor I left my poor rusticated friend early the next morning, chewing the cud of the unedifying and well-worn theme: *Tempora mutantur et nos mutamur in illis*— Time is changeful and changes us, too.

THE PARSON AT VEJLBYE

[*Præsten i Vejlbye*, 1829]

I. JUDGE ERIK SÖRENSEN'S JOURNAL

In the name of Our Lord Jesus Christ! Now at last, by the will of God, and through the generosity of my dear patron, I am elevated, all unworthily, to the office of county sheriff and judge over this people. May He who judgeth all men vouchsafe me wisdom and grace and uprightness so to fulfill my duties that I may find favor in His sight.

"Every man's judgment cometh from the Lord." Proverbs 29:26.

❖

It is not good for man to be alone. Inasmuch as I can now keep a wife, ought I not to look about me for a helpmeet? The daughter of the pastor at Vejlbye is well spoken of by all who know her. Since the death of her mother she has managed the household affairs of the parsonage with thrift and good sense, and as there are no other children with the exception of one brother, now a student at the University, it is likely that she will come into a tidy fortune when the old man passes away.

❖

Morten Bruus from Ingvorstrup was here this morning and wanted to give me a fatted calf; but I remembered the warning of Moses, "Thou shalt take no gift," and refused it. This Bruus is much given to lawsuits, I am told, and is moreover contentious, and a great braggart; I will have nothing to do with him outside of my office as judge.

❖

I have now taken counsel with my Heavenly Father and with my own heart, and it is clear to me that Mistress Mettë

Qvist is the one person with whom I wish to pass my life until death. Yet will I observe her quietly for some time. Favor is deceitful, and beauty is vain. Nevertheless, she is without a doubt the fairest woman I have seen in all my days.

This Morten Bruus is to me a most odious person, though I am scarce able to say why. He somehow reminds me of a bad dream, but so hazy and indistinct is the memory that I cannot even say whether I have ever really dreamed about him. It may well be that it is a kind of foreboding. He came here again this morning to offer me a pair of blooded horses—splendid animals, dappled gray, with black manes and tails and black fetlocks. I know that he bought them separately at a cost of seventy dollars for the two. Perfectly matched as they are, the pair are well worth a hundred, yet he offered them to me for seventy. It was this very cheapness that gave me pause. Is it not a bribery? I am sure that he must have some lawsuit in mind. I do not want his dappled grays.

Today I visited the pastor at Vejlbye. He is a God-fearing and upright man, but hot-tempered and domineering, intolerant of any opposition to his will. And he is close-fisted besides. When I arrived at the parsonage, there was a peasant there who wanted his tithe reduced. The fellow was a sly one, for his tithe was not too high, and Pastor Sören seemed well aware of it, for he talked to the man so that a dog would not have taken a piece of bread from his hand; and the more he scolded, the angrier he himself became. Well, Heaven knows, every man has his faults. Qvist means no harm by his outbursts, for immediately afterwards he directed his daughter to give the man a piece of bread and butter and a good glass of beer.—She is assuredly a comely and well-behaved maiden. When she saw me, she greeted me in a manner so kindly and yet so modest that I was strangely moved, and scarce able to say a word to her.

My farm steward worked at the parsonage upward of three years before he came to me. I shall question him skilfully and find out how she treats the domestics and anything else he may know of her. One may often get the most trustworthy information about people from their servants.

Zounds! My man Rasmus tells me that this Morten Bruus not so long ago went courting at Vejlbye parsonage, but was refused. The parson was willing enough at first—for Bruus is a well-to-do man—but the daughter would have none of him. I understand that in the beginning her father took her sternly to task, but when he saw that she was unalterably opposed to the match, he let her have her own way. It was not pride on her part; for Rasmus says that she is as humble as she is good, and does not hesitate to admit that her own father is peasant-born as well as Bruus.

Now I understand what the Ingvorstrup horses were to do here in Rosmus; they were to draw me from the straight path of justice. It is a matter of Ole Andersen's peat-bog and adjoining meadow. That prize was no doubt worth the value of the horses. Nay, nay, my good Morten, you do not know Erik Sörensen. "Thou shalt not wrest the judgment of the poor."

Pastor Sören of Vejlbye was here for a short visit this morning. He has hired a new coachman, one Niels Bruus, brother to the Ingvorstrup farmer. This Niels, the parson complains, is a lazy fellow and impudent and quarrelsome besides. Pastor Sören wanted him punished and put in prison, but he lacks the necessary witnesses. I advised him to dismiss the fellow at once, or else to try to get along with him somehow until his time is out. At first he answered my suggestions very shortly, but when he had heard me to the end and weighed my argument a little, he admitted the strength of my reasoning, and thanked me warmly for my advice. He is a hot-headed, quick-tempered man, but not difficult to reason with when he has had time to cool a little and compose himself. We parted very good friends indeed. Not a word was spoken about Mistress Mettë.

❖

This day I passed most agreeably at the Vejlbye parsonage. Pastor Sören was from home when I arrived, but Mistress Mettë greeted me warmly. She was spinning when I came in, and it seemed to me that she blushed deeply.

It is curious how long it took me to find some subject of conversation. When I sit on the bench in my judicial robes, I seldom lack for words, and when I cross-examine a prisoner, I can think of questions enough to ask; but before this gentle, innocent child I stood as confused as a chicken-thief caught red-handed. At last it occurred to me to speak of Ole Andersen and his lawsuit, his peat-bog and meadow; and I do not know how it came about, but the talk turned from meadows to roses and violets and daisies, until finally she conducted me out into her garden to see her flowers. Thus pleasantly we passed the time until her father returned home, and then she retired into the kitchen and did not appear again until she came to bid us to supper.

Just as she stepped into the doorway, her father was saying to me, "I should think it is high time for you also to enter into the state of matrimony." We had just been talking about a magnificent wedding which had been celebrated at Höjholm manor. Hearing this last remark, Mistress Mettë blushed as red as a rose. Her father smiled slyly, and said, "One can see that you have been bending over the fire, my daughter."

I have taken the good pastor's advice to heart, and, God willing, it shall not be long now before I shall go courting at the parsonage, for I consider her father's words a subtle hint that he would not be averse to having me for a son-in-law. And

the daughter?—why did she blush, I wonder? Dare I take that
as a favorable sign?

And so the poor man is to keep his peat-bog and his meadow
after all; but assuredly the decision made the rich man my
mortal enemy. Before the judgment of the Court was read,
Morten Bruus stood and stared scornfully at Ole Andersen.
At the words, "It is the verdict of the Court," he looked around
the courtroom and grinned slyly, as if certain of a favorable
decision. And that he was, indeed, for I was told that he had
remarked, "It's foolish for that beggar to think he can win
against me." Yet that is just what happened.

When Bruus heard the verdict, he shut his eyes and pursed
his lips together, and his face went white as chalk. But he managed to control his rage, and said to his opponent, as he went
out of the courtroom, "I wish you joy, Ole Andersen. Losing
that peat-bog won't beggar me, and the Ingvorstrup oxen will
doubtless get what hay they need elsewhere." But outside I
heard him laughing loudly and, as he rode away, cracking his
whip till it echoed and re-echoed in the woods.

The office of a judge is indeed a heavy burden. He makes a
new enemy with every verdict he pronounces. But if we can
only keep on good terms with our own conscience! "Endure
all things for conscience's sake."

Yesterday was the happiest day in my whole life; my betrothal to Mettë Qvist was celebrated at Vejlbye parsonage. My
future father-in-law spoke from the text, "I have given my
maid into thy bosom," Genesis 16:5. He spoke very movingly
of how he was giving me his most precious treasure in this
world, and of how he hoped I would be kind to her. (And that
I will, so help me God!)

I had scarce believed that the grave, even stern man could
be so tender. When he concluded, his eyes were filled with

tears and his lips trembled with the effort to keep from weeping. My betrothed wept like a child, especially when he referred to her sainted mother; and when he said, "Thy father and thy mother shall forsake thee, but the Lord shall take thee up," I too felt my eyes filling. I thought of my own dear parents, whom God long since took to Himself in the everlasting habitations, and yet He has cared so graciously for me, poor fatherless child that I was.

When we had plighted our troth, my sweet bride gave me her first kiss. May God bless her! She loves me fondly.

At the table the merriment was unrestrained. Many of her mother's kinsfolk were present, but none of her father's, for they are but few and live far up by the Skaw. There was food and wine in abundance, and after the tables were cleared there was dancing until well-nigh dawn. The neighboring parsons from Aalsöe, Lyngbye, and Hyllested were all present; the last became so tipsy that he had to be put to bed. My father-in-law also drank mightily, but did not seem the worse for it; he is as strong as a giant, and could doubtless drink all the parsons in the county under the table. I noticed, too, that he thought it would be good sport to see me a little fuddled, but I took good care that he should not. I am no lover of strong drink.

Our nuptials will be celebrated in six weeks. May God give His blessing thereto!

❖

It is a pity that my father-in-law should have got this Niels Bruus in his service. He is a rough fellow, a worthy brother to him of Ingvorstrup. He ought to be given his wages and shown the door; that would be far better than to soil one's fingers in a fray with such a brute. But the good parson is hot-tempered and stubborn, and two hard stones don't grind well together. He is determined that Niels shall serve his time out, even though it means daily vexation for himself.

The other day he gave Niels a box on the ear, whereupon the rascal threatened that "he would see to it that the parson was paid back." But to all this there were no witnesses. I had the fellow up before me, and both admonished and threatened him, but I could do nothing with him. There is evil in the man.

My betrothed, too, has entreated her father to rid himself of the fellow, but he will no more listen to her than to me. I scarce know how things will go when she moves from her father's roof to mine, for she shields the old man from a great deal of trouble and knows how to smooth over everything.

She will be to me a tender wife, "as a fruitful vine by the side of thy house."

❖

It was an unlucky business—and yet lucky, too, for Niels has run away. My father-in-law is angry as a German, but I rejoice silently that he has thus got rid of this dangerous person. No doubt Bruus will try to avenge his brother at the first likely opportunity, but thank Heaven we have law and justice in this land, and the law will protect us.

It seems that Pastor Sören had set Niels to digging in the garden. When he came out a little later to see what progress had been made, he saw the fellow stand resting on his spade and cracking nuts which he had picked off the bushes. He had done no work at all. The parson upbraided him. Niels answered impudently that he was not hired for a gardener, whereupon he got a couple of blows on the mouth. At this he flung away his spade, and berated his master foully. Then the old man's fiery temper burst out, he seized the spade, and clouted him with it. He should not have done so, for a spade is a dangerous weapon, especially when lifted in anger and in the hands of a strong man. The rascal let himself fall as if he were dead, but when the parson became frightened and attempted to lift him, he jumped up, ran across the garden, leaped the hedge, and disappeared into the woods just back of the parsonage. So my father-in-law himself described the unhappy affair.

My betrothed is much distressed about it. She fears that Niels will avenge himself in some way or other—that he will work some harm on the cattle, or even set fire to the house. God helping, I think there is small danger.

Only three weeks more now, and then I can lead my bride into my home. She has already been here and taken stock of everything, both within and without. She seemed well pleased and complimented us on the orderliness and neatness everywhere. The only thing she seems to regret is that she will have to leave her father; and he will surely miss her. Yet I will do whatever I can to compensate him for his loss. I will exchange for his daughter my own good Aunt Gertrude, a capable woman about the house, and active for her age.

My betrothed is indeed an angel! Everyone speaks well of her—I am sure I shall be a most happy man. God be praised!

❖

What can have happened to that fellow! I wonder if he has fled the country. In any event it is a sorry tale, and people around in the parish are beginning to gossip about it. I am sure that these calumnies must have their source back in Ingvorstrup. It would be a pity for my father-in-law to hear of them. Had he only followed my advice! For the wrath of man worketh not the righteousness of God. Yet I am but a layman, and should not presume to rebuke one of God's servants, especially one so much older than I. We can only hope that all this talk will die away of itself. Tomorrow morning I will go to Vejlbye, and I shall soon learn whether he has heard aught of the gossip.

The goldsmith has just been here with the pair of bracelets that I ordered; they are very handsome, and will, I am sure, give pleasure to my dear Mettë. If only they fit her. I took the measurement of her wrist hastily and in secret with a blade of grass. The bed will be a credit to my aunt. The fringes are particularly fine.

❖

I found my father-in-law quite depressed, indeed I have never seen him in such low spirits before. Busy tongues had already brought him some of the stupid rumors which, more is the pity, are common talk in the neighborhood. Morten Bruus is reported to have said, "The parson will have to bring back my brother Niels, even if he has to dig him up out of the ground."

It may be that the fellow is in hiding at Ingvorstrup. At any rate, he is gone, and no one has seen hide or hair of him since he ran away. My poor betrothed is allowing it to prey too much on her mind; she is disturbed by portents and bad dreams.

Lord have mercy upon us all! I am so overwhelmed with sorrow and terror that I can scarce guide my pen; a hundred times already it has slipped from my hand. My heart is full of fear and my mind so distracted that I scarce know how to begin. The whole thing has burst upon me like a thunderbolt. Time has ceased to have any meaning for me, morning and evening are as one, and the whole terrible day is like one jagged stroke of lightning which has burned down in a moment my proud temple of hope and ambition.

A venerable man of God, my betrothed's father, in jail and in chains!—and that as a murderer and malefactor! Of course there is always the hope that he may be innocent, but, alas! that hope is but as a straw to the drowning, for the circumstantial evidence against him seems very heavy indeed. And to think that I, miserable wretch, should be his judge! And his daughter my promised bride! Lord my Saviour, have mercy on us! I am helpless!

❖

It was early yesterday morning, about half an hour before sunrise, that Morten Bruus came here to the house, bringing with him one Jens Larsen, a crofter from Vejlbye, together with the widow and daughter of his former shepherd. Bruus declared to me at once his suspicion that the parson at Vejlbye had killed his brother. I answered him that I, too, had heard gossip to that effect, but that I regarded it all as a silly and vicious slander, unworthy the attention of honest men, inasmuch as the pastor had told me that Niels had risen and run away.

"Had Niels actually run away," Bruus retorted, "I am sure that he would have come to me at once, and told me all about it. But that the facts are quite different, these good people"——he indicated his three companions——"can bear witness, and I therefore ask you, as judge, to examine them."

"Bethink yourself well, Bruus," I warned him, "and you, good folk, bethink yourselves well before you bring accusations against an honorable man in good repute and your pastor at that. If, as I strongly suspect, you are unable to prove your charges, then it will go hard with you."

"Parson or no parson," Bruus cried wrathfully, "it is written, 'Thou shalt not kill,' and it is also written that the government beareth not the sword in vain. We have law and justice in this land, and a murderer cannot escape his just punishment—even if he had the governor for a son-in-law."

I ignored the sneer, and replied with dignity, "Very well, be it as you will. What do you, Kirsten Madsdaughter, know of this crime of which Morten Bruus accuses your pastor? Tell me the truth, as you would tell it before the great judgment seat, and as you may be required to tell it to the Court later on."

Thus admonished, she told the following story:

Shortly after noon of the day when Niels Bruus was said to have run away, she and her daughter, Elsë, had passed along the path outside the parsonage garden. Just as they came about midway by the stone fence which encloses the east side of the garden, they heard a voice calling Elsë. It was Niels Bruus. He was standing just inside the hazel hedge that borders the stone fence, and had bent the bushes aside to ask Elsë if she wanted some nuts. Elsë took a handful of them, and asked him what he was doing there. He answered that the parson had told him to spade the garden, but that he would rather pick nuts; the garden could take care of itself for a while. At the same moment they heard a door slam, and Niels said, "Listen, now we're going to get a sermon." They soon heard the two brawling. They saw nothing, for the wall was high and the hedge thick. One word led to another, and at last they heard the pastor cry out, "I'll

give you a beating, you dog! You shall lie dead at my feet!"
Whereupon they heard a couple of smart blows, as when one
receives a slap on the mouth. At this they heard Niels Bruus
revile the pastor, calling him a hangman and a scoundrel. To
all this the pastor answered not a word, but they heard two dull
blows, and saw the blade and part of the handle of a spade fly
up in the air a couple of times; but whose hand it was that
wielded the spade they were unable to see, for the hedge was
thick and high. After that all was quiet within the garden, but
the shepherd's widow and her daughter had become so thoroughly frightened that they hastened away to their cows out in
the pasture.

The girl Elsë confirmed her mother's story in every circumstance. I asked them if they had not seen Niels Bruus come out
of the garden, but they both denied this, though they assured
me that they had looked back a number of times.

All of this agreed completely with what the pastor had already told me. That the witnesses had not seen Niels coming
out was to be explained by the fact that the woods were just as
near the south side of the garden, and, according to the pastor,
it was in this direction that he had fled. So, after weighing the
testimony of the women, I declared to Morten Bruus that their
tale threw no new light on the case, inasmuch as the pastor had
already told me the whole story himself.

At this Bruus smiled bitterly, and asked me to examine his
third witness, which I proceeded to do.

Jens Larsen, after I had admonished him as I had the first
two witnesses, told the following story:

Late one evening—not the evening of the disappearance of
Niels Bruus but, as far as he could remember, the following
night—he was returning home from the neighboring hamlet of
Tolstrup, and walking along the path which ran by the east
side of the parsonage garden, when he heard from within the
sound of some one digging. There was a bright moon that
night, and, though somewhat frightened, he decided to see who
it was that was digging, and what he could be doing at so un-

usual an hour. So he took off his wooden shoes, scrambled up the stone wall, and made a little peephole through the thick hedge with his hands. There in the garden, flooded with moonlight, stood the figure of the pastor in his long green robe and his white cotton nightcap. He was smoothing the surface of the ground with the back of a spade. Suddenly the pastor turned, as if conscious of being watched, and Jens Larsen, being frightened, slid hastily down the wall and ran home.

Although I thought it strange that the pastor should be out in his garden at that time of night, I was still unable to find any valid grounds for suspicion of the imputed murder. This conclusion I communicated to Morten Bruus with a solemn warning not only to retract his baseless charges but to put an end to the rumors by a public declaration of his retraction. To this admonition Bruus merely replied, "Not until I know what the parson was burying in his garden at that hour of night."

"By that time," I warned him, "it may be too late; you are gambling your honor and welfare on a very dangerous chance."

"I owe that much to my brother," he rejoined. "I hope that our rightful rulers will not refuse me the aid and support of the law."

Such a demand I could not ignore, and so I was forced to investigate Bruus's charges. I hastily made what preparations were necessary, and, accompanied by Bruus and the three witnesses, drove over to Vejlbye. Heavy of heart I was, and sore depressed, not from fear that I should find the fugitive Niels in the garden of the parsonage, but at the thought of subjecting the pastor and my betrothed to such vexation and indignity. All during the trip my thoughts dwelt on how I might make the defamer of innocence feel the full weight of the law. Ah, Thou merciful Heaven, what a shock was in store for me!

I had planned, as soon as I arrived, to take the pastor aside and forewarn him, thus giving him time to compose himself. But Morten anticipated me, for, as I drove up to the parsonage, he rode past me on his horse, dashed up to the door, and, as the pastor opened it, cried out, "Folks say that you killed my brother and buried him in your garden. Here's the judge come with me to search for him."

This rude announcement so disconcerted the pastor that he was unable to say a word before I jumped out of my carriage, and, hurrying to him, seized his hand, and said, "You have heard the charge, and without beating about the bush. By virtue of my office, I am bound to comply with this man's request. But your own honor now requires that the truth be brought to light, and the mouths of the slanderers stopped."

"It is indeed hard," the pastor replied, "that a man in my office should be required to refute so abominable an accusation. But enter if you will, my garden and my house are open to you."

We passed through the house and into the garden at the back. There my betrothed met us, but when she saw Bruus behind me she trembled with fear, and her eyes looked at me appealingly.

"Be not alarmed, dear heart," I whispered to her hurriedly. "Go into the house, and fear nothing, your enemy is rushing headlong to his ruin."

Morten Bruus led the way to the hedge over toward the east. I and the witnesses followed him, then came the pastor with his servants whom he had himself ordered to bring spades. The accuser stood still for a moment, looking around until we came up to him; then he pointed to a place on the ground, and said, "That looks as if it was dug up not so long ago. Let us begin here."

"Dig, then," the pastor ordered angrily.

His men set to work with their spades, but after a few moments Bruus, who was watching their progress with obvious impatience, tore the spade from the hands of one of the men and joined in the work with great energy. When they had spaded about a foot beneath the surface, they came to ground so hard that it was clear it had not been disturbed recently— probably not for years.

All of us—with one exception—were vastly pleased, the pastor most of all. He began already to triumph over his accuser, and taunted him with the sneer, "Well, you slanderer, did you find anything?"

Bruus did not vouchsafe him an answer, but stood thoughtfully for a moment, and then, turning to Jens Larsen, asked, "Jens, where was it you saw the parson spading that night?"

Jens Larsen had been standing with folded hands looking at the work. Now he seemed to wake from a dream and pointed to a spot three or four fathoms from the place where we were standing. "I think it was over there," he said.

"What is that, Jens?" the pastor exclaimed with some asperity. "When did you ever see me spade?"

Without heeding this interruption, Morten Bruus beckoned the men over to the designated corner. He brushed away some withered cabbage stalks, branches, and other rubbish, and ordered the digging to begin at once.

I stood quietly by, well satisfied with the course of events so far, discussing with my father-in-law the misdemeanor for which the accuser had made himself liable and the punishment which could be meted out to him, when one of the spaders screamed, "Jesus Christ!"

We glanced quickly over at them. The crown of a hat had been uncovered.

"I think we'll find what we're looking for right here," Bruus said. "I know that hat well, it belonged to Niels."

My blood froze in my veins, and I saw the whole hope of my life crumble to earth.

"Dig, dig!" the terrible blood-avenger bawled, redoubling his own efforts.

I looked over at my father-in-law; he was pale as death and trembling, but his eyes were wide open and fixed in a sort of fascination on the dreadful spot.

Another scream! They had uncovered a hand stretching up at them through the earth.

"Look," cried Bruus, "he is reaching up after me. Wait, brother Niels, you'll soon have your revenge."

Presently the whole body was uncovered, and it proved to

be that of the missing Niels, beyond any doubt. The face was scarcely recognizable—the flesh had already begun to decay, and the nose was broken and smashed flat; but the clothes, especially the shirt with Niels's name sewed on it, were immediately identified by his fellow servants. And in the left ear they even found the leaden ring which Niels had worn constantly for several years.

"Now, parson," Morten cried, "come and lay your hand on the dead if you dare."

The pastor sighed deeply, and raised his eyes in a mute appeal to Heaven. "Almighty God," he said, "Thou art my witness that I am innocent of this crime. Strike him, that I did indeed, and bitterly do I repent it now. Strike him I did, but who buried him here, that Thou alone knowest."

"Jens Larsen knows it, too," Bruus interrupted with a sneer, "and perhaps we shall find others besides. Sir Judge"—he turned to me—"doubtless you will wish to examine the servants, but I demand that you first place this wolf in sheep's clothing under lock and key."

Alas, Thou merciful God! no longer dared I doubt; the evidence was too plain. But I was ready to sink into the ground with horror and loathing. I was just about to tell the pastor that he would have to submit to arrest, when he himself spoke to me. He was ghastly pale, and shaking like an aspen leaf. "Appearances are against me," he admitted, "but surely this is the work of the devil himself, and I know that there is One above who will bear witness to my innocence. Come, Sir Judge, in chains and in prison will I await His disposition of me, poor sinner that I am. Comfort my daughter! Remember she is your promised wife."

Scarce had he finished speaking, when we heard a moan and then a body fall behind us. We turned quickly, and I saw that it was my betrothed who had swooned and lay prone on the ground. Would to God I might have lain down beside her and neither of us ever awakened again! I lifted her up and held her in my arms, thinking she was dead; but her father tore her from my grasp, and carried her into the house. At the same moment I was called away to inspect a wound in the head of the slain man, which, though not deep, had cracked the skull, and had clearly been caused by a spade or some such blunt weapon.

After this we all went into the parsonage. My betrothed had already regained consciousness, and when she saw me she rushed to me, flung her arms around my neck, and implored me by all that was sacred to save her father from the great danger which threatened him. Afterwards she begged me, for the sake of our great love, to allow her to go with him to prison, which request I granted her. I myself accompanied them to the jail at Grennaae, in what a state of mind God alone knows. During the whole of that melancholy ride none of us spoke a word, and I parted from them with a bursting heart.

The body of Niels Bruus has been placed in a coffin which Jens Larsen had ready for himself, and tomorrow it will be honorably buried in Vejlbye churchyard.

Tomorrow, too, the first witnesses will be heard. May God strengthen me, miserable creature that I am!

❖

Fool that I was to strive so eagerly for this office of county judge! Would that I had never obtained it! It is a dreary business to be a judge. I would fain change places with one of the talesmen!

When this servant of God was led into Court this morning, his hands and his feet in chains, I was reminded of Our Lord before the judgment seat of Pontius Pilate, and methought I heard distinctly the voice of my sweetheart—alas, she is lying ill at Grennaae—whisper to me, "Have thou nothing to do with that just man."

Would to God that her father was such a one, but at present I cannot perceive the slightest possibility of his innocence. Jens Larsen, the widow, and her daughter Elsë were the first witnesses. They reaffirmed on oath the entire story which they had previously told me, and that almost word for word. Nothing was retracted, nothing added. Besides these, three new witnesses appeared, Sören Qvist's two menservants and his milkmaid. The two men said that they had been sitting in the servants' hall the afternoon of the day of the murder, and that through the open window they had distinctly heard the voices of the pastor and Niels raised in angry altercation and that they had heard the former cry out, "You dog, you shall lie dead at my feet!" Their testimony, therefore, coincided with that of the widow and her daughter. They affirmed further, that they had twice before heard the pastor abuse and threaten Niels, that when the pastor was angry, he did not hesitate to use whatever weapon came to hand, and that he had once struck a servant with a wooden maul.

The maid deposed that, on the same night when Jens Larsen had seen the pastor in the garden, she had been unable to sleep, and as she lay there wide awake she heard the door from the hall to the garden creak on its hinges. She sprang from her bed and went over to the window to see what it could be, and saw the pastor in his long robe and nightcap in the garden. She was unable to see what he was doing out there, but about an hour later she heard the garden door creak again.

When all the witnesses had been heard, I asked the defendant whether he had anything to say in his own defense, or whether he was prepared to make a confession. He folded his hands over his heart, and said solemnly, "I am speaking the truth, so help me God, and I swear by His holy word that I know no more of this matter than I have already confessed. I struck the deceased with a spade, though not so hard but that he could run away from me and out of the garden. What happened to him afterwards, or how he came to be buried in my garden, I do not know. As to the testimony of Jens Larsen and my maid that they saw me out in the garden at night, I can only say that, either they are lying, or else the whole thing is a phantom from hell. But I can clearly see that, miserable creature that I am, I have no one to defend me here on earth, and if my Heavenly

Father chooses to remain silent, then verily I know that I am lost, and I bow to His inscrutable will." When he had finished speaking, the old man heaved a deep sigh, and bowed his head upon his breast.

Many of those who were in the courtroom could not restrain their tears, while others whispered that maybe their parson was innocent after all; but this was merely the natural result of the emotions and sympathies which he had aroused. My own heart, too, argued for his innocence, but the reason of the judge cannot be swayed by the counsels or pleading of the heart; neither pity nor hate, gain nor contempt, can weigh by so much as a grain of sand in the even scales of justice. My own well-considered judgment did not allow me to conclude other than that the accused had killed Niels Bruus, though not with deliberate intent or purpose. True, I knew he had been in the habit of making threats against those who provoked his anger, saying that he "would remember them when they least expected it," but he had never before been known to carry out such threats. That the defendant now persisted in his denial was doubtless due to the instinct of self-preservation and the desire to vindicate his honor.

Morten Bruus (there is a churlish brute, ugly enough before and worse now since his brother's murder) began to talk about means to force confession from an obdurate sinner, but I shut him up quickly. God forbid that I should put so venerable a man on the rack! What is it after all but a trial of physical and mental strength?—he who withstands the torture and he who succumbs to it may both be lying, and a forced confession can never be trustworthy. Nay, rather than resort to that, I would give up my office and the duties that have become so irksome to me.

Alas, my sweet darling! I have lost her in this world, and yet I loved her with all my heart.

❖

I have just gone through another heart-rending scene. As I sat reviewing this terrible case in my mind, trying to find some solution, the door flew open and the pastor's daughter—I scarce dare call her betrothed who perhaps will never be my wife—rushed in, threw herself at my feet, and embraced my knees. I lifted her into my arms, but it was some time before either of us could speak for tears. I mastered my emotion first, and said to her, "I know what you are come for, dear heart— you would ask me to save your father. Alas, God have mercy on us poor mortals, I can do nothing. Tell me, dear child, do you yourself believe your father to be innocent?"

She put her hand on her heart, and said, "I do not know," and with that she began to weep again most bitterly. "Surely, he did not bury Niels in the garden," she went on, when she had recovered somewhat, "but I suppose the man died out in the woods from the blows that my father had given him—alas, it must be so."

"My dear girl," I said, "both Jens Larsen and your maid saw him out in the garden the following night."

She shook her head slowly. "Perhaps the foul fiend may have hoodwinked them."

"Lord Jesus forbid that he should have such power over Christian folk," I replied.

She began to weep again, but after a while she said, "Tell me, my affianced husband, tell me frankly, if God does not vouchsafe further light on this matter, what verdict will you pronounce?" She looked at me full of fear, and her lips trembled.

"Were I not sure that any other judge would be more severe than I," I answered her, "I would resign my seat at once—yea, gladly lay down my office forever. But, since you demand an answer, I dare not conceal from you that the mildest sentence decreed by the laws of both God and the King is a life for a life."

At this she fell to her knees in despair, but in a moment she was on her feet again. She retreated a few steps, and then advanced toward me, crying, as if distracted, "Will you murder my father? Will you murder your betrothed?" She held her hand up to my eyes. "Do you see this ring?" she asked me. "Do

you remember what my unhappy father said when you placed
it on my finger?—'I give my maid into thy bosom'—But you—
you pierce my bosom."

Merciful God, every word she said pierced my own bosom.
"Dearest child," I sighed, "say not so! You tear my heart with
red-hot pincers. What is it you want me to do? Do you ask me
to set free one whom the laws of God and man condemn?"

She was silent for a moment, lost in thought, and I continued, "One thing I will do, and if it is wrong, then I pray
God not to lay this sin to my charge. Listen, dear child. If this
trial is concluded, then we both know that your father's life is
forfeited. There is no escape but in flight. If you can evolve any
plan of escape, I promise to shut my eyes and keep silence. Nay
more, I will give you every assistance. Look you, as soon as
your father was imprisoned, I wrote to your brother in Copenhagen, and we can expect him almost any day now. When he
comes, let him help you, and meanwhile try to win the jailer
for your plan; if you need money, all that I have is yours."

When I had spoken this, her face flushed with hope, and
she threw her arms around my neck, and cried, "God reward
you for this advice! If only my brother were here now, then I
know we should succeed." She stopped, and was silent a moment. "But where could we go?" she asked, "and if we were
able to find refuge in some strange land, then I should never
see you again."

She said this so plaintively that I thought my heart would
burst. "Dearest child," I consoled her, "I will find you and
come to you, no matter how far you may travel. And if our
resources are not sufficient for our support, then these hands of
mine shall work for us all. They have wielded the axe and the
plane before, and they can do it again."

At this she was exceeding happy, and kissed me many times.
Then we prayed together that God might see fit to further
our plan, and when she left me she was buoyed up with hope.

I too began to hope that we might find some way. But no
sooner had she gone, than my spirits were assailed by a thou-

sand doubts, and all the difficulties which seemed at the moment so easy to overcome now appeared like mountains which my weak hands could never remove. Nay, out of this darkness and terror only He to whom the night shineth as the day can lead us!

✧

Morten Bruus was here this morning and announced two new witnesses with an air that boded little good for us. He has a heart as hard as flint and full of poison and gall. The new witnesses are to appear in Court tomorrow, and I am as despondent as if it were myself that they were to testify against. May God give me strength!

✧

All is over! He has confessed everything!

The Court was convened, and the prisoner led forth to hear the testimony of the new witnesses. They deposed: That, on the now famous night of the day after the crime, they were walking along the road that runs between the woods and the garden of the parsonage, when they saw a man emerge from the woods with a large sack on his back, walk quickly over to the garden, and disappear behind the fence. The man's face was completely concealed by the sack, but the moon shone full on his back, and they saw distinctly that he was clad in a long green robe, and that he wore a white nightcap.

No sooner had the first witness completed his testimony than the pastor's face went ashen gray, and it was with the greatest difficulty that he stammered in a weak voice, "I am ill." He was given a chair and sat down heavily. Bruus turned to the spectators, and said, "That helped the parson's memory, didn't it?" The pastor did not hear the sneer. Instead he beckoned to me, and when I came over to him, he said, "Let me be taken back to prison. I want to talk to you." It was done as he requested.

We drove off to Grennaae, the pastor in the cart with the jailor and the clerk, and I on horseback. As we opened the door to the prison, there stood my betrothed making her father's bed. On a chair at the head of the bed hung the telltale green robe. When she saw us entering together, she gave a cry of joy, for she concluded that her father had been freed, and that I was coming to release him from jail. She dropped what she had in her hands, rushed over to her father, and flung her arms around his neck. The old man wept so that his eyes were blinded with tears. He did not have the heart to tell her what had just happened in the courtroom, and instead sent her on some errands in town.

Before she left us, she ran over to me, took my hand and pressed it to her heart, and whispered, "Have you good tidings?" To conceal my own confusion I kissed her on the forehead, and said merely, "Dearest, you shall know everything later on. I cannot tell yet whether what has happened is of great importance one way or the other. Go now, and fetch us what your father asked for."

Alas! what a change from the time when this innocent child lived, carefree and happy, in the pleasant parsonage, to the dreary present here in this dismal prison, with grief and terror for companions.

"Be seated, my friend," the pastor said to me as he himself sat down on the edge of the bed, folded his hands in his lap, and stared down on the floor as if lost in thought. At last he roused himself, sat up, and fastened his eyes upon me. I waited in breathless silence as if it were my own doom I was about to hear—as indeed in a sense it was.

"I am a great sinner," he began at last, "how great I do not myself know. God alone knows, and I am firmly convinced that He wishes to punish me here in this world so that I may receive grace and eternal blessedness hereafter. Praise and glory be unto Him!" With this he seemed to gain more quietness and strength, and he proceeded as follows:

"From my earliest childhood, as far back as I can remember, I have been of a quarrelsome nature, proud and hasty, impatient of opposition, and always ready to resort to blows. Yet have I seldom let the sun go down on my anger, neither have I borne malice toward any man. When I was but a half-grown boy my ungovernable temper led me to commit a deed which I have often since bitterly repented and which, even now, I cannot recall without pain. Our watchdog, a gentle beast who had never harmed any living creature, ate up my lunch which I had for the moment laid on a chair. I flew into a rage and kicked him so hard with my wooden shoes that he died, moaning miserably in his agony. That time it was only a dumb animal, but it should have been a warning to me not to lay violent hands on any creature. Again, some years later, when I was a student at Leipzig University, I picked a quarrel with a Bursch, called him out, and gave him a wound in the chest that came within a hair's breadth of killing him. So you see I have these many years deserved what I am now to suffer, but now my punishment falls with tenfold weight on my sinful head: An old man, a pastor and messenger of peace, and—a father, O merciful God, that is the deepest wound of all!" He sprang to his feet and wrung his hands so that I could hear the joints creaking. I would have said something to console him, but could find no words.

When he had regained control of himself, he sat down again, and continued, "To you, formerly my friend and now my judge, I am about to confess a crime which I can no longer doubt having committed, but which I still do not fully understand."

I started in surprise and wondered what he meant, for I had prepared myself for a full and open confession.

"I want you to pay the closest attention to what I am about to relate," he continued, "and try to understand me. I have already confessed all that I know; that I struck the wretched fellow with a spade—whether with the edge or the flat side I cannot remember—and that he fell down, jumped up, and ran away into the woods. The rest, alas! has been told by four witnesses: that I fetched his dead body and buried it in my garden the following night. And though of all this I know nothing myself, I am forced to accept it as the truth, and you shall hear my reasons.

"On three or four occasions earlier in my life I have walked in my sleep. The last time I know of having done this was some nine or ten years ago; it was the night before I was to hold funeral services for a man who had met a very sudden and painful death. I remember it all distinctly. I remember that I was at a loss for a suitable text, when the words of one of the Greek philosophers occurred to me, 'Call no man happy before he is dead.' But to use a heathen text for a Christian service would never do, and I was sure that I should be able to find the same idea in about the same words somewhere in the Bible. I hunted diligently, but without success, and since I was already tired from other work, I undressed and went to bed, and soon fell asleep. The next morning when I went to my study to find a proper text and outline my talk, I was dumbfounded to see, lying on my desk, a piece of paper with the words: 'Call no man happy until his days are told. Sirach's Book, 11th chapter, 34th verse,' written in large clear letters. But this was not all; beside it lay a funeral sermon, brief but well-constructed—and all in my own handwriting. No one had been in the room. The door was bolted on the inside, because the lock was worn and easily sprang open. No one had come through the window, for it was frozen fast to the casement. I had composed and written the whole thing in my sleep.

"Nor is this the only instance of its kind. It was indeed but a few months previous to this that I had, while sound asleep, gone into the church to fetch a handkerchief which I distinctly remember having left on my chair behind the altar.

"And now, my friend, it must all be plain to you. When the first witness was giving his testimony this morning in Court, I suddenly remembered these earlier occasions of walking in my sleep, and I remembered, too, another incident which, until that moment, had completely slipped my mind: when I awoke on the morning after the body had been buried, I found my green robe, which I always hang over the back of a chair beside my bed, lying on the floor. The miserable victim of my ungovernable temper must have fallen dead in the woods, and I must have found him there, brought him to my garden, and buried him—all in my sleep. Yes, God have mercy upon me, it must be so."

He ceased speaking, buried his face in his hands, and wept bitterly. As for me, I was utterly astounded and full of misgivings. I had from the beginning believed that the murdered man had died on the spot where he was attacked, and that the pastor had hastily covered him over with some dirt—though how he was able to do this in broad daylight without being seen was a mystery to me—and later had buried the body deeper in the ground. Now the last witnesses had just testified that they saw the pastor carrying a sack from the woods. This struck me as most extraordinary, and it had occurred to me at once that their testimony might conflict with our earlier version of the case, and the man's innocence thus be demonstrated. But now, alas, all the facts fitted together only too well, and his guilt was established beyond the shadow of a doubt. Only the curious aspect which his sleepwalking had given the case continued to perplex me. That he had committed the murder was certain, but whether the last and the less important half of the crime was carried out in a waking or a sleeping condition remained a puzzle to me. The pastor's whole conduct, his testimony in court, all bore the hallmark of truth, yea, for truth's sake he sacrificed his last hope of life. Yet perhaps he still hoped to preserve a certain remnant of honor; or, on the other hand, perhaps he was really telling the truth. Such spells of sleepwalking are not unknown, nor is it beyond the realm of possibility that a man who was mortally wounded could have run so far.

The pastor paced quickly to and fro, then stopped in front of me. "You have now heard my full confession," he said, "and I know that your lips will be forced to pronounce sentence on me and condemn me, but tell me, what says your heart?"

"My heart," I replied, though I could scarce speak for pity, "my heart bleeds for you, and it would gladly cease beating at this moment could it thus save you from a shameful and terrible death." Our last resort—flight—I dared not even mention.

"You cannot save me," he said hurriedly. "My life is forfeited, my death just, and I shall serve as a terrible warning to succeeding generations. But promise that you will not abandon my poor daughter. I had hoped, once, to give her in thy bosom." At this the tears welled up in his eyes, but he mastered his emotion, and continued, "That hope I have myself destroyed, for you cannot wed the daughter of a malefactor! But promise me that you will take care of her as a second father."

Mournfully and with tears I gave him my hand.

"I presume you have not heard from my son of late?" the pastor continued when we had both recovered our composure. "I hope that he may remain in ignorance of this misery until it is all over, for I do not think I could bear to see him." He buried his face in his hands, turned and rested his forehead against the wall, and sobbed like a child. It was some time before he was able to speak.

"Now, my friend, leave me—and let us not see each other again until we meet in the house of stern justice. And then— give me one last token of your friendship—let my sentence be pronounced soon, tomorrow if possible, for verily I long for death. I hope that through the infinite mercy of Christ it will mean but the beginning of a happier life than this, which now has nothing to give me but anguish and terror. Farewell, my kind and compassionate judge, let me be brought before you tomorrow. And send at once for Pastor Jens in Aalsöe, for I want him to minister the last sacrament to me. Farewell, God bless you and preserve you." He averted his face, but stretched forth his hand to me. I stumbled out of the prison, scarce knowing what I did.

I should perhaps have ridden home without speaking to the

daughter, had she not been awaiting me outside the prison wall. She must have read the death sentence in my face, for she paled and seized my arm. She looked at me imploringly, as if begging for her own life, but could not ask—or dared not.

"Fly, fly—save your father!" was all that I could say. I threw myself on my horse, and was home before I knew it. Tomorrow, then!

❖

The sentence has been pronounced, and the guilty man heard it with greater fortitude and composure than he who pronounced it possessed. Every one in Court, with the exception of his obdurate enemy, showed the most profound sympathy for the condemned, and there were those who whispered that it was a cruel sentence. Yea, cruel it is indeed, for it deprives one man of his life and three others of their happiness and peace of mind forever. May the merciful God judge me more leniently than I, poor sinner, dare judge my fellow man.

❖

This morning she was here and found me sick in bed. There is no longer any hope. He refuses to escape.

❖

Everything was arranged. The jailor had been won over. A fisherman, a cousin of her sainted mother, had promised to transport them all to Sweden, and had his fishing smack in readiness; but the repentant sinner was not to be persuaded. He will not flee from the sword of righteousness, for he is firmly convinced that through his own death and his Saviour's, he will find salvation hereafter. She left me as unhappy as she came, but without a single unkind word. God help her, poor child, how will she ever live through the terrible day! And here I lie, sick in body and in soul, unable to give comfort or aid. Her brother has not yet arrived.

Farewell, bride of my heart! Farewell, in this dreary world until we meet again in a better one. May it not be long, for I am wearied of this life and ready for death. Would that I might pass over the border ahead of him whom stern duty forces me to send thither.

"Farewell, my beloved," she said to me. "I leave you without bitterness, for I know that you did only what was your stern duty; but now farewell, for we two can never meet again." She made the sign of peace over me, and left me. God give me soon eternal peace!

❖

Merciful God, where will she go? What are her plans? Her brother is not yet here—and tomorrow—at Ravens' Hill. . . .[1]

❖

(At this point the Journal of Judge Erik Sörensen comes to an abrupt end. For the elucidation and exposition of this terrible tragedy we can refer to the written account of the parish pastor of Aalsöe, neighbor and friend of the lamented Sören Qvist, which follows below.)

II. THE NARRATIVE OF
THE AALSÖE PASTOR

In the seventeenth year of my pastorate there occurred in this neighborhood an event which filled all men with terror and consternation and reflected shame and disgrace upon the cloth. The pastor at Vejlbye, the Reverend Sören Qvist, in a moment of anger, killed his coachman and buried him at night in his garden. He was duly tried in the regular Court, and, after hearing the damning testimony of several witnesses, confessed the dreadful crime, and was sentenced to be beheaded. This sentence was carried out here in Aalsöe meadow in the presence of thousands of spectators.

[1] The knoll on Aalsöe meadow just outside of Grennaae, where Pastor Sören Qvist was beheaded, is still called Ravnhöj (Ravens' Hill).

The condemned man, whose spiritual adviser I had formerly been, requested that I be allowed to visit him in prison and bring him the solace of religion, and I can truthfully say that I never administered the last sacrament to a more repentant and believing Christian. He confessed with deepest contrition that he had hardened his heart and been as a child of wrath, for which God had humbled him deeply and covered him with shame and bowed him with sorrow, that he might again be raised up through Christ. He maintained his composure to the very end, and, standing on the scaffold, spoke to the assembled throng a few words full of power and grace, which he had composed during his imprisonment. His homily dealt with anger and its terrible consequences, and was replete with moving reference to himself and the great sin into which his anger had led him. His text he took from the Lamentations of Jeremiah, Chapter two, sixth verse, "The Lord hath despised in the indignation of His anger the king and the priest." Upon the conclusion of his moving discourse, he disrobed, tied the cloth before his eyes, and knelt down with folded hands, and as I said the words—"Be of good cheer, dear brother! Today shalt thou be with the Saviour in Paradise," the sword fell, and his head was severed from his body.

That which made death most bitter to him was the thought of leaving his two children. The elder, a son, was away at the time of the execution—we thought in Copenhagen, but we later learned in Lund—wherefore he only arrived in the evening of the day on which his father paid the supreme penalty. The daughter—who, to the still more heart-rending woe of herself and her lover, had been affianced to the judge who sentenced him—I took home with me, more dead than alive, after she had said a last farewell to her father. When I returned home from what was the most painful duty of my whole life, I found her fairly composed, and busied with preparing her father's shroud—for it was permitted him to be buried in consecrated ground if the interment were conducted in quiet and privacy. She no longer wept, but neither did she speak. I too was silent, for what indeed was I to say to her. I who was myself bowed down with sorrow and foreboding?

About an hour after my return home, my cart arrived with the body, and shortly afterwards a young man on horseback dashed into the yard. It was the son. He threw himself upon his father's body, and thereafter into his sister's arms; brother and sister clasped each other in a long embrace, but neither of them was able to say a word.

That afternoon a grave was dug hard by the side door of Aalsöe church, and there, at midnight, were laid the last mortal remains of the former Vejlbye pastor. A stone with a simple cross, which I had earlier prepared for myself, marks the grave, and reminds every churchgoer of the sinfulness of man and his ultimate salvation through the Cross of Christ.[2]

The next morning both the two fatherless children had disappeared, and no one has since been able to discover any trace of them. God alone knows in what secluded corner they have hidden themselves from the world.

The county judge continues to be ailing and is not expected to live. I myself am sore afflicted by sorrow and anguish, and I feel that death would be the greatest boon to all of us together. We are in the hands of God. May He suffer us to be governed by His wisdom and His mercy.

Lord, how inscrutable are Thy ways!

In the thirty-eighth year of my pastorate, and just twenty-one years after my brother pastor, the Reverend Sören Qvist of Vejlbye, was sentenced to death and beheaded for the murder of one of his servants, it happened that a beggar came to my door. He was an elderly man with grizzled hair, and walked with the aid of a crutch. None of the maids were present at the time, so I went out into the kitchen myself to give him a bite to eat, and, while he was munching his bread, I

2 This marker is still standing in the Aalsöe churchyard.

asked him whence he came. He sighed, and replied, "From nowhere."

I then asked him his name. He looked timidly around, and said, "They used to call me Niels Bruus."

I felt a cold shiver run down my spine, and said to him, "That is an ugly name; a fellow of that name was murdered here about a score of years ago."

He sighed even more deeply, as he muttered, "I ought to have died then; it has gone badly with me ever since I left this country."

I could feel my hair stand on end, and I shook with terror; for now it seemed to me that I recognized him, and further, it was as if I saw standing before me the living image of Morten Bruus whom I had buried three years earlier. I started back and made the sign of the Cross, for I thought that this must be a ghost.

My visitor seated himself heavily on the edge of the fireplace, and said, "Alackaday, parson, I hear my brother Morten is dead. I went to the farm at Ingvorstrup, but the new owner didn't know me and drove me away. Is my old master, the Vejlbye parson, still alive?"

Then suddenly the scales fell from my eyes, and I understood the meaning of this whole miserable affair; but I was so profoundly shocked that I quite lost the power of speech for several minutes.

"Heigh-ho," he was saying, as he greedily ate his bread, "it was all Morten's fault. But did any harm befall the old parson?"

"Niels, Niels," I cried, full of horror and loathing, "you have a bloody crime on your conscience. On your account an innocent man lost his life at the hands of the executioner."

The beggar started back so that he almost fell into the fire; the bread dropped from his hands, and his crutch rattled to the floor. "God forgive you, Morten," he groaned, "God forgive you and me, but it was none of my doing. . . . But tell me," he looked at me appealingly, "it's not true? You're only trying to scare me. I have come here from far on the other side of Hamburg, and not a word of this have I heard on the way. No one has known me, except you, parson, but when I passed through Vejlbye I asked if the pastor was still alive, and they said Yes."

"That's the new pastor," I told him, "not he whom you and your wicked brother did to death."

At this the poor fellow began to wring his hands and moan and whimper with such evident sincerity that I could easily see that he had been but a blind tool in the hands of the devil. He even aroused my pity, and I invited him into my study, where I spoke to him a few words of comfort until he was somewhat quieted, and was able to tell me, brokenly, the whole story of their hellish plot.

The brother Morten—a man of Belial—had conceived a deadly hatred of Pastor Sören Qvist at Vejlbye from the day that the pastor had refused him his daughter in marriage. When therefore the pastor rid himself of his coachman, Morten told his brother Niels to seek the position. "And have a care now," he told Niels, "when the chance comes we'll play a trick on the black man, and you shan't be the loser by it." Niels, who was rough and stubborn by nature and was egged on by Morten, was soon quarrelling with his master, and the first time the pastor struck him he hurried over to tell his brother at Ingvorstrup.

"Just let him strike you once more," Morten said, "and he shall pay dear for it. If he does, you come to me and tell me at once."

It was shortly after this conversation that Niels picked a quarrel with the pastor out in the garden, and when the pastor had felled him with a blow from the spade, he ran without delay to Ingvorstrup. The brothers met outside the farmhouse, and Niels told Morten what had just happened in the parsonage garden. "Did any one see you on your way over here?" Morten asked him. Niels thought not. "Then," said Morten, "we'll give the parson a fright that he won't recover from in a fortnight."

Morten then led Niels by a secluded way to the farmhouse

and concealed him there until night. As soon as every one was in bed, the brothers stole forth to a corner in the meadow where, two days earlier, they had buried the body of a youth about the age, size, and general appearance of Niels. (He had worked at Ingvorstrup, and hanged himself in his room, some said in desperation over Bruus's tyranny; others, in grief over an unhappy love affair.) This body the brothers now dug up, despite the protest of Niels, and carried back to the farmhouse which was nearby. Then Niels was compelled to take off all his clothes, and the dead body was dressed in them, piece for piece, even to Niels's earring. When this work was completed, Morten gave the corpse a blow on the face with a heavy spade, and one over the temple, and then threw the body into a sack until the following evening, when they carried it into the woods just outside the parsonage at Vejlbye.

Time and again, Niels assured me, he asked his brother what all this ado was about, but the latter always replied, "That is none of your affair; you leave all that to me." Now when they were come to the woods, Morten said to him, "Run over and fetch me one of the parson's gowns—try to find the long green robe I have seen him go around with in the morning."

"I dare not," Niels replied, "his clothes are all hanging in his bedroom."

"Then I dare," said Morten, "and I will do without you. Now you go away at once, and never show your face here again. Here is a purse with a hundred dollars; that ought to last you until you get to the South—but remember—far away—where no one will know you or recognize you. Take another name, and never set foot on Danish soil again. Travel by night, and hide in the forests by day. Here is a bag with food enough for you until you get out of the kingdom. Now hurry, and don't come back if you value your life."

Niels, who was accustomed to obeying his brother, did as he was told, and there the brothers parted, nor did they ever see each other again. Niels had suffered much in foreign lands. In Germany he was conscripted for the army and served in many campaigns in which he lost his health. Poor, weak, and miserable, he resolved to revisit his birthplace before he died, and after encountering much hardship and suffering he had managed to make his way back to this neighborhood.

Such, in brief, was the story which this unhappy wretch told me, and I was forced to accept its veracity. Thus it was revealed to me that my unfortunate brother pastor had fallen as a sacrifice to the infamous villainy of his mortal enemy, to the delusion of the judge and the witnesses, and to his own too ready self-deception. What, indeed, is man that he dare set himself up to judge his fellow men! Who dares say to his brother, "Thou art deserving of death!" Judge not, that ye be not judged. Vengeance is mine, I will repay, saith the Lord. Only He who gives life can take it away. And may He compensate you for the bitter martyr death that you suffered here with the gift of everlasting life!

I did not feel disposed to surrender this broken and repentant sinner to the law, all the less as the judge, Erik Sörensen, was still living, and it would have been cruel to let him know of his terrible mistake, before he left this world for one where all things are to be revealed. Instead, I strove to give the returned prodigal the solace of religion, and exhorted him by all that was sacred to conceal his real name and the real story of the Vejlbye crime from everyone. On this condition I promised him a refuge and care at the home of my brother, who lives far away from here.

The next day was a Sunday. When I returned home late that evening from my parish of ease, I found that the beggar had gone, and before the evening of the following day his story was known all over the neighborhood. Driven by his uneasy conscience, he had hurried over to Rosmus and there revealed himself as the real Niels Bruus before the judge and all his household. The judge was so deeply affected that he suffered a stroke and died before the week was out. And on Tuesday morning they found Niels Bruus lying dead outside the door of Aalsöe church, across the grave of the sainted Sören Qvist.

GYPSY LIFE

[*Kjeltringliv*, 1829]

I HAVE two things to apologize for: the title and the story. The first is low, vulgar, and perhaps disgusting to a refined and delicate taste; the second is like unto the first.[1]

True, the account of great villains is the most interesting aspect of history and romance; but in the first place we don't call them that, and furthermore such racy characters must be people of high degree, or at least of honest degree, not people with whom no farmer would eat from the same dish. Who can deny that Claudius and Messalina, Pope Sergius and Marozia, Front de Beuf and Ulrica lived the life of villains, but, be it noted, in palaces and not in sheepcots? That which is becoming in royal personages and holy prelates, or in Norman barons, is not proper in Jutland nightmen. Nero was a great monster— Jens Long-Knife a vulgar scoundrel. It never occurs to a well-bred person to moralize over the manners of the Turkish Sultan *in puncto sexti;* when he keeps three hundred mistresses, while a Christian prince often gets along with three, that is gallantry on a grand scale. But if a travelling glazier has three wives, it is quite rightly called lewd conduct. Our moral sense is outraged when a gypsy throws his stick to anyone he fancies, but if a king desires the wife or daughter of one of his subjects, we smile and say, "He throws the handkerchief."

It is not the thing itself that is weighed on the scales of justice, but who does it and how it is done. To steal from an enemy country is called to levy a contribution; to kill and maim thousands of people is called a brilliant victory; to burn a city and lay waste a province is called conquest. But when our Jutland nightmen levy contributions, it is stealing. When a gypsy wins a

---

[1] *Kjeltring*, the word applied to the Danish gypsies, means "rogue," "villain," although Blicher claims, in his introduction to this story, that it had lost much of its obnoxious meaning. Blicher's friend, N. V. Dorph (see note on page 303), thought it should be written *Keldring* and that it was originally *Kedeldreng*, from *Kedel*, "kettle," and *Dreng*, "boy," having reference to the skill of the gypsies as tinkers.—TRANSLATOR.

decisive victory in a duel with thorn-staves and clasp knives, it is murder, and if he should burn down a straw hut (which very rarely happens), it is genuine arson. To steal a country, as everybody knows, is a grand undertaking; to steal a pig or a sheep is a vulgar theft. Attila and Semiramis get their places in history; Stoffer One-Eye and Big-Margret get theirs in Viborg jail.

But I am myself in danger of talking like a villain and, instead of my intended apologies for the villainous life of my heroes, I am straying into a kind of defense of them. Yet that was not my purpose! I have enough to do defending myself; I am really at my wit's end, and have no recourse but to say: a good friend asked me to do it. But let no one think I am lying in this matter, too, or that I am guilty of the usual prudery. No, this time I am speaking the unadulterated truth, and I could even name my man, if I were not afraid of compromising him. "Write a story about the gypsies," he has said several times, "it might be amusing enough."—"Faugh," I have always replied, "that's a vulgar subject."—"Why so?" he has answered. "Don't the 'Egyptians' have their places on the canvases of Scott, Goethe, Müller, and others? Our Danish 'nightmen' are the same breed. Call them 'Egyptians' if you like." But that does not appeal to me. *Kjeltring* is a good Danish word, which I mean to keep.

But before I end this Introduction I must add a few words of explanation. *Kjeltring* [villain] is the name which the common people in Denmark give to the vagrant "nightpeople" particularly, but one which these people do not themselves own. The word as the peasants use it in this sense does not involve any criminal tendencies, and they can perfectly well say "a decent Kjeltring." The true *Kjeltringer*—not those who are found in all classes of society—constitute an isolated association, a state within the state; and therefore a certain French traveller spoke more truly than he knew when he said: "*En Danemarc il y une nation, qui s'appelle Kieltrings, elle n'est pas si bien cultivée comme les autres danois.*"

This nation calls itself "Travellers." A name that hits the bull's-eye! For life is to these people more than anything else a journey. They journey, in the most literal sense, through life, for they have no fixed habitation, but wander from one town to another; they have no home, but only a shelter. They are born, marry, and die—all while on the road. But if anyone on that account should call them tramps or vagrants they would feel very much insulted, and rightly so. They are nomads, just as much as Kalmucks or Bedouins. They are travellers, just as much as Mungo Park, Belzoni, or Colonel Sundt—men whom nobody thinks of characterizing as vagrants, because their vagrancy is on a large scale; that is the difference. And I find it an attractive feature in the small *voyageurs*, contrasted with the great ones, that they wander about incognito, without pretensions or letters of introduction, and do not torture us afterwards with "Travels" which are more wearisome to read than to perform. Would we might learn from their silence! Would that many might imitate them, instead of filling whole volumes with misinformation and wrong opinions —with looks askance at the great men or prominent writers who have not made enough of them—with still more shameless and impertinent praise of others who have had no desire to be dragged out and displayed to the public view in payment for a meal or a bed—with kaleidoscopic landscape paintings and enthusiastic ravings, both equally obscure and incomprehensible— or with menus which are sometimes the fattest morsels in the book and, so far as they arouse the appetite, the most inoffensive.

So much for the Introduction.

THIRST—THE *PRÆVLIQUANTS*[2]—*LAKVIRUM*[3] —GYPSY LATIN—GYPSY WEATHER

THE day was sultry. A strong southeast wind swept the heat down over us—a veritable sirocco. Whitish red thunder-clouds were piling up above the horizon both in the east and the west.

[2] Persons who speak a fine (gypsy) language. [3] Bad weather.

They looked like a distant range of snow-capped mountains, their summits gilded by the sun, their bases divided by deep, dark valleys. One by one the clouds lost their sharp contours, were thinned and spread out in lighter, more tenuous strips—a sign that "the artillery of heaven" was about to thunder; but the noise was drowned in the bluster of the wind, as the gleams of lightning were in the golden effulgence of the sun.

I walked on between the two fire-spewing batteries. Driven by my thirst, I walked fast, in spite of the intense heat, bent on reaching a bog which I was certain must be found in the general direction in which I was headed. How far away it was I could not tell, for on the flat expanse of heath there was no elevated object that could have guided me, and even had there been one, the quivering of the hazy air would have obscured and confused the outlines. At last I caught sight of the tops of some scrubby willows and a pale green strip in the heather. My dog, who was suffering even more from thirst than I, sniffed the air and ran on ahead. I envied him his greater speed. Alas, without reason! I soon saw him scraping the ground, and knew that the bog was dried out. There we both stood, baffled in our ardent longing. I threw myself down on the ground, discouraged; but my poor companion howled and panted and eagerly scraped aside the dry grass in order to cool his heaving chest in whatever slight moisture the meadow retained.

Pity us not, kind reader! I have known a man—a darling child of fate, a pet of fortune and of men—who plumed himself on never in his life having known real hunger or thirst. Pity him! The unhappy man did not know the taste of water, still less what it means, when reeling with heat and burning thirst, to plunge into the cool, invigorating embrace of the waves. This luxury awaited me only a short mile from the dried-out bog, where I found a lake surrounded by heather and bog myrtle.

Revived for new exertions, with an unspeakably pleasant tingling of all my nerves, I sat a little ways up from the lake on the windy side of a grave-mound—the only one in the vicinity as far as my eye could reach. The dog lay at my feet and shared my ambrosial repast of bread and cheese, when an animated object attracted his attention; he raised his head a little, pricked up his ears, drew his eyebrows together, growled, and emitted a few short yelps.

I turned and saw a spectacle approaching that might well astonish both men and dogs. It was in fact an amphibious creature, or a hermaphrodite, an enormously tall Holofernes in petticoats, a creature that was man above and woman below. The apparition came toward me carrying a lance in either hand —my thumb automatically pressed the trigger of my gun. But in a moment I discovered that the lances were only sticks, and that the creature was a double figure with two heads, four arms, four sticks, and four legs—to put it briefly and clearly: a man carried by a woman. A boy a little less than half grown walked close behind them. The path ran below the mound on the opposite side, but as the approaching trio had the sun in their eyes, they could not see me. The dog was silent, either from fear or amazement.

A man who—figuratively speaking—patiently carries his domestic cross through life, or who from love of his wife carries her on his hands, is no great rarity, but a female cross-bearer in a literal sense, actually with her husband on her back, was something I had never encountered. The story about *die Weiber von Weinsberg* has always seemed to me a little suspicious; it happened far away and long ago. At any rate, it was only a question of a short walk and no more; *einmal ist keinmal*. And these celebrated women were moved by fear of widow-hood, perhaps also by a desire to make a sensation among the officers of the enemy. Here on the wide, barren heath there must be other motives; the first one, I discovered, was that the man lacked both his feet.

When the little party had arrived at a spot right in front of the mound, they made a halt. The woman turned her back to the slope, leaned over, and allowed her burden to slide down.

Then she straightened up, stretched her limbs, drew a few long breaths, and sat down between the man and the boy. The latter laid a little bag in her lap. Food was taken out and eaten in silence. When the scanty meal was ended, they began a brief conversation, of which I only caught a word now and then; for it was carried on in a language which—from such expressions as *jup*, *brall*, *pukkasch*—I soon realized was the so-called Romany. In a few minutes the topic seemed to be exhausted, and all three lay down to sleep.

Now I rose and went around to the other side of the mound to examine the group of sleepers. The man was of a small but —barring the fact that he lacked feet—well-shaped figure with a fresh face of a brown complexion; he seemed to be in the prime of life. The woman was of a much darker color; had thick, black eyebrows which almost met, a short nose, full cheeks, a rather wide mouth with thick lips which, when parted, revealed snow-white teeth that anyone might envy her. Torso and limbs were large and strongly built; she looked as if she could throw a man or carry him.

So far I had come in my observation of this strange pair, but what have we seen of a human being when the shutters hide the windows of the soul? No more than the binding shows of a book.

I had already turned away and was about to go on, when the boy cried out, "*Madrum, padrum*, a dog, a hunter!" The woman opened a pair of black, deep-set, serious eyes, slowly rose to a sitting position, and nodded to me in the peculiar manner these people use when they greet anyone. In the same instant the man opened the shutters of two large, light blue, merry and lively eyes. He took off his hat, but did not stir from his relaxed position.

I like to speak foreign languages, not to show off my linguistic accomplishments, but because there is something particularly pleasant about getting on familiar terms with foreigners, for without this means of communication, we should have to regard each other as deaf mutes. The magic words loose the tongue, open the hidden treasure trove of the soul, and stimulate that barter of thoughts by which both parties are gainers. Moreover, there is the sweetly tingling surprise: when a traveller who is laboriously trudging along in a strange language suddenly is addressed in his beloved mother tongue, then thoughts and speech get life and wings, words pour out in an unbroken stream—the stranger is suddenly at home, he is among friends and kinfolk.

Not for any of these reasons—but rather without reason, as we so often speak and act—I had a fancy not to hide my gypsy light under a bushel. I returned their nods with a *"Goddeis Genter."*[4] A quick smile played over the Asiatic features of the woman, but the man raised his body, supporting himself with the palms of both hands, and looked suspiciously first at me, then at the lady.

"Is she your *Maie?*"[5] I asked.

"Sibe, sibe,"[6] he said quickly and gave her a kindly look.

"It must be hard work for you to carry your *Knasper,*"[7] I said to her. *"Nobes,"*[8] she replied curtly, and whipped the heather with her stick. I then put my hand in my pocket, gave the boy a few coppers—for which the man thanked me politely —said good-bye, and left.

It was not till I had gone some little distance that I began to regret not having questioned these people more closely. But that is always the way; the nearer we are to the unusual, the remarkable, the less it awakens our interest. A man may live ten years at Möen and not see the chalk cliffs, but may travel to Switzerland to see Schreckhorn or Staubbach. Another man has twice been to see the Rhine falls, but has never once seen the Western Ocean, although he can hear its mighty thunder every day. When I visited Rosenborg, it was in the company of four Copenhageners—and all five of us were there for the first time. Anyone who had the time and the means might easily get a notion to run down to Norwood or Siebenbürgen

---

[4] Good-day, folks. [5] Wife. [6] Yes, yes. [7] Man. [8] No.

to see a gypsy camp, but our Danish pariahs can pass him every day without being thought worthy of a glance.

How strange, I thought afterwards, is not this little caravan! How unselfish, how strong, faithful, even heroic is not this woman's love for a helpless cripple, whom she has carried on her shoulders—heaven knows how far or how long! How mighty is not the invisible power that has united these two beings—wild children of a wild and barren nature! And yet it is against the fundamental principle of nature, for usually it is the vine that clings to the elm, the weak woman who seeks protection from the man; here it is just the opposite.

Filled with these thoughts, I turned back to retrieve my neglect and learn more about this strange couple and their—no doubt—strange fate. I walked back about a mile to the mound, but the caravan had already disappeared; as far as my eye could reach, there was not a living creature to be seen.

It was toward evening; I had to think of the night. The town where I had intended to spend it was six miles distant, and in the intervening stretch there was not—so far as I knew —a single human habitation.

"Southeast squalls and women's quarrels are apt to end in water," the Jutlanders say. The latter may fail, if the person in question is allowed to remain in possession of the field and the last word; but the truth of the former was soon brought home to me in a very forcible manner.

The wind had gone down, but the sky was hidden by black, low-scudding clouds. The rumbling of the thunder became louder and louder, and an occasional flash of lightning appeared here and there in the distance. I realized that I could not escape the storm, and I therefore prepared myself for a wet coat, but also for the enjoyment of the most impressive natural spec- tacle our country can show. "Heath—night—thunder and lightning," such is the description of the stage on which Lear's madness rages more furiously than the elements. Here I had the same setting and the same scenery, the same stage machin- ery, and—I was alone. Unchecked, undisturbed, my imagination could fly on the wings of the storm and ride on the bolts of the thunder.

Fear not, grave reader, that I shall jar you out of the staid and measured ambling of your soul! This time I shall not plague you with what I thought and felt; for some of it is of such a nature that I want to keep it to myself, and some of it is such that I could not tell you even if I wanted to. If this story should happen to fall into the hands of one who has allowed himself to be drenched through in order to witness a thunderstorm at night, such a one will know what I mean. Others must be satisfied with what I saw and heard.

Evening came; night came. The storm was around me, was over me. Thor's chariot rumbled; the axles blew sparks, the feet of his goats clattered up and down the hills and vales of the clouds; rain and hail poured down in torrents. Pitch dark and blinding light alternated. One moment I walked in a darkness that one could see and feel; the next moment the heath lay before me in a baffling light, and for an instant the sky showed me its curtain rent asunder. In such moments nothing was lacking but the witches of Macbeth.

PENNEKAS[9] — DRALLERS[10] — GYPSY BALL

SOME distance ahead of me there appeared a stationary light, which was blotted out each time the lightning illuminated the sky, but shone again in the darkness that followed. I knew just about where I was on the heath, and I knew that there could not be—at least there had not been a few weeks ago—any human dwelling here. I stood still now and then in order to see whether the light moved. No! Then it could not be a lantern or a will-o'-the-wisp, but perhaps one of those mysterious meteors that are thought to mark the spot where treasure is hidden, or where a corpse is buried. I did not fear the latter, still less the former; so I walked on. The light became larger and clearer.

[9] Shelter.   [10] Dancing.

I had just made a halt when a terrific flash of lightning revealed an object in front of me which looked like a house without a roof. I was startled, and involuntarily I thought of those shifting ballrooms which the underground people are said to build for their nightly orgies. And yet—what sensible hill man or hill woman would care to dance above ground on such a night as this? The light of the heavens was extinguished, but this earthly light was lit again. I stared, I listened—faint tones of a stringed instrument, sometimes lost in the din of thunder and the howling of the wind, reached my ears. So then it was a dance—at night, here on the wild heath, in the wild storm! Should I stay where I was, or go back or forward? Curiosity prompted me to go on, for I had never before been in an assembly of witches or a festivity of hill people. (My adventure at Dagbjerg Dos was, to be honest, neither more nor less than a dream.)

Again I walked on, determined to penetrate this horrible mystery, but if I should find here one of the castles of the seductive Morgana, to beat a hasty retreat. Now I was so near that the light took shape as a square—it shone from a window in the enchanted castle. Again I made a halt. The music sounded quite distinctly; it was a fiddle and no harp. This circumstance reassured me as to any seductive Morgana, but on the other hand it made me think of picnics at which the fiddlers were billy goats. I listened; the music was mixed with shouts and laughter. I stared; dark figures moved back and forth inside the window. I was in a strange mood.

Meanwhile the storm had passed; the rain had stopped; a few stars glistened here and there with "weeping" eyes through the quickly drifting clouds of mist. The outlines of the oriental house were now plain. I ventured to stretch out my hand to find out if it was made of earthly stuff or of such materials as the elves and fairies use. I felt, I saw; the hut was built of heath turf, as substantial, as real as anything could be. So there was a human shelter here; *ergo* there could be one, and I had come to a false conclusion a little while ago, as one often does when one deduces from *posse* to *esse*. A man of firmer principles would have said, "Here is no house, for there cannot be any." But I, who am not so strong in *logica*, accepted the bona fide house for a house, and merely wondered how it came there, and for what purpose.

I must make a digression; it is neither long nor uncalled for. Anyone who really loves dancing is never at a loss for a ballroom. When the French (who are a genuine dancing nation) had stormed Constantinople, they danced in the Sophia Church, just as sweaty and bloody as they came from the city walls. When they had stormed the Tuileries, they danced in the royal halls, where the floors were painted with bloody roses. When the Bastille had been levelled with the ground, they danced on the site. This last pleases me best; and the brief inscription, "Dancing here," on the simple monument that marks the site of the prison, seems to me clever, poetic, and pregnant. There—right there—where people sighed and groaned, where there was nothing but wailing and gnashing of teeth, where the victims of despotism were thrust living into the grave, where there should have been the same device as over Dante's hell, "Leave hope behind!" And here, too, on the barren heath, four miles from the nearest house, where a short time ago nothing was heard but the soughing of the wind in the heather and the shrieking of the plover, where the wanderer trudged on in the darkness of night, languishing for a warm stove and a dish of warm groats—here, too, they are dancing. I felt cheered and went close to the window to get a good view of the ballroom and the dancers.

Where shall I find a Netherland brush with which to paint this netherly scene? How shall I describe for the reader who is quite a stranger to such a stage set the "pleasant" room with ceiling of clay, walls of clay, floor of clay? How picture for him the noble simplicity of the furnishings?—benches of rough pine boards, dun-colored oak chests littered with black clay pots and dishes, with green brandy bottles, and bright glasses on wooden feet. How convey to him an idea of the *clair-*

obscure caused by four tallow dips stuck on the walls? And above all the living figures? I shall confine myself to these last.

In the middle of the room two couples were whirling around in the well-known *schwabischen Wirbeltanz,* but the rotations were so vehement that I could not see what the faces of the dancers looked like. On the bench opposite the window two other couples were resting, their flushed faces showing that they had just left the floor. To one side the fiddler sat on the corner of a flat chest, beating time with the heel of his wooden shoe, and on the other side two ragged children were scraping the burnt crusts out of the bottom of a black kettle.

Now the waltz was over, but at that moment a person appeared who had hitherto been hidden from me. I saw only his profile, but that was enough for me to recognize the chap. When I say that he was a thickset fellow, had hanging shoulders with an enormous head set on them, that he had a horse face, a wide mouth with thick lips, small eyes which seemed to be constantly flitting—much as those of the Bushmen are said to do—that his big, pock-marked face showed rapid transitions from surly gravity to rough mirth, that the whole figure moved with such a firm, hard, rapid step that one only had to see his back in order to say, "That fellow is one who wouldn't stop at sticking his knife into anyone who interfered with him"—when I thus describe him, there are certainly at least three people besides myself who would remember having seen him, though only one of them has profited by his special knowledge of the gypsy language. It is hardly necessary to complete my description by saying that he had the image of the Crucified One tattooed on his left arm.

Presently our professor in the gypsy and Romany language stepped backward out on the floor, looked around at the fiddler and nodded, stamped hard on the floor a few times, and twined his arms together across his chest. In this position he awaited the lady he had just engaged, whom in my present position I could not yet see. The music began; it was a kind of reel in a quick two-quarters beat.

Like a—like what shall I say? Like a fury? No, for that she was too good-looking. Like a Penthesilea *furens, quæ mediis in millibus ardet?* No, not that either; for that she was too stocky, too plump, too simply and peacefully dressed. Like Madame Schall in a gypsy dance? That comes a little nearer, but I think I had better use similes of my own invention and according to my own taste. Like a peg top, a teetotum, a whirligig, darted out on the floor and in front of and behind and round about the lightly skipping professor—who? None other than the cross-bearer, the woman with the man on her back.

It was a genuine gypsy dance which I had the good luck to be a spectator of. The lady's feet moved like drumsticks and hit the clay floor with quick taps. The arms, too, were in motion, as were the fingers, which successfully imitated the clatter of castanets. With all this, her movements and play of expression had nothing of the bayadere or dewidoschi; on the contrary, her face was so cold, sulky, even defiant that it was in complete contrast with that of the professor. His whole face was spread out in a constant, unchanging, immovable grin; his small eyes were wide open, the mouth half open, the upper lip almost touching the nose, the lower hanging down halfway to the chin; teeth and gums were revealed—unquestionably he had, during this dance, a very "open" face.

I was not the only one who was entertained by the skill of the dancers; the spectators who stood in a half circle around them gave their delight both audible and visible expression, by cries of astonishment, bursts of loud laughter, by lifting their shoulders, rubbing their arms, and clapping (with the back of the right hand in the hollow of the left). At the same time they turned their faces, glistening with perspiration and pleasure, from one side to the other. I could not help thinking of the trolls in Thor's masquerade: "In their innocent merriment, with goat horns in their brows, they butted again and again." And really there was nothing except this Jotunheim decoration lacking to make the illusion perfect. Certainly the gypsy woman made a very passable Gerda.

This dance, too, came to an end, and Gerda returned to the place from which she had darted out. I moved quickly to the other side of the window in order to see what became of her. Ah, there stood a chest, and on top of it sat the legless wanderer. His brisk partner in the dance of life turned her back to the chest, rested her hands on it, and vaulted up to him. Just then I heard a door creak, and the learned gypsy scholar came out to me. In the light from the room, we stood face to face, and he—knew me just as quickly as I did him, and with even greater surprise.

I told him that I was bound for Örre, that I had missed my way in the storm, and had gone after the light from this house. He obligingly offered to show me the way, and I accepted his kind offer gratefully, not so much because I needed a guide as because I wanted to learn something about the scene I had just witnessed and especially about the strange couple. What he told me I shall now set down.

PETER LEGLESS AND GYPSY LINKA

THE mysterious house had not been built with the aid of Aladdin's lamp or a sorcerer's wand, but—so my companion told me—by the poor relief of Örre parish upon order from the county, to house the well-known traveller Johannes Axelsen whom the gypsy described to me (1) as a learned man, for he could both read and write; (2) as a clever man, since no one hitherto had been able to get anything on him; (3) as a mighty champion who in strength yielded only to "Jens Munkedal, Chresten Strong in Hveisel, and Chresten Jensen in Örre" (three athletes who—judging by descriptions and sworn facts —must have been comparable to Milo, Palydamas, and Eutellus—to Starkodder, Bue Digre, and Orm Storolfsen—to August the Second, the Marshal of Saxony, and Frank).

This subject gave me a natural opening to speak of the gypsy woman who must also possess more than ordinary strength, since she could carry her man from town to town.

"Gypsy Linka," he said, "is strong as sin. I found that out once I tried to be a little sporty with her. She socked me one in the jaw—I never want a better one. But we're just as good friends for all that."

"Then she's faithful to her cripple?" I asked.

"True as gold," he replied; "if anyone tries to get near her in that way, she's fierce as a bandog."

"How did it happen," I went on, "that those two people got together?"

"I'll tell you the story," he said. "Peter Legless—as we call him—and I were born in the same place—"

"Where?" I interrupted.

"That I don't know," he answered laughing. "My mother said it was somewhere on the heath here."

"Then it was in a big house," I remarked.

"So it was," he nodded laughing, "the roof was high and the walls were wide. I and Peter travelled together till we got big, and then we thought we'd like to look around in the world. In White-Matini—"[11]

"That was a long jump," I broke in.

"It's many thousand miles," he said with all the smug self-satisfaction of a great traveller. "From Blue-Matini we'd been in the company of gypsies. Then it happened neither worse nor better than that we'd made our quarters for the night in a great big wood, and in the morning when we got up there was war all round us, an uproar everywhere. The gypsies knew about a cave in a mountain a good ways off, and we tried to get there and crawl in for shelter. But the fighting came nearer and nearer, and the cannon balls whizzed around us and

[11] *White-Matini*, Austria. *Blue-Matini*, Prussia. *Buffalo-Matini*, Mecklenburg. *Matini* means "state," "realm," "kingdom." According to Dorph, gypsies named the countries after the most prominent color in the soldiers' uniforms. Denmark was called *Red-Matini*. Possibly, *Buffalo-Matini* refers to the jerkins of buffalo hide worn for protection against the enemies' weapons.—Translator.

chopped branches off the trees. One of them fell right on the head of a half-grown girl, and that was none other than Linka —Gypsy Linka we call her, Peter's *Maie*—and she dropped on the ground. All the gypsies went on running, and no one wanted to wait for Linka; for she didn't belong to any of them, she'd been stolen some place way down South. 'Let's see if she's really dead,' says Peter. 'Let her lay,' says I. But she wasn't dead, only pretty well smashed up and one arm broken, and she begged and prayed that we take her along. So then Peter picked her up, and we set off after the others. When we came to the cave we were all right, and there Linka was taken care of. But when the war had passed by and we were going to start out again, there was nobody but Peter who wanted to carry Linka; she couldn't walk, and the gypsies were going to leave her a little food and let her stay in the cave. So he kept on carrying the girl for many days and a long way, till she could begin to put her feet on the ground. So it isn't for nothing that she carries him now; it's paying off old scores."

"Well, then," I broke in, "the first part of the payment was that she married him."

"Oh, yes," he smirked, "sure, they were married a couple of years later—in a way. You know how we do it. But it's just as good as if parson and clerk had tied the knot. If they want to serve strange gods, or to run away from each other, it's all the same whether they came together on the road or in a *Siongert*."[12]

I did not feel called upon to answer such an impudent jibe; I felt it was beneath my dignity to defend respectable people against such a scamp. He continued his story.

"But Peter and Linka stuck together. Then it happened neither worse nor better than that we were caught by a bunch of soldiers. What became of the gypsies I don't know, but I know that Peter and I got each a white *Rokkelpoj*[13] and a *Sneller*[14] and more lickings than money till we learned soldier-

[12] Church.   [13] Coat.   [14] Gun.

ing. So then we fought the Frenchmen, and Linka went along in our regiment with the other women and the baggage. When we weren't fighting she was always with Peter and did everything she could for him. It was hard enough, for first she was with child and then she had the youngster to drag along—the same little fellow that's with them now. But she never croaked.

"For a year or maybe three, things went fairly well, but then one day we got into a big battle, and there poor Peter got both his feet spoiled by a cannon ball. I didn't know what had become of him till evening when we were in our quarters, and there came Linka with him on her back and carried him into the sick-room. The surgeon cut both his feet off, and when he was cured, they let him go wherever he pleased. He had his discharge—there was nothing the matter with that, but they forgot about the pension. So Linka took him on her back again and the youngster by the hand, and set out in the world. She had a tough time, I'll wager, for she had to earn the food for them all three. But she was never at a loss—she was good as a man. She begged, and she danced, and she told fortunes—for she knows how to tell fortunes," he added in all seriousness, "both in coffee grounds and cards, and from people's hands. And what she says comes true—that's sure.

"So she had struggled through, all the way from a river out there they call *die Donau* and up to Buffalo-Matini.[15] There I happened to find them again, and so we came home together."

"But," I interrupted, "you have both your feet, how did you manage to get your discharge?"

"I took it," he replied grinning. "I thought that war had lasted too long. One day I was standing guard in a big wood —the same one where Linka had got her arm broken—and I got to thinking I'd like to get back to Denmark again. So I chucked the *Rokkelpoj* and *Sneller* and cartridges and the whole outfit and took to my heels, and it went fine."

During this story, which was much more long-winded, more epic and episodic than I have thought necessary to tell it, we

15 Mecklenburg.

had reached a more beaten track to Örre. My travelled companion went back, and I went forward, although I should have liked to see more of the faithful gypsy couple and to talk with them. I never saw them before or since.

I cannot deny that this tale filled me with many thoughts, feelings, conjectures, but most of them never saw the light of day—nor will they. One I still remember—a fancy—whether Romany or romantic I don't know: what if this nightman's lady, who is now dancing in a turf hut on Örre heath, should be a Hungarian countess or baroness? What if she were destined by birth to dance at court balls in Vienna—to see barons, counts, and princes at her feet—instead of, as now, carrying a gypsy without feet through life? Perhaps her cradle stood in "golden halls," and her grave will be in a corner of a Jutland rural graveyard. But it may be that her faithful love is written down where imperial palaces and turf huts stand side by side.

THE HOSIER AND HIS
DAUGHTER

[*Hosekræmmeren*, 1829]

"*The greatest sorrow, or far or near,*
Is to be parted from him you hold dear."

SOMETIMES when I have wandered across the great moor with
nothing but brown heather round about me and blue sky over
me; when I have strolled far from human beings and the marks
of their piddling here below—mere molehills that time or some
restless Tamerlane will level with the ground; when I have
flitted, light of heart, proud of my freedom like the Bedouin
whom no house, no narrowly bounded field ties to one spot, who
possesses all that he sees, who lives nowhere but roams as he
pleases everywhere; when in such a mood my roving eye has
caught sight of a house on the horizon which arrested its airy
flight unpleasantly, then I would sometimes wish—God forgive
me the passing thought, for after all it was nothing more—
would that this human dwelling were not there! For it harbors
trouble and pain; there people quarrel and wrangle about mine
and thine. Alackaday, the happy desert is both mine and thine,
is everybody's and nobody's.

A forester has proposed that the entire colony development
be wiped out, and that trees be planted in the fields and on the
site of the razed villages. I have sometimes been seized by a far
more inhuman idea: what if we still had the heather-grown
moor, the same that existed thousands of years ago, undisturbed,
its sod unturned by human hands! But, as I have said, I didn't
mean it seriously. For when, exhausted, weary, languishing
with heat and thirst, I have longed intensely for the Arab's
hut and his coffeepot, then I have thanked God for a heather-
thatched cottage—though miles distant—promising me shade
and refreshment.

And I was in just such a state one calm, hot September day,

some years ago, when I had walked far out on that same moor which, in an Arabian sense, I call my own. Not a breath of wind stirred the reddening heather; the air was sultry and drowsy. The distant hills that bounded the horizon swam like clouds around the immense plain, and took on marvellous shapes of houses, towers, castles, human beings, and animals, but all in dim, formless outlines, wavering and unstable like dream pictures. One moment a hut was changed into a church and the church into a pyramid; there a spire shot up, and there another sank down; a man became a horse, and the horse an elephant; here rocked a boat and there a ship with all sails spread.

For a long time my eye feasted on the contemplation of these fantastic images—a panorama such as only the sailor and the desert-dweller have an opportunity to enjoy. But presently, feeling tired and thirsty, I began to search for a real house among the many false; I earnestly desired to exchange all my magnificent fairy palaces for a single human cottage. And my search was successful. I soon discerned a real house without spires or towers; its outlines became clearer and sharper as I approached, and the peat stacks flanking it made it seem much larger than it really was.

The people living there were strangers to me. Their garments were poor, their furnishings plain. But I knew that the heath-dweller would often hide precious metals in an unpainted box or a dilapidated hanging cupboard, that he would often carry a thick wallet under a patched coat. When, therefore, my eye was attracted by an alcove stuffed full of stockings, I rightly surmised that I had entered the home of a well-to-do hosier. (Incidentally, I never knew a poor one.)

An elderly, gray-haired, but still hale and hearty man rose from the table and held out his hand to me, saying, "Welcome! By your leave, where does this good friend come from?"

Reader, do not take umbrage at such a direct and indelicate question! The peasant on the heath is just as hospitable as the lairds of Scotland, but slightly more inquisitive, and after all one cannot blame him for wanting to know whom he is entertaining. When I had told him who I was and where I came from, he called his wife, who at once set before me the best the house could afford, urging me with kindly courtesy to eat and drink, though indeed my hunger and thirst made all urging superfluous.

I was in the middle of my meal and in the middle of a political discussion with my host, when a young and very beautiful peasant girl entered. I would without fail have taken her for a disguised young lady, perhaps fleeing from cruel parents and a repugnant marriage, if her reddened hands and genuine peasant dialect had not convinced me that no masquerading had taken place. She nodded pleasantly, glanced under the table, and came back with a dish of bread and milk, which she set down on the floor with the words, "Perhaps your dog may need something, too."

I thanked her for the attention, but this attention was directed entirely to the big dog. Hungry as he was, he soon emptied the dish and tried to thank the giver by rubbing himself against her, and when she lifted her arm a little timidly, Chasseur took it as an invitation to play, and forced the screaming girl backward against the alcove. I called off the dog and explained to her that he meant no harm. Nor should I have related such a trifling incident except to remark how every movement became her, for this peasant girl, in everything she said and did, had a certain natural grace which could not be attributed to coquetry, unless one would designate an inborn, unconscious instinct by that name.

When she had left the room, I asked the old people if she was their daughter. They said she was, and added that she was an only child.

"You are not likely to keep her long," I said.

"Mercy, what do you mean?" asked the father, but his self-satisfied smile showed well enough that he understood my meaning.

"I imagine," said I, "that she will have no lack of suitors."

"Hm," he growled, "there are plenty of suitors, but if they are good for anything, that's another question. To come courting with a watch and a silver-mounted pipe isn't enough. There's more to driving a horse than just to say giddap!—I declare," he went on, supporting himself with both fists on the table, and bending to look through the low window, "if there isn't one of them now—a herdsboy who has just crawled up from the heather—heh, one of the fellows who run around with a couple of dozen pairs of stockings in a knapsack—stupid dog! Proposing to our daughter with two oxen and three and a half cows—aye, fool him! The beggar!"

These outpourings were not directed to me but at the new arrival, on whom he gazed with darkened eye, as the young man approached the house by a path through the heather. He was still so far away that I had time to ask my host who he was and to receive the information that he was a son of the nearest neighbor—who, however, lived two miles away—and that the father had a little place on which he even owed the hosier two hundred dollars; that the son for the last few years had gone around peddling woollen wares, and finally that he had had the temerity to propose to the beautiful Cecil, but had got a flat refusal. While I was listening to this story, she herself had come in, and from her troubled look, which was turned alternately on the father and the wanderer outside, I could guess that she did not share the old man's view of the case.

As soon as the young peddler came in at one door, she went out of the other, though not without a quick but tender and yearning look.

My host turned toward the newcomer, grasped the table top with both hands as if he needed support, and answered the young man's "God's peace and good-day" with a dry "Welcome."

The other remained standing a little while, took from his inner pocket a pipe and from his back pocket a tobacco pouch, emptied his pipe on the stove at his side, and refilled it. All this was done slowly and with measured movements, while my host stood immovable in the position he had assumed.

The stranger was a very handsome young man, a true son of our Northern nature which induces a slow but vigorous and lasting growth, light-haired, blue-eyed, red-cheeked, with a fine down on his chin which the razor had not yet touched, though he looked to be fully twenty years old. He was dressed after the fashion of peddlers, with a little more pretension than an ordinary peasant or even than the wealthy hosier, in coat and wide pantaloons, a red-striped vest, and a blue-flowered neckerchief. He was no unworthy admirer of the lovely Cecilia. Furthermore, he made a pleasant impression on me by his kindly and open countenance, expressing honesty, patience, and tenacity—leading traits in the North Cimbrian character.

It was quite a while before either of them said anything, but at last the host broke the silence, asking slowly, in a cold, indifferent tone, "Where are you bound for today, Esben?"

The young man answered, while he struck fire, and lit his pipe in a leisurely way, with a few long puffs, "No farther today, but tomorrow I am off for Holstein."

There was again a pause, during which Esben examined the chairs, chose one of them, and sat down on it. Meanwhile the mother and the daughter came in. The young peddler greeted them with an expression so calm and unruffled that I might have imagined he cared nothing about the lovely Cecilia, had I not known that in such a heart love may be strong, however quiet it seems; that it is not a flame which leaps and throws sparks, but a glow which gives a steady and lasting warmth. Cecilia, with a sigh, took a seat at the lower end of the table and began to knit rapidly. The mother, with a low-voiced "Welcome, Esben!" sat down to her spinning wheel.

"I suppose that is in the way of business?" the host now asked.

"That is as may be," answered his guest. "I am going to look for some way of making money in the South. What I came here for today is to ask that you will not be in too great a hurry to marry Cecil off before I come back and we see what luck I have."

Cecil blushed, but did not look up from her work.

The mother stopped the spinning wheel with one hand, dropped the other in her lap, and gazed fixedly at the speaker. But the father said, as he turned to me, "While the grass grows, the mare dies. How can you ask that Cecil shall wait for you? You may be gone a long time—may happen you won't come back at all."

"If so it will be your fault, Michel Krænsen," Esben broke in. "But I tell you that if you force Cecil to take anyone else, you sin greatly against both her and me."

With that he rose, shook hands with the two old people, and bade them a curt good-bye. To his sweetheart he said in a slightly lower and softer tone, "Good-bye, Cecil, and thanks for all your goodness. Think kindly of me if you can. God be with you—and with all of you. Good-bye!"

He turned to the door, put away his pipe, tobacco pouch, and tinder each in its proper pocket, took his stick, and walked away without once turning to look back.

The old man smiled as before; his wife sighed, "Ah, yes," but tear after tear coursed down Cecilia's cheeks.

Here I had the most appropriate occasion for a lecture on the principles that ought to guide parents in regard to the marriage of their children. I could have reminded them that wealth is not enough for wedded bliss, that the heart also must have something to say, that wisdom bids everyone look more on honesty, industry, and ability than on money. I could have reproached the father—for the mother seemed at least to be neutral—with his harshness toward his only daughter. But I knew the peasants too well to waste words on this subject. I knew that worldly goods go before everything else in their class—and I wonder if things are very different in other classes! Furthermore, I knew the firmness, even obstinacy of the peasant on this point, and was aware that in controversies with his superiors he would often seem to yield, and pretend to adopt their view, while he was most inexorably bent on following his own head.

Furthermore, there was another reflection that bade me not to put my finger between the knife and the wall, between the door and the frame, between the hammer and the anvil, namely: is not wealth after all the most tangible of all good things on earth?—at least of those which, according to the classification of Epictetus, are "not within our power." Is not money the best substitute for all sublunary benefits—the unexceptionable representative of food and drink, raiment and shelter, respect and friendship, yes, even to some extent of love? Is not wealth, finally, that which gives us the most pleasures, the greatest independence, which compensates for most shortcomings? Is not poverty the rock upon which friendship and even love is often wrecked? "When the stall is empty the horses bite each other," says the peasant; and what say the others when the intoxication of love is evaporated and the honeymoon is at an end? True, it would be well if Cupid and Hymen could always be companions, but nevertheless they do want Pluto as the third.

After this view of the world as it is—more rational perhaps than some would expect and others would like in the author of a novel—my readers will at least give me credit for consistency when I refrained from mixing in the romance of Esben and Cecilia, all the more as on the part of the former it might be an interested speculation directed less toward the beauty and affections of the daughter than the full alcove and heavy hanging cupboard of the father. And although I knew that pure love is not entirely a poetic invention, still I was aware even then that it is found more frequently in books than outside of them.

When therefore the beautiful Cecilia had left the room— probably to give vent more freely to a flood of tears—I merely threw out the remark that it was a pity the young man was not warmer, since he seemed to be a decent chap and fond of the girl. "If he could come back," I added, "with a score of hundred-dollar bills—"

"And if they were his own," said old Michel slyly, "yes, that would be another matter."

I went out again into my empty and careless heath. Far away and to one side I could still see Esben and the ascending smoke from his pipe. So, I thought, his sorrow and love go up in smoke, but what of poor Cecilia? I cast a glance backward at the house of the wealthy hosier and said to myself that, if it had not existed, there would have been fewer tears shed in the world.

✧

Six years passed before I visited that part of the heath again. It was a warm, quiet September day just like last time. Thirst drove me to look for a house, and as it happened that of the hosier was the nearest. It was not till I recognized the good Michel Krænsen's solitary dwelling that I brought to mind the beautiful Cecilia and her sweetheart; and then curiosity to learn how this idyl of the heath had turned out impelled me just as strongly as my thirst. In such circumstances I am very prone to anticipate the real story; I make my conjectures, I imagine how things could and should have been, and try whether my charting corresponds with the course steered by fate. Alas, usually my guesses are very much at variance with the actual happenings! It turned out so this time. I pictured Esben and Cecilia as man and wife, she with a baby at her breast, the grandfather with one or two bigger ones on his knee, the young peddler himself as the active and successful manager of the expanded hosiery business—but things proved to be very different.

As I stepped into the entry, I heard a soft feminine voice singing what at first I took for a lullaby, and yet the tone was so sad that my high hopes immediately suffered a downfall. I stood still and listened: the song was a plaint of hopeless love. The expression was simple, yet true and touching, but my memory has retained only the refrain which came at the end of each verse:

> "The greatest sorrow, or far or near,
>   Is to be parted from him you hold dear."

Filled with dark forebodings, I opened the door to the living room.

A middle-aged, large and stout peasant woman who sat carding wool was the first person I saw, but it was not she who was singing. The singer turned her back to me. She sat rocking herself quickly back and forth and moved her hands as if she were spinning. The nearer of the two rose and wished me welcome, but I advanced in order to see the face of the other.

It was Cecilia, pale but still beautiful, until she looked up at me. Alas! Madness shone in her dully gleaming eyes and in her sickly sweet smile. Then I noticed, too, that she had no spinning wheel; but the one she imagined herself treading must be of the same stuff as Macbeth's dagger.

She stopped both her singing and her airy spinning, and asked me eagerly, "Are you from Holstein? Did you see Esben? Is he coming soon?"

I realized how I had been caught and answered just as quickly, "Yes, he will soon be coming. He sent greetings to you."

"Then I must go out and meet him," she exclaimed happily, started up from her stool, and leaped toward the door.

"Wait a bit, Cecil," said the other woman, putting down her cards, "let me come with you." She winked at me and shook her head—gestures that were quite superfluous.

"Mother," she cried in a loud voice turning toward the kitchen door, "here's a stranger. Come in, for now we're going." She ran after the mad girl, who was already outside.

The old woman came in. I did not recognize her, but took for granted that she must be the unhappy girl's mother, though she was worn with grief and age. Nor did she remember me from my last visit, but after a "Welcome! Sit down," she asked the usual question. "By your leave, where does this good man come from?"

I told her, and reminded her that I had been there some years ago.

"Good God!" she said, and struck her hands together, "is it you? Please sit down by the table while I cut some bread and butter for you. Perhaps you are thirsty, too?" Without waiting for an answer she hurried into a pantry and soon came back with food and drink.

Although I was eager to learn more about poor Cecilia, a premonition of something especially tragic subdued my curiosity and kept me from direct questions about that which I both wished and dreaded to hear.

"Is your husband at home?" was the first thing I asked.

"My husband?" she said. "The good God has taken him. It will be three years come Michaelmas that I have been a widow. Have another slice! Please—though it's nothing but peasant food."

"Thank you," I replied, "I am more thirsty than hungry.— So your husband has passed away? That was a great loss, a great sorrow for you—"

"Yes, indeed," she sighed, while the tears came into her eyes; "but that was not all—Good God! You saw our daughter?"

"Yes," I said, "she seemed a little strange—"

"She is quite out of her mind," she said, bursting into tears. "We have to keep a woman only to take care of her, and she can't do much else. She's supposed to spin and knit a little, but it doesn't amount to anything, for she has to run after the girl sixteen times a day, when she gets to thinking of Esben—"

"Where is Esben?" I broke in.

"In heaven," she replied. "So you haven't heard that? Yes, God ha' mercy! He got a miserable death; such wretchedness was never known.—You mustn't be too grand, but eat and drink what we have—please! Yes, indeed, I have gone through something since you were here last. And times are difficult; the hosiery trade doesn't pay when we have to hire strangers to look after everything."

When I saw that her grief over the past, mingled with worry over the present, was not so great but that she could bear to tell about her troubles, I asked her to do so. She willingly complied with my request and told me a story which— omitting irrelevant matters—I will repeat as well as I can in the simple and artless style of the narrator.

"We and Kjeld Esbensen," she began, after she had drawn a chair to the table, seated herself, and made ready her knitting, "have been neighbors ever since I came to the place. Kjeld's Esben and our Cecil became good friends before anyone knew it. My husband was not very happy about it, nor I either, for Esben had little and his father nothing at all. Still we thought the girl would have had more sense than to set her heart on such a green boy. To be sure, he ran around with a few pairs of stockings and earned a few pennies, but what would that amount to? Then they came and proposed, and my husband said No—as anyone would—and at that Esben went to Holstein.

"We saw that Cecil got a little down-hearted, but we didn't pay any attention. 'She'll forget him when the right one comes,' said my husband. And it was not long before Mads Egelund— I don't know if you know him? He lives a few miles from here —he came courting with a farm fully paid for and three thousand dollars out at interest. That was good enough. Michel said Yes right away, but Cecil—God help us!—she said No. So my husband got angry and scolded her. It seemed to me he was too hard, but my poor dear husband always wanted his own way, and so he and Mads's father went to the parson and had the banns read for them. It went very well the first two Sundays, but on the third when he asked, 'Does anyone know any impediment?' Cecil rose and said, 'I do. The banns have been read three times for Esben and me in Paradise.' I tried to hush her, but it was too late, everybody in the church had heard it and looked over to our pew—we were put to great shame.

Still I didn't think that she had gone out of her mind, but before the parson got down from the pulpit she started a rigamarole about Esben and Paradise and bridal dress and bridal bed, and so on, all topsy-turvy. We had to get her out of the church. Poor dear Michel scolded her and said she was trying to play a trick on us, but God help us! it was no trick. She was in dead earnest. Crazy she was, and crazy she remained."

Here the woman allowed the stocking she was knitting to sink down in her lap, took the ball of yarn from her left shoulder, turned it round several times, and looked at it from every direction. But her thoughts were elsewhere; after a few minutes' pause she pressed the ball against her eyes, hung it on its hook again, and began to move her knitting needles quickly, as if she were thus taking up the thread of her broken narrative.

"She talked about nothing but how she was dead and had come into Paradise and how she was to marry Esben as soon as he was dead, too; and she kept on with this, night and day. Then poor dear Michel understood how it was. 'It's God's doing,' he said. 'His will no one can resist.' But he felt bad about it anyway, and as for me, it's many an hour I have lain awake and cried when all the others were asleep. Sometimes it seemed to me it would have been better if the two young people could have been married. 'Perhaps,' said my husband, 'but it wasn't to be.'

"The first few months she was very unruly, and we had a hard time with her. Later she quieted down. She didn't speak much, but sighed and wept all the time. She didn't want to do any work, for 'in heaven,' she said, 'there's a holiday every day.'

"So half a year passed, and it was about twice as. long since Esben had gone south, and no one had heard from him, either good or bad. Then it happened one day, just as we were sitting here, poor dear Michel and Cecil and I, that Esben came in at the door. He came right from his journey and hadn't been home, so he didn't know how things were here, until he looked at the girl; then of course he saw there was something wrong.

" 'You have waited long,' she said. 'The bridal bed has been made for a year and a day. But tell me first: are you living or dead?'

" 'Good God, Cecil,' he said. 'Surely you can see that I am living!'

" 'That's too bad,' she said. 'Try to lie down and die as soon as you can, for Mads Egelund is trying to get there first.'

" 'This state of things isn't so good,' he said. 'Michel, Michel, you have done us a great wrong. Now I'm a man of five thousand dollars or more. My mother's brother in Holstein is dead; he wasn't married, and I'm his heir.'

" 'What are you saying?' said my husband. 'It was a shame we didn't know it before, but take your time, the girl may get well yet.'

"Esben shook his head, and went over to our daughter to take her hand. 'Cecil,' he said, 'now try to talk sense. We're alive, both of us, and if you'll only be rational, your parents will give their consent to our being married.'

"But she put both hands behind her back, and cried, 'Get thee behind me! What have I to do with thee? You are a human being, and I am an angel of God.'

"Then he turned around and began to weep quite bitterly. 'God forgive you, Michel Krænsen,' he said, 'for what you have done against us two human beings.'

" 'Wait a little,' said my husband. 'It may turn out all right. Stay here overnight, and then we'll see what she says tomorrow.'

"It was in the evening, and there was a bad storm brewing with thunder and lightning—the worst I've ever seen—just as if the world were coming to an end. So then Esben made up his mind to stay with us, and as soon as the storm quieted down a little, he lay down in the best room. We went to bed, too, but for a long time I could hear through the wall how he sighed and wept, and I think he was also praying to God in heaven. At last I dozed off. Cecil was sleeping in the alcove over there, right opposite to Michel's and mine here.

"It might have been an hour or so past midnight when I awakened. It was calm outside, and the moon was shining in through the window. I lay thinking of all the trouble that had come over us, but least of all could I have foreseen that which I am now going to tell you.

"It came over me that everything was so quiet at Cecil's. I couldn't hear her breathing, nor did I hear anything more of Esben. Somehow I felt that there was something wrong. I stole out of my own bed and over to Cecil's. I peered in. I felt for her with my hand, but she was not there. Then I became really frightened, ran out into the kitchen, lit a candle, and went up into the other room. Alack, God help us in His mercy! What did I see! She was sitting on Esben's bed holding his head in her lap; but when I looked more closely his face was pale as a corpse, and the sheets were red with blood. I screamed and fell to the floor. But Cecil beckoned to me with one hand and patted his cheek with the other. 'Hush, hush,' she said, 'now my dear is sleeping the sweet sleep. As soon as you have buried his body, the angels will bear his soul to Paradise, and there our wedding will be held with great rejoicing.' Alackaday! Merciful God and Father! She had cut his throat—the bloody razor was lying on the floor by the bed."

Here the unhappy widow hid her face in her hands and wept bitterly, while horror and pity wrung my heart. At last she regained control of herself, and went on with her story.

"There was great sorrow and lamentation both here and at Esben's. When our people came driving with him to his parents —they had thought he was safe and sound in Holstein—there was a screaming and crying aloud as if the house had fallen. He was an honest fellow, and now had come into money and wealth, and yet he had to die so miserably in his youth, and at the hands of his sweetheart, too. Poor dear Michel could never forget it; he was never himself again. A few months later he took to his bed, and then Our Lord let him depart from me.

"The very day when he was buried Cecil fell into a deep

sleep and slept for three whole days and nights. When she awakened, her mind had come back. I sat by her bed and expected that Our Lord would make an end of her troubles. But then, as she lay there, she fetched a deep sigh, turned her eyes on me, and said, 'What has happened? Where have I been? I have had a strange dream; it seemed to me I was in heaven, and Esben was with me.—Good God, mother, where's Esben? Have you heard nothing from him since he went to Holstein?'

"I hardly knew how much I dared to say. No—I said—we hadn't heard much about him. She sighed. 'Where's father?' she went on. I said her father was well off, that God had taken him. Then she cried, 'Mother, let me see him,' she begged. I said, 'No, my child, you can't see him, he is buried already.' 'God help us!' she shrieked. 'How long have I slept?' I realized from this that she didn't know what condition she had been in. 'If you have wakened me, mother,' she said, 'it was no kindness. I slept so sweetly and dreamt so beautifully; Esben came to see me every night in shining white garments and with a wreath of red beads around his neck.'

At this point the old woman sank into her own melancholy thoughts again and heaved a few deep, heartfelt sighs before she could go on.

"The poor child had got her mind back, but God knows if it was any better for her! She was never happy, but always quiet and sad, didn't speak unless she was spoken to, and tended to her work properly. She was neither sick nor well.

"The rumor spread round about in the neighborhood, and after three months Mads Egelund came and proposed to her again. But she didn't want to have anything to do with him —not on any account. When he saw that she couldn't abide him, he got angry and wanted to hurt her. I and our people and all who came here were always very careful not to say a word about how in her madness she herself had killed poor Esben; and she most likely thought that he was either dead or married down South. But one day when Mads was here and urging her to say Yes, and she answered that she would rather die than marry him, then he said right out that he was not so eager to marry a girl who had cut the throat of her first sweetheart, and with that he told her everything that had happened. I was standing out in the kitchen and heard part of what he said. I dropped what I had in my hand, ran in, and cried, 'Mads, Mads, God forgive you, what are you doing?' But it was too late. She sat on the bench as pale as a whited wall, and her eyes were staring. 'What am I doing?' he said, 'I'm only telling her the truth. It's better she should know it than to make a fool of her by letting her go and wait all her life for a dead man.—Good-bye! I won't trouble you any more.'

"He went away; but she had had a relapse, and I don't suppose she will ever get her mind back in this life. You can see for yourself how she is. Whenever she isn't sleeping she sings the song she made up when Esben went to Holstein, and then she thinks she is spinning thread for the bridal sheets. Otherwise she is quiet—God be thanked!—and doesn't harm the smallest creature. Still we don't dare to let her out of our sight. God look upon her in His mercy and give us both peace soon!"

As she spoke the last words, the unhappy girl came in with her companion. "No," she said, "I can't see him today, but tomorrow I am sure he will come. I must make haste if I am going to get the sheets ready." She sat down quickly on her little stool and, with hands and feet in rapid motion, she began her plaintive song again. A long, deeply drawn sigh each time preceded the refrain, "The greatest sorrow, or far or near, Is to be parted from him you hold dear." Then her beautiful pale face would sink down toward her bosom, hands and feet rested a moment; but soon she straightened up, began another verse, and set her shadowy spinning wheel going again.

Filled with melancholy thoughts, I went my way. My soul had taken on the color of the desert. My imagination hovered around Cecilia and her dreadful fate. In every distant mirage I seemed to see the hosier's daughter, how she sat spinning and rocking and beating the air with her arms. In the plaintive call of the plover, in the mournful, monotonous trilling of the lonely heath lark, I heard only those sad, true words expressing the deepest feeling of thousands of wounded hearts,

> "The greatest sorrow, or far or near,
> Is to be parted from him you hold dear."

MARIE

A REMINISCENCE FROM THE WESTERN OCEAN

[*Marie, En Erindring fra Vesterhavet*, 1836]

THE narrow strip of land which the Danish peninsula shoots out into the North Sea is almost entirely covered with quicksand, cast up by the Western Ocean, and carried farther inland by its ally, the storm. It is as though that dread element would mock the earth with this sterile gift, while undermining its foundations and robbing it of its fertile soil. But as yet the enemy has not been strong enough to drive out the indomitable people who live there. They take compensation for their losses from the sea itself, and they fight the onslaught of the sand with a kind of grass that will never allow itself to be choked, but always comes out on top. By means of it, hills and valleys are formed, in ever-changing variety, extending all the way down to the western coast. Seen from a distance, with the sun behind them, they delude the wanderer by their deceptive likeness to forest-clad slopes. But farther inland there are still wide naked mounds of sand which in the distance look like snow-covered mountains; year after year they conquer bits of the tillable plains from which painstaking labor once wrested a scanty harvest. All the way along the coast the landscape bears the same stamp.

In one of these desolate regions the narrator, then a young man, climbed a dune covered with beach grass, in order to look out for the first time upon the real ocean. The sun was setting. The sea was liquid fire; the sand-hills were glowing embers. The winds were slumbering; only the muffled sound of the ground swell on the beach told of their late battle with the waves. A more melancholy reminder of the might of storm and ocean in united onslaught was a wreck, stuck on the nearest sand bar, and stretching its blackened boards up through the sand.

The sun might have set over my silent transport, and darkness alone might have awakened me from unutterable dreams, if a party of fishermen with their oars and nets had not arrived near the spot where I was standing. Before I could see them, I heard their footsteps grating on the sand as they wended their way down through the narrow valleys. When their fishing-gear had been placed in the boat lying in a break of the cliff, they separated, going some to one side, some to the other, stemmed their backs against the gunwale, and pushed the boat down to the water's edge to the tune of a chantey sung in hollow tones by a gigantic fisherman. The refrain was quite jolly: "I hoist, you haul"—"Hurrah, hurrah, hurrah!" came the chorus—"I drink, you pay for all"—"Hurrah, hurrah, hurrah!" The merry words were in strange contrast with the deep tones and the dark seriousness with which they were sung—and with which the men all at once turned around, took off their caps, and knelt with their brows against the gunwale. For a few moments they remained in this position, but not a sound was heard from their lips; silently they prayed to the Lord of the winds and the waves. Silently they rose, pushed the boat out on the water, sprang into it, and seized the oars.

Under their steady pulling, the small craft glided over the surface of the water. I followed it with my eyes till it was lost in the dim distance.

One man remained behind. He was very old, but age had not yet whitened the reddish brown locks of hair that shaded his wrinkled face, although it had somewhat bent his broad back. He stood a long time immovable, his hands in his side pockets, looking after the men as they sailed out. Then he turned, walked slowly over to me, and greeted me with a hearty "Good evening."

I seized the opportunity to learn something about these men and their laborious means of livelihood, as well as about the shipwrecks that frequently occur on this dangerous coast. He replied very intelligently, and especially described the last wreck—the remains of which were standing near by—so clearly and vividly that, in my youthful levity, I wished I might once witness such a terrible tragedy.

I accompanied the man to his home, an attractive, well-furnished house a little farther inland, near one of the largest dunes. Shortly before reaching it, he stopped, and, as we were walking down the last hill, said thoughtfully, "The weather's not to be trusted."

"What do you mean?" I asked.

"Only that we're in for a change," was the answer. Thereupon he invited me to have supper and spend the night. I accepted the kind offer, and he and his wife, who was as old as he, entertained me with a hospitality that could not have been heartier in the tents of the Bedouins. Feeling a pleasant sense of peace and safety, contrasting with the hardships and dangers of the fishermen on their expedition at night over the treacherous sea, I fell asleep on the soft featherbed of my hosts.

Before daybreak I was awakened by a mixture of noises in the living room adjoining my bedroom: talking in voices, some strident and some low, clatter of wooden shoes, creaking and clanking of doors opened and shut. I sat up and listened. In more quiet intervals it seemed to me that I heard a hollow whistling or a deep and monotonous roaring. I jumped up, dressed quickly, and went into the other room. The whole family was astir and busy. The man of the house was coiling a rope; the housewife was at the hearth, raking the embers together, and putting on the kettle; two young women—one the daughter, the other the son's wife—fully dressed, were tying shawls over their heads as if they were starting out on a long journey. My "Good morning" was answered curtly, and when I asked what was the roaring I heard, the old man answered as curtly and briefly, "The sea."

"Where are you going, my good man?" I asked further.

"Out to look for our folks," he replied. "We're getting dirty weather."

These words acted upon me like an electric shock, and I instantly resolved that I would go with them to face their dreaded neighbor. In a few minutes we were ready and left the house.

The sun was just rising. Its dark red disk glowed between strips of cloud. No wind was noticeable, but the incessant roaring of the ocean sounded louder. Silently we went to meet it, I full of tense and anxious expectation.

I climbed the outermost cliff. To my great surprise the sea was not very much disturbed. It was only near land that the ground swell broke against the beach and rolled in with a rumbling noise. Even now the air was calm, but my old weather-forecaster assured me that it would not be long before I should feel the west wind. He was right. Soon the cruel lord of the North Sea came in full force, swathed in murky fogs. Now the sea far out began to stir; it showed white specks which all the time grew larger and came nearer, it seemed with the speed of the wind. But the wind ran past them. All at once it came with ominous sighs and sharp whistling in the harsh clumps of beach grass. No boat was yet to be seen. But along the dunes people appeared, one after another, chiefly women and half-grown boys. They came, as we did, to look for the delayed fishermen, then disappeared, and returned again, or perhaps it was others that came in their places.

The velocity of the wind increased, the turbulence of the waves likewise; the beach was a mass of foam. I trembled for the poor fellows out there and had already given them up in my own distressful thoughts. Then the old man, who was shading his eyes with his hand, cried out, "There they are," and the same cry was repeated far along the beach. But I could see nothing, and my anxiety grew. At last the pointing of the others guided my eyes to a darker speck in the distance, which often disappeared, but always came again, and each time larger and nearer. The uproar of the sea increased; the white-caps became more numerous and broader. The three sand bars which, with narrow spaces between them, ran parallel to the land, were marked by continuous strips of foam, stretching to the south and north as far as the eye could see. These bars are a menace to seafaring men, but a triple guard to the coast, for they break the power of the tremendous waves that often rise higher than the cliff itself, and, without this resistance, would soon break down the feeble ramparts and flood the low land along the western coast.

The boat was coming on fast. Already we could see the heads of the men when it rode the crest of the waves. But when it ran as if down a hill and disappeared in the trough of a wave, I often thought with dread, "Will they come up again?" A cry of fear escaped me; but the old man, who stood near me with arms crossed, said grimly, "What's the matter? There's no danger yet."

They had reached the outermost bar. There they stopped, nay, even rowed backwards with all their might; and in this way they successfully cleared several enormous waves. As these broke into surf, there was for a moment a strip of quiet water, and the men seized the chance to row across it with the speed of a bird. The second bar was passed in the same way. But now came the most dangerous moment. All the onlookers ran down to the edge of the water and, as if by a command, sank on their knees, lifting clasped hands to heaven. Then all sprang up just as quickly and caught each other by the hand. I did not at once understand the meaning of this chain; I was soon to see.

The boat had reached the innermost bar, not a stone's throw from land. It dashed into the breakers, pursued by a gigantic wave that lifted its white comb high over the boat—caught up with it; the boat turned to one side—was overpowered—capsized. A shriek, piercing, heart-rending, went up from the women and children. Life or death hung in the balance. The shipwrecked men were washed ashore by the wave; some reached firm ground and got a footing right away, but others did not come so far up. Then the chain broke in several places; the one standing nearest reached a hand to the man struggling in the breakers, the others in the chain pulled with all their might to rob the sea of its victim; for the same wave that had cast them up would have sucked them back again, and then there would have been no way of saving them. Terrible moments! But they passed so quickly that I hardly saw what happened till all were saved. Just as quickly the boat—that trusty carrier over the abyss and faithful aid in many a danger—was hauled in. Not till the boat with the abundant catch of the night was well beached, did the men greet each other with vigorous handclasps, and many a sailor, for all his dripping garments, was clasped in loving arms. And now the mothers, wives, and daughters who had stayed home hurried to the beach with mugs of warm ale. Every one of the returned men grasped his mug with both hands and did not let it go till the bottom turned up to heaven. (These hardy men never carry food or drink with them on the ocean, but when they land are always received with a heartening drink of warm ale.) Then the catch was divided. All went home; I went with my host and his family.

A tasty meal was quickly prepared from the gifts of the sea; but even before it was over, a man thrust his head in through the half-open door and cried, "A ship aground!" Everybody jumped up and asked, "Where?"—"Here," replied the man quickly, and the head was withdrawn, as he went on to carry his important message farther. My host, his son, and two other young men who had been along on the fishing expedition last night rushed out. I followed.

The gale had risen to a storm. The ocean roared in its most wrathful mood. The sand from the dunes whipped our faces, and the froth flew over our heads like snowflakes. With wide open eyes I rushed out on the cliff; it seemed to shake under my feet. The dark waters were churned into froth; the fine spray almost hid the view, and the thundering of the waves deafened my ears.

"Where?" I called to the man nearest me.

He stretched out his arm; now I saw the unfortunate ship, little more than a gunshot from us.

"Can she save herself?" I asked.

"Not if she was the only ship on the ocean," was the answer. "She can't keep clear of the land—She *must* run aground."

Reeling and staggering, the ship came on. "Now!" everybody called at once. "Now she's at the first bar." "She's struck!" cried one. "No," cried another, "there's a wave coming, that may help her."

It came—the ship was lifted on the gigantic wave—sank again. "She's over," they cried. My heart leaped, but I didn't know the Jutland coast. A few seconds later they cried, "There, she's stuck!" It was on the middle bar. To me it looked as if she were still coming on, but it was only the rolling and pitching of the ship aground.

It was only the distance of a musket-shot from land where it had stopped. I hoped, therefore, that the people could be saved. They lowered a boat, and two men jumped into it, but then came a great wave and carried it away; it was crushed into bits and thrown up on the beach; the men never came up again. The screams of the crew when it vanished pierced through the howling of the storm and the roaring of the breakers.

Now a succession of waves from out there came tumbling in, higher, heavier than any that had gone before—nine, the shore-dwellers say, follow one upon another, the last one biggest of all. When the first one hit the ship, it lurched to one side—a scream, louder, wilder than the first came from the frightened crew. The next wave turned the ship still more and washed over the foredeck. The sailors climbed up into the rigging and tied themselves fast. With each successive wave the ship swung more and more around until at last it turned its broadside full toward us. The ropes in the rigging were loosened, and thrown hither and thither; the masts were toppling.

After this violent blast there was a moment's pause, as if the ocean were gathering its forces for a new and more ferocious attack. The terrified sailors stretched out their hands, sometimes to the darkened heaven, sometimes toward land—the land that was so near and which they nevertheless would never reach alive. Their cries cut my young heart like knives. But there was no possibility of helping them; and it was in vain that the people on shore called to them that they should tie ropes to casks or barrels and throw them overboard. Either they did not hear or they did not understand.

A new, touching sight appeared. A man came out from the deckhouse, a woman after him. He cast a glance at the sea and then at the land. It must have been the captain and his wife. They were clasped in each other's arms, but suddenly they released each other, ran into the deckhouse, and came back carrying a large bundle between them. By means of a rope they lowered it to the water. Both knelt on the deck and stretched their arms beseechingly toward us. The bundle did not sink, though it bobbed up and down in the breakers. Soon it was cast up on land; a man caught it, carried it higher up, and loosed the rope. Not till then did the two on board jump up, with a cry that sounded like joy. Quickly he tied her with one end of the rope fast to a board—too late! A new succession of waves broke over the wreck. The first tumbled over it, roaring and frothing, and entirely engulfed it. One mast went overboard with all who clung to the rigging; the captain and his wife were no longer to be seen. The people on land pulled with all their might at the rope—she was hauled up on land, but with head crushed. The next wave took the other mast, too; the hull capsized. The last wave rose like a mountain from the abyss. The old man, who was standing near me, cried, "If she can stand that, she can stand anything!" Scarcely had the words been spoken before the wave lifted its broad back still higher, formed a comb, and dashed down over the wreck like an avalanche with a crack that sounded above the noise of storm and breakers—it was crushed! Its splintered boards whirled and danced in the churning foam.

The captain's body was never found. Nor was it possible to learn the name of the skipper and ship or its home port.

While everybody was busy saving the bits of wreckage drifting in, I took upon myself to examine the bundle that had been hauled in first. It consisted of bedclothes tightly bound together and strapped to a cabin door. I bent down and loosened them, hoping I hardly knew what. To my happy surprise I heard a faint whimper; I cut the strings—turned back the pillows—a living child lay there before my eyes. Quickly I wrapped it up again and ran as fast as I could to the home of my hosts with this precious bit of salvage.

There was no one home except the aged housewife and her three-year-old grandson.

I laid my find on the table. The child—a girl scarcely half a year old—was wet with sea-water, but showed no signs of having swallowed any of this bitter drink of death. It began to whimper, probably with hunger. When the woman heard it, she left her coffeepot on the hearth and, catching sight of the baby, struck her thighs with the palms of her hands, and cried, "Little Lord Jesus! Where did you get that?"—"From God," I replied, and asked for dry clothes and some of the warm milk that was standing on the hearth. The little one drank it eagerly and then submitted without a sound to be divested of her wet swaddling-clothes and dressed in dry underwear. I took her in my arms while a cradle was being prepared. Soon her head sank down on my shoulder, and she was sound asleep even before she had been put to bed.

It touched my heart to see the sweetly sleeping baby which a little while ago had been with its father and mother, and was now in a strange country, torn from those who gave it life. When you open your innocent eyes again, you will look for them, but not find them. Never to pronounce those names —the first we learn and the most precious—poor little delicate flower from a distant land, perhaps from the gentle South, now cast up here to be transplanted into the cold, barren sand of the North. Perhaps you will wither early, and no one will miss you, no parting tear will fall on your pale cheek. You will be as a stranger in a strange land, unloved in life, forgotten in death.

"What are you crying for?" asked the woman. "Is it for those whom the sea has taken? Don't we all owe the Lord a death? My first husband died at sea, and my father died at sea, and my brother died at sea, all on the same day. Then I cried, but now—"

"I am not grieving for the dead," I broke in, "but for the living. Don't you think this little one is to be pitied?"

"Yes—oh, yes," she said, while she went on with her work. "Our Lord still lives." There was something in these words that dried my eyes and made my heart expand. I left the house to go and look at the salvage.

Midway to the beach I met some of the people carrying great loads of wreckage. When they told me there was nothing more to do down there, I went back with the family to the house where I was staying. None of them knew anything about my salvage, and they opened their eyes wide when they saw the child in the cradle. The grandson of my host—the little three-year-old—stood by the side of it and peeped into it with delighted curiosity.—I explained what had occurred.

"That's all very well," said the master of the house, "but what are we going to do with it?"

"The parish will have to take care of it," said the son.

"We had better bring it to the minister," said the son-in-law. "Then he can do with it whatever he thinks best."

While they were consulting about the fate of the orphaned child, the young woman stood at the foot of the cradle, gazing fixedly at the sleeping baby, with both hands on her hips.

"Mother," said the little boy, "is that my sister?"

In the same moment the child opened its eyes, looked round, then let them rest on the boy. He held out his hand to her— she grasped it—he shrieked with joy.

"Good God," said the young wife, and tears glistened in her eyes—"isn't she like our little Marie?"

"Where?" I asked looking around, "where is she?"

"In heaven," she sighed. "It's now three months since she

died." Then she glanced at her husband, saying, "Couldn't we keep this one instead?"

"Hm," he said slowly. "That's not for us to say."

Now she looked at her parents-in-law as if appealing to them. "What do father and mother say? It looks at us in such a friendly way, the little lamb."

"Hm," said the old man. "Where there's food for ten there's food for eleven, too—take it then."

The baby smiled as if it understood, and reached out its little hands to its new mother. She quickly turned back the coverlet, took the child in her arms, and kissed it with motherly tenderness. The little boy jumped around, clapped his hands, and cried, "Thank God, we've got Marie back."

"Yes, what's her name? What shall we call her?" said the old man.

"Marie, Marie!" exclaimed the young wife jubilantly. "So little Jörgen says." All agreed to this. But the mother of the house folded her hands in her lap and, with a feeling of which I had not believed her capable, said, "In Jesus' name! She's a loan of God's from the sea."

✧

Thirty years had passed since my first visit to the wild coast of West Jutland, when last summer I found myself there once more. Much water had run into the sea, as the saying is, and many an eye had been closed out on the sea, I thought, as again I gazed at it stretching before me. The events—the storms—of a generation had weakened the memory of the story I have just told and of all its dreadful effects; just as the storm itself effaces the footprints of the wanderer in the sand on the dunes. But the sight of the ocean, and the coasts that for thousands of years have defied its might, awakened my slumbering memories. From the beach along which I was strolling I turned in among the dunes, climbed one of the highest sand-hills, and looked around for the house where I had stayed. I could not discover it anywhere and supposed, therefore, that I

had not gone in the right direction but—as can easily happen—
had lost my way in this monotonous but ever-changing region;
for sometimes the wind levels a mountain and again sweeps
together a new one, and even the huge dunes move, change
contour or direction, just as snowdrifts do under the alternating
winds of winter.

The sun was high in its course; the air was mild, and a light
easterly breeze blew from the land and softly moved the pale
green leaves of the beach grass; the heath larks sang. I sat down
facing the sea. It was calm and reflected the light blue of the
cloudless sky—how different from the wild uproar in which I
last saw it. But is it the same ocean? I asked myself. Why not?
I know a far sadder transformation: the face of a child is also
the clear mirror of joy and innocence, yet the time comes when
it is darkened by the clouds of sorrow and the fogs of sadness,
when it is stirred and furrowed by the violent gusts of passion.

I was about to leave my solitary resting-place when an unexpected sight detained me. A white-haired, bent old man came
slowly tottering forward. In his right hand he held a stick which
he used incessantly to feel his way; his left hand was clasped in
that of a little boy of five or six years. In the sand valley right
north of me they stopped.

"Are we there now, Terkil?" said the man.

"Yes, greatgrandpa," answered the little one.

With the help of the child, the old man sat down, his face
turned to me and the sun; he grasped his staff in both hands
and set it as a support for his bearded chin. The little boy began
to collect stones and arrange them in ordered squares.

After a few moments of silence, the old man asked, "Are
you there? What are you doing?"

"Building houses, greatgrandpa," said the boy.

Build, my child—thought I—we old folks, too, build on
sand.

"Where's your mother?" the blind man asked presently.

"Now she's coming," said the boy. I turned my eyes in the
direction from which the man and boy had appeared. A well-

dressed peasant woman with an attractive though pale face hurried toward them with a light, quick step. On her shoulders she carried a spade. As soon as she caught sight of me, she stopped, stuck the spade down in the sand, and put the backs of her hands against her hips. A strange smile played around her mouth; she looked at me with half closed eyes, nodded familiarly, as if we were old friends, and then began to sing in a merry tone and with a shrill voice:

> "The young men are so false to the bottom of their hearts,
>   They plight their troth with hand and mouth,
>   But—devil take—it comes not from their hearts.
>   Heyomdick, heyomdack, come fallerah!"[1]

At the refrain she made a little jump, and struck out with her arms. The blind man sighed, and said crossly, "Good God! That ugly song you keep singing all the time. But Jörgen wasn't false to you—you know that very well."

At these words the ghastly merriment of the young woman suddenly changed to the deepest sadness; her hands fell down against her body as if they had lost their strength; the beautiful, pale face was bent to one side, and a deep sigh lifted her bosom and shoulders.

"Yes, that's true, greatgrandpa," she whimpered. "Now I'll see if he's here." At that she grasped the spade and began to dig in the sand. But soon she ceased, rested her hands on the handle, shook her head, and said, "He isn't here—no, no! Mahanster[2] has been talking to him and taking him away from me—we know them!" She straightened up and sang in the same tone as before, and with the same arch look:

> "The young men we love them, ay from our hearts' core.
>   But what is the use that we love them?
>   They go away and don't come back any more.
>   Heyomdick, heyomdack, come fallerah!"

The little fellow, who hardly knew yet what insanity meant, joined in the refrain, merrily kicking over his pebble buildings.

---

[1] Jutland peasant song.   [2] Maren Hansdaughter.

But the old man hid his face in his hands and beneath them
his tears dripped on the sand. I sat as if transfixed. I had not
the heart to ask questions. Nevertheless, I presently got an
explanation which later I almost regretted that I had sought.

The mad woman slung the spade over her shoulder and
went her way, singing:

"So many a one wears palest cheek for her very dear friend
 But shame upon them, but shame upon them
 Who from another lures her very dear friend.
 Heyomdick, heyomdack, come fallerah!"

When she was gone, the old man folded his hands over his
trembling knees, and lifted his face to that heaven which he
could no longer see, but from which even the blind draws light
for his soul and hope for his sorrowful heart. When he had
ended his silent prayer, he said, "Come, Terkil, come and kiss
your greatgrandpa."

The boy laid both hands on his and kissed him. The old man
rose with the help of the child, and both walked slowly away in
the direction from which they had come.

Deeply moved, I turned toward the sea. An elderly woman
was walking along the beach with her wicker basket on her
back. Old and poor people gather in their baskets amber, bits of
wood, and anything else that the greedy sea casts up again.

I called to her. She came and greeted me with a "God's
peace and good-day." I told her what I had seen. She put down
the basket, seated herself by the side of it, and told the following
story:

"The blind man is old Terkil—he doesn't know how old he
is, but he must be over five score. God have mercy on us all!
He was once a warm man and had money out at interest. He
lived over there—his house was right there in the edge of that
big sand-hill. But first the quicksand took his land, and then
he had to move farther in and begin all over again. I tell you,
young man—wherever you come from—you people in the East
little know what we have to fight against here—between the

water and the sand. Look, out there where ships are sailing now,
there my cradle stood."

Now I knew that I had not been mistaken in the location of
the house where I once enjoyed hospitality, and I knew also that
my one-time kind host was still living, blind and poor in his
old age.

"But the mad girl—or whatever she is," I asked further, "is
she his daughter or—?"

"She doesn't really belong to him at all," was the answer.
"Many years ago a ship was wrecked here; all the people were
drowned except a little baby who sailed ashore in her cradle.
And that very baby is Crazy-Marie whom you saw here a little
while ago. Terkils took her as their own, and she thrived and
grew up into a good-looking girl. Terkils had two children—
you must know—a daughter who was married and who died
many years ago without leaving any children, and a son who is
also dead. But that time he was alive and married and had one
boy, but not any more children. That boy and Marie, when they
got bigger, fell in love with each other. The parents didn't like it
so overly well, for she didn't have anything except the swaddling-clothes she came sailing in with. But however it was, the
young people were sweethearts, and—the old story—she had
a child by him—it was that little chap you saw here. Then his
parents didn't want her in the house any more with her brat,
which was not to be wondered at. Old Terkil wanted to keep
them, but he had nothing to say any more, he'd given up the
place to his son; and the old woman was dead before then.
Well, as I was going to tell you, then Terkil and Jörgen—that
was the name of the young fellow—they got my husband to take
both mother and child. But that I was sorry for many a time,
for there was no peace by night or by day. It's miserable never
to be happy—as the saying goes—and poor Marie, she sighed
and moaned and cried early and late; and the baby whined,
too, for I can tell you, Marie's eyes gave more water than her
breasts gave milk. Many a time she would lie by the hour on
her knees in front of the cradle and rock and sing and cry all

at once. Then when the child at last was quieted, she would throw herself in her clothes across the bed and pray so hard to Our Lord that He should take them both. To be sure, Jörgen came as often as he could to see how she was, and gave her money, and tried to cheer her. But it was no use. 'Jörgen,' she said to him many and many a time, 'you mustn't come any more. Why should I make trouble between you and your parents?' But Jörgen kept on coming—he wouldn't leave her on any account.—Sometimes she would say to me, 'Kirsten,' she said, 'I would to God I'd drowned with my parents! I am a stranger and an alien here in this sinful world. Oh—if it wasn't for the child there—' She said no more, but I knew well enough what she meant.—About that time Stig over there lay down and died, and he had money, and his widow was young and fine. She asked Jörgen to marry her. He said No. If things had been bad before, they got worse now. The parents worked upon him, but he wouldn't for little or for much. Marie got to hear of it, and she said to him, not once but many times, 'Jörgen, marry Mahanster. It's best for all of us.' But, no—he wouldn't. At last she said to him, 'If you don't marry her, I'll go back where I came from'—she meant the sea.

Then he began to cry, and ran away like a crazy man. When he had gone, she was sorry for what she had said, and cried and wrung her hands till I thought her knuckles would crack. Jörgen didn't come back. He stayed away for two days and for three. Now people said that he was going to marry Mahanster. Marie said nothing, but looked as if she might do most anything. My husband and I kept an eye on her, for we were afraid. But then one night he came running over to our house and threw the door wide open and caught Marie around the neck and took the child up from the cradle and kissed and fondled it. —The meaning of it all was that now at last he'd got leave, and they were going to be married. You should have seen Marie —poor thing; she couldn't say one word. Alackaday, it was the last happiness they had in this world, and it was short.

It was midnight before he left; he went away, and we

didn't think of anything. In the morning they came from Ter-kil's to ask for him. He was gone. We searched and we searched; at last Marie found his hat—right on the spot below us where you just saw her and the others. To make the story short: under it he lay and had been choked by the quicksand. For there had been a high wind that day, and the water had washed in. He must have got out in the sand where it was wet, and then there's no help; they sink and they sink till they're all covered.—Marie went out of her mind right away, and never got it back and I don't suppose she ever will.—So now, that's all there is to the story, and now you know what she's digging for, and why old Terkil on a fine day sits here and suns himself and sighs and weeps with his blind eyes. Alackaday! God comfort all who are sorrowful!"

With these words she rose, slung the basket over her back, and gave me "God's peace and farewell." She descended to the water's edge again, and as she went she said to herself, "Oh, no, there's no peace for us in this world till we're lying with spade and shovel crossed over us."

THE GAMEKEEPER AT
AUNSBJERG

[Skytten paa Aunsbjerg, 1839]

As a lad I had to stay, or rather I was imprisoned, on this estate oftener and longer than I wished. The owner, Counsellor Steen de Steensen, was my mother's uncle. He and his wife—née Schinkel—had no children; I was named for him, and he was a good-natured man. She, too, was really fond of me, but she was a "thoroughbred," as they say, and we know that people of this breed are not free from crotchets, which even the "permanent guillotine" has not been able to eradicate. She wanted to dominate, that was all.

"Where is your will, little Steen?" she would often say to me—but only when strangers were present. I was a doll, an automaton; and she had taught me to answer, "In grandmother's pocket."

The poor boy's usual consolation was, in her absence, to tease her favorite dog, Manille, which, between you and me, had a very fretful and irritable disposition. By the way, I had the satisfaction that it once got tangled up in the tether of an eagle, which was also imprisoned, but on a grassy spot in the garden, and there this king of birds murdered the favorite and ate him for breakfast. To be sure, the reigning queen commanded that a summary court martial be held, and the sentence, shooting, was instantly executed by the gamekeeper, Vilhelm.

This gamekeeper was *my* favorite; and I was never happier than when I was allowed to visit him in his room, look at his guns, play with his dogs, and listen to his hunting stories. His name was really Guillaume, which means the same in French as Wilhelm in German, and he was a Frenchman. Now I know that I have a reputation for lying, and possibly someone may accuse me of a forgery, but I can authenticate what I say, and I like to be authentic. General Numsen, who at one time,

within the memory of men now living, commanded a regiment
of horse then stationed in Randers, had, before he entered the
Russian service, been an officer in the French Army. There the
trooper Guillaume had been assigned to him as a servant, and
inasmuch as they were both tired of the *Kehraus* at Rosbach,
which the Pompadour general—did not lead, for old Fritz did
that—but in which he retreated down the Rhine, and inasmuch
as both Numsen and his servant got their throats full of the
powder that blew from the French perukes, they said good-bye
to the petticoat government, and went to Denmark together.

Vilhelm was a stocky, square-built man with thick black hair
and eyebrows and small brown eyes in a broad, rather pale, but
nevertheless handsome face. Contrary to the usual French temperament, he was so serious that I cannot remember ever having
known him to laugh. Even a smile was a rarity with him, and
there was something in his smile that did not please me. Furthermore, he was taciturn and said no more than was absolutely
necessary, except when he was minded to tell me stories, and
then I thought his face took on a look quite different from its
everyday expression.

The squire—as grandfather was usually called at home—
made more of him than even of the manager of the estate,
and often said that he was "honest as the day." Her ladyship
did not like him much, and it seemed to me that she purposely
avoided speaking to him; at least I was often charged with
bringing him her commands, even if he was no farther away
than from one door to another. He had almost as little to do
with the other servants on the estate—with one exception. This
was a young and, according to connoisseurs, very pretty housemaid by the name of Mettë. One might have supposed it was
because she resembled him in temperament and manner, but
she was just his opposite. She was always cheerful and merry,
and yet so proper in all her demeanor that the butler who could
not do without—and very rarely did do without—a little
lovemaking, sometimes with one, sometimes with another, called
her a prude—but not so that either she or Vilhelm heard it.

The manager, the gardener, and the overseer all gave her similar fine names, but of course not in the presence of the master or mistress.

It often puzzled me and I could not understand what was the reason of it, but when Vilhelm and Mettë were together, he looked more cheerful and she more serious than usual, and still less could I understand why, after a while, both looked serious, whether they were together or apart. And the longer this went on, the worse it became, and sometimes I noticed poor Mettë crying when only I, small boy that I was, saw her. And when I asked why she cried, she said that her teeth ached. But of this more later. I shall now ask leave to narrate something that occurred about the time the housemaid's teeth began to ache.

The squire had sent the gamekeeper south—I don't remember where or why. On the way home, toward evening, he came riding to Them Inn about four miles west of Himmelbjerget. Wanting his horse to bait for a couple of hours, he entered the common room and found a seat between the bed and the big stove (fired from the kitchen) in order to snatch a nap in that warm corner.

Meanwhile several peasants drifted in; they sat down at the table, and each got a mug of ale and a pipe, but none of them noticed the gamekeeper.

A few weeks earlier an accident had occurred in the neighborhood; a team of horses pulling a wood cart had run away and had overturned it, with the result that a girl who was driving, and was alone in the cart, had got her head crushed against a tree. This event was the subject of the talk in the inn. Two of the men had been along on the trip to the woods, but had been so far behind that they had not seen just what happened. A young peasant had been driving the cart right behind the girl, but he too said he did not know what had frightened the horses, and those farther back had not been able to see the two carts at the head. That the young man had not seen anything they could only explain by saying that he must have been asleep.

As they were talking this over, the very same young man came in, and sat down at the table. Immediately the others began to ask him to explain once more just what had taken place. After wetting his whistle with a glass of brandy and a draught of ale, he complied with their request. But evidently his story did not satisfy his listeners, for first one and then another interrupted him, to say that what he told now didn't jibe, in this or that particular, with the explanation he had given right away. At last he became angry, stiffened his back against the wall, and cried out to the one who had made this remark,

"What's the matter with you? You don't suppose that I'm to blame for Karen's death? That"—he banged the table with clenched fist—"that you'll have to prove, devil take me!"

The man so addressed was quite taken aback, and said no more; but one of the oldest men present tried to calm the angry fellow by assuring him that of course no one had said or thought any such thing. At that moment Vilhelm rushed out from his hiding-place, hit the table in front of the fellow a doomsday blow, and thundered, "You murdered her—I'll prove it." The horrified company jumped up from their seats, but the accused slipped down from the bench till only his face, pale as death, was visible above the table, and stammered with teeth chattering, "So I did—and I want to confess."

The gamekeeper had, of course, not been asleep, but had followed the conversation closely, and had made up his mind that the young man was the murderer. When he appeared so suddenly, like a ghost or an avenging angel, and shook the sin-burdened conscience, then the hardihood of the criminal was melted, his forced courage was crushed, his effrontery destroyed.

The man was bound and taken to the district judge, where he declared that the girl had been with child by him, that he was tired of her, and that her everlasting reproaches and threats to betray him—so as to prevent his intended marriage with another girl—had made him determine on her death. At a cer-

tain place in the woods, where a turn in the road hid his cart
and hers from those that followed, he jumped down, hit her
a deadly blow in the neck with the back of his woodman's axe,
then lashed the horses with his whip; and the animals, feeling
that no one was driving them, ran away at full speed.

The criminal suffered the punishment he had deserved, but
Vilhelm was generally regarded as one who "knew more than
his Our Father"—in other words, as something of a wizard.

It is not merely in order to characterize the leading person
in this true story that I have described the murder and the
scene of its discovery. Rather I have done so because I am inclined to believe that the latter had something to do with another death of which I shall presently tell. But now we must
go back with the gamekeeper to Aunsbjerg.

A few days after he had returned home, the counsellor was
sitting in the living room hearing me read my lesson, when his
wife came storming in. She left the door wide open, but when
she had reached the middle of the room, she stopped, threw out
both her arms, and stood there as if nailed to the floor, with
staring eyes and trembling lips.

"God help us, mamma," he said without getting up. "What's
the matter?"

"Mettë, Mettë!" she cried.

"What about her, mamma?" he asked quietly.

"Mettë is with child," she stammered in horror.

"Why, then, so help me"—that was his only form of swearing—"she must have had to do with a man."

"She must leave! Out of the house," she cried, "and that
right away! And he, too!"

"Who is the *he*, mamma?" he asked.

"The gamekeeper," she replied, "the gamekeeper, dear heart,
that wicked creature!"

"Dear mamma," he answered, "I do believe, so help me,
you're—I came near saying—Vilhelm is just as innocent as I
am."

"That's what you say, dear heart," she went on, "because

the wicked wretch has always stood so high in your favor. But he has owned it himself. I have long had a suspicion of the baggage, that all was not right with her. So I took her to task in the pantry, and when I pressed her, she confessed, but she would not on any account tell who was her paramour. But now listen, dear heart. As I was pressing her with all my might, the pantry door was opened, and who do you suppose appeared? Vilhelm, dear heart, and then he said—I didn't ask him, neither did the girl—then he said, 'If Mettë is getting ready for a birthday party, I'll take the part of the father of the child!'—What do you say to that, dear heart?"

The counsellor rose with an impetuosity I had never seen in him, saying, "I believe, we must be in the dog days—mamma, call them both in."

She hurried out; he threw the book on the sofa, and walked up and down the room with his hands on his back. The sinners came, she with face red from weeping, he with his usual quiet and serious aspect. Her ladyship stood behind them with both fists planted in her sides. The counsellor met them with *his* hands still on his back.

He hardly looked at the girl, but fixed his eyes on Vilhelm's unmoved face. "Man," he said after a pause, "I would not have believed such a thing of you—an old fellow—fifty if a day, I think—and that young child—"

"Mr. Counsellor," said the gamekeeper with undisturbed composure, "may I speak a few words to you in private, sir?"

The squire was silent for a few seconds, then he said, "Come," and went into an adjoining room. Vilhelm followed him; the door was closed.

No one could distinguish what they said to each other in there, for they spoke in low voices, and nothing was heard except an occasional, "So help me," from the squire.

While this secret negotiation went on—and I think it lasted half an hour—there was absolute silence in the living room. Mamma threw herself down on the sofa and looked, sometimes at Mettë, sometimes at the door of the other room. Mettë stood as if carved in wood, the tears rolling down her face, which grew paler and paler. I sat on my own little stool, looking in my book and wondering about what was going to come out of all this, which was just as mysterious to me as hieroglyphics now are to the learned.

When the squire came out from the secret negotiations, followed by his servant, he lifted his handkerchief to his nose— and I thought to his eyes, too. But Vilhelm's face had brightened.

"Mamma dear," said the squire, speaking slowly and hesitatingly, "these two are to be married very soon—for I suppose you are willing to have him, Mettë?" She curtsied, and bent her face still deeper. "And then we will not speak any more of the past, mamma! Vilhelm, there is a house right next to the blacksmith's up in Vium that's not leased—you can have that, and it won't hinder you from continuing your service with me."

The gamekeeper bowed, and said to his betrothed, "Thank the counsellor and her ladyship, Mettë." The girl hurried over to the squire and curtsied sobbing, first to him and then to the mistress, after which she tottered out of the room. The gamekeeper followed her slowly, but when he had reached the door, the squire called after him in a lively voice, "Oh, Vilhelm, take a look in the alder-bog and see if the snipes should have come last night. It's the twenty-first today." Vilhelm nodded with a quiet smile, and went out.

Aunsbjerg lies in Lysgaard district and belongs to the parish of Sörslev. The church has a historical association. It was there —so the story goes—that the Jutland nobles gathered for the deliberations which ended in their renouncing allegiance to Christian II, and Magnus Munk was by lot assigned to the dangerous task of apprising His Majesty of the resolution. But the churchyard has to me another and more vital interest, though this too has to do with the dead. There is—I hope it is there yet—a fairly large mound set about with hewn stones and furnished on the south side with an iron-work gate or wicket.

Beneath it rest the earthly remains of my youngest brother and sister who died in infancy, of the squire and his lady, and several others of our kin. But the first two were yet unborn and the last two were very much alive when we attended the wedding of Guillaume Marteau and Mettë Kjeldsdaughter in Sörslev church.

The newly married couple moved to Vium that same day. I remember, however, that Vilhelm, after escorting his wife to her new home, came back late at night, and I remember that this did not please my gracious grandmother, which puzzled me just as much as her anger when, a short time afterwards, he called his son by my name.

Soon everything went on as before, except that sometimes, when the weather was fine, I was allowed to go along on the hunt—that is, the kind of hunt in which the game is driven in by hounds or beaters to a hunter standing still in one place. I was now posted behind my grandfather, and always with the admonition not to stir. This order I obeyed in a much better spirit than I did when my "dear grandmother" set me down on my stool at home.

Just as Vilhelm, after his marriage, seemed to have risen still higher in the good graces of his master, so I rose in Vilhelm's favor because of my early-awakened love of the chase. But I must go on with my story, all the more as I am anxious to get that which is now coming over with.

It was a day in the autumn when the gamekeeper was ordered to ride out on the heath and shoot black cocks. He did not come back that evening; they thought he had stopped at Vium. But he didn't come the next day either. In the evening a messenger was sent up to his home—his wife had not seen him since the morning of the foregoing day, when on his way out he had passed by there and called at the house. Now grandfather began to worry and with good reason feared that an accident might have befallen him.

Two reliable men were sent out to search for him and inquire about him in the colonies. Toward noon on the following day they came back with the report that two days earlier he had stopped at Haverdale Inn, and the innkeeper said that he had gotten something to eat for his horse and dog and for himself, too, and that he had started in good time for Aunsbjerg. At that the squire himself mounted his horse and set out with the manager of the estate and a couple of under-gamekeepers. He was gloomy and anxious, and I already began to weep for Vilhelm.

To me it was a long day. Toward evening they returned, followed by two carts; on the first lay Vilhelm's lifeless body, on the second his dead horse, while his dog trailed along behind with drooping head and empty stomach. On the heath, where now the royal forest stands, there was at that time nothing but heather. The work of preparing the ground had begun, however, in the very year that the events just narrated took place. Even now the strip of heath first reclaimed for the cultivation of a forest, situated a couple of thousand feet from the ranger's house, is known as "the old plantation." In this strip, square pits had been dug, according to the rules of woodcraft, and the turf piled on the side. It was here that poor Vilhelm was found at last after long searching of the wide heath, which here is quite hilly. His pointer led the searchers to the spot.

After first trying to trace him in the colony and among the scattered heath-dwellers of Vium parish, and then in heathery valleys and turf pits, they suddenly heard the pitiful whine of a dog far in the distance. They rode in the direction of the sound, which was repeated at intervals; and when they came nearer, the counsellor exclaimed, "So help me, it's Vagtel!" Coming closer still, they caught sight of the white dog which now lifted its head and howled, now buried itself deep in the heather. They hastened to the spot—and there, among the pits in the newly laid-out plantation, they found hunter and horse, the man in front of the horse's head; and the dog by its side. It looked as though, through carelessness, the horse had stumbled, and the rider had been pitched over its head and had broken his neck. Both were beginning to putrify already. But the counsellor had his own opinion. He called on the officers of justice to make investigations, but nothing came of them. True, there was a hole in the chest of the horse, but that might have been made by a sharp stone; and moreover, the stench got worse and worse, and nobody could or would undertake a post-mortem examination of either.

The burial of the gamekeeper's body could no longer be postponed. I followed it to the grave where my dear father threw the first three spadefuls of earth on the coffin and pronounced the formula that consigns to corruption and transfiguration. But the grave was not filled up or the mound shaped till several days later, when the counsellor at last saw that all his efforts to find out anything were futile.

The horse was buried the same day in the home-field where it had been laid, and the dog—dear reader, whoever you are, do not take offense at the womanish weakness of an old and poor poet! And do not laugh at him, even if you think he is entering on his second childhood!—the dog Vagtel, my dearest playmate at serious Aunsbjerg, he who so many a time had shared my sandwiches with me, and more than once had found and brought back a lost handkerchief or glove, yes, I admit it freely, I wept over Vagtel, too. Was it because of Vilhelm? Possibly—I hardly know it myself. As long as the gamekeeper's body was unburied, the dog stuck close to it. He would have followed it to the grave, but was too feeble. When we closed the gate in order to keep him in, he dragged himself into the home-field and lay down by the grave of the horse. We set his favorite food before him—he turned his head away—he starved and grieved himself to death. He was buried near the horse. Grandfather, too, cried over him.

But there was one who wept even more than I—Vagtel was not alone in grieving himself to death over Vilhelm. Both while the grave was open and long after it had been covered with green turf, the widow would visit it every evening to mourn—weep she could not, for she had no more tears left. The grave was a little to the north of the church tower—I could go right to the spot now as unerringly as half a hundred years ago—there she sat leaning back against the wall, her hands folded in her lap, and stared in silent despair at the mound hiding the friend who had been torn from her in such a horrible manner. My father visited her every day, but his consolation found no hearing. "My only friend on earth!" was all she could say.

The child suffered from the mother's sorrow. It pined away, and three weeks after the father's death it was laid by his side. The loss of it seemed hardly to make any impression on the widow. She did not care about the little body, but gave it only an indifferent glance. Neighbor women had to dress it and prepare it for burial.

Hardly a month had passed before the mother was laid by her husband's other side.

❖

Nine years had gone by, and I was in the upper class preparing for entrance examinations to the University, when in the dog days I visited my great-uncle at Liselund, a small place under Aunsbjerg which he had saved as a home for his old age, when he sold the rest of the estate.

I had to give a report of my progress in scholarship and answer many other questions which the inquisitive old gentleman amused himself by putting to me. Our talk drifted back to old times, and each reminiscence from my childhood brought others in its train. It was not strange, therefore, that I recalled the events with which the reader is now familiar. I mentioned them, and expressed a desire for any possible information on matters that seemed to me obscure and even sinister.

The old man looked at me, blinking with his red-rimmed eyes. "Hm!" he said, "I hardly know whether it is good for you to know such things—and yet—perhaps. In God's name! I will reveal to you what I know; and then you will have to use your own common sense and draw a lesson from this miserable affair."

He sat silent yet a while with his chin resting on his breast, took his snuffbox, tapped the side of it with his finger three times—which is the proper way if one wants to take snuff gracefully—but he didn't take any; he held the box on his knee, lifted his face, looked fixedly at his favorite gun, which was hanging on the wall opposite him, and said:

"That fowling piece—well, now I don't use it much—my eyes are not so good any more—that piece has belonged to Guillaume de Martonnière—*de Martonnière!* Take note of that, my boy! I got it in exchange for another, which was really better, but didn't suit me so well, and into the bargain I gave him this powder horn that you see there, inlaid with silver— I bought it back at the auction after him. It is just nineteen years since he came from my brother-in-law at Hald to me. I have never had a better gamekeeper or a better man in my service." Here he wiped a tear from his eye, saying, "My eyes are running badly these days—it is a sign of bad weather coming. Fetch me the eye lotion, my boy; it's standing on the stove in there." I did so; he bathed his eyes, and went on, "You remember when he overwhelmed that murderer in Them Inn and by his fierce demeanor forced him to confess his crime?" I nodded. "But you probably don't know that that wretch was Mettë's sweetheart—you remember, the girl Guillaume married—and that he was the father of her child?"

"No!" I exclaimed, horrified.

"Hm!" he went on. "Weren't you in the house on the day when Mettë's condition was discovered by my poor, dear wife, and when he was closeted with me in the small room inside the parlor?"

"Yes."

"It was then he told me about himself and gave me a good clear account, which I shall now repeat to you. While the trial was in progress, Vilhelm had to go there several times in order to be confronted with the murderer. Shortly before sentence was to be pronounced, the judge admonished the criminal to confess anything else that he might have on his conscience.

Then for the first time he burst into tears, and was so over-whelmed with emotion that he could not speak. The judge told his secretary to dip his pen, but the sinner said, 'What I have to confess is something that only God in His mercy can punish me for, and it is of no use to write anything about it. And besides, I want to ask that I might be alone with the judge and this man';—it was Vilhelm—'otherwise I can't say a word.'— The judge granted his request. And then he revealed that his real sweetheart, whom he had meant to marry if the devil hadn't ensnared him, was Mettë Kjeldsdaughter, who at that time was our housemaid. For he had worked here, under my tenant Hansen, and had become good friends with her. Then it happened on Whitsunday that they had a merrymaking in the horse pasture here, as they have every year, and then she allowed herself to be seduced by him. Alas, my dear boy, sin— mark it well!—sin is the ruin of human beings. No doubt they would have been married, for he was genuinely fond of her, and the parents of both were well-to-do. But then it happened at a wedding which he attended in his home district that he also wronged another girl, her whom he afterwards murdered in order to marry Mettë. 'And now I beg and implore you,' he finally said to Vilhelm, 'you are the one who is sending me to gallow's hill, but that I can't complain of—I thank you for it—but I beg you for Jesus' sake that you will do whatever is in your power to comfort Mettë and help her in her great trou-ble and misery, and don't let anybody know that she has been got with child by such a criminal as I—unless it should be the Aunsbjerg squire, if you think it might benefit her.'

"Of course I was greatly shocked to hear it," the old man went on, "and asked him just what he meant to do. He passed his hand over his forehead, and said, 'I have robbed the girl of her lover—although that I can never regret—but she is inno-cent of his crime, and I owe it to her to make up for it as well as I can. Besides'—and here his face took on a look more gloomy than I have ever seen on it before or since—'besides'—

at this a shudder passed through him, and he walked quickly over to the window as if he needed a breath of air, then turned toward me, and said, 'Are you satisfied with my decision, Mr. Counsellor?'—I not only answered this question in the affirmative, but assured him that it increased my esteem for him. And so this brief and joyless marriage came to pass.

"Never as long as I live shall I forget the morning he was killed. Before he rode out he asked that he might speak with me. And he said very quietly and philosophically—as if he were talking about wind and weather—'Counsellor Steensen,' he said—he did not ordinarily add my name—'if today or another day something should happen to me, and I should not have a chance to speak with you again, I want to ask you, for the sake of the kindness you have always shown me, to comply with a request I have directed to you, and which you will find as the first thing in my pocket book. It lies in the middle drawer to the right in my escritoire, and here is the key.' This speech made me feel very uncomfortable—for surely, my boy, you don't doubt that there are such things as forebodings, and this one, as you know, was only too true! Well, I took the key, and explained to him the ground where I wanted him to shoot the black cocks that day. He rode away—"

Here the old man again had to resort to the eye lotion, and this time it seemed to require a longer time before it helped. At last he continued his story. "I had a suspicion from the first that he had met a violent death, and I also suspected who had perpetrated it, none other, in fact, than the brother of the first murderer. Not so much because Vilhelm had brought his brother to justice as because not long before he had caught the fellow poaching, and had taken his gun away from him. By the way, I forgot to tell you that the rascal had got himself a house out there in a spot very handy for that kind of traffic, and he came from a region, out there by Silkeborg, Them, and Mattrup, where people were in the habit of poaching—and still are, I dare say. What I supposed was this: Vilhelm, as he rode from Haverdale, skirting the old plantation, may have caught sight of the poacher, for it is a good place to lie in wait for the red deer when they come down to the water at Aaresvad, and he started after him, and when the scoundrel saw that he could not escape, he fired and hit the horse. But even if one had found the bullet in the half-rotten carcass, *whose* bullet was it?"

❖

I wept again after all these years for my dear Vilhelm, and when the old man saw it, he had to resort to the eye lotion again.

"But," he went on, "it was not till he had been laid out that I remembered the key he had given me, and opened his escritoire. Here—take my key, go into the bedroom there and open my writing-desk. In the bottom drawer in the center there is a folded paper tied up with a black silk string. Bring it here."

I fetched it.

"Take my spectacles—but, no—you can read it yourself, but aloud!"

I read, "If it should be the will of Providence that I should come to a sudden and untimely end, without having an opportunity, that is, to dispose of the things I have, I would ask Counsellor St. de Steensen to take charge of them as follows. My few books I will ask him to keep in memory of me. My clothes, my guns, and anything else that will bring money are to be sold and the proceeds given to my wife or, if she should be dead, to the little one, and if he too should be gone, to her next of kin. Finally, in a secret compartment there is a bundle of letters which the counsellor will please take into custody, and what is further to be done with them is stated in the package itself. To find the secret compartment it is only necessary to press with a sharp instrument such as an awl"—The rest was unreadable because of ink that had been spilled on it.

"The cat did that," said the old man. "It jumped up on

The Gamekeeper at Aunsbjerg 269

the table as I was reading and overturned the inkwell. But you see down below that he has signed his name Guillaume de Martonnière. So he was a nobleman. But the compartment I have never been able to find, however much I tried."

"But you still have the escritoire?" I asked.

"Yes, indeed I have it, for I bought it at the auction I arranged after his death. I have never been able to make up my mind to chop it to pieces, all the more as there was no sign of any secret compartment, for all the drawers seem to be equally large and to extend way to the back. If he has possessed the documents he mentioned, they must have been in some other place."

❖

So he ended, and so I must end. When he died, and his effects were sold, I was far away, and I don't know what became of the escritoire or whether it still exists. But if it does, and if anyone who reads these pages should know of it, he could do me, and possibly others, a service by letting me know. For I am convinced that the letters mentioned must be found in this piece of furniture, and that most likely they will give information about Guillaume de Martonnière's life and experiences before he came here and would reveal how this French nobleman came to end his days as a humble gamekeeper for a Jutland squire.

❖

Dear and highly-honored readers! Do not be wroth with me because this little story, which is scarcely more than an incident, is so fragmentary, obscure, and sad. Is not all our knowledge down here fragmentary? Is not all our wisdom obscure? And the greater part of our experience—yes, let it stand here—sad? Many a time in the days of my boyhood I have stood in Vium churchyard where Mettë had sat and looked at the graves of her husband and child. I have sat there when the sun went down in the northwest back of Lyshöj, and have listened to the sad song of the bittern over there in Bastrup parish. I sorrowed, too, but there was no bitterness in my sorrow, still less of doubt or fear. There was something, there was much, that resembled joy, that *was* joy. The animal does not sorrow, except perhaps in relation to human beings. Sorrow is the birthright of men.

AN ONLY CHILD

[*Eneste Barn,* 1842]

WHEN in the year 1815 I was in Copenhagen, I happened one day to be visiting the friend whom I have mentioned in my story "Eva." The doorbell rang, the door was opened, and in came, with a deep and elegant curtsy, a woman who, judging from her appearance, was a little more than middle-aged. Her entire costume was shabby genteel. There were holes in her hat and also in her dress, though they were small and had been carelessly drawn together. On the third finger of her left hand she wore a cheap ring which looked more like brass than gold. In her right hand she carried a parasol which had long since passed its days of beauty, as had its owner, whose long, thin, pale face matched her costume.

When you come across an acquaintance you instinctively seek to have eye meet eye. But of hers even the lower half evaded you; the immovable lids closed the windows of the soul —I mean the eyeballs, those round peepholes. She had been fairly tall, but had now shrunk a little; she was round-shouldered. When she spoke, she straightened up for a moment, but soon sank down again. She was begging; one could hear that she used a formula which she repeated by rote. A certain haughtiness that life had not yet beaten down was revealed in her speech and posture.

"I have not the honor to know you personally, sir," she said, "and you probably don't know me, but you can believe me when I say that I have seen better days than these"—a slight shrug of the shoulder accented this remark. "I have been told that you are a man of generous mind, and I venture to ask you for a contribution—in any amount you please—toward my rent."

He took two or three steps in the direction of his desk, but turned abruptly toward her with the question, "Your name, madam?"

She shuddered, bent her head, and lowered her lids till they hid the eyes completely, as she answered slowly and in a ghastly tone, "My name? I lost that long ago, and now I have almost forgotten it—as the rest of the world has forgotten me. I have received another, but it belongs to a large family—it is Care-and-Want." Here she wiped her dry eyes.

Without further questioning, Smith gave her a few bills. She curtsied, straightened up again, and left.

During this scene I had been looking at the genteel beggar woman with a strange feeling. It seemed to me that I knew— or had known—this face, this voice. But I could not fix the vague, dim memory either in time or place. Though I was awake, she seemed to me a dream picture, as when the imagination projects forms that we think we know, but when we try to grasp them, they change or vanish.

"Hm!—strange," said Smith. "She didn't want her name to be known. You looked so fixedly at her—do you know anything?"

"Hm!" I replied. "I have seen her before, but I can't think when or where. Did she go out?"

"I can see her out in the street," he said. "She's walking down toward the Church of Our Lady. If you want to find out anything about her, you'd better skurry."

I did so, caught up with her, and followed her, but at some little distance.

As she turned the corner of the bishop's residence, she took a paper from her pocket and, still walking, looked alternately at the paper and the numbers on the houses. When she had passed Crystal Street, she stopped for a few minutes, and then turned in at a doorway. I continued in the wake of the old sailer—up to the second floor. While she rang the bell, I went up another flight and peeped down between the balusters.

The door down there was opened. A servant maid came out and said pertly, "Oh, it's you. You call on us rather often, but my master and mistress have ordered me to tell you it's no use that you come before Saturday week—the first of the month, you understand—good-bye!" With that she slammed the door and bolted it.

The woman who was thus shut out tapped the floor with her parasol, stiffened her back, opened her eyes fully, stood there a few moments as if she were turning over important matters in her mind, and then walked—or rather tripped—rapidly down the stairs. I followed. She went back by way of North Street, turned into Crystal Street, and then into Peter Hvitfeld's Lane, where she entered a humble-looking house. I surmised that she lodged there, and found it to be so.

In the basement there lived a cheesemonger, whom I took to be the owner, or at least the person who by virtue of his business must be posted on the people in the house. He was not at home, but there was a woman who in answer to my question told me she was his wife. I made a purchase and asked her if such and such a person lodged there and who she was.

"Yes, she rooms here," was the answer, "but I can't remember what her name is. My husband knows, for he comes from the same place over in Jutland. I know only that he was born on the estate her father owned. He was a chamberlain or something like that, and a rich man, and she was an only child; but they say she behaved badly, married against her father's wish, and then ran away from her husband—serving strange gods, as the saying is. And now things are pretty bad with her; she always has a bill here, and the rent is never paid on time, but my husband is kind of easy on her, because they come from the same place.—There he is. Now he can tell you all about it."

"About what?" he asked.

"The gentleman," said the wife as she was about to go, "wants to know the name of the woman on the third floor to the left."

He looked hard at me, and said, "May I ask who you are?" I told him my name and where I was born. At that he became very friendly, struck the counter with the palm of his hand, and gave me the information I wanted. This, together with the story of the beggar woman's youth, on which I was much better posted than the cheesemonger, I retailed to Smith about as follows.

✧

As far back as my memory serves me, I remember Miss S——, and though I was a madcap when I could have my fling, it seemed to me that she was even more mad than I. She would take me on her lap, rock me, and kiss me, and then she said that when I got older I would understand such things. I didn't know what she meant, nor did I bother my head about it; but whenever I could I would escape to the room of her mother, who suffered a great deal from rheumatism and—as I have since thought—also from heartsickness; she always caressed me and always had sweets that she would put into my little mouth. I never saw her outside of her chamber until she was carried out in the well-known little black *porte-chaise*. Her husband, the chamberlain, did not stand nearly so high in my regard. When he turned his small green eyes on me, I felt a vague antipathy, although he never said a harsh word to me, but only played some little harmless tricks with me—and those not always of the most delicate kind, but I understood them as little as those of his daughter.

This old-fashioned nobleman was a veritable aristocrat: any peasant girl on the estate to whom he threw the handkerchief had to yield to him, and any peasant with whom he got angry would have it taken out on his back. Sometimes he would strike too hard, for he was strong, and once he got a lawsuit on his hands, because he had beaten a man so that he died of it. The case went all the way to the High Court. The chamberlain was acquitted, of course, and that was the end of that story. But I am going to tell another story, which also ended in death and destruction, but which was nevertheless very amusing.

At H. there was a herdsboy who could run and jump as if

he had learned it in Nachtigall's Institute. It happened one summer that the functioning bull all of a sudden went mad, broke his tether, and chased the other cattle and the horses, till they all ran amok in the squire's rye. He called together the men on the estate and promised a crown to anyone who could bring him the runagate dead or alive. The herdsboy said, "I'll try, but then the rest of you'll have to shut the gate when I get him in."

All the men armed with pitchforks, axes, and scythes and posted themselves to wait for the bull, while my good Thomas had already run him down in the rye field. He stuck out his tongue and boo'ed at the brute, which immediately went for him. Thomas's two feet were quicker than the bull's four, and several times he had to stop in order to lead it on. He succeeded; Thomas dashed triumphantly into the yard—the bull after him—and out on the dunghill, where it found a dirty death.

Thomas not only got his crown, but also a blue coat with silver braid and an even more dazzling cap. In other words, he became a running footman, and in this capacity conferred great credit on the chamberlain. The squire liked to drive fast, but Thomas could run still faster, and no matter how hard the coachman would drive, the running footman was always far ahead and sometimes would make circles around the carriage, cracking his whip as if he wanted to challenge both coachman and horses. In spite of his brilliant gifts, however, Thomas Runner would not have figured in this story if he had not done any other running than that in front of the chamberlain's carriage.

The time had come when our young lady was to be married. Papa had picked out a handsome young baron for her, who was a lieutenant to boot, and there was nothing to hinder the marriage except this: that the daughter had picked out someone else. It had happened so secretly that the squire knew nothing about it, and therefore could not understand why she objected to such a suitable match, for she hid the reason carefully.

Her secret choice was unfortunately nothing but a minister's son, but his uniform was blue and his beard was black, whereas the baron had only a few yellow wisps on his chin.

Our racer, Thomas, became the carrier pigeon of the lovers, and the office was the back of Niels Bugge's portrait in the vestibule.

But the correspondence was discovered—not the mail-carrier, however, for he ran between H. and W. when everybody else was sleeping. One day a learned historian and antiquarian arrived from Copenhagen, because he had heard of the abovementioned picture. The chamberlain himself showed it to him. The stranger looked for the painter's signature, and failing to find it on the right side, turned the picture around, and what should he find there but a little three-cornered billet-doux which didn't look in the least antiquarian. The chamberlain silently took possession of it. When the stranger had departed, the squire opened the letter, and thereby got full light on the state of his daughter's affection.

The coachman was instantly ordered to harness the horses to the carriage, and the young lady was told to get ready for a journey, and soon the four light bays were conveying the squire and his daughter to A. It was a polite prison in which the young lady was placed; the master and the mistress—her father's sister—were the keepers. But there was a slip: before the prisoner was out of the carriage, the running footman had been informed of the new post office which she had established on the way—the mouth of one of the wild men that stood as guards at the head of the front steps.

The baron arrived the very same day. Everything was very loving; she kissed him and caressed him, and no one could believe but that she was over head and ears in love. And so she was, but not with the poor baron.

The prisoner was confined to a chamber on the second floor, and the servants took turns keeping watch in the passage that led to the only exit and entrance door of the manor.

One morning when the master and mistress and my small

person were seated at breakfast, one of the servants entered with a handkerchief which he had found beneath the young lady's window.

"Take it up to her," said the master.

But the mistress, who had a finer scent, took the handkerchief from him and examined all the corners, while she allowed the servant to go. "Halloo!" she said, "That's not Lotte's handkerchief—see, there's a B. I'll wager that this Mr. B—— has been with her last night. You go out, dear heart, and look carefully in the garden and on the wall to see if there should be other signs of a secret assignation."

"Indeed I will, so help me," he said, and went out.

His search led to the following results: the dew had been brushed off, the grass trampled under foot; in a walk leading to the north wicket there were footprints in the sand pointing both ways; outside the wicket a horse had been tied and had trampled and scraped the ground with its hoofs.

"So help me!" he ended his account, "I'd rather watch a hundred goats than one young girl if she gets notions in her head. If you agree with me, mamma, we'll send her back this blessed day. Then your brother will have to look after her as best he can."

"Yes, dear heart, let us do that," she said. "But," she added, "would it not be safest that we accompany her? For if we send her away alone, who knows what she might do? And as for the coachman and the servants, we can't trust them."

"You're right, mamma!" he replied. "The worst is, how are we going to get her away from here decently?—for I'm certainly not going to use force. It's the first time I've undertaken to act as guard, and so help me, it'll surely be the last."

"Let Steen go up to her," said the mistress, "and ask if she would like to take a ride to H." I went, and yes, she would like to go, and she came down dressed for the trip before the old people were ready. Nothing was said about the suspected window-climbing, and we drove off, the four of us.

About midway between A. and H. there is a little town, the

name of which I don't care to give. In the town lived a clergy-man whose garden stretched down to the road that we had to travel. As we approached, we saw the pastor's gardener—who seemed a very courteous man, a Copenhagener. He was pick-ing flowers and tying them together in bouquets. He seemed not to notice us till we had come just opposite him. Then he greeted us, jumped over the ditch, and came close to the car-riage, while he asked the coachman to stop.

"May I have the honor," he exclaimed, "to offer your lady-ships some of my ten weeks' stock? I believe you will hardly find as perfect ones anywhere else in Jutland." They thanked him and accepted the gift of flowers. "When you come to the town," he added, "where you will perhaps spend the night, it would be well if the bouquets were loosened and the flowers separately put into wet sand; in that way they keep much longer. Perhaps her young ladyship would undertake to do that —it is well worth the trouble."

He said this with a rather serious face and with a look at the young lady which I did not then understand, but of a kind that I am now old enough to have seen quite a few. I am usually able to detect in a pair of eyes if there is an important secret within them.

Our young lady was much pleased with her nosegay; she smelled it every few minutes, fingered the flowers and praised them, as we drove along. Once when she pulled a little more at them, I saw something white in the middle of the posy, but she covered it up again at once.

"Why!" said I in my childish innocence, "I think there's a white carnation in the middle of it."

"Carnation—nonsense!" she said smiling, and hid the bou-quet on her bosom. But it seemed to me that her stays were not strong enough to hold the flowers, for they rose and fell— and that I couldn't understand.

Nor did I bother my head long with the matter. There were other things to occupy my attention: the picturesque and varied landscape, which I will not describe here, but which anyone can allow his imagination to paint in green, yellow, light blue, and brown colors, and to mould in high hills and deep dales.

The chamberlain was surprised and displeased when he saw us; he murmured something that I didn't understand. "You can go into your room for a while—and take the child with you," he said to his daughter.

We went. In there, she whispered quickly and, I might say, confidentially, "Take that glass and fill it half full of the white sand, you know, and bring me."

I took the glass and ran. As I turned at the door to shut it, I saw that when she cut the string that held the flowers together, a little piece of folded paper fell out; but she caught it in mid-air with one hand, while with the other she threw the flowers pell-mell on the window sill.

I fetched the sand she asked for and came in again. As I opened the door, I saw that she pressed a piece of paper—the same, no doubt—to her lips and when she saw me, dropped it in her bosom.

"Did you see anything, you little scamp?" she asked, as she fluttered over to me and bent her face down to mine.

"I saw you kissing a strip of paper, nothing else," I replied.

"Not at all," she said, "I was only smelling it, because it smelt so nicely of the flowers—and besides you're not to tell any human being what you happen to see in here; for—see, here are two macaroons, and you shall have more if the little mouth doesn't tattle."

(I promised—and have kept my promise till now, that is a little over half a century. My listeners must not therefore mind if I speak freely of an incident which is many thousand years old and yet will be new as long as the world stands. The bag has been opened and the contents will out.)

"Listen," she went on. "I am not well, and I am going to bed now. In a little while you can come back and read to me from *Siegvart* as you used to; the part where Kronhelm carries off Therese—it's so sweet. And now go down to father and talk with him about the bays."

I went down and talked about the bays, both that day and the next. And the baron joined in—for he was a cavalry officer. Sometimes he and the chamberlain went to see the sick young lady, but when they came she was always sleeping. (It was funny, when I came alone she was always awake.)

When I was about to go, she would say, "Try to get hold of Thomas Runner, and ask him if he hasn't got anything for me." I did so, but he didn't have anything before the evening of the second day after the young lady got sick. Then he gave me such a queer letter; it was not folded in the usual way, but in the shape of a bowknot. It must have been a remarkable letter, for as soon as she had read it, she was well again, jumped out of bed, and dressed herself. I asked if I shouldn't read from *Siegvart*, but she said, "Never mind him! I have another Siegvart—he'll be coming soon. Wait—stay here with me! Here's the whole box of macaroons."

I tackled the macaroons. She packed dresses and clothes and ornaments into a valise, while she looked out of the window every minute. When I had finished the macaroons, I looked out of the window, too, in order to see what it was. And there came a carriage with four bays—but they were not the chamberlain's, nor was the coachman his.

The young lady slammed the valise shut, took the key, and grasped my hand. "Come with me," she cried, "and help to receive the visitors." She ordered her maid, who was standing in the passage, to carry down the valise and put it in the entry.

Just as we arrived there, the carriage drove up to the front door, and the chamberlain came out to us. He started when he saw his daughter, and in travelling dress. "What does this mean, Lotte? Are you so well now?"

"Yes, papa, now I have quite recovered," she cried with an arch smile.

In the same moment the visitors—a man with a yellow key on his right coat tail just like our chamberlain, and two others without keys—stepped in through the door.

The strange chamberlain greeted ours with an ironic smile,

and began, "In accordance with His Majesty's royal order, and by virtue of the authority vested in me——"

"I don't care a straw for the authority vested in you!" Chamberlain S—— interrupted him angrily. "But where is His Majesty's order? And what is the import of it?"

"The order is here," replied the other, as he took out a big document through the first page of which shone the red seal of His Majesty.

Our chamberlain reached after it, and bellowed out, "Let's see!"

"Your worshipful honor," said the other with a malicious smile, "is hardly in such a state of mind that I venture to entrust His Majesty's letter directly into your hands. But if you will allow the young lady your daughter—whom the order especially concerns—to step this way, I will read it aloud in her presence and yours, and will furthermore allow these witnesses to examine it."

"Call the young lady!" he thundered at a servant standing at some distance, and she herself came from the opposite direction, dressed for the journey and carrying a small bundle in one hand. Her father looked her over from head to foot once or twice, and said gruffly, "Whither away, mademoiselle?"

The stranger took upon himself to answer for her, and said with affected solemnity, "Inasmuch as the two parties concerned are now both present, I will read His Majesty's communication which has been entrusted to me and which is as follows: 'Upon the humble supplication of Lieutenant B—— of our Royal Navy, alleging that he, being engaged to Miss Ch. S——, has learned that the father of said young lady Ch. S—— keeps her in dire captivity in order to force her against her will to marry another, you are to investigate and find out the true foundation of this complaint, and furthermore you are to confront the father with the daughter and from her obtain a statement regarding the alleged captivity, and particularly to learn which of the two rivals she chooses. If it should be the supplicant, Lieutenant B——, and if it should be her firm resolve to be united in marriage with him, then in case the father does not willingly allow her to go, you are to remove her with the aid of the civil and military power, which we graciously put at your disposal.' "

While this document was being read, our chamberlain clenched first one hand, then the other, and then held both stiff arms slantwise along his hips, exactly in the posture assumed by an old-fashioned prizefighter. When the stranger, having finished reading, was about to hand the document to him, he gave it a fillip with his right forefinger, and began to stamp with one foot and then with the other—his fat little body looking not unlike a statue trembling in an earthquake.

"Well!" said the other with unchanged sunny expression, "and you, Miss, what do you want to do? You are free to choose."

"You're not going to run away from your father?" shouted the father to the daughter.

"She won't have to run," the strange chamberlain said, "for she can ride with me—if she wants to. Are you going to stay here, or may I offer you my arm?" She accepted it and bowed to her father.

"Then go, you trollop, go to the end of the world with your ruffian sailor! But don't dare ever to set your foot within the limits of your paternal estate. It's lost to you. You're disinherited."

With that, father and daughter parted. They had seen each other for the last time.

The chamberlain did not go to bed till morning. Sometimes he would write, sometimes he would walk up and down in his bedroom, now with firm, quick steps, now slowly like one who is brooding or who has just risen from an illness. Though he had not eaten anything since the day before, he at last threw himself down on the bed without undressing, rang for his servant, and asked to be wakened in two hours. At the appointed time the servant went in, but was unable to waken him; for he was dead. A sudden stroke had ended his wicked life and

choked his plans for vengeance in their birth. The hated son-
in-law became his heir.

The latter never established residence at H., but would visit
it every summer to look after the management of the farm and
the estate and to go through the accounts. His wife never
accompanied him; she preferred to remain in the capital, where
of course she could amuse herself better. Perhaps the disinclina-
tion of Mrs. B—— to revisit her birthplace and native country
moved her husband after a few years to sell the entire property.
This transaction and the many details that had to be settled
on the estate kept him there longer than usual.

When he returned, he found his house, his children, and his
servants, but his wife he didn't find. It was lightly come and
lightly go.

Whether time had hung heavy on her hands while her husband was away, or whether she had gotten tired of him—
which I think most likely—however that might be, she had
acquired another lieutenant to pass the time. But a few days
before she expected the right lieutenant to come home, the two
had absconded with all the precious metal they could find in
the house—people thought they had gone to Sweden. At least,
a friend of mine told me the following tale:

"In the summer of 1805 I was in Christianstad on business
for our house. There I met one day the lieutenant who had
absconded with Mrs. B—— a few weeks earlier. I had known
him well in Copenhagen, and had lent him money now and
then—which I never got back. 'Is that you, R——?' he exclaimed. 'What are you doing here? Come home with me and
see how I live!' I went with him and saw that he lived in
a small way, but fairly well. He went over to a door and called
out through the crack, 'Madam, may I ask you to bring breakfast for two?'—I expected to see Mrs. B——, but this was
quite another person, and when she brought the breakfast, I
heard her speaking Swedish. When she had gone out and
closed the door after her, L—— made a wanton grimace, and

said, 'She's neither among the youngest nor the handsomest, but she's a dependable friend—you understand?'—'I understand you well enough,' I replied, 'but I thought you had an older friend.'—'Ah,' he said, 'have had—yes. You knew Mrs. B——, —there was no getting along with her. She'd run away from her father and from her husband, and so she ran away from me, too, the devil.'—'Whom did she run with this time?' I asked, 'and where is she now?'—'She ran back to Denmark with a counterjumper, who had filched some cash from his employer, but what happened to her after that—I don't know anything about. Have a drink!' "

❖

About ten years later I had occasion to visit H. Alas, what a change!

The old aristocratic manor with its solid foundation was gone, and a half-timbered house with thatched roof was now the modest dwelling of the middle class owner. Within the house one was constantly reminded of the mutations of everything human. "Now" is never the same as "before." "New" is joined to—or rather apart from—"old." Here it was like grandparents in the company of grandchildren: a ponderous oak press in the fashion of bygone days confronting a little mahogany bureau; an ottoman with gilding—mostly worn off—on its wooden frame and leather seat opposite a sofa with veneered woodwork and home-woven cushions; and some large paintings of unknown, long since forgotten gentlemen and ladies interlarded with and abutted by copperplates representing the battle of April Second or Napoleon's victories.

I went out into the garden—there was none! All the old fruit trees had disappeared, flowers and herbs had given way to rye, barley, oats, cows, and sheep. I ran down to the lake, where in my boyhood I had angled from a balcony overhanging the water—there was no balcony, there was no boat—there was nothing but water and the woods on the other side. I thought I

could still hear faint echoes of the salutes that used to introduce
the festivities I had so often attended in my boyhood years. All
was still. I paid my childhood memories the tribute of a long,
dreary sigh, and thought: There will come a time when you
too are still.

THREE HOLIDAY EVES
A STORY OF JUTLAND ROBBERS
[*De tre Helligaftener, En jydsk Röverhistorie,* 1841]

EASTER EVE

IF YOU, dear reader, have ever been on Snabs Hill where the assizes were held in olden times, and if you have looked toward the south, you may have seen a scattered little hamlet called Uannet. None but peasants live there now or have lived there in the past.

A couple of hundred years ago there lived a man called Ib. What his wife's name was I have never been able to find out, but so much I know that he had an only daughter whose name was Maren, and for everyday use they called her Ma-Ibs. She was a comely and dapper young woman, and wherever she went the young men looked after her, but she had eyes only for Sejer. He, too, was an only child, and his father, too, lived in Uannet.

As I was about to tell you, it happened on Saturday before Easter that a stranger called at Ib's house. He was dressed as a peasant, was well-grown and strapping, and had an air of assurance; his age might be about thirty. There was no one at Ib's who knew him, but he said he was a Wood-Louning,[1] that he had lately leased his father's farm, and that he was on his way north to see about selling his charcoal. The silver buttons on his coat and vest showed well enough that he was no beggarly lout. Well, they gave him both food and drink, and while he was eating he talked of one thing and another.

So then he said to Ib, and smirked a little as he said it, "My mother's getting old, and it's about time I get someone in. Can't you put me on the track of a handy woman? It doesn't matter so much about money, we can always agree on that, but she

---

[1] A man from the wooded region of Lou near Silkeborg.

must have a pair of brisk, capable hands, and she oughtn't to be too old either."

Ib didn't let on that he understood; he scratched himself behind the ear, and said, "Hm, such a one doesn't grow up from the heather-tufts every day." He glanced at his daughter, and simpered slyly. But the daughter was none too well pleased with such talk, and made an excuse to leave the room.

When the stranger was about to go, they asked him what his name was. "Oh," he said, "my father was called Ole Breadless, and I suppose I'll have the same name." With that he left, but when he had gone a little ways, he met Ma-Ibs, who had been over to Sejer's, and he said to her, "It's no use handing out a lot of talk. I am here to see you and for nothing else. At Whitsun I'll be back, so you can think it over in the meantime. And now, good-bye."

Ma-Ibs was not very happy about that suitor. When she came in, she took a seat at the lower end of the table, crossed her hands on her lap, and sighed from the bottom of her heart.

"What's the matter?" asked her father.

"I don't like that Wood-Louning—or whatever he is," she replied. "Can't Sejer and I ever get married?"

"On what?" said the old man. And that was the end of that. Father and daughter both took their knitting.

A little later Sejer came in. "God's peace," he said.

"Thanks," said they.

"Now I am going up to the house," said he, "to talk to the squire, for it's no use beating about the bush any longer."

"It won't do any good," said Ib. "The squire is set against you, and he'll perhaps send you for a soldier."

"That may be," said Sejer, "but anyway we'll put it to the test." With that he went away.

Now when he came to Aunsbjerg and went in at the gate, he met the squire himself. The squire's name was Jörgen Marsviin.

"Have you come to see about leasing a farm again?" he said. "It's no use—I've told you that so many times."

"Oh, please, master," said Sejer, "I beg you—"

The squire looked angrily at him, drew his eyebrows together, and frowned. One might have thought he was ready to fly at the man and beat him. But then he seemed to think better of it, and his face took on a milder expression, as he said, "Listen! You have heard about the robbers that have been plundering and killing people so long. They're said to have their den somewhere here on the heath. If you can hunt them down for me and bind them, you shall get your lease and not have to pay a penny for it. And you shall marry Ma-Ibs, and on top of that I'll let you take a cart and two horses out of Aunsbjerg. Now you know my mind."

"Then God have mercy upon me," said Sejer, and slunk away, looking very downcast. He didn't eat anything that night, and Ma-Ibs was none too happy either. It was a miserable Holiday Eve for them both.

WHITSUN EVE

So then the time passed as best it might from Easter to Whitsuntide, and with the two young people things were very much as they had been; they were not utterly downcast, for they put their faith in the future and in Him who is the Lord of the future.

Whitsun Eve Sejer went over to Ib's—as he often did, I dare say—to ask if his sweetheart might go with him to Aunsbjerg wood the following afternoon when they came from Sörslev church. For it was an old custom in those parts—and is yet, I dare say—that on the first day of Whitsuntide the young people would gather in the woods for a dance. The Saturday in question Sejer found his sweetheart already decked out in her best.

"Good-day, Maren," he said, "what's going to happen that you're so fine today?"

"It came over me," she said, "that perhaps I should go up and see the mistress and get her to say a good word for us to the master."

"Hm," he said, "that might turn out well. I'll go with you and wait outside while you're in the house."

While she went up to the manor, he sat on a stone by the driveway. As he was sitting there, a cart came from the woods with a huge oak log that was going to the sawmill. But the horses were small and worn out, and right outside the gate they stopped. The man—it was a peasant who was doing his socage-service—whipped the poor nags, but they couldn't budge the cart. Then the forester came, and he grumbled, and then the bailiff, and then the honorable and well-born Jörgen Marsviin himself. And they all scolded the peasant for coming to do his socage with such miserable jades—I dare say they were the best he had.

Sejer sat and looked at this, and now and again he smiled to himself at the fuss they were making.

The master noticed it, and said, "What are you grinning at?"

"It looks to me," he said, "that the load isn't so heavy but that I could pull it alone."

"Hey, unharness the horses!" cried the squire to the driver. And when that was done, he turned to Sejer, "Now you take hold! and if you can pull the cart, I'll give you what's on it, but if you can't, you shall take a ride on the wooden horse."

The young man began to excuse himself, saying that he was only joking. But the master said that he would teach him not to joke in his presence, and it was one or the other.

"Well, if I must, I must," said Sejer. With that he went over to the cart, took off the pole, grabbed the traces, bent forward, and tugged—and the cart moved; but his wooden shoes were splintered, so hard did he set his feet on the ground.

"You're no weakling," said the squire, and for the matter of that he was none himself; for they still tell of him that he could catch hold of an iron ring in the crossbeam over the gate and lift his horse up from the ground with his legs. "Now take the log, but you'll have to get it home yourself. And as for the lease, we'll see about it."

Happy was Sejer! He thanked the squire, rolled the log off the cart, sat down on it, and looked in through the gate after his Maren. He waited and waited, and when at last she came, she looked woebegone.

"God help us miserable people!" she said, and she could hardly speak for weeping. "We can never get married."

"That's bad tidings you're bringing," said Sejer. "The squire just now half promised me—what's got into him?"

"And the mistress the same," she said. "But now I'll tell you what bad luck I had. Just as I came up the steps and into a narrow hall, I met a bigwig, and he looked closely at me—I couldn't get past him, for he stood in front of me—and then he said, 'You're'—and how he swore!—'the prettiest maid or wife, whatever you are, I've seen in the country. Listen, will you love me?'—'No,' I said, 'I mayn't.'—'If you will,' he said, 'then you may. I am Baron'—now I don't remember what he called himself. 'You just come here this evening, my servant will be on the lookout for you and take you in to me.'— 'No,' I said, 'it would be a sin, and besides I have a sweetheart, and I can't be unfaithful to him.' Then he took out a handful of money and jingled before me, but I slipped past him and in to the mistress. She was very gracious to me, and the squire came in, and it seemed that he was going to grant what I asked. But then that baron had been listening at the door, and he came in and said, 'If it's a decent fellow she wants to marry, he ought not to take her, for she's a shameless creature; I saw how she stood and flirted with one of the servants out there in the hall.' So after that wretch had lied about me, the squire and the mistress scolded me and told me to be gone and never show myself there again."

"Good God, Maren," said Sejer, "is that all you get for your honesty and your faithfulness to me? Poor girl! But God still lives. We'll not be downcast; I feel sure somehow that we'll get married yet—even if there were as many lords and ladies as there are leaves on the trees in Aunsbjerg wood."

Ma-Ibs sighed as if her heart would break, but answered

nothing. She hardly spoke till they came to Uannet and were about to part and go their separate ways. Then she said, "Good-night, Sejer, and thanks for today."

"Thanks yourself, Maren," he said. "You're having a bad time for my sake. I don't know how I'm ever to make it up to you—but Our Lord will."

"Do you want to go to the dance tomorrow?" the girl asked.

"Do you?" he turned her question back.

"No," she said, "I don't care for it."

"Neither do I," he said.

"Then good-night," she said and held out her hand.

"Good-night yourself," he said, and so they parted.

But there was more trouble waiting for poor Maren before she could get to rest. When she came home, there sat the Wood-Louning, Ole Breadless. "Well, here you are, my little girl," he said. "Have you thought it over?"

"Thought over what?" she said.

"Have you forgotten that?" he said. "It's no longer ago than last Easter—it was about moving to my place. And see here! So you shan't think I'm courting you with small beer and dry bread, I'll give you this for a betrothal gift," and with that he pulled out a heavy silver necklace with a heart of silver hanging from it. "If you'd known the one who wore it when she was alive, you wouldn't have called her a barefoot wench." With these words he made such a strange sign to the father that the daughter was gripped by a secret terror. The old man looked startled and hardly knew whether he could believe his own eyes. Neither of them said a word.

"Well, do you want it?" repeated Ole.

"No," stammered the girl, and was about to run out to seek comfort from her sweetheart. But the terrible suitor caught her arm with one hand, and putting away the necklace with the other, he said, "When I come a third time, I won't take No for an answer." And without further farewells he picked up his cap and stick and went his way.

"Here's the boy with the cows," said Ib, and sat down on

a three-legged stool. Ma-Ibs went out to do the milking, but she didn't sing as she usually did at this work. Sejer was watering his father's horses, but he didn't whistle as he was in the habit of doing. It was a miserable Holiday Eve for them both.

CHRISTMAS EVE

It was twilight when an old beggar came tottering and dragging himself to Uannet to ask for a little something in God's name. So then he also came to Ib's. They told him to sit down by the kitchen door and promised they would give him something to eat and a little in his bag.

When he had eaten, he began to groan about how late it was and how cold; he didn't see how he was going to walk farther that day, and he asked the people to let him stay overnight. They consented and told him to lie down in the oven which was still a bit lukewarm from the baking, and there the old fellow crawled in.

It was getting late. They had eaten their sweet porridge and whatever else they had; the animals had received their extra feed; the outside door had been barred, and they had sung a Christmas hymn, as usual, and were getting ready to go to bed. But now you shall hear what the old beggar did. He crawled out of the oven, pulled the bar from the door, and unhooked it, and no sooner had he done so than five tall, sturdy young men entered the room, and the beggar with them, and now he could step on the floor as firmly as any of them. For, you must know, it was the robbers whom the Aunsbjerg squire wanted Sejer to hunt down and bind; and the beggar was the father of the other five.

Things looked bad for the poor folk at Ib's. The man and his wife and daughter thought their last hour had come, and were so shaken with fear that they hardly had wits left to beg for their lives.

The biggest and oldest of the young robbers—and he was none other than the Wood-Louning—was the spokesman, and said, "Now first dish up whatever you have, and we can talk about the rest later."

Ma-Ibs lifted the latch of the door, but the robber said, "You just stay here and let the old woman wait on us. You might take it into your head to run away, and we want to have a little sport with you after we've had something to eat and drink."

The girl sat down on a chair and almost fainted with fear. Ib sat on the bed and prayed to God who has power to save whom He will. The old woman set out on the table everything they had of food and drink, and it was all she could do to keep up.

But now you shall hear the rest of the story. Ib had a herds-boy, a half-grown little chap. He was sleeping in a turn-up bed behind the stove, and heard everything. Without making a noise, he pulled on his breeches and stockings, and sneaked out behind the old woman as she went into the kitchen to light the candle, which one of the robbers had accidentally put out. And he ran over to the neighbor's and in to Sejer and told him what was happening at home.

Sejer lost no time making his plan. "Take that mouse-eared horse of ours," he said, "and ride like a streak to Aunsbjerg. Tell them what's happening and tell them to come as fast as they can; then maybe they can catch all the robbers before they leave."

The boy out, and up on the horse, and away!

Sejer seized a heavy oaken flail and ran over to Ib's. There sat all six scoundrels on one bench with their backs to the windows. "What kind of a fellow are you?" they cried to him. "Maybe you want your stomach ripped up!" At that they were just about to jump up and catch him. But he was too quick for them, grabbed the table top, tipped the oak table over them, and squeezed them against the wall with the edge of it. "Now I'll see if I can squeeze your stomachs," he said; and while he held them fast with one hand, he swung the flail and prom-ised he'd break any arm that stirred. The oldest of them tried to push the table back, but instantly got such a whack across his arm that it hung limp. After that they all sat quiet as mice and only begged Sejer please not to squeeze quite so hard.

Now Ib's courage came back; he grabbed an axe and took his place at Sejer's one side, and on the other his sweetheart stood with a poker. Such was the state of things, and it was not very cheerful for either side. The robbers were tortured by fear of how this terrific squeeze was going to end, and they were at a loss to understand what the visitor meant to do or how long it would last—which made the agony all the greater. Ib and his daughter were equally uncertain, for of course Sejer couldn't blurt out the story of what he was waiting for. And you may trust me, it was a long wait; for if the people from the manor should delay too long or shouldn't come at all—the boy might have been thrown from his horse—what then?

At last they came, the Aunsbjerg squire with seven or eight men, and he was not the hindmost when the door flew open. But there they stood. The room was quiet, and although there was a moon outside, they couldn't see anything plainly in the house, for the candles had been tipped over with the table.

Then Sejer cried, "Where have you got the pine-sticks? Light a couple of them on the hearth."

"There are some in the wood box," said the old woman.

They were lit and illuminated the room.

"There you can see, master," said Sejer. "Now I've found them and bound them, too—in a way. If you want them better tethered, there's a coil of rope over in that corner, I see."

They took the rope, and cut it into as many pieces as there were robbers. And then they dragged them out from under the table one by one, tied their hands behind their backs, tied their feet together also, and threw them on the floor in a row. Then the squire began to ask them questions: where they came from, where they had their den, if there were more of them, and so on. But he couldn't get so much as half a word out of them, though he threatened them with gruesome tortures.

Then the old robber said—not to the squire, but to his sons,

"Let him do what he will, for now he has the power. But as he does to us, so it shall be done to him and his. The three in the hill at home won't forget either him or the good folks in Uannet. And now you keep your mouths shut till the rope opens them."

But this threat was of no avail, for when the Christmas days were over, Jörgen Marsviin put them on the rack, first the old man, and then the young fellows. They all held out except the youngest. He confessed all their crimes and told where their cave was. That very same day it was searched and the robber wife and her two remaining sons were taken. They were hanged together with the other six. In the cave were great piles of silver and gold, and among the things was a ring that was recognized as belonging to the baron whose lying charges had done so much harm to Ma-Ibs. Now she got her reward. The squire himself held the wedding for her and Sejer; he did all he had promised them, and in addition gave them a number of the things that had been found in the robbers' den.

Strong-Sejer (by which nickname he was known afterwards) lived with his wife for many, many years. Their children and children's children after them kept the nickname. But now it has probably died out, just like the name and the whole noble family of the strong squire.

But the Holiday Eve I have told about ended happily at Aunsbjerg, and most happily of all at Uannet.

BRASS-JENS

[*Messingjens*, from *E Bindstouw*, 1842]

RASMUS OWSTRUP, in his turn, told the following story:

As I was just saying, it was the time of the war, when the British had made such a to-do in Copenhagen; so then I wasn't let stay home either. The recruiting officer came and ordered me to the Session, and there they put me in a regiment of horse. I learned to ride and to kill people. But we didn't get any beatings, for I tell you how it is; they only beat us in peace time, but when there's a war on they're afraid we might turn on them. In peace time they've got the upper hand, but in war we've got it—that's the difference. I brought lots of good food in my bag when I came to the school, and I got more from home later, and that didn't do me any harm with the sergeant who drilled me. I got to stand well with him and with the captain, too.

So one day I'd given the sergeant a sausage and a couple of cheeses—for he was a married man, you must know—and then he said "Listen, do you know Brass-Jens?"—" 'Twould be strange if I didn't know him," said I. "He's the best horse in the regiment."—"Now," said he, "Watrup who rides him is sick, and it looks as if he's going to die."—"That may well be," said I.—"If you want Brass-Jens," said he, "I'll try to get him for you, but then you must remember my wife."—"I'll remember her," said I, "with a leg o'mutton and a bit o' bacon, if I can get Brass-Jens. And besides I'll give her a score of eggs and a couple o' pounds of butter as soon as my mother comes to see me."—"Agreed," said he. And sure enough, I got Brass-Jens, though it was quite a fracas, for everybody wanted him—but after all he couldn't carry more than one at a time.

The first time I went to take him, he certainly looked at me as if he wanted to ask me: what kind of a fellow are you? But

I talked sense to him, and told him that Watrup was in the hospital and not likely to get out of it, and the sergeant had said I should ride him, and it was no use to set himself against it. That he understood—for all those who knew him said he alone had as much sense as two cuirassiers. And it was true; all he lacked was that he couldn't talk, and that wasn't his fault.

I'll never forget when I told him that Watrup was so poorly; then the horse sighed just like anyone else. I tell you, we two had a lot of talk together, and to everything I said he would neigh or he'd whinny or he'd snort, and I always understood what he meant.

As I was going to tell you, we went down south, and we marched one day and another day, and then we got just a little tired of riding, and got a little sore in the part that's uppermost when you're picking chips. So the men got down and walked, now and then, with the bridle rein thrown over their arm. I walked, too, but I let Jens take care of himself. He followed me very faithfully, and if anyone came too near him, he would neigh—he had the spirit of a stallion—and would both bite and kick.

Well, then, we came to a village down near Aabenraa, and I got my quarters with a farmer. He was well-to-do, but he was a stingy dog, and we hardly got enough to eat. But then there was one of the daughters—he had six of them—and I liked her and she liked me, too, for the matter of that, and she gave me a good extra portion that same evening; and the next day—for we stayed over there—she was still kinder to me and wanted to do everything she could for me. The second morning when we were going to start, she came out in the stable where I was busy currying.

"Rasmus," said she, "now you're going to leave, and then it's hardly likely we'll see each other again."

"It might happen," said I.

"No," said she, "you may lose your life, or you may get a sweetheart out there."

"Do you know," said I, "whether I live or die, I don't want any sweetheart unless you'll be it, Hellë!"

"God help us," she said. "My mother'll never let me, and not my father either. They have picked out someone else for me."

"Hellë," said I, "if you really mean it that you'll come to me, then wait for me a little while and see if I get back. I'll soon have my discharge and my father's farm, too, and then we'll get married, if you're willing to run away from here and follow me to my home."

Then she put her arms around my neck and kissed me, and cried a little, and slipped out again.

Brass-Jens looked after her, and I put saddle and bridle on him and rode away with the others.—It was a bad time we had; sometimes we got something to eat and sometimes we didn't, but I always divided my bread—when I had any—with Jens; and just as soon as we came to quarters I took care of him first of all with straw and with oats, and with anything else I could find for him, sometimes rye and sometimes barley and sometimes wheat, just as it happened.—We went far away. I don't know where we were, but we didn't see anything of the war. After a long time we got orders to go home.

Hellë had hardly been out of my thoughts on the whole march. When we came near enough to see her village, I rode over to our captain and told him how things had happened when I was there last, and what we had in mind to do, and I asked him for leave to take the girl along. "Brass-Jens," said I, "can carry us both easy, and I know he'll do it with right good will."

The captain smiled and said, "You're a devil of a fellow, but how do you think you'll get away with stealing a girl like that? They'll follow right on your heels and take her away from you. You'll pay dear for it—and I can't save you."

"That'll be no trouble," said I. "I'll give her my stable clothes to put on, and then nobody'll know her. I'll tell our boys and anybody else who asks that it's a sick dragoon from Fyn who had been left behind in the village there."

"Very well, you rogue," said he, "I'll talk to the colonel and get him to consent. But I won't give away your trick; I'll make him think it's Brass-Jens himself who out of pure compassion insisted on taking the sick dragoon on his back."

Everything went off as it should. We rode into the village, and there big and little were standing outside the gates and doors to wish us welcome. I looked for Hellë—yes, sure enough, she was there, and when she caught sight of me and I greeted her with my sword, her whole face shone as if she'd been out hiring maids, as the saying is.

I didn't let on anything; I said good-day to old and young, but I made no difference. When we'd had our supper (and it was nothing but buckwheat mush and poor at that, and nothing but thin half-sour milk to dip it in) then I went out to feed my horse—I'd stolen a piece of bread out of the drawer under the table.

Jens whinnied when he saw me and smelt the bread.

"Now I'm giving you this over and above your ration," said I. "D'you s'pose then you can stand to carry someone else besides me?"

"Hohohohohohoho!" said he.

"Now you're talking," said I. "And you won't be sorry—"

Just then Hellë came. She was both happy and sad; now she smiled and now she cried, and sometimes both at once. Now that the running-away was getting real, she felt a little bit bad about it. "They're my parents, after all, and I was born on the farm here, and now I shall never in my life see them again. I'm going among strangers, and I have only one friend. Rasmus, Rasmus! Will you be good to me?"

"You can see," said I, "how I am to Jens, though he's only a dumb brute. I share my last mouthful of bread with him— how then could I ever be unkind to you?"

"But how am I to get away from here?" said she.

"I've thought of that," said I. "Don't be afraid."

Then I gave her my stable clothes, cap and blouse and the whole outfit, a pair of stockings and a pair of shoes, and asked her to go into the menservants' room and take off her clothes and put on mine. Those she took off she was to throw in the lake near the farm so they'd think she'd made away with herself. Then I pasted a big moustache on her upper lip. I'd made it out of the ends of Jens's mane. At that she laughed.

"Go now," said I, "along this road here, till you come to the village that's about four miles from here. Then you can go into the inn and wait till we come. It won't be long. But you must act as if you were done up."

Well, she did everything just as I'd taught her. A couple of hours later, as day was dawning, the squadron started off. When we came to the inn and halted there, sure enough she came staggering out, and asked if one of us would take her along.

"What's the matter with you?" said I.

"I'm done up," she said. "I can't walk any farther."

I looked at the captain and asked permission.

"Certainly," said he, "but then where the deuce will you put—someone else, you know?"

"That'll be all right," said I. "I bet on Brass-Jens."

"Very well," said he, "you and Jens will have to settle it."

"We've settled it already," said I, and so no more was said.

The boys in the platoon looked at the little dragoon with the big whiskers, and laughed a little at him; but they didn't talk to him, because they thought he was sick.

Well, it's no use spending a lot of words on these doings. We came home safely, and we had our banns read in church and had our wedding as soon as we could, and—but here I'm almost forgetting to tell what happened to Brass-Jens afterwards. When we came to Horsens, he got his discharge, too, and was sold with some other army horses. I bought him, though the price was too high.

But I said to him, "Brass-Jens," said I, "I want to keep

you and feed you and curry you in your old age, for that you've earned."

"Hohoho!" said he; he was pleased. And I didn't fool him either. I kept him for near seven years, and he had an easier time than I did, for he had nothing to do except that I rode him to town sometimes, and in seed-time and harvest he might do a bit of work now and then.

But we can't live forever—Jens's time came. It was once I'd been away for four days, and when I got back there wasn't a living soul to be seen on the place, either up or down, except my old mother who was stirring the porridge over the fire.

"God's peace!" said I. "What's the matter? Where are all the others?"

"They're out in the pasture with Brass-Jens," she said. "Seems like he's going to drop."

I went out there. They all stood around him, Hellë and both our children, and the manservant and the maid; and Jens was lying there on his side.

"I'm afraid you're in a bad way," said I. He lifted his head and looked at me, kind of pleading like, and sighed, then laid his head down again, stretched out his legs, and died.

"Hellë," said I, "he must have a decent burial. I wouldn't for anything in the world have his skin taken off him; and he must be buried in the garden, for I don't want either pigs or dogs to be rooting around him." And so he came to lie under the old apple tree that my father grafted. Every time I look at the tree, I think of Brass-Jens.[1]

❖

That was a fine story, said Mads Uhr, even if it was only about a horse.

[1] There are even now (1842) several people living who knew Brass-Jens in his prime, and his fame still lives, so far as I know, among the Slesvig Cuirassiers.—AUTHOR'S NOTE.

NOTES

THE JOURNAL OF A PARISH CLERK

THIS story is based on the same events that inspired J. P. Jacobsen fifty years later to write his novel *Marie Grubbe*. The "Thiele" of Blicher's story is the same as Tjele, the childhood home of Marie Grubbe. Jacobsen calls his heroine by her real name and follows history in having her marry Ulrik Frederik Gyldenlöve, natural son of Frederik III of Denmark.

(Page 50) "To arrange for my dinners," and (page 51) "while I sing at people's doors in Viborg." Poor students were given their dinners certain days in the week in the homes of prosperous families. They further eked out a subsistence by singing at the doors of the townspeople, for which they were given food and sometimes money.

THE ROBBERS' DEN

(Page 85) The references to the comedies on the stage in Copenhagen and later to the "Danish Pasquino" are no doubt aimed at Johan Ludvig Heiberg. Gammel Strand is an old street in Copenhagen where fishwives used to offer their wares.

(Page 87) The writers whose identity is thinly veiled by initials were all German authors of the sentimental, tear-starting type, whose books by the score were translated into Danish and much enjoyed.

The exception is W . . . . . S . . . . , which of course stands for Walter Scott, whom Blicher admired, though he protests against the inference that he is imitating him.

(Page 118) The festivals on the Aunsbjerg grounds at Whitsuntide became an institution. It is said that the last was held in 1848 as a benefit for the soldiers in the war with Germany.

ALAS, HOW CHANGED!

(Page 150) La Fontaine . . . see note under "The Robbers' Den," page 87.

THE PARSON AT VEJLBYE

Sören Vasegaard in his notes to the 1922 two-volume edition of Blicher's stories gives the historical foundation of "The Parson at Vejlbye." The events have been very freely treated, and almost the only basis of fact in the story is that the pastor, Sören Quist, was unjustly accused of murder by his enemies, and was executed (1625), that many years after his death his innocence was proved, and the witnesses confessed that they had sworn falsely.

GYPSY LIFE

(Page 202) Jens Long-Knife was a famous Jutland robber who lived toward the end of the sixteenth century.

(Page 203) Stoffer One-Eye and Big-Margret were well known gypsies in Blicher's time.

(Page 213) "Only one of them has profited" . . . Blicher refers to N. V. Dorph, a teacher in Viborg, who wrote a small book on the Danish gypsies (1837) containing a glossary of their language. Dorph got most of his information from the gypsy whom Blicher calls "the professor."

Dorph carried on his studies largely in Viborg jail, where the gypsies were often imprisoned for vagrancy or other offenses against the law. At one time Blicher went with him. Dorph in his book tells of how he saw there the originals of the couple described by Blicher, and it was true that the wife carried the husband who was a cripple, but the romantic story of the war is pure fiction.

(Page 214) Madame Schall, a noted ballet dancer at the Royal Theater in Copenhagen.

"Thor's masquerade" refers to Thor's trip to Jotunheim to redeem his hammer.

(Page 215) Johannes Axelsen was found by the Danish author Meïr Goldschmidt, in 1867, in Horsens jail, sentenced for making counterfeit money. He was then ninety-one years old.

THE GAMEKEEPER AT AUNSBJERG

Although Blicher calls this "a true story," Sören Vasegaard thinks it had little foundation in fact. There was a gamekeeper at Aunsbjerg, who was killed while out riding, but he seems to have had nothing to do with the murder at Them, and it is doubtful if he was even French. As usual, that which gives beauty and significance to the story is Blicher's own addition.

(Page 255) "The Pompadour general" was Marshal Charles de Rohan, a favorite of Madame Pompadour. He was defeated at Rossbach by Frederick II of Prussia.

AN ONLY CHILD

Like many of Blicher's stories, "An Only Child" had its point of departure in an incident which he remembered from his childhood, but unlike most of them, it follows the facts rather closely. Probably because some of the persons concerned were still living, he suppressed names and used only initials.

H. stands for the historic castle Hald (several times rebuilt) which in the fourteenth century belonged to the patriot Niels Bugge. An old painting which hung there in Blicher's time, and which he calls "a portrait of Niels Bugge," is of unknown origin.

The owner of Hald who appears in this story was Judge and Chamberlain Frederich Schinkel, whose sister was married to Blicher's great-uncle, Steen de Steensen of Aunsbjerg manor, who figures in "The Gamekeeper at Aunsbjerg." The unsavory record of Schinkel's quarrels and lawsuits is set down in detail by Jeppe Aakjær in his three-volume work, *Blichers Livstragedie*, where he devotes a large part of one volume to the historic background of the stories. It is true that Schinkel tried to force his daughter Charlotte to marry a baron, that he kept her in a kind of captivity guarded by her aunt at Aunsbjerg, and that her lover, naval Lieutenant Martinus Braëm, appealed to the King. The King sent the governor of Viborg diocese, Chamberlain Niels Sehested, to Hald—although the letter he reads in the story is fictitious—and the lovers were married from his home in 1792. Blicher was then ten years old. The couple were divorced in 1809 on the grounds that Charlotte had an affair with a married man, and Braëm petitioned that she might be denied the right to use his name—hence the remark of the old lady in the beginning of the story, "My name? I lost that long ago." She died in 1861 at the age of eighty-nine.

Many people knew Charlotte's history, and Blicher was criticized for using it, thus thinly veiled, while she was still living.

THREE HOLIDAY EVES

(Page 287) Jörgen Marsviin was a real person, who died in 1671. The last scion of this old Danish noble family died in 1768.

(Page 288) Aunsbjerg wood . . . see note under "The Robbers' Den."

BRASS-JENS

This story is taken from *E Bindstouw,* a small volume in which Blicher collected his most important stories and poems in the Jutland dialect. The setting is a knitting-bee, held in the schoolmaster's house.

The stories and poems, thirteen in all, are put into the mouths of the different knitters.